W9-BAF-285

Daniel was different from any other man she'd ever known.

He was kind. Patient. Funny. Appealing. Watching him play with the boys, she noticed the graceful way he moved, as if he were comfortable in his own skin.

Her gaze lingered, and a tingle ran through her. Well, of course, it was hard to be a female and not tingle at the sight of him. He was great to look at, but he wasn't just a pretty face. He radiated energy and life, and when he smiled, he could take her breath away.

There was danger here.

He must have sensed her looking at him, because suddenly he stopped and then, slowly, sent her that smile of his. Lilah felt attraction dance down her spine like a caress, and without thinking, she found herself smiling back.

A Dog
Between Them

Daly Thompson & C.J. Carmichael

Previously published as *One of a Kind Dad*
and *Her Cowboy Dilemma*

If you purchased this book without a cover you should be aware that this book is stolen property. It was reported as "unsold and destroyed" to the publisher, and neither the author nor the publisher has received any payment for this "stripped book."

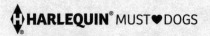

ISBN-13: 978-1-335-98855-3

A Dog Between Them

Copyright © 2020 by Harlequin Books S.A.

One of a Kind Dad
First published in 2009. This edition published in 2020.
Copyright © 2009 by Barbara Daly / Mary E. Lounsbury

Her Cowboy Dilemma
First published in 2013. This edition published in 2020.
Copyright © 2013 by Carla Daum

Recycling programs
for this product may
not exist in your area.

All rights reserved. No part of this book may be used or reproduced in any manner whatsoever without written permission except in the case of brief quotations embodied in critical articles and reviews.

This is a work of fiction. Names, characters, places and incidents are either the product of the author's imagination or are used fictitiously. Any resemblance to actual persons, living or dead, businesses, companies, events or locales is entirely coincidental.

This edition published by arrangement with Harlequin Books S.A.

For questions and comments about the quality of this book, please contact us at CustomerService@Harlequin.com.

Harlequin Enterprises ULC
22 Adelaide St. West, 40th Floor
Toronto, Ontario M5H 4E3, Canada
www.Harlequin.com

Printed in U.S.A.

CONTENTS

Daly Thompson is a collaboration between Barbara Daly and Liz Jarrett, both multipublished authors. Barbara brings to this joint effort her passion for reading, the characters she's collected from the diverse places she's lived and the jobs she's held, and a firm belief in happy endings. She began writing when she discovered she'd need a mobile career in order to follow her academic husband from coast (the Atlantic) to river (just across the Mississippi), and at last found her own happy ending in writing romance.

Liz has been writing stories since she was a child. After graduating from college, she was a technical writer for twelve years before she decided to stay home with her children. During their naps, she started writing her favorite type of stories—romances. This enjoyable pastime is now her full-time career.

Books by Daly Thompson

One of a Kind Dad
Surprise Dad
Dream Daddy

Visit the Author Profile page at Harlequin.com.

ONE OF A KIND DAD

Daly Thompson

Thanks to Johanna Raisanen
for her expert guidance...
and to my Vermont friends and neighbors.
I wish I could have named a town after each of you.

Chapter 1

Nick's screams jolted Daniel into action before he was entirely awake. Barefooted, with his pajama bottoms flapping around his ankles, he raced down the hall, pausing outside Nick's room to take a deep breath and will his heartbeat to settle down. Not until he'd accomplished that did he step into the room.

"Nick," Daniel said softly. "It's okay. I'm here." He switched on the bedside lamp, a figure of a baseball player in a Red Sox uniform. In the subdued glow of the light, he saw the boy sitting up in bed, eyes wild and face drained of color, his screams still bouncing off the walls.

Daniel sat on the edge of the bed and smoothed Nick's tousled red hair. It was wet with perspiration. "It's okay," he said again. "I won't let anything hurt you."

Gradually, the screams faded into sobs, then to gasps for air. Nick didn't reach out his arms to be hugged until his terror passed. He'd been one of Daniel's foster boys for almost two months now, and still didn't trust him enough to seek him out for comfort. What could have happened to a boy so young to make him close his heart so completely?

No one knew. A woman in a larger town nearby had found Nick, all alone and unable to give his name or his parents' to Child Services. How old was he? The pediatrician who examined him had put his age at seven. Daniel's hands clenched. He'd solve the mystery of Nick one day, and when he did, the responsible parties would deeply regret what they'd done to this child.

"What's wrong?" Daniel asked, gently rubbing Nick's bony shoulder. "Tell me about it."

With one final gasp that ended on a sigh, Nick mumbled, "It was just a bad dream."

"What about?"

"Nothing."

"You'd feel better if you told me. We could talk about it."

"I don't remember. Sorry I woke you up."

Nick always said, "I don't remember." He was calm now, safe behind the invisible wall that protected him from the demons he couldn't confront.

"How about a little bedtime reading, then?" Daniel suggested. "What would you like to hear?"

"The Swiss Family Robinson?" It was not a statement so much as a question. *Is that okay with you—or am I asking too much?*

"Terrific," Daniel said. "My favorite."

In less than a minute he was back in Nick's room with the book, an old copy with yellowing pages. *The Swiss Family Robinson,* in which the father was able to solve any problem that threatened his family's survival.

If only. The book offered a dream world in place of a nightmare world, and Nick clearly needed a glimpse of a dream world.

That's what Daniel had needed at Nick's age, as well. Routinely beaten by his father as his mother cried and wrung her hands, often before being knocked unconscious in her attempts to protect her son, Daniel had finally appeared in the local emergency room one time too many. Based on the testimony of medical staff and neighbors, he'd been taken from his parents and placed in a foster home.

But not a good foster home like the one he was giving Nick. In a series of miserable places, he'd slept on sofas, cut school to take care of younger children in his foster families, gone hungry, worn dirty clothes and been whipped for any infringement of a rule or shirking of a duty.

Daniel ran away from each of these homes, getting picked up, every time, only to be turned over to another family.

He lost his trust in human beings, thinking that no one would ever love him or even be kind to him. Still in his teens, he ran away again, and this time he was determined to run so far that no one could find him. He stole a bicycle and what little money his foster parents had around the house, grabbed a jar full of coins donated to charity from the general store counter and rode north as fast as he could. When he made the mistake of trying to cross over the border into Canada with a fanciful story but no ID, the border guards detained him for questioning. He could still feel the rage and frustration that made him fight back, injuring one of the guards before they could get him under control. Cuffed and helpless, he was sent back to Vermont and placed in juvenile detention. It was the best thing that could have happened to him, because there, at last, he'd found a family.

He and two other boys, Mike and Ian, discovered they had the same goal, to leave their unhappy pasts behind and become law-abiding and productive citizens. Slowly but surely, he'd learned to trust them. The three formed a strong bond, and when they were released from the facility they became "brothers," changing their surnames to Foster, and set out to change their lives.

Knowing he had people he could trust absolutely had been the turning point in Daniel's life. It had led him to taking in foster children—he had that one thing he could teach them, that in him they had someone they could trust, and that trust could eventually extend to other people, too.

So far, each of his foster kids had come to do that. And someday Nick would, too. But when? How could Daniel break through the boy's silence? Weekly visits to a psychiatrist hadn't worked any better than Daniel's own efforts.

Nick didn't want to be found by his real parents, and that told Daniel the whole story.

When the boy's eyes closed in spite of his attempts to stay awake, Daniel went back to his own room and fell into bed, emotionally drained, to struggle with his own nightmares.

"We're going to be fine, honey. I know it's scary to leave home for a new place, but I wouldn't bring you here if I didn't know it was the right thing to do, would I?" Lilah Jamison slid a sidelong glance at her son. Jonathan was scrunched down in the passenger seat, looking smaller and younger than usual, scared to death by this sudden upheaval.

Was it the right thing to do? She had $290, three-quarters of a tank of gas to get her from Whittaker, her hometown in the Northeast Kingdom of Vermont, to Serenity Valley, many miles south, a cooler packed with the contents of her refrigerator and not even an inkling of what she would do to support the two of them. But they'd be safe there. She'd researched every corner of Vermont before deciding that Serenity Valley was the perfect place to hide.

She had to hide, had to protect Jonathan and herself from her ex-husband, Jonathan's father. He'd been imprisoned for defrauding investors who'd trusted in him. Only a few people knew he'd also abused her. And now he was being released from prison. She'd been the one to blow the whistle on him, and she knew he was going to come after her as soon as he had the opportunity. Her muscles tightened, and her hands balled into fists on the steering wheel.

"Where will we live?" Those were the first words Jonathan had spoken in the past hour.

"We'll start by finding a special, secret place to park the car and set up housekeeping," Lilah said in a conspiratorial whisper.

"Are we hiding out from the bad guys?" Jonathan turned toward her for the first time, looking interested.

She couldn't tell him the only "bad guy" in their lives was his father. She said, "Hmm. I was thinking we'd be more like *The Boxcar Children*." It was one of his favorite books. She hoped it would conjure up a positive image in his mind, even if it was less exciting than escaping from "the bad guys." "As soon as I get a job, we'll find a real house."

Or a one-room apartment like the one they'd lived in after she'd sold their three-bedroom cottage in Whittaker and used the money to pay off Bruce's remaining debts.

"What kind of work will you look for?"

"Well, I used to be a nurse," she reminded him. "Then, when you came along, I stayed home with you and did your father's bookkeeping." She could hardly bear to say the words. "And you know what I've been doing the past three years."

"Home care," Jonathan said. "For a nice, old lady."

"So I can look for several kinds of jobs. And you'll like your new school," she went on. "I just know it, because you make friends easily and you're a great soccer player."

"Yeah." He sighed. "Are we almost there?"

"The exit's coming up now. We'll take Route 30 for a few miles, and then we'll start looking for our hideout."

Daniel wasn't a churchgoer himself, but he firmly believed in Sunday school for children. The boys griped and dragged their feet sometimes, but many of their best friends were kids they'd met at the Churchill Congregational Church, where they learned more about kindness than they did about any particular religion.

He'd finally herded the four of them, their hair still damp from showering and a few hands undoubtedly still sticky from pancake syrup, into the van. "Are we gonna have breakfast at the church?" Will asked.

"You just had breakfast," Daniel said, glancing into his rearview mirror to catch the eleven-year-old's eyes. "Seven pancakes, I think. A personal best."

"I know," Will said, "but sometimes they have real good stuff."

"I should hope so," Daniel said. "If you guys were ever ready in time to get there thirty minutes early, instead of eating breakfast at home in ten…"

"Yeah, yeah." Mutters came from the backseat. Daniel smiled. Kids who arrived thirty minutes before Sunday school began were served a hot breakfast. It had been his idea, and he still supported it financially. So much poverty existed in and around Churchill that he'd thought it would be a valuable service to the community. Besides, he owed the church something in return for suffering through an hour a week with his unruly gang. The program had been a big success.

As he pulled into the yard, he saw a small car, many years old, parked at the curb well away from the entrance to the building. It was dusty, as all Vermont cars were after negotiating the dirt farm roads into the town center, but otherwise it looked as if it had been well cared for.

A woman sat at the wheel, probably waiting for one of the children the breakfast program was intended to benefit. He could see little of her, just blond hair hiding her face as she bent over the steering wheel, reading, maybe, or just resting. His boys had already tumbled out of the van and gone on their way to rattle the cages of their long-suffering teachers.

Daniel thought about going to speak to her, offering to drive her child home after Sunday school so she wouldn't have to wait, but he decided against it. If she'd wanted company, she'd have gone into the church for the adult class.

Besides, he had a whole hour to himself, and what

was he going to do with it? What any normal, virile, macho man would do. Go to the grocery store.

Lilah saw the children begin to stream out of the church and looked anxiously for Jonathan. When she saw him, he was in deep discussion with a freckled red-headed boy about his age. Her muscles tightened. What she hated most about her situation was that she and Jonathan had to lie about themselves. But what if someday he forgot?

She got out of the car. She had to end the conversation before Jonathan became too chatty. When he saw her, he gave the other boy a wave and came running toward her, his eyes bright. She forced a big smile. She had to calm herself down—she couldn't start quizzing him about his conversation right away. "Did you have fun?" Lilah asked as they pulled away from the curb.

"Yeah." Jonathan looked happy.

"How was breakfast?" As she'd searched the grocery store bulletin board for job possibilities the day before, she'd seen a flyer inviting children to come for "breakfast and Bible study." Feeling desperately shy, she'd taken him into the church this morning, where he, to her relief, was greeted warmly.

"Great. We had pancakes and sausage and chocolate milk."

Lilah's stomach growled. "That does sound good," she said. She felt terrible about asking someone else to feed her child, but he hadn't had a hot meal in more than a week.

"And I made a friend."

"Now that is wonderful. What's his—or her—name?"

"His," Jonathan said, directing a brief "I hate girls" scowl at his mother. "Nick. He's nice."

"Tell me about him." *Please tell me you asked all the questions and didn't answer any.*

"He told me he's a foster child. What's a foster child?"

"Well, sometimes," Lilah said, dreading the inevitable consequences of giving Jonathan a definition, "parents can't take care of their own children. They have to let other people take care of them until they can get their lives in order."

"Is your life in order?"

"You and I are together and we always will be," Lilah said with a forced steadiness. "That's what I call having your life in order." How long could she keep up this pretense? A week of job-hunting had netted her nothing. But tomorrow could be different. *Would* be different. Because she'd never lose Jonathan to foster care, no matter how good that care might be.

"Who are Nick's foster parents?"

"He lives with a guy named Daniel. A vet…veternar…"

"Veterinarian," Lilah said.

"Vet-er-in-ar-ian. Some other boys live there, too, and a sort of grampa. His name is Jesse. Nick says they're all real nice."

"Really nice," Lilah said automatically.

"Yeah. But he looked real tired—*really* tired—and I asked him why, and he said he'd had another nightmare last night."

"Another nightmare?"

"He says he has 'em all the time."

"That's terrible," Lilah said, her heart going out to this child she didn't even know.

"Remember when I had those bad nightmares?"

How could she ever forget? Jonathan hadn't had one since he was three, when his father went to prison. Her child might be living in a car, eating cereal and sandwiches, but every night, when she'd tucked him into the backseat, he slept like Rip Van Winkle.

"I told him you made me a dreamcatcher, and I didn't have 'em anymore. I told him maybe you'd make one for him." He looked at her, the question in his eyes.

"Of course I will," Lilah said. "You could give it to him at Sunday school next week." She couldn't tell Jonathan the dreamcatcher had nothing to do with his nightmares going away. Even at three, he'd been far too aware of his father's brutality. He'd even tried to shield her from Bruce's fists with his small body. His father was his nightmare, and hers, but he'd left his nightmares behind with their source. Lilah still had a few. She hadn't found a job, and now she was down to $215.

"What color do you think he'd like?"

"Red and white. He likes the Boston Red Sox."

"Just like you." Lilah smiled. "Okay, red and white it is. Wow, that was quite a talk you had with Nick." Now, the quizzing. Lilah's hands tightened on the steering wheel. "Um, what did you tell Nick about yourself?"

"What you told me to. My father's dead and we moved here. And Mom, guess what the Sunday school lesson was about."

"What?" She was so relieved she could barely breathe.

"Telling the truth."

God, forgive me.

Looking out his window, Daniel saw the woman get out of the car and watched the boy run toward her. He might have called her pretty if she hadn't been so painfully thin and drawn. Her clothes were wrinkled, and her hair, although it was neatly combed, was dull and lank. But her posture was confident—determined was more like it—and it was clear that she and the boy loved each other. He was curious about her.

"Okay, spill it," he said to his passengers as they moved away from the curb. "How was Sunday school?"

Jason, almost sixteen and the oldest of his boys, spoke up first. "Not bad."

"The usual." Maury, a few weeks younger, was Jason's sidekick. "Another life lesson."

"Which *life lesson?*" Buzz words irritated Daniel, even when they came from the mouth of a Sunday-school teacher.

"Being honest."

"Us, too," Nick piped up.

"Ah," Daniel said. "A coordinated curriculum."

"Whatever," Nick said. "So this new kid asked me a question and I told him the truth."

A breakthrough! Had Nick told this boy the truth about where he came from?

Act casual. "What'd you tell him?"

"He said I looked tired, and I told him about my nightmares."

"What they were about?" The other boys had fallen silent, as if they were all holding their breath.

"I told you," he said. "I don't remember."

Hopes dashed, Daniel asked for and got a full report, not on the sin of lying but the inefficiency of it. And then they were home. Home to the scent of braising pot roast, to the comforting sight of Jesse carefully removing an apple crisp from the oven, to the racket of four boys shouting, arguing, laughing, racing up and down the stairs of the huge, creaky old Victorian house and the family dog, Aengus, barking, delighted they'd come back.

To Daniel, it sounded like the sweet strains of the Westminster Abbey boys' choir.

"Lilah Jamison?"

"Yes." Lilah gave the portly manager of the Ben Franklin dime store a confident smile. *Don't be modest. Sell yourself. You have to, for your sake and Jonathan's.* "I saw that you're looking for a person to handle your crafts section. I'm a crafter myself, and…"

"Already filled," the woman said. "Retha, she's one of our cashiers, says her daughter wants the job."

It wasn't the first time she'd gotten this response. Jobs in Churchill went to relatives of current employees. Lilah wanted to say, *But have you interviewed Retha's daughter? Does she know anything about knitting? Or decoupage? Or tole painting?* But it wouldn't matter. All that mattered was that she was Retha's daughter.

"Well," Lilah said, forcing another smile, "thanks for talking to me." She couldn't ask the woman to call her if she had another opening. She hadn't been able to afford a cell phone since Bruce had gone to prison. Her address, at the moment, was CWC 402, her license plate number. "While I'm here, I'd like to look at yarn."

Now that Lilah was a customer rather than a job applicant, the woman was all smiles. "You picked the right day," she said. "We're having a sale."

Lilah fought the tidal wave of discouragement threatening her belief that leaving Whittaker had been the right thing to do. First, she'd gone to the hospital to look for work as a hospital nurse or a home caregiver. "No openings in nursing," said the head of personnel, looking at her warily.

"I also have bookkeeping experience," Lilah said. "Would you have anything in Accounting?"

"No, but if something comes up, I'll give you a call."

But, of course, Lilah didn't have a phone number.

Since she'd arrived in Churchill, she'd followed up on every job offer on the grocery store bulletin board and in the classified ads of the local newspaper. There weren't many. Apparently Churchill folks didn't hire cleaning ladies. And the school didn't need cafeteria workers or teachers' aides.

She dropped in at the local diner. "My husband's the short-order cook, my daughter and I are the waitresses, and we hire the intellectually challenged to bus tables and clean up," the woman at the counter told her. "Sorry."

Before she picked up Jonathan at the park, where she'd discovered the town ran an informal, drop in, drop out, day care in the summer months, Lilah took one last look at the grocery store bulletin board. No job offers, but a brightly colored poster caught her eye:

Fair Meadows Soccer Camp
Attention, future soccer stars aged five to sixteen!
Coach Wetherby and the Town of Churchill offer
you this opportunity to sharpen your skills for
competitive team play!
Nine to noon, Monday through Friday
at Friendship Fields.
All Serenity Valley students welcomed.
Sign up now!
Registration fee includes...

Lilah's eye stopped at "registration fee." Jonathan excelled at soccer. He could make friends at the camp, and then he wouldn't have to enter second grade as the "new kid." The fee wasn't much, but she couldn't afford a fee of any size.

It was the last straw. "Go team," she whispered. They'd have to go without Jonathan. His mother had missed one goal too many.

She hurried out of the store before she fell apart. What was she going to do? Would she have to move to a larger town outside the valley, where she'd find more job opportunities?

"I have an idea," she told Jonathan when she picked him up, giving him a smile that took all the optimism she could muster. "Let's blow it all out at the diner—hamburgers, French fries, the works—and then we'll drive back to our secret hideout and make Nick a dream-catcher."

Chapter 2

Daniel eyed the mountain of laundry on the basement floor, started a load, stalked up the steep stairs and said, "Jesse, we need a housekeeper."

"Last thing we need's a woman around here," Jesse said. "They don't have their priorities straight. Want things to look pretty before they really do anything."

A typical reaction from Jesse O'Reilly. A long-retired marine and a widower for many years, he'd been renting the apartment over the carriage house when Daniel bought the property. Because any income to offset Daniel's investment was a plus, he'd encouraged Jesse to stay.

Then, when Daniel took in his first foster child, Jason, a rebellious, fighting-mad fourteen-year-old at the time, Jesse had told Daniel if he ran into a problem, he should just call and he'd keep an eye on the boy. And slowly, Daniel had begun to trust Jesse. He took in more boys, and Jesse became even closer to the family, somehow having dinner ready before Daniel got back from picking up the kids after school, somehow producing stacks of laundered clothes, a full cookie jar.

Last year Jesse had fallen down the apartment stairs, and Daniel had talked him into moving into the house. Now he was chef, chauffeur, child-sitter, homework supervisor—and Daniel's best friend, next to his brothers. More like a father than a friend. A grumpy father with a heart of pure homemade spaghetti sauce.

"Let me put it another way," Daniel said. "You work sixteen hours a day, the boys have their chores, we all help clean on Saturday, but if you could see the condition upstairs you'd have us court-martialed." He was exaggerating, but not by much.

Jesse, who was even now engrossed in dinner preparations while the boys—Jason and Maury, Will and Nick—did their homework at the kitchen table, spun around from his stovetop. "It's dirty?" he gasped.

"Criminally," Daniel assured him. "If Child Services came around, they'd take the kids away." Thinking that might scare the younger boys, he gave them a wink, and they gave him a thumbs-up. "Then there's the laundry. Imagine Mount Everest."

"You're the one won't let me go down those stairs any more," Jesse grumbled.

"For good reason," Daniel said. "The housekeeper doesn't have to be a woman, but whoever it is, I won't let him or her get in your way."

"Well, okay, look around." His nose in the air, Jesse turned back to the stove. "Just don't let anybody mess with my kitchen."

"Why would I do that?" Daniel asked. "It's the cleanest room in the house."

"This is a funny way to wash clothes," Jonathan said.

"But it works," Lilah told him, smiling brightly and trying to hide the sickness she felt inside. "The sun dries them, they smell fresh and sweet… This is the way the pioneers did their laundry. How about a bologna-and-cheese sandwich before I take you to the park?"

Their hideout hadn't been easy to find. After scouring the back roads of the three towns that made up the valley, Lilah had found, just outside Churchill, a lumber road that led up to a forested area, beautiful and serene, with no heavy equipment around to indicate that the trees were marked to be cut any time soon. This is where she and Jonathan were living. They slept in the car, bathed in the icy stream and washed their clothes there, leaving them to dry in the dappled sunlight.

They ate cereal and milk, sandwiches made of the least expensive sandwich meat and cheese, or peanut butter and jelly, with a piece of fruit for Jonathan each day. Lilah ate as little as she could without making herself feel faint, saving everything possible for her son. They'd been living like this for almost two weeks now. She couldn't hold out much longer. It wasn't fair to Jonathan.

"What do you think about the dreamcatcher?"

"It's great," Jonathan said, his face lighting up.

Together they admired her handiwork. She'd cut a circle out of a cereal box and had painted it with scarlet nail polish she'd found among the things she'd hastily thrown into garbage bags when they left Whittaker. When had she ever worn bright-red nail polish? Long years ago, when she was still in love with Bruce and had no idea what he would eventually do to her, to their lives? The love hadn't lasted long. The bottle of polish had been almost full.

When the polish dried, Lilah filled in the circle with the yarn she'd bought, a twisted red and white, and then she attached red-painted twig arms and legs, crocheting fanciful feet and hands to fit over the twigs.

In a moment of whimsy, she crocheted a baseball cap and attached it to the top of the circle. A Boston Red Sox dreamcatcher. And then, giving it one last critical look, she decided it needed a catcher's mitt.

"Is Nick rightor left-handed?" she asked Jonathan.

Jonathan looked at her as if she'd asked a pretty dumb question, but then he thought about it. "Left," he said suddenly, "because when there's a new kid at Sunday school everybody writes himself a name tag, and Nick was sitting over here," he gestured to his right, "so our elbows kept bumping and we thought it was funny and that's when we started talking."

"You're a great detective," Lilah congratulated him. So she'd crocheted the mitt onto the left toothpick hand, smiling to herself as she worked.

Making the dreamcatcher had been as good for her as she hoped it would be for Nick. It was the first time in ages she'd found anything humorous to think about her in life.

"Okay, kiddo," she said, giving him that forced bright smile. "Off to the park."

And back to her desperate job search. This week, she didn't even have to buy the *Valley News*. Someone had left a copy on a park bench, which she spotted after dropping Jonathan off at the soccer field. In the classified ads section, she read, "Single father is seeking housekeeper. Call 802.555.4432. References essential."

It was as if an angel had left the newspaper for her to find. She felt a glimmer of excitement, and then the glimmer began to shine. It would be a perfect job for her.

She had no references, however. If she asked for one from the son of the woman she'd cared for these past three years she'd be letting him know where she was, and she didn't want anyone in Whittaker to know where she was. She raised her chin resolutely. She'd have to convince this single father that she'd be the housekeeper of his dreams, references or not.

Gathering change from the bottom of her handbag, knowing every penny had to be spent carefully, she sought out the pay phone on Main Street and dialed the number. If no one answered, she'd just have to call again and again. In her mind's eye she saw dollars and dollars clinking through that slot…

"'Lo."

She blinked. She hadn't expected such a gruff, grumpy voice. "I'm calling to apply for the housekeeping job," she said. The assured voice she'd planned on using came out timid and shaky.

"He's working now," the voice said, skipping several conversational steps. "What's your number? He'll call you back tonight."

This time, Lilah got her voice to cooperate. "I don't have phone service just now," she said. "Is there a time I could drop by?" She held her breath and crossed her fingers.

Silence. Then, "Ay-uh. Might talk to you around five. In his office." He gave her the address. "Side door," he added.

Limp with relief, Lilah almost slid to the sidewalk. She had an interview. At five o'clock this afternoon she *would* get that job. She had to.

"Another applicant," Jesse told Daniel.

Daniel blew a breath into the hands-free mouthpiece of his cell phone. "When can I talk to her?"

"She made an appointment. I told her five—figured that would work."

Daniel sighed. "I didn't realize how much time it would take just to hire a housekeeper. What's your take on that first one I talked to last night?"

"She gossips. Everybody knows it."

"Hmm. The next one had an excellent reference."

"From Shaw's Supermarket, yes. If you were needing a butcher, then she'd be your woman."

Daniel had disliked the other two he'd met after five minutes with each of them. "You're not much help," he grumbled.

"I'm not too excited about this housekeeper idea."

"Duh," Daniel said, and frowned. "Well, okay, I'll make the decision about the one who's coming in this afternoon. I'm not even going to let you see her."

"Humph," Jesse said, and hung up.

It was a busy afternoon. Jesse had caught Daniel on the way to the Dupras farm to check on Maggie, a prize-winning pig who should be delivering her piglets in the next few days. After he'd seen Maggie, he went back to the office to see two cats, a dog, a mynah bird who called him "pond scum" in a radio announcer's voice and a boa constrictor that kept wrapping itself around Daniel's arm.

He was still a little rattled by the snake's fondness

for him when Mildred, his receptionist—actually, she did everything except practice medicine—put her head through his office door and said, "Your five o'clock is here. No pet." She gave Daniel a quizzical look.

"Housekeeper applicant," he said.

"Hmm," she murmured. "Can you see her now?"

"Sure. Whoever she is, she can't be worse than the snake."

Mildred shuddered and went back to the waiting room.

A minute later, he heard a timid knock on the door. The woman who stepped in wasn't what he expected, not at all like the other applicants. She couldn't be more than thirty, but her face looked old with worry. She was tall, or at least not short. Her sedate dress was clean but wrinkled, and her blond hair hung limply around her shoulders...

Hadn't he said the same thing to himself about some other woman recently? Yes, she was the woman he'd seen at the church, the one whose little boy had made friends with Nick.

She hadn't seen him there, he thought, so he wouldn't mention it. He stood and held out his hand. "Daniel Foster," he said.

"Yes," she said, shaking his hand, "Lilah Jamison."

Her hand was damp, and she was trembling. "Good of you to come by," Daniel said. "Have a seat. So you're new in town?"

"Yes." Her voice grew firmer. "My husband died, and my son and I needed a fresh start."

He nodded. "You have references?"

She flushed, but she looked him straight in the eye. "I'm afraid not. I've never worked as a housekeeper but

I've always kept a spotless house, even though I worked full-time." She stared him down as if she expected him to say, *Sure you did.*

"What sort of work did you do?"

When she told him she'd been a nurse doing home care, it occurred to him that it wouldn't be bad having a nurse in the house to deal with four risk-taking boys. But his attention was distracted by how desperate she looked.

She wasn't merely thin, but haggard. The half-moons under her eyes, which were dark blue, indicated sleep deprivation and worry; lusterless hair suggested a poor diet. A modest sundress showed off arms that were too thin. Ivory skin that might once have been beautiful was now dry and lifeless. Her husband's death must have thrown her a knockout punch. Either he had been much older than she, or he'd died tragically young.

And she had a little boy. His blood suddenly ran cold. How could she take care of a child in her condition?

This was hitting him too close to home. The boy—what kind of life was he living? Nick had liked him. Nick was scared of his own shadow, so her son couldn't be a bully or a troublemaker. But still, Daniel was looking for a housekeeper for *his* kids and he was taking no chances.

"Why didn't you take a nursing job?" he asked, keeping his voice gentle. "The Churchill hospital is—"

"Filled with nurses already." He saw her face tighten, but she didn't sound bitter.

"I understand," he said, and he did. "Nepotism" wasn't in the local vocabulary. It was simply understood that jobs were passed down from generation to generation. "You seem like a pleasant person, which is important to me, since you'd be keeping house for four foster children. But without references—"

She seemed to sag in her chair.

"Tell you what," he said, starting to think that perhaps because this woman needed help so badly he could trust her to do the job well. "Give me your address and phone number and I'll call you with my final decision. I've had several applicants," *dreadful ones,* he reminded himself, "and I need to think things over."

"As you said, we're new here. No phone service yet." He could tell she was trying to be matter-of-fact, but he could also see the pain in her eyes. "I'll come by the clinic in a few days. You could leave a message with your assistant."

She stood up, too, and just as Daniel held out his hand to shake hers again, he heard a familiar sound, one of the boys coming to tell him about some wonderful—or terrible—thing that had just happened.

"Daniel!"

"Mom!"

His job applicant rushed toward the boy who'd yelled, "Mom," and said, "Honey, you were supposed to stay outside…"

But Nick drowned her out. "This is Jonathan, the one I was telling you about. I saw him in his car, and he said he had a present for me. Look what his mom made!"

Daniel, not as rattled as he had been about the snake but close to it, moved around his desk to stare at the weird thing Nick held in his hand. It could be a voodoo doll. No voodoo in his house. Or it might be a Satanic totem.

A Satanic totem that looked like a Red Sox baseball player?

He tried to clear his head. "That was kind of you," he

said to the mysterious Lilah Jamison, who had an arm around her son. "What is it?"

"A dreamcatcher," she answered for Nick. Then she relaxed her hold on Jonathan and turned her attention to Nick, her voice soft and musical. "It captures bad dreams before you dream them. You told Jonathan you have nightmares, but if you really and truly believe in it, we're sure this dreamcatcher will bring an end to them."

"I do believe in it," Nick said reverently. "Jonathan told me it worked for him. Look at it, Daniel," Nick said. "It even has a catcher's mitt on its left hand!"

Daniel admired this thing they called a dreamcatcher, then gazed at Lilah's son. He was a little taller than Nick, with his mother's blond hair and deep-blue eyes. But he didn't have his mother's look of despair. Whatever had befallen them, Jonathan was a happy child.

His gaze moved toward Lilah, and she must have had that feeling of being watched, because she looked up at him at once. "I think you've just provided your reference," he said, ruffling Jonathan's hair, "and he's an excellent one."

Her eyes widened. "Thank you," she said.

He'd decided he could trust her to be good with the boys. Even if she wasn't a perfect housekeeper, any assistance would be an improvement. He needed help, she needed help—they could help each other and everybody would be better off.

"I'd like the rest of the family to meet you before I make a final decision, and you should meet them so you know what you'd be getting into," he said. "Stay for dinner. It's the best way to catch them all at once."

He saw Jonathan's gaze turn on her, but she gave him a quick glance and said, "Oh, I'm not sure we should…"

"It's some kind of chicken stew, it smells great, and there's apple pie for dessert."

"Mom?" The look in Jonathan's eyes was a dead give-away.

"Well, I…" She was wavering.

Then she turned to Daniel. Her determined expression made him sure she'd say no, but she surprised him. "Thank you for your invitation," she said formally. "We accept."

Nick and Jonathan sped away, cheering. Lilah looked limp. "Thank you for seeing me," she said. "I know you're busy, so I'll just wait outside."

"Look around, if you want to," Daniel said. "I'm warning you. It's a big place." He opened the back door of the clinic, which led into the house.

She gave him a slight smile. "I'm not afraid of hard work."

You're afraid of something, Daniel thought as she ignored the open door and went instead through the waiting room into the yard. He shook his head. She was running scared, and he wished he could figure out why.

In the yard, Lilah tried to still the trembling of her hands. She wanted and needed this job so badly. But she hadn't intended to become a member of Daniel Foster's family. She'd imagined herself slipping in at nine and out at five, a human vacuum cleaner, nothing more. This situation might be too intimate. She'd wanted to stay invisible. But she had to have a job. For Jonathan's sake. And this one was her best bet.

Worry was wearing her out. To distract herself, she studied the house. The patterned wood shingles were painted lavender, with the molding details picked out in dark purple and turquoise. It was an enormous place, with a turret rising into the sky. She'd entered the clinic through a separate entrance that had its own stoop and overhang, with a discreet brass plaque on the door that read, Serenity Valley Veterinary Clinic, Daniel Foster, DVM. and in front of it, the small graveled parking area where she'd left her car.

She gazed back at the fancifully painted building. The man she'd just met didn't look like a lavender, purple and turquoise kind of person. She'd read his name on the door plate, wondered if he could be the Daniel who was Nick's foster father, and was expecting to see an old, fatherly country vet, not someone close to her own age, undeniably masculine, tall, lean and muscular. She'd felt a moment of fright when she walked into his office, and she wondered—would the sight of a large, powerful man always have this effect on her?

The thought was enough to dim her mood, her hopes, the illusion of confidence she'd been able to maintain after that first uncomfortable minute. If Daniel offered her the job, she'd stay as far away from him as she could.

He *seemed* to be a kind person. His sandy hair, which fell across his forehead, made him look boyish. His eyes were an interesting color—mocha, she'd call it. They were thoughtful eyes, assessing, analyzing her while they talked.

But you never knew. Bruce had been attractive, too. And she'd let herself become dependent on him; too dependent to run away from his abuse, too afraid she couldn't raise Jonathan on her own.

His years in prison had changed her. Now, even though she had no money, she was independent. Confident in her ability to give Jonathan the important things—love, support, emotional security. She'd never again let a man take control of her life. But just being a housekeeper wouldn't be taking a risk, would it?

Daniel appeared at the back door. "Come on in," he said. "Dinner's almost ready."

Here we go. My future and Jonathan's depend on the next few hours.

Daniel hadn't called the boys to dinner yet. He wanted them to barrel in one or two at a time, as they usually did, so Lilah wouldn't grab her son and run screaming from the chaos.

The fact that the kitchen was relatively empty seemed to unnerve her for a second, but then he saw her face as she took in her surroundings. The old-fashioned maple cupboards, which rose high enough so that even he needed a stepladder to reach the upper ones, the big range and the even bigger refrigerator. The old brick floor, worn smooth by the feet of several generations of occupants. The round table that sat in the middle of the room surrounded by mismatched chairs. The table centerpiece: a bicycle helmet instead of flowers.

He couldn't read her expression. Was she thinking it wasn't quite as clean as a kitchen should be for a houseful of children? Was she appalled by the oilcloth cover on the table? If that was it, was she out of her mind? Did she have any idea what laundry problems real tablecloths and napkins would cause?

He reminded himself to postpone showing her the laundry piled in the basement until after she'd accepted the job.

"Jesse, meet our job applicant, Lilah Jamison. She and her son are staying for dinner."

Jesse, stirring something in a gigantic pot, wheeled around on his good leg. "Major Jesse O'Reilly at your service, ma'am." Having done his duty, he whirled back to the stove. Jesse didn't want a housekeeper, and he'd spoken pretty crisply. Then he stopped stirring, and slowly turned back to take another look at Lilah. His expression changed. Daniel could tell that now he was seeing her not as a potential interloper, but simply as a nice-looking young woman who needed feeding.

Jesse dipped a spoon into the pot and held it aloft. "Mind tasting this stuff?" he asked her. "Might need more salt."

She joined him at the stove, instantly looking comfortable with the situation she'd walked into. "It's just right," she told him, licking her lips.

"When's dinner?" Nick and Jonathan shot through the door, Nick yelling the question at Jesse.

"Hold on, hold on," Jesse grumbled, and focused his attention on Jonathan.

"This is Jesse," Nick said to Jonathan.

"And this is Jonathan, Lilah's son," Daniel explained.

Jesse gave Jonathan the same thoughtful gaze he'd given Lilah. "I need a junior opinion on this stew," he said, and handed spoons to the boys.

Daniel wondered if Jesse was starting to look a little obvious. At just the right time, Will raced in through the door. "Brunswick stew," he shouted. "I could smell it all the way upstairs."

"Hey, Will, you almost knocked Nick over."

Daniel smiled at Jason, noticing how his voice had deepened even more in the past few weeks, seeing how he ruffled Will's hair and smiled even as he scolded him.

"You said four boys?" Lilah murmured, looking stunned by the sudden frenzy of activity.

"Yeah, it just feels like more. That's why we do a lot of yelling around here. Have to, if you want anybody to hear you. Meet Jason, he's the blond one—and Maury, the one who looks like a football player, which he is. This is Lilah, and this is Jonathan. Did anybody let Aengus in?"

"I'll do it," Jason said.

"We're moving in on it, kids," Jesse said. "Grab a couple of those round loaves of bread out of the pantry, Sergeant Jamison. Step lively. It's that door over there." He pointed with his stirring spoon and juices dripped on the floor.

"The rest of you boys get that table set and everybody sit down. You're startin' to make me dizzy."

Nobody's life could be this good. The boys threw cutlery and plates haphazardly onto the table and sat down at once, including Jonathan. Shyly, Lilah joined them.

"What can I get you to drink? Water? Wine? Beer from my secret stash?"

"Water, please," she said, "and thank you." Secret stash? He was a closet drinker? While he harbored a houseful of foster boys, he drank himself into oblivion night after night?

"Good choice," he said. "I was down to my last beer—I have one every Saturday night after I get the kids to bed, and the wine is the stuff Jesse uses for his fancy beef stews. The alcohol boils off," he explained, as if he thought she might be planning to report him for serving wine to children.

So. Not a big drinker. He had to have a different fatal flaw. All men had a fatal flaw.

Or maybe just the ones who'd had some impact on her life.

Already stretched as tight as a bungee cord, every bone in her body went stiff when the biggest dog she'd ever seen leapt into the room and ran directly toward Jonathan. She gasped, jumping up so rapidly she knocked over her chair.

Before she could rescue her son, if it was possible to rescue him from a beast this huge, the dog had set to work licking Jonathan's face. Jonathan was giggling uncontrollably, hugging the animal.

She picked up her chair and sat down. "I see he's friendly," she said, feeling limp as a frozen celery stalk. "What—is he?"

"An Irish wolfhound," Daniel said, "who's way too big to be way too friendly." In a quiet tone, he said, "Aengus. Sit."

Aengus sat.

"Stay," Daniel said.

Aengus stayed.

Jason came back and Jesse called out over the cacophony of voices, "Chow's on!" He put a huge serving of stew in front of Lilah and another in front of Jonathan, then began serving the rest of them, including a plate for the dog, who didn't move until Daniel said, "Okay." A basket of hot bread and a stick of butter in a plastic refrigerator container followed, then a huge plastic bowl of salad. The noise level was deafening as the boys ate and talked at the same time.

The stew was delicious, a rich combination of chicken and vegetables. Lilah tried to eat slowly, signaling to

Jonathan not to gobble his food. But all the kids were eating as if they hadn't eaten in months.

"Everything okay?" Daniel said.

She turned to look at him. "It's excellent. Thank you," she said, hearing the faintness of her voice. She felt overwhelmed by...

By what, she wasn't sure. When she turned back to her plate, she saw that Jesse had refilled it. Out of the corner of her eye she saw him putting not one but three pies into the oven to warm.

What overwhelmed her was the realization that this was a happier family than either she or Jonathan had ever known. Her parents had been poor and they'd resented it, never showing her the love they must have felt for her, their only child. They'd never shared a meal like this one, gathered around a table and laughing together. As for Jonathan's life with her and Bruce... Lilah's throat tightened, and she rose from the table.

"This has been wonderful, but we should go now," she managed to say before Daniel leapt up just as rapidly.

He took her arm and turned her away from the boys, saying, "I'd like to talk to you for a few minutes. You guys get on with it. Save us some pie." He closed the door on the chaotic scene and began to hurry her down the hall.

"No!" she said, tugging her arm away from him. "I'm fine. Let me go back to the kitchen."

Taken aback, Daniel halted and turned to look at her. She glared back at him. "Why?" was all he could think of to say.

"I don't want to leave Jonathan alone."

"Alone with four other boys and a retired marine?"

"Alone without me. And I don't want to be alone with you."

He spoke as soothingly as he could. "Look, something upset you in the kitchen, and I thought you might like some privacy."

"I would," she said. Her voice was strained. "I really appreciate your hospitality, but now I want to take my son home."

"As soon as we talk." Lilah was chewing off her own foot, taking herself and her child away from something they'd both obviously enjoyed.

"All right. We'll talk." Stiffly, she followed him into the living room. And that was the right word for it—signs of living were everywhere, with books, games, bats and balls, this and that dropped here and there.

"Have a seat. How about some coffee? Relax a minute and I'll bring you some." Daniel knew she wouldn't leave without her son, but he hurried out anyway, leaving her sitting straight as a fencepost on the cracked leather sofa. When he came back she was still sitting there, looking slightly less combative.

He handed her one of the coffee mugs, stretching out his arm as far as it would go and not coming any closer to her than he had to, as if she were a feral cat. Then he sat down in the chair that was farthest from her chosen corner.

"I suppose this means I've lost my chance to get the job," she said as if she'd rehearsed the lines in his absence. "I did get a little…upset. I guess I'm tired and overemotional."

He nodded. "Moving is stressful. But, no, you haven't lost your chance. In fact, you seem to be exactly the housekeeper we've been looking for."

It was painful for Daniel to see the relief that flooded her face. "So give me your address, and I'll drop you a note."

"As I said earlier, I'll come to the clinic in a few days to find out what you decided."

Daniel's chest tightened. "You don't have a phone, you don't have an address—you're homeless, aren't you?"

She flushed with embarrassment. "That's none of your business."

"Lilah," he said, "look around you. Making sure kids are being taken care of *is* my business."

"I'm taking very good care of Jonathan," she said. Her voice shook and her eyes glittered with tears. "He's the most important thing in my…"

"Mom!" Jonathan ran into the room, so excited he looked as if he might pop. "Can I spend the night with Nick? He thinks I'd help the dreamcatcher work better."

Aengus bounded in right behind Jonathan, and Nick followed with a precariously loaded tray holding wedges of apple pie. He pushed aside the things that already littered the coffee table and set down the tray. "Please?" Jonathan said. His eyes were shining.

Daniel desperately wanted Lilah to say yes—for Nick, who looked so happy, and for Jonathan, her homeless son. "That sounds like a great idea to me," he said, raising a hand to warn Aengus against stealing the pie.

"Jonathan, we've imposed ourselves on these people long enough. It's time to go home. So say goodbye and thank you and we'll—"

"But Mom, we don't—"

Lilah stiffened, and Jonathan grew quiet.

"Tell you what," Daniel said easily, "your mom and

I will discuss it. You guys can find something to do for five minutes, right?" He'd had a brilliant idea.

When the boys had left, he faced Lilah, whose face was pale and rigid. "You do understand that what I need is a live-in housekeeper," he said.

Her expression changed. "Sure," she said bitterly. "I knew there was a catch. No, thank you. I don't need a job that badly."

"Not living in this house," he said. Exasperation rose in him, too, in response to her implication. "There's an apartment over the carriage house—Jesse used to live there. You can stay there tonight and check it out."

"I'd be very glad to take the housekeeping job," she said. Her lips were drawn and white. "But not a live-in job."

"I'm afraid," he added, even more determined now, "that I'll have to insist on the housekeeper living on the premises. With all these kids, she can't help but be a housemother, too."

"Thank you, but I'm going home, and tomorrow I'll look for a job that won't require us to live in." She started toward the door.

"Think about Jonathan. Do it for him."

She spun toward him and pushed back her hair. "I think about nothing but Jonathan," she said. "And I think about how I'm never going to let him fall under the spell of a man who's all nice and charming at first and then…"

When she pushed back her hair, Daniel saw the scar on her forehead—a jagged scar than ran from her temple to just above her eyebrow. It wasn't a fresh wound, but it was too recently healed to have been the result of a childhood accident. A car wreck, maybe, or a serious fall on the ice, but somehow he didn't think so. A blow from her deceased husband? A recent boyfriend? Daniel's protective instincts boiled up inside him. Where had her son been when this happened to her?

"Then what?" he asked, saying it as casually as a shop clerk might say, "Anything else?" And all the while, his gut clenched and twisted, just as if the young, suspicious Daniel was struggling to get loose.

Her lips tightened. "Nothing. Goodbye."

"The carriage house door has a lock. The apartment door has a lock. You'll be safe, and Jonathan will be right next door. A night in a good bed, a hot shower, one of Jesse's breakfasts, and you'll be in much better shape for job-hunting."

She hesitated, turned back, searched his face, and thank God, she must have seen only the calm adult Daniel. Or she'd thought about the good bed, the hot shower, a big breakfast. But he had a feeling she was seeing it for Jonathan, not for herself.

She loved her son, and he loved her. She could have faked it, but a child couldn't. That, to Daniel, was the key to what she was as a person—a caring human being, a woman who'd somehow lost control of her life.

All at once she seemed to deflate. The embarrassment and anger were gone, and resignation took their place. "One night," she said. "And Jonathan may spend the night with Nick."

Daniel's face still felt tight. "Fine," he said. "Jesse has the carriage house keys. You can give Jonathan the good news. I'll stay out of your way." He stalked toward the door, then turned back to face her. "The job is yours if you want it." He glanced at the coffee table. "Don't forget your pie."

It was a relief to turn his back on her startled face.

When he got to his room, he sank onto the bed. It hadn't been a pretty scene, but he'd gotten the result he wanted. Lilah would spend the night in the carriage house instead of her car, and Jonathan would be safe and warm and surrounded by boys who were delighted to have him there, especially Nick, who needed one more little leap of faith to help the dreamcatcher do its work.

Lilah's scar lingered in Daniel's thoughts, entered into his dreams and then kept him awake until the midnight call that meant he had to throw on clothes, alert Jesse that it was his watch and speed to the Dupras farm, where Maggie, the prize sow, had gone into labor.

A woman in distress always got him up and running, even when she was a pig.

With a feeling that she was falling into a trap, Lilah made her way through the darkness to her car to retrieve the big trash bag into which she'd thrown her clothes before leaving Whittaker. She took note of the silver van and bright red pickup parked where a carriage would once have sat, then slowly climbed the stairs to the living quarters.

She unlocked the door, stepping inside to find a self-contained apartment, clearly a man's world, but neat and clean. No coachman had ever lived in such splendor. Lilah set down her modest bag of possessions and put the wedge of pie next to the bed. She was stunned by all that had happened in just a few hours. She'd broken her own promise to herself and had put her life and Jonathan's into someone else's hands, even if it was only for a night. What had she been thinking?

Slowly she went toward the door that had to lead to

the bathroom, opened it and looked inside. For the first time in two weeks, she could take a shower!

Giddy with excitement, she dug out her toiletries and arranged them on the granite counter, stripped off her clothes and turned on the water. She stepped under the steaming spray and let out a deep sigh of pleasure.

The water streamed through her hair, over her shoulders, down her back. She reveled in it, washing away all her worries, if only for a few minutes. She poured shampoo into her hand and lathered it into her hair. It smelled faintly of flowers. Flowers in the rain. She wanted to stay in the shower until everything was all right again.

The bathroom was warm when she stepped out, wrapped herself in a towel and looked in the mirror. She looked different, she felt different. Something buzzed through her body, making her feel alive again. With a start, she realized that what she was feeling was hope.

Chapter 3

Lilah woke early, more rested than she'd felt in years. She took another shower and spent a few minutes styling her hair as well as she could without a hair dryer—she'd forgotten hers, and why would an ex-marine with a buzz cut have a hair dryer? A swish of mascara, a bit of powder on her nose, lip gloss.

She didn't want Daniel's charity. He'd given her and her son shelter for the night. She had to pay him back, and she'd figured out how she might do it.

She dug into her bag of clothes and searched for something relatively clean and not as wrinkled as the sundress she'd taken off the night before. Tan trousers and a pale-blue shirt were the best she could do. Leaving the apartment in perfect order, she set off toward the main house.

Daniel's big silver van was still in its spot, but the little red pickup was gone. She stepped through the dewy grass toward the house where Jonathan slept now, happier than he'd been in weeks.

Shivering in the chill of a June morning in Vermont, Lilah approached the kitchen door to find it locked. Inside, she could hear Aengus barking. In trying to surprise them, she'd probably awakened the whole household.

She spent a minute biting her lower lip, then circled the building, wondering which room was Nick's. When she saw a Red Sox pennant taped to a window, she smiled. That was a clue.

She tapped on the window and called Jonathan's name, softly at first, then a little louder. Apparently even Aengus couldn't wake up these boys.

A tousled blond head appeared at last, and Jonathan raised the window. "Mom?"

"Good morning," she said, smiling at him. "Unlock the kitchen door for me, okay? I want to surprise everybody and cook breakfast."

A second tousled head appeared. "Can we help?" Nick asked.

"You really want to?" she whispered. "You don't want to go back to sleep?"

"I'm not sleepy anymore," Jonathan said.

"Me, either," Nick agreed, looking both proud and surprised. "I slept all the way through the night."

"What great news!" Lilah said. "Okay, meet me at the kitchen door and we'll get to work."

They met her so quickly that she wondered if they'd slept in their clothes. Jonathan was wearing shorts that weren't his own. Nor was the oversize T-shirt, which said, Fair Meadows Soccer Camp. Her heart wrenched, but her optimism level steadied almost immediately when she entered the wonderful old kitchen. "Okay, Nick, help me out here. What do you guys usually have for breakfast?"

"We have four different breakfasts." Nick recited them. "Eggs and sausage, pancakes and bacon, oatmeal and toast and French toast with ham."

No cold cereal? "Which is your favorite?"

He sighed. "French toast, but we had that yesterday and ate all the ham."

"Second choice?"

"Scrambled eggs and sausage. J.J., do you like eggs and sausage?"

J.J.? She'd ask about that later.

"Oh, yeah," Jonathan said.

She opened the refrigerator. Three dozen eggs. Three wrapped rolls of sausage. She lifted an eyebrow. That should do it. A carton of buttermilk at the back of the shelf gave her a bright idea. "Where's the flour?"

"In here," Nick said.

In the cupboard she found everything she'd need. "Do you like biscuits?"

"Yeah," Nick breathed. "Jesse makes 'em sometimes."

"Okay, we have our menu," she said briskly. "You two can set the table while I'm getting the biscuits started."

Jonathan was cutting out biscuits and Nick was shaping sausage into patties when the door opened and Daniel walked in. His shirt and jeans were filthy. His hair was uncombed, and it seemed to have bits of straw in it. He looked exhausted. "What's going on here?" he asked.

All he'd said was "what's going on?" But even that scared her. Her feet nearly left the ground.

"Sorry I surprised you." He tried to smooth his hair.

"I can see what's going on here. You're cooking breakfast."

Then he took a second look at Lilah. She wasn't the same woman she'd been the night before. Now, she looked clean, fresh and wholesome, well-rested. Pretty. Her hair swung around her shoulders, silky and shining, and her eyes, even bluer than her shirt, looked capable of sparkling. In fact, they probably had been sparkling until he'd walked in.

Lilah gave him a faint smile, then went back to whatever she'd been doing at the sink. Nick had apparently been too excited to sense the tension in the air. "We're making eggs and sausage," he said. "Lilah's making biscuits—and I slept all the way through the night!"

Daniel leaned over to hug him. "I don't know which one of those news flashes is the best one," he said. Looking up at Lilah, he started to wink, then thought better of it.

"Were you in a car wreck?" Jonathan asked.

"Jonathan!" Lilah said.

"I look like it, don't I? But," he sighed, "it was just piglets."

Jonathan swiveled with the biscuit cutter still in his hand, and a raw biscuit plopped onto the floor. "You were attacked by piglets?"

"Of course not!" Lilah reached down for the dough, tossed it in the trash and vigorously scrubbed her hands.

All at once, Daniel felt less tired. "No, I delivered them. Eight of them."

Nick said, "Can we have one?"

"No," Daniel said in synch with another "No!" trumpeted from the hallway. Daniel fell heavily into a kitchen chair and groaned. When Jesse saw his kitchen had been invaded, World War III was likely to break out.

"No pigs in this house," he insisted as he came through the door. "We have enough—" He halted when he took in the scene, and Lilah seemed to tense, as if she were seeing it through Jesse's eyes.

She was whipping eggs. Jonathan was cutting out biscuits. Nick occupied the remaining counter space with his sausage operation. This was *Jesse's* kitchen, *his* biscuit cutter, *his* wire whip. Feeling as tense as Lilah looked, Daniel waited to see how it was all going to come down.

Right before his eyes, she changed. "Jesse," Lilah said, giving him a sunny smile, "I hope it's okay for me to help with breakfast. My goodness. The way you keep this kitchen puts me to shame. I thought I was neat, but your refrigerator is in perfect order, and I found all the biscuit ingredients lined up in the same cupboard, so it didn't take me any time at all to make them. Everything is spotless, and I promise you it will be, well, almost as spotless when we're through."

Daniel nearly let out a whoosh of breath that would have given away his nervousness. Jesse grumbled a little, scraped his foot against the brick floor and said, "The military does that to you. Everything shipshape, you know."

"The military does wonderful things for young men," Lilah responded earnestly. "Teaches them routine, and order, and a sense of responsibility. I could learn a lot from you."

"I'll give you some kitchen management tips when we have some time," Jesse said with the arrogance of a man who's been told he's perfect, which he knew anyway.

Daniel couldn't believe it. The tough marine was melting like butter on a hot griddle. "The boys know," Lilah went on, "that breakfast won't be as good as if you'd cooked it, especially the biscuits, but I wanted to say thank you and this was all I could think of."

"Mighty thoughtful of you," Jesse said. "I have to admit my war injuries are kicking up this morning."

"You got hurt in the war?"

Daniel figured Jonathan's morning was getting off to a pretty exciting start. One man with piglet wounds and another with war wounds. Lilah was left to finish the cooking while Jesse entertained the two boys with a harrowing story of capture and escape due to the hero- ism of his buddies. Daniel wandered away to his room and made fast work of a shower and a change of clothes. The usual sounds of the morning began to fill the house, the clatter of footsteps, shouting, laughing, barking, and then the barbarian attack on the kitchen.

Joining them, he glanced down at the table. To the left of each place setting was a paper napkin folded into the shape of a pig. Lilah saw his expression. "Origami," she said. "We had a few extra minutes while the biscuits baked." She looked ever so slightly defensive, as if she expected the pigs might make him mad.

"Aw," Daniel said. "You did it in Maggie's honor."

"Maggie?"

"Maggie the sow. You know, instead of cigars, pig- let napkins."

She laughed, actually laughed. Her face lit up and her eyes sparkled. "Of course," she said. "Congratula- tions, Dad."

He hadn't felt this good since—since he'd delivered Maggie's last piglet. It was fine, as all the others had been, and she was fine—which she wouldn't have been if he hadn't helped her out.

Maggie trusts me. Why doesn't Lilah Jamison?

The boys were wedged in around the table, Jesse among them—any more boys and Daniel would have to turn this table into an oval—and when he pulled out his chair, he paused, looked around, counted and observed, "We need one more place setting."

"Oh, no," Lilah said. "I have to be running around serving. It's what Jesse did last night…"

"But not what we're doing this morning," Daniel said. "Everybody crunch closer."

Twenty minutes later, when not a scrap of food was left anywhere except on the oilcloth and the boys' shirts, Daniel said, "You guys have to get off to soccer camp, and I mean right now."

They were all wearing Fair Meadows Soccer Camp T-shirts. Lilah felt her face flush. "Jonathan and I must be going as soon as we clean up the kitchen."

"Jonathan's going to soccer camp, too," Daniel said.

"Hop to it, men," Jesse barked, moving away from the breakfast table and herding the boys out the door. "Brush your teeth, comb your hair, get your gear."

Three seconds from chaos to silence. Lilah was alone in the kitchen with Daniel. She got up and began to load the dishwasher with lightning speed. "Daniel, Jonathan, unlike every other child in Serenity Valley," she said, cold on the inside and cold on the outside, "isn't signed up for soccer camp."

"Yes, he is," Daniel said. "Last night when I was seeing everybody off to bed Nick reminded me about soccer camp. So I called the coach and registered Jonathan."

She fixed her eyes firmly on the lower dishwasher rack. "Sorry," she said, "but I can't afford it right now."

"I get a group rate," Daniel said, "which I richly deserve, so I told him to add one more to my group."

She swiveled to stare at him. "But he doesn't have the clothes or the shoes…"

Daniel gave her a look that suggested she'd almost exceeded the limits of his patience. "Lilah, we have so many hand-me-downs in the attic we could open a thrift shop. I don't throw anything away until it's a rag, because I never know what size boy might be arriving next. Jonathan is wearing…" He counted on his fingers. "Nick's shorts. The shoes Will outgrew. A shirt of Jason's that got washed in hot water and shrank. We got the gear together last night. So *don't worry.*"

"Okay," she said, turning back to the dishes and registering the stunned silence behind her.

"Okay?"

"What else can I say? I'm sure Jonathan's terribly excited about the camp, and you've dressed him for it. It's out of my hands now."

"Doesn't it feel good for a change?"

"It won't last forever," she said, scrubbing viciously at a huge frying pan. "Jonathan's expectations have risen, and I can't do the same things for him that you can."

"If you take the job I'm offering, you can."

It was blackmail, pure and simple. What she'd feared last night was becoming a reality. She was falling headlong into Daniel Foster's tender trap.

The more Daniel thought about it, the more determined he was to hire Lilah. The carriage house would be all hers. Jonathan could stay there with her or room with Nick. She'd have a salary, plus free room and board. It was a real job—was it ever!—so she'd feel independent financially.

From his point of view, he could keep an eye on her and Jonathan, make sure they were eating enough, know that they had what they needed and that whatever demons were chasing her wouldn't be able to find her. That was all he wanted, to help her get back on her feet.

"No," he heard her say. Her tone was cool. "I know what you're doing, Daniel, but we're not a charity case. I'd like to be your housekeeper, but I need my own place to live. I can't be dependent on you, and frankly, you can't depend on me in the long run." He looked question marks at her. "Churchill is an experiment," she explained. Her voice quavered. "We might have to move on if it doesn't work out."

"Then I'd hire somebody else," he said. "Think about it some more. The boys help with the cleaning, which is why," and he aimed a rueful smile at her rigid back, "the house lacks a certain…polish. That'll give you time to help the kids with homework and Jesse with the cooking. You'd be more like an ordinary mother than a housekeeper. These boys need a mother badly."

She turned to look at him again, thoughtfully. He thought he had her hooked, but the hint of interest in her eyes died as quickly as it had come to life. "I like the boys very much," she said, "but my life is too uncertain right now. I wouldn't want them to become attached to me."

"As I said, just think about it." He wasn't letting her go yet. "In the meantime, will you work for me today, catching up on the laundry? With Jesse so stiff and sore, he can't go up and down the stairs to the basement."

Daniel could see her batting that option back and forth. He was gaming her, which he hated doing. But when he thought about Lilah and Jonathan sleeping in that small car, eating cold food, counting every cent, he couldn't stand it. He couldn't stand to let her do that to her son. Anything he could think of, any lie he had to tell, would be worth it in order to keep her here.

"Well, I suppose I could work for you today. I have the dishes to finish, and I have to wait for Jonathan anyway." She looked at him somewhat hopefully as she rationalized a decision she hadn't wanted to make.

"Jesse will be very grateful. He rarely complains, but…"

She was still gazing at him, the dirty dishes temporarily forgotten. "Some war wounds never completely heal," she said. "I understand they have a certain random quality. For example, one evening a man can leap around a kitchen, cooking dinner for eight people, and the next morning he can hardly move."

Was that a twinkle in her eye or was she being sarcastic? He couldn't tell, and he was afraid to assume anything. He wondered if his face was red, because it felt red. *And* he'd just banged his knee on a table leg. Clumsy as a teenager. "Well, it's time to get those boys off to camp. Come on, guys," he shouted, "time to go."

They came in a platoon, with Jesse lining them up for inspection at the bottom of the stairs. "Okay, Jesse," Daniel called into the hallway. "Load the car and get this show on the road. And buy out the grocery store on the way back."

Jesse really was hobbling when he stepped into the kitchen. In an unsteady voice, he said, "Miss Lilah, do you think you could do the driving? I'm still feeling sort of punk. I'll go along and navigate, and I can help out at the grocery store." He paused for a second, then added, "Help out the best I can, anyway." He offered the keys to her.

What in the heck was he up to? Except for Sunday mornings, when Jesse liked to watch PBS news-in-depth, he wouldn't hand over the keys to that van unless you knocked him down and sat on him. Furthermore, his leg was as fine as it ever would be. The four boys were staring at Jesse as if he'd morphed into an alien. But they weren't saying a word. *Good boys. Keep it up. We have a situation here.*

Lilah put down her scrubbing brush. "I'd be happy to help you, Jesse," she said. "You're sure you feel like going along? The boys probably know where the camp is."

"Of course I feel like going along," Jesse snapped, apparently forgetting his new persona. "Don't think I should be driving these kids, though, with my shaky leg and all." He'd segued directly back into the frail old-man voice.

"Then let's go," Lilah said, and headed for the carriage house where the van was parked.

Daniel had to sit down again. It was as if they all knew; as if they were all helping him out. And then he thought, *What is it exactly they're helping me out with?*

Maybe they're helping themselves out, already imagining her as a mother figure and liking the idea.

He pulled himself together. He had a full schedule today, including a trip out to the Edwards farm to give the Jersey milk cows a thorough examination. This evening he had a meeting that was important to him—one that could shape the rest of his life.

* * *

"We got here first!" Nick shouted.

They'd reached a tree-fenced field on the outskirts of Churchill. A stocky man, obviously the coach, waved when he saw the van. "Bye, Mom," Jonathan said. He leaned over the seat to give her a hug. *I'm being dragged into all of this because of Jonathan,* she thought before she reached behind her to return the hug. "Show them your stuff, Tiger," she said.

The boys sped off to meet the coach, who greeted them warmly with high-fives and manly punches to their shoulders, acting as if he couldn't think of anything he'd rather do on a beautiful summer day than play soccer with a bunch of kids. More cars arrived. Moms, already looking tired in their shorts or work clothes, and dads looking proud, waved their carloads of boys and girls onto the field.

Lilah watched, seeing Jonathan mix right in with the others, and couldn't help feeling a glow of happiness. At the same time she was thinking, *not for long*.

Jesse said, "Wish I could run like those boys. Can't even walk fast anymore. And this morning…"

"Jesse," Lilah said, turning a direct glance on him, "I know when I'm being worked on. So cut it out. We're going to hit that grocery store like an attack force. I have laundry to do." But then she smiled at him, enjoying the sheepish look on his face.

Jesse put the groceries away while Lilah stared at the laundry piled beneath and around an old-fashioned clothes chute. She'd never been in the back of a professional laundry, but she couldn't imagine that even one of them would have so many dirty clothes on hand. Mountains of them. Mixed in with sheets, towels—she half expected to find a dead body in there.

The washer and dryer were huge. She filled the washer with many sheets as she dared to and started the first load. While they washed, she'd sort the rest of the laundry.

Darks, lights, whites, towels, more sheets. Flinging the items into one pile or another, she came across the tan plaid shirt Daniel had been wearing when he came home from delivering the piglets. For a moment she held it in her hands, fingering the soft fabric, as scenes of Daniel and his boys danced through her mind. She pressed it to her face, taking in the manly smell of soap, warm skin and straw. Then she quickly tossed it into the "lights" pile. There was something all too comfortable about Daniel. She'd told him she didn't want the boys to have time to become attached to her. But she didn't want to get attached to them, either. And even more importantly, she didn't want to become attached to Daniel or vulnerable to his opinion of her. Or vulnerable to any other man, ever again.

At eleven-thirty she started another load of washing, then went upstairs to the kitchen. Aengus stared at Jesse with rapt attention as he piled something onto hamburger buns, dozens of them. "Hot tuna salad sandwiches," he explained. "For lunch. The guys love them."

"I'll be on my way to pick them up," Lilah said.

"*I* pick them up," Jesse said, sounding sort of huffy, and then he caught himself in his own trap. "I mean," he said, shuffling his feet, "I'm feeling a lot better now."

"I'm *so* glad to hear it." She shot him a sidelong glance. "I was terribly worried about you."

He glared at her. She smiled back. "So I'll just go on with the laundry."

A half hour later, silence exploded into chaos above her head. Ah, the boys were home. Almost immediately, footsteps thumped down the stairs to the basement. "Mom," Jonathan said, "we practiced making goals, and I made more than anybody my age!"

She dropped the towel she was folding and gave him a hug. "You are the best soccer player ever."

While she was at his level, he whispered in her ear, "I even made more than Will, but don't tell him I told you."

"Not a word," she said, "but that's really something. He must be…ten, maybe?"

"He's eleven," Jonathan hissed.

"Wow!" Now she had to bring him back down to earth. "Honey, we were going back to our hideout when you got home, but I said I'd stay today and do the laundry."

"Good," Jonathan said, "because after lunch everybody goes to the pool."

Lilah sighed. The tender trap tightened around her every moment Jonathan spent in its embrace. "Okay," she said. "Run over to the carriage house and get the sunscreen out of my bag. Your swimsuit's in the car."

"Nick's loaning me a swimsuit," Jonathan said, "but I don't know about the sunscreen. You coming upstairs for lunch?"

"Well, I—"

"Lilah," Jesse shouted down the stairs, "lunch in ten minutes!"

"I guess I am," she said.

Jonathan paused at the bottom of the steep basement stairs. "Mom," he said hesitantly, "did you get the job?"

"Dr. Foster offered me the job," she said carefully, "but it might not be quite right for me."

"I really hope you take it," he said. "I like it here."

His steps were slow as he climbed the stairs. Lilah sank her face into her hands. What was she going to do?

It was close to four o'clock when Jesse yelled down at her again. "You don't have to bring up the clothes," he said. "Everybody gets his own."

She was, at that moment, wearily heading for the kitchen cradling a basket in each arm, wondering if Jesse had ever been able to negotiate those stairs or if Daniel and the boys had been trying to manage the laundry themselves. "Thank goodness," she moaned. She dropped the basket onto the kitchen table. "Here are the dish towels and cloths," she said. "I'll take up the sheets and bath towels and leave everything else. I had no idea what belonged to whom. Can the boys figure it out?"

Jesse turned away from a steaming pot that was giving out a delicious smell of tomatoes, garlic and basil. "They pick things up by size," he said. "Somehow it all works out. I bet you could use something to drink before the mob gets home. Lemonade?"

"Sounds wonderful. Jesse, do you think Daniel would mind if I used the computer in the living room for a few minutes?"

"Of course not. I'm off to the pool, so enjoy the peace and quiet while you can."

Lilah took the glass of lemonade he handed her, cold, tart and delicious, and sat down at the computer. In a few minutes she was into the Web site of *The Kingdom Dispatch,* the weekly newspaper that served Whittaker and the rest of the Northeast Kingdom, reading the news clips.

The city council was fighting again, this time over a new truck for the volunteer fire department. The principal of the elementary school had resigned.

But those newsy tidbits weren't what Lilah was looking for. She stiffened. There on the screen was Bruce's face, a study in remorse. "Bruce Jamison was recently released from Northeast State Correctional Facility after serving three years of his five-year sentence. 'He's been a model prisoner,' says Prison Supervisor Lex Holt. 'We feel he's ready to return to his community and live a useful life.'"

"Right," Lilah muttered, "a useful life." She read on, feeling more disgusted by the minute.

"In a recent interview, Jamison expressed his regret to God, the community and his family. 'I don't know what made me do it,' he said. 'I'm not the kind of person to take good money from hardworking folks. While I was getting my mind straight in prison, I realized I was glad they caught me so that those folks could get their money back.'"

Not all of it, however. Lilah had had to make up the rest, and doing so had left her penniless.

"'I feel the worst about my family. My wife and my son have left me, and I understand why. But I'm going to move heaven and earth to find them and try to win back their love and respect. If anybody knows their whereabouts, I would appreciate the information.'"

Her flesh crawled. He will find us. He'll punish me for the rest of my life for turning him in. And Jonathan... Jonathan...

Her hands were icy as she acknowledged the truth: There was no safe place for her and Jonathan.

She got up from the computer and stared at Daniel's

homey, untidy living room. Unless it was here. Even if
Daniel wasn't quite as great a guy as he seemed to be,
they'd still be safer here than they would be running
from Bruce at his most determined. Maybe it was the
only choice she had.

The house suddenly filled with noise, and above all
the boys' voices she could hear Daniel's. "How many
goals? Good grief, Jonathan, I'm harboring a celebrity.
Yes, I mean you."

Lilah could imagine the scene in the kitchen. Daniel
would ruffle Jonathan's hair, give him that infectious
grin, and Jonathan would beam back. She closed the
Web site and stepped into the kitchen.

While Jason and Maury stood back, looking indul-
gent when they meant to look bored, the younger boys
gave Daniel a blow-by-blow description of their day, sur-
rounding him like adoring fans. Then, at Jesse's suggestion—command was more like it—they flooded into the
basement, returning with armloads of clothes and calling, "Thanks, Lilah," as they raced away to their rooms.

She felt exhausted but she had something to say, and
she had to say it now, before she lost her nerve. While
Jesse was microwaving popcorn, she said quietly to Daniel, "May I talk to you a minute? In private?"

He stepped into the hall with her. He looked worried,
which made her feel more determined to get it over with.
She drew in a deep breath. "Daniel, if your job offer's
still open, I'll accept it."

Chapter 4

Daniel was elated to have the housekeeper search over and done with, even though the way Lilah had accepted the job made him think she might just as well have been saying to her doctor, "Yes, I'll have the spinal fusion. Without anesthetic." And after delivering the message, she'd fled so quickly that he hadn't even had time to talk to her about her salary.

Why did he make her so nervous? He could understand that she wouldn't want to become involved with anyone so soon after losing her husband, but hell, he wasn't asking her to get involved. He'd only been trying to give her a job that included room and board! He hadn't flirted with her and asking her to have dinner in the kitchen with his family and his dog surely couldn't be confused with asking her for a date. It had been her own idea to interview for the job; she needed one desperately, and he'd practically had to force it on her. What was her problem?

Even if she was somewhat neurotic, however, he felt he'd made a good decision. Jonathan was his proof that she'd be good to the boys, which was all that mattered. Shaking his head, he wandered back into the clinic, where he'd have a brief window of time in which to think about the meeting of the Serenity Valley Regional Development Board this evening. There he planned to bring up some new business, the dream he'd been cherishing for the past several years.

Taking in foster children had made him a whole man again, but there was a limit to the number of kids he could handle on his own. And in Vermont there were dozens, maybe even hundreds of children going hungry, being neglected, some of them being physically abused, as well. He could do more by himself, but not enough.

On fifteen acres of Ian's sheep farm in Holman, the town at the tip of the valley, he wanted to build a foster care center to meet the needs of several dozen children. He'd already consulted an architect and talked to some government agencies and private foundations about funding. Daniel felt ready to test the waters.

He was thinking about what he'd say at the meeting when Mildred appeared in the doorway. "Betty brought Tiffany in with a sore paw," she whispered. "Can you take a minute to see her?"

Daniel groaned. "Sure," he said. "A sore paw could be fatal."

"How's business?" Ian Foster stuck his head through the door of Daniel's examination room.

"Steady, as you can see." His current patient, a giant Maine coon cat, glared balefully at Ian.

"Don't look at me," Ian growled. "He's the one who's sticking the needle into your—"

"Language," Daniel said automatically.

"Hey, it's me," Ian said. "I'm in charge of my own language."

"Okay, Tiffany, you're all set," Daniel said to the cat.

"Tiffany?"

"I don't get to name the patients, Ian, I just get to stick needles into them. Tiffany's good to go," he called out into the waiting room.

"Why isn't Tiffany's owner in here with her in her time of trial?" Ian rolled his eyes as he said the cat's name.

"These," Daniel said, pulling off a pair of gloves a steelworker might find adequate. "We don't want Tiffany's mom to know that her kitty is one of the most vicious… Betty! Here she is. Her paw's going to be fine."

The stout gray-haired woman swept the cat into her arms and said, "Ooh, was Mommy's little precious a good girl for Dr. Foster? Of course you were, you little sweetums."

Ian looked as if he might upchuck. The woman bustled out, carrying the cat, who was purring now, upside down in her arms like a baby. Mike, the middle Foster brother, came in in her wake, carrying takeout containers in much the same way Betty had carried the cat. "Dinner," he said succinctly. "It'll be a long, tough meeting. We need fortification."

"You don't have to be at the restaurant?"

"It'll be fine. Almost everybody ate early anyway. My guess is they're all going to the meeting. I dropped off last night's leftovers at the house, too."

"You don't want to eat last night's leftovers with the kids?"

"Not tonight. Seems the table would be too full." Mike narrowed his eyes. "Who was that vision of beauty in the kitchen with Jesse who ran like a gazelle as soon as she saw me?"

Ian gave Mike a long, contemplative look, then turned his gaze on Daniel.

Daniel hadn't thought of her as a "vision of beauty," but now that Mike mentioned it, she had cleaned up well. "That's Lilah Jamison," he said, feeling uneasy. "She's, well, she's my new housekeeper. I told you about the housekeeper, and you agreed I needed some help…"

"We agreed you needed a housekeeper," Mike said. "I was expecting a different sort of person."

"What do you know about her?" Ian said.

"She's a widow."

His brothers waited for more. "Where does she come from?" Mike asked.

"I don't know. We haven't talked that much."

Ian and Mike stared at each other. "Where'd you find her—or *vice versa?*" Ian chimed in.

Daniel sighed. "She saw my ad and asked for an interview. She has a son, six or seven years old. I finally figured out they were homeless. I turned the job into one for a live-in housekeeper."

"Omigod," Ian moaned. "Don't tell me. She said, 'Oh, my, I just don't know, but, well, yes, I can do that.'"

"I had to con her into accepting the job," Daniel snapped. "They've been living in their car, and I have an empty apartment. And besides, Nick met her son at Sunday school, they hit it off, and she made Nick a dreamcatcher."

"A what?" Ian said, scowling.

"It's a thing. A totem. A good luck charm. Wards off bad dreams." He took off his lab coat, washed his hands and gestured both of them into the waiting room.

Mike lined up the carry-out cartons on the receptionist's counter and started heaping food onto plastic plates. Beef cooked in wine, some fancy kind of scalloped potatoes, asparagus, crusty bread.

"Looks great," Daniel said enthusiastically. "What do you call those potatoes? And is this the daube or the bourguignonne?"

"Don't change the subject. Have you moved her into the house?"

"The carriage house. Before she even agreed to take the job, she cooked breakfast, did the laundry…"

Mike and Ian gave each other another one of those irritating looks. This was a common occurrence, but Daniel liked it much better when he and one of them was giving the third one that look. Ian settled himself in a seat against the wall, and Daniel sat down a chair away for elbow room. Mike chose a spot facing Daniel. Plate in hand, he said, "Daniel."

"What?" Daniel replied, knowing what was coming and already feeling cross.

"Do you remember the dog you brought home just before you were going off to vet school, when we were waiting to close out our jobs? The one who ripped up the kitchen floor? Which the landlord made Ian and me replace, when we were living on spaghetti *without* meatballs? Sometimes without sauce?"

"You did good things with spaghetti," Ian said. "A little oil, some cheese…"

"Shut up, Ian. We're not talking about my cooking."

"It wasn't the dog's fault," Daniel protested. "He missed me. You brought him with you when we joined up again, and he was the best dog…"

"And that girl," Ian said, "also homeless, who moved in with us and left with every penny of the paychecks we'd just cashed?"

"That disappointed me," Daniel said. "She'd had a terrible life, though, and—"

"The old man selling magazine subscriptions?"

"Mike, every family should subscribe to a high-quality news magazine—"

"And every old man should have a good hot meal—a twenty-dollar good hot meal. Daniel," Mike said, "you're doing it again. You're taking in another stray."

"Lilah? She's nothing like that girl we took in. She's a good person who needs a break."

"How can you tell she's a good person?" Mike asked. "How much time have you spent with her? Thirty minutes?"

"I can tell from her son. They're crazy about each other. He's a homeless kid who feels sure his mom can turn things around. And," he added, "say what you want to about dreamcatchers, but Nick didn't have any nightmares last night."

"Well, that's something," Mike said. "All it took was a dreamcatcher."

Daniel and his brothers were always honest with each other. "And her son, Jonathan, spending the night. That probably had more to do with it than the dreamcatcher."

"Great," Ian said. "They probably stayed up all night throwing pillows at each other. No time for nightmares."

"He's a great kid," Daniel insisted. "He went to soccer camp with the kids this morning and they said he…"

"You paid for him to go to soccer camp."

"I couldn't let him feel left out. Look, you two," Daniel said, fed up with his brothers' doubts. "She's lost her husband. She has a scar on her forehead. I can't put it all together yet, but something bad has happened to this woman. She's not the kind of person you'd ever expect to be homeless and penniless. I just want to help her, that's all."

For a second he thought they were going to jump him and wrestle him to the ground. Not that they really would, but they looked as if they'd like to. He stood up. "Great dinner, Mike. We have a few minutes before the meeting. So come meet her—officially, I mean. And act nice," he said, glaring at them.

When a man about Daniel's height, but somehow *bigger,* had walked into the kitchen without knocking, Lilah instinctively fled, even though she was supposed to be tossing a salad to go with Jesse's lasagna. *Who is he?* In the few minutes she heard him talking to Jesse, he'd sounded like a stand-up comedian.

At last she sneaked downstairs to finish the salad. At the bottom of the staircase, she became aware of footsteps and voices coming from the clinic. It was too late to flee again. Daniel and his companions had spotted her.

"Lilah Jamison," Daniel said, "meet my brothers, Mike and Ian."

The hallway was crammed with Fosters, tall, imposing Fosters: Mike, the one who'd come into the kitchen without knocking, and the third one, who glared at her as if he disliked her even before he'd met her. She was trapped. She held out a shaky hand to each of them.

"I'm Ian."

The one who glared.

"Mike," said Mike. His smile was guarded, as if he was testing her.

Lilah tried to take them in. Mike was a little taller than Daniel, and Ian, a little shorter. While Daniel had sandy hair and light-brown eyes—Ian's hair was dark, as were his eyes, both dark and brooding. Mike's head was shaved, but his red-brown eyebrows and faint freckling gave him away. A redhead with spectacular green eyes.

She took a second look. "You don't look anything alike," she blurted out, then realized they might have been adopted. She blushed. "Oh, I'm so sorry. I shouldn't have said that."

"We get that a lot," Daniel said quickly, probably to fill the sudden silence. "And we're pretty darned grateful for it. Aren't we?" he added, when the other two remained silent.

"Uh-huh," Mike murmured, staring at Lilah. Ian, on the other hand, just kept glaring.

"Well," Lilah said, feeling dismissed, "I'm glad I got to meet you."

The brothers muttered something that might have been "nice to meet you, too," and then Ian said, "We're late for a meeting." His voice was steely.

But Daniel smiled at her. "Everything under control here?"

"Absolutely," she said, afraid to smile back. "Don't worry about a thing."

When they left, she collapsed on the stairs. The two brothers Daniel hadn't mentioned didn't like her. Didn't want her here. She'd had no idea Daniel had brothers who might have a say in his hiring her. Fearing that

Bruce would find her, she'd made a commitment to Daniel, to Jonathan, to Jesse and to Daniel's boys.

But her most important commitment was to herself and Jonathan. If his brothers didn't like her, how would Daniel come to feel about her? And if he began to dislike her, to regret his job offer, might she and Jonathan find themselves living in close proximity with and dependent upon a man like Bruce? She'd leave now, with Jonathan, before it could fall down on her.

"Mom!" In the dimly lit hall, Jonathan barreled into her on his way out of the kitchen. "Guess what? We're having lasagna for dinner, and Uncle Mike brought all kinds of pies! Jesse says we can have them for dessert."

Already, the enemy was "Uncle Mike." Lilah sighed, then joined Jesse in the kitchen to finish dressing the salad.

After a brief argument, Mike got to drive and Ian copped the front seat. Daniel compressed himself into the backseat of Mike's Subaru wagon. "Ian, you could at least move your seat forward," he grumbled.

"What the hell's wrong with you?" Ian asked as soon as they were on their way to the Town Hall for the meeting. "Taking that woman in without checking her out."

Daniel knew his brothers were just trying to protect him, but he was an adult now and able to protect himself. "I asked Child Services to check her out," he snapped. "She has a great kid, she has Jesse kissing her feet, and the boys seem to want her around."

"So now you're letting the boys choose the housekeeper?"

"I've learned to trust people, okay? A skill you could stand to work on."

"Time out!" Mike said. "We all need to calm down

here. Daniel, you can't get mad. How this meeting goes tonight will affect the rest of your life, and you won't do it right if you're mad. So," and now he raised his voice, "if you guys can't stop fighting in the car, Mom and I aren't taking you to Disneyland next summer."

A brief silence, then Daniel chuckled. A second later, Ian snorted. He turned around in the car seat. "I was counting on Disneyland," he said, his voice and his face as gruff as ever.

"So pull yourself together for the meeting, Daniel," Mike said.

"Don't worry. Five minutes of sulking and I'll be in top form." He had to be. His project, his dream, meant too much to him. He couldn't blow off this chance to do something really important, to protect more children than he could possibly fit into his house on Prospect Street.

Discussion at the meeting droned on forever. It was an open board meeting, which meant all Serenity Valley residents could attend, but Daniel still couldn't imagine why so many of them had come out. He fidgeted in his seat, waiting for the words, "The floor is now open for new business."

If anybody took the floor before he did, he thought the veins in his temples might explode.

The moment arrived, and he shot from his seat. "Mr. Chairman."

"Daniel. Yes." The chairman of the board gave him a nod. "State your name, please, and present your business."

He stated his name as requested, although everybody in the room already knew who he was, and then he began his pitch, trying to sound easy and casual. "Most of you know I take in foster children," he began. "And that has

gotten me interested in the whole foster home situation."
He went on, respectful of those who already were foster
parents, but emphasizing the number of children who
probably needed foster care and weren't getting it.

"Many communities," and he named various other
places, "have built foster-care centers designed to house
a number of children in individual homes staffed by
couples, with common rooms in a larger main building
that would also house…"

The local pediatrician was nodding. So was the
head of Child Services in the valley. On the other hand,
the Churchill minister's wife, Virginia Galloway, was
frowning, and several members of the Women's Auxiliary had their heads together with hers. Daniel was
sure she was a good person—she taught the teenagers'
Sunday school class and she hadn't expelled Jason or
Maury yet—but he'd never been able to work up much
enthusiasm for the woman. Ironically, he was probably
going to have to persuade these godly women to be kind
to others who were less fortunate, while the inebriated
man who'd staggered into a backseat at the last minute
would turn out to be 100 percent in favor of the project.

"My brother Ian has volunteered to donate land for the
project, if it receives your approval. The kids will have
playing fields to share with the rest of the valley, and a
safe, protected environment. I've consulted an architect,
and I've researched the grants that might be available.
But I'll need your support to move on to the planning
stage, and I'd like to hear your opinions."

"The floor is open for discussion," the chairman said.

When the minister's wife raised her hand, Daniel's
heart sank. The chairman acknowledged her, and she

asked, "Would any of these children come from locations outside the valley?"

"Yes," Daniel said politely. "The facility would be available to any child in Vermont."

"Aren't you at all concerned that this foster center would bring undesirable elements into the valley?"

Daniel was gritting his teeth to keep from snapping, "No," when he heard Ian's voice. Startled looks came from the audience. Ian wasn't noted for contributing verbally to any cause.

"Ian?" the chairman said doubtfully.

Daniel held his breath. If Ian spoke the way he usually did, it could mean the end of the center. His gruffness and reserve put people off. God knew what he might say. The townspeople should focus on what he's done, Daniel worried, donating that land, and not what he… And then his eyes widened. Was that calm, even voice Ian's?

"Ma'am," Ian said, directing his gaze toward the minister's wife. "With all due respect, we're not talking about 'elements' here, we're talking about children."

Daniel was gratified to hear a ripple of laughter run through the room.

"The children aren't undesirable. Is any child undesirable?" He pinned his gaze on the woman, who shifted in her seat.

"Many of the parents of these children aren't undesirable, either," Ian went on. "They're poverty-stricken, or they're sick, or one parent is fine but the other is abusive. Sometimes the parents really care about their children, but they know they can't afford to take care of them."

Just as abruptly as he'd stood up, Ian sat down.

Daniel was stunned. He'd never heard Ian speak so eloquently. He'd never heard him speak eloquently at all.

The pediatrician, who was legendary for his lack of tact in situations not involving his patients, leapt to his feet. "Don't be an idiot, Virginia," he said to the minister's wife. "As Foster said, the children aren't criminals. Just because they're foster children doesn't mean they're going to raise hell."

"The sins of the fathers are visited on the children," intoned the minister from the back of the room.

He and his wife were a perfect couple.

"The sins of the fathers, speaking generically," the head of Child Services spoke up, "often result in the need for foster homes for the children. In that sense I agree with you."

Other objections arose, along with other statements in defense of the project. Daniel felt exhausted, and now, as if Mike were tuned in to his thought process, he raised his hand.

"Daniel's been talking to Ian and me about this project for a long time," he told the group in his smiling, easygoing way, "so I'm not exactly objective."

The group smiled back at him. Of the three of them, Daniel thought dolefully, Mike did the best job of fitting in with the community. Nothing like having the best restaurant—the only real restaurant—in the valley. People had a vested interest in staying on his good side.

"But I do think you folks need to know more specifics. Mr. Chairman, I'd like to propose that Daniel deliver a formal presentation with all the details at the next board meeting."

In seconds, the chairman had a motion and a second from the floor, and the show of hands was impressive. Apparently the townspeople wanted to know about the center, at least.

Daniel's heart swelled with affection for Mike and Ian. Whatever their disagreements, their bond stood firm. All for one, one for all.

"Well, not a coup," Mike said on the way home, "but a good start. Virginia Galloway lost this one."

"We need a mole in the Women's Auxiliary," Ian growled. "Or a hit man."

"I'd prefer the mole," Daniel said.

"You would," Ian said.

"Disneyland?" Mike said.

"Okay," Daniel said. "When we get back to my place we're all going in to see if Lilah has bruised, mutilated or killed the boys, and then we'll come to an agreement about whether she's a suitable housekeeper." He waited through the silence.

"Okay, fair enough," Mike said.

Daniel released a deep breath. *Dear God, let everything be okay.* Because Mike and Ian were the constants in his life. If they disapproved of Lilah, he couldn't let her stay.

When all three of them had finally set out on their careers, Ian had taken the legal steps to incorporate them. They'd struggled to educate each other in their chosen fields, and following that they'd decided to share the wealth, such as it was. Their income went into a corporate account, out of which they paid themselves equal salaries. Hiring Lilah didn't represent a cost for Daniel alone, but for all three of them.

And maybe Daniel's brothers were right. Maybe he'd taken this trust thing too far.

Chapter 5

"The house is too dark," Ian said, as Mike pulled into the parking area.

"Not the living room," Daniel remarked. "I imagine they're all in there."

"Tied up," Ian suggested. "Begging for their lives."

"Ian!" Mike said.

"Oh, okay, but I think we ought to sneak in and catch her at whatever she's doing."

"All right," Daniel said, getting out of the car. "Come on." He was sure everything was fine. Had to be. It would be, wouldn't it? Sure it would.

Through the window he saw Lilah standing in the living room, wearing an evil expression. "What the hell—"

She rushed toward the sofa with her arms outstretched. He launched into a run, with his brothers breathing down his neck, and almost ripped the front

door off its hinges. As he lunged through the foyer and
into the room, he heard a scream, then Jesse said from
the far corner, tilting his chair forward and almost falling out of it, "What the heck are you doing, Daniel? You
scared us out of our wits."

Daniel came to a stop so suddenly that Mike and Ian
rear-ended him. It was Lilah who had screamed, and
now she seemed to be breathing hard and trying to pull
herself together. Jonathan clung to her. The boys simply stared at Daniel.

"Well," he said to Lilah, reluctant to look her in the
eye, "we were coming in from the car, and I saw you,
um, rush forward, looking…"

He sent another glance toward the sofa, where the
boys were lined up, all perfectly fine and still staring at
him. Bowls of popcorn sat on either end of the coffee
table, and in the middle was a low, spreading bouquet of
heavy white blossoms picked from the snowball bushes
that hedged his property.

He didn't think he had any vases. He took a closer
look. The container was Jesse's sacred bean pot.

Then he took a look around the rest of the room. Jesse
had relaxed back into the rocker, his cane resting against
the wall, and Aengus was lying on the round rag rug,
standing guard. The room was neater than he'd ever
seen it. The wide planks of the maple floor, original to
the house, looked funny. They gleamed. Had someone
scrubbed them?

"We were playing charades," Jonathan said, "and
Mom was acting out the Wicked Witch of the West."

"From *The Wizard of Oz*," Will said, as if Daniel
might have missed out on it.

Behind him, Daniel heard a snicker. He'd remind his

brothers later that they were the ones who'd gotten him stirred up.

"I thought it might make a nice change from television and computer games," Lilah said. Her face was pale, but she'd recovered enough to glare at him.

"When we did *Pirates of the Caribbean*," Nick added, "Jason was trying to show us the ocean making waves and…" he began laughing "he fell over."

"The waters were rough," Jason said.

"Want to play?" Will asked.

"Sure!" Mike said.

"I guess so," Ian growled. "What do I have to do?"

"It's nine o'clock," Lilah said. "I believe that's bedtime."

Daniel exchanged a look with her. He tried to tell her with his eyes how stupid he felt, how sorry he was. "I think we can bend the rules once in a while," he said. "It's summertime, and there's nothing I like better than seeing Ian and Mike make fools of themselves."

Her slight smile was almost like forgiveness. When Mike and Ian launched into the game, he did, too. He had a feeling they'd changed their minds about Lilah.

Talk about bending the rules, it was almost eleven when Daniel sent the boys up to bed and walked Mike and Ian to their cars. The fun hadn't ended when the game was finished. Jesse had brought out wedges of the pies Mike had brought, lemon and chocolate meringue, coconut cream and something absolutely delicious called key lime pie. It was a first for Lilah, and it embarrassed her to realize she'd eaten two pieces of it.

While they ate until nothing was left but crumbs of crust, which Will picked off the serving plate with a finger he'd licked, Daniel, his brothers and the kids engaged in lively conversation about everything under the sun, politics and soccer, recycling and movie ratings, the culinary arts and baseball. Lilah saw how Jonathan entered into the discussion and had clearly been accepted, even celebrated, and it made her feel warm inside.

But the boys were in bed now, even Jonathan, who was having a ball being with other boys, knowing she was a shout away. She and Daniel were alone, and for the first time she didn't feel like running away.

"I'm sorry I freaked out," he said as soon as the house was quiet. "I have this overprotective streak."

"Your entrance was a little overdramatic, I have to admit."

"I should go into show business?"

"I said *over*dramatic." She couldn't understand why she felt comfortable enough to tease him. "Daniel…"

He'd been headed toward the door, but he turned back.

"I know you're exhausted," she said, "but sometime I wish you'd tell me about each of the boys. It would help me know what they need from me."

"What about right now?" Daniel said, although she could see that he was drained to the core by the tensions of the evening. "We should have a glass of Jesse's cooking wine and unwind."

She feigned horror. "You'd veer from the Saturday-night beer and have a glass of wine? Off schedule?"

"I have to save that beer for Saturday night. And besides, my whole household is off schedule."

"You have a point. I'd love a glass of wine."

He came back with wine and gestured toward the empty bowl of popcorn. "Wine and snacks," he said.

"How good are your teeth? We seem to have a few un-popped corns left."

"My teeth are excellent, but I've had so much pie I could care less about any more snacks."

He joined her on the sofa. "Before we talk about the boys, I have something for you." He handed her a cell phone.

Lilah shook her head and tried to return it. "Thanks, but no."

Daniel wouldn't take it back. "You might need it. I put you on the family plan, so it won't be expensive. But you should be reachable in an emergency."

She looked at him, then at the phone. Finally, she nodded. "Okay. Thanks."

"Now, about the boys." He settled back on the sofa. "Starting with the oldest, Jason's family lived in an aban-doned school bus out in the woods, where his father was growing marijuana. His idea," and Daniel's jaw tight-ened as he explained this, "was that Jason could deliver the pot. Who's going to be suspicious of a twelve-year-old kid on a bike?"

Lilah moaned. "Horrible," she murmured. "How could a parent do something like that?"

"Well, the parent could, but the son couldn't. When Jason refused to make the deliveries, his father kicked him out of the house. He lived on the street for a year before a social worker caught up with him and put him into foster care. Two other families gave up on him be-fore he came to me. He was mad at the whole world."

"I wouldn't have believed it," she said. "He's kind and helpful, and he has a wonderful, dry sense of humor…"

"And he's a big brother to the younger kids. So's Maury," Daniel went on, "whose past is even more tragic. His parents moved, and moved and moved again, trying to escape their debts. To his mother's credit, she kept him in school—he was in fourteen schools in eight years, never knew where he'd be the next day. One day his dad just fell apart and shot Maury's mom and then himself."

Lilah wondered how she'd ever thought her life had been hard. Her family had been poor, but that was all. Her heart bled for these boys.

"Mike's the one who turned Maury around," Daniel said. "Maury's a born foodie, just like Mike. He spends every minute he can at Mike's restaurant, and as soon as he can drive himself, Mike will give him a regular part-time job. We're bringing up a chef here."

"Do these boys have any idea how lucky they are to be with you?" Her face felt hot. She shouldn't have said something so personal. "I mean," she stammered, "they have you, and Jesse's just like a grandfather, and your brothers are great with them—" She halted suddenly. Her only hope was to change the subject immediately. "Tell me about the other two boys."

"Quick sketches," Daniel said and swallowed a yawn. "Will's parents want him back as soon as they've recovered from really bad injuries in a car accident. And Nick…" His brow furrowed. "Nick's the most complicated case I have."

He rested his forehead in his hand. "Apparently he was abandoned—or maybe he ran away. All he'll say is that he can't remember where he comes from. I can't stand thinking what those nightmares must have been about."

He got to his feet and looked down at her. When he spoke, his voice was soft. "You've done more for him with that dreamcatcher you made than I've been able to do in the last three months. I'm very grateful."

Lilah stood up, too. "I'm so glad it helped."

When she turned toward him, he suddenly seemed too close. She could see his fatigue, the shadow of a blond beard on his cheeks and a vulnerability in his eyes she hadn't noticed before.

Why should he feel vulnerable to anything? He and his brothers had obviously had happy childhoods, Daniel was well-off, and she suspected Mike and Ian were, too. What did Daniel have to be sad about?

And what was it about him that made her feel drawn to him instinctively, just as Jonathan was?

"One more thing," she said. "The kids are calling Jonathan J.J. It's okay, but I just wondered…"

"We're big on nicknames around here," he said, smile lines crinkling around his eyes. "It sort of says we're all buddies, so everybody has a nickname. Except Jason," he added, as if he were realizing it for the first time.

"And you."

Their gazes locked. He opened his mouth, but before he could say anything, a voice shouted, "Daniel!"

It was Jonathan's voice, and he'd called for Daniel, not for her. Daniel was already moving, Lilah on his heels, when Jonathan spoke again. "Nick's got a splinter in his hand. A big one."

Daniel turned at the door and gave her a crooked grin. "Can you get home okay? I have to make one of those late-night house calls."

"Daniel, do you have a minute?"

Daniel was attending to a Jack Russell terrier, the beloved pet of Reverend and Mrs. Galloway. He slid a needle into the little dog's plump haunch and allowed himself a moment of self-congratulation—this was the goosiest dog in the world and he didn't even flinch— then looked up to see Dana Holstead standing in his doorway. "Dana!" he said. "Come on in. I always have time for you."

Dana, the head of Child Services in the valley, had been his first real friend in Churchill and also the woman who'd examined every nook and cranny of his character before changing his life by allowing him to become a foster parent. In her fifties and childless, she took each child who came into the Child Services system as a personal responsibility.

"I can't find anything negative about Lilah Jamison," Dana said. "How's she working out?"

It was Dana's job to be interested. Daniel probed the dog's body for cysts and otherwise painful areas and said, "Great so far. Come to dinner next weekend and check her out."

"How is Banjo?" asked Virginia Galloway, sailing through the door like a ship's figurehead, her substantial bosom leading the way. Apparently, she'd milked Mildred of all her gossip at last.

"In perfect health," Daniel said, thinking to himself that the dog was pampered, overfed and yet, somehow, as overactive as any other Jack Russell.

"Of course he is," Virginia replied, then turned to direct a critical gaze toward Dana and an accusing one toward Daniel. "Dana," she said without much warmth.

"Virginia," Dana said with considerable warmth. "How nice to run into you. Banjo is such a darling."

Dana wasn't a gushy person. If she was pandering to

Virginia Galloway, she must have an agenda. "How old is he now?" she went on.

"Fourteen," Virginia said.

"I would have guessed he was just a puppy!"

Had Virginia thawed at all? Daniel couldn't tell. She swept regally from the room, almost certainly on her way to protest the amount of her bill.

"Lovely person," Dana said.

"Salt of the earth," Daniel replied.

"You think she could stall the foster center?"

"Absolutely. She has enormous power in the community. I can't imagine why."

"What can we do about her, short of rat poison?"

"I don't know. You did your best to soften her up, and it didn't work."

"We have to find her weak spot."

"Good luck." Daniel felt gloomy about the prospect.

"Okay, now the good news. I got a letter today—three former foster children who've grown up and done well want to launch a fund-raising effort for your center."

He suddenly felt great. "That makes my day. Looks like our financial prospects are pretty good."

"Hailed from without, condemned from within," Dana said dramatically.

"A prophet without honor in his own country," Daniel intoned.

Dana snickered, then began to fill Daniel in on the details of the offer. Suddenly, she seemed to hear the barking and yowling coming from the waiting room, and the raucous squawk of the poetry-quoting parrot, Robert Frost, Bob for short, named for the famous Vermont poet. The bird had an impressive repertoire of his poems. Even now Bob was screeching, "And miles to go before I sleep."

"Sorry," she said. "I forgot you had a job. Gotta run before Bob Frost launches into 'Birches.'"

"This looks great, Jesse."

"Tell Lilah. She cooked it." But Jesse was beaming like a proud father. "I gave her some tips, of course."

"If he hadn't, it wouldn't look—or taste—half this good," Lilah said. It was true. She glanced with pride at the huge dutch oven filled with big chunks of pork in barbecue sauce, the giant bowls of rice and pinto beans and the basket containing three dozen corn muffins, which might or might not be enough. Without Jesse's advice, that the pork didn't have to be browned for a dish like this, she'd still be browning it.

"Mexican food night," Daniel said. "Perfect time for a serious family council."

Lilah felt uneasy, but the boys leaned forward, chewing happily. They were not at all dreading a "serious family council" but anticipating something interesting. Will dashed to the line of dishes on the kitchen counter to grab another corn muffin, and Daniel waited patiently for him to return.

"It has come to my attention," he said, forking up a bite of pork and rice, "that Jason's sixteenth birthday is next week and Maury's is just two weeks later. That means they'll be eligible for junior driver's licenses."

The younger boys stared at them with awe bordering on worship.

"A license piles a lot of responsibility on the driver's shoulders," Daniel continued.

Lilah listened. In her world, a driver's license had just

piled more responsibility on her. It had meant she had to do the grocery shopping, had to pick up her mother and then her father at work, because they only had one rattletrap car, and if she was going to take it to school in the morning, she had to pay the price in the afternoon. Homework had to wait until she'd fulfilled her family duties.

"Not to drink," Jason said.

"Not to pile a bunch of kids into the car and take them places they're not supposed to be," Maury said.

"And to help with some of the errands," Daniel added.

"No problem."

Lilah could tell both boys were trying to hide their excitement. "Buy groceries when we're out of something important. Like popcorn," Jason said, twisting his mouth into a smile that was so like Daniel's it made Lilah smile. Daniel was Jason's superhero, and as far as she could tell, he'd chosen a darned good one.

"Let's see. What else?" Daniel frowned.

"Getting to their jobs on time?"

That came from Jonathan. Lilah stared at him, amazed that he knew more about the dynamic of this family than she did.

Daniel explained, "When they can drive themselves, Jason will be doing odd jobs on Ian's farm every afternoon, and Maury can go to Mike's Diner afternoons and weekends." He paused, and the pause was dramatic. "Which means we have to add two cars. Used cars, naturally, so we're going shopping for trendy junkers on Saturday. All of us," he said, glancing at Lilah and Jesse. "Forget the cleaning. Hamburgers on the grill for dinner. This is a big event. We need everybody's imput."

Lilah could think of worse ways to spend a Saturday

than that. She attacked her own dinner at last, allowed herself a second corn muffin slathered with butter and thought about Jonathan. One day, in Daniel's world, he could have a car, too. The rules for being a responsible licensed driver would have been drilled into him from the experiences of Jason and Maury, and she'd be able to relax, knowing everything that could have been done or said had been done or said.

But surely it wasn't possible for life to be that predictable. There had to be a catch somewhere.

Chapter 6

They stood awestruck in a semicircle around two distinctively different vehicles. Jason gazed, starry-eyed, at a miniscule sports car, its once bright yellow paint dimmed to lemon and scratched in spots, a noticeable dent in its right front fender. The black leather upholstery was cracked with age, and the hood, also black, creaked ominously as the boy tenderly raised it. The car was old, but it would never be a vintage classic.

Maury stood at the rear of a station wagon just like Mike's, but ten years older. Those extra years hadn't been easy, either. He opened the rear hatch, examined the interior and closed it again. He'd done that five or six times while everyone waited for the salesman on the used car lot to finish the paperwork.

"He's figuring the volume and how to pack the food

containers," Daniel murmured. "When he's eighteen, he can help Mike haul food to his catering jobs."

He sighed, a sigh of satisfaction. "Well, we did it. Yes," he said to the salesman who'd just joined them, "where do I sign?"

A few minutes later he said, "Jesse, you can ride shotgun with Maury. Lilah," he turned toward her with an imploring look on his face, "would you mind taking Will and Nick and Jonathan home? Because I," he said grandly, "get to ride in the sports car."

"It'll be a treat for me. I've been wanting to spend some time alone with these guys."

The boys raced for her car without a protest and settled themselves into the backseat. Pulling out of the lot, she glanced into the rearview mirror and saw Daniel gazing at her, and the expression on his face startled her. There was warmth in that gaze, but Daniel was always warm. This was something else. Longing? When their eyes connected, she felt a stab of electricity that sizzled through her from head to toe. For a moment she held the contact, looking into the depths of his mysterious milk-chocolate eyes, unable to break the connection. Nor could he. She saw a flash of surprise cross his face, as if the brief spell had startled him as much as it had her.

"Are you okay, Mom?" Jonathan sounded anxious.

She turned her gaze back toward the road, away from Daniel, breathless and quivering inside. "Just great," she said cheerfully. "Let's go home and have ourselves some fun."

"Wow, that was cool," Jonathan said. "I'm going to have a car when I'm sixteen."

"You turn sixteen and you get a car?" Will sounded hopeful.

Lilah didn't feel exactly like herself, so it took some effort to sound normal. "Well, no, it's not quite that easy." She smiled, still seeing the image of Daniel in her mind although they were now blocks away from the car lot. "You also have to learn to drive."

"I hope mine's a Porsche," Jonathan said.

"Dream on," Lilah said. "You'll be thrilled with whatever it is. Hey, when we get home, we should get to work on dinner."

"Daniel says it's warm enough for a picnic," Nick said.

"Yep," Lilah agreed, "and it'll be just like the Fourth of July. Jesse has baked beans in the oven, and we made potato salad last night." She remembered something else she'd been thinking about. "You know, July really is birthday month around here. Jason's, then Maury's, and then Daniel's. Jesse told me."

"Jason told me they have parties on their birthdays," Will said.

"Jesse says Daniel won't let us give him one," Nick said.

Maybe it was just seeing the expression on Daniel's face a few minutes earlier, but Lilah felt like doing something special for him, and the bud of an idea began to blossom.

"Maybe we should give him one anyway," she said slowly. "A surprise party."

The minute they got home, the boys began setting up the backyard for a picnic. A black-and-white checked oil-cloth tablecover, its edges trimmed with pinking shears, covered the picnic table. From each corner a weight dangled, not a decorative weight, either, but a rock wrapped in cheesecloth and tied on with kitchen twine.

Lilah smiled. Daniel ran a no-frills operation for sure. While the boys were in the house gathering the tableware, she made a bouquet of dark pink peonies cut from the plants that had just begun to bloom at the side of the house. She stood in the yard holding them, frowning. Daniel was getting a proper vase for his birthday, whether he liked it or not. In the meantime…

She found a clear plastic pitcher in a cupboard, and once she'd lined it with huge, bright-green hosta leaves, it looked pretty nice filled with peonies.

She put it down in the center of the table, where the boys were fitting flimsy paper plates into wicker holders. Under each holder and plate was a paper napkin, and on top, a knife and fork from their everyday stainless steel held everything down.

"No plastic forks?"

"Jesse said if we bought plastic forks, we'd probably start washing them and using them again," Nick explained. "So why buy plastic?"

Now everyone was home and everything was under control. Lilah sat on one of the lawn chairs that were arranged around the backyard and relaxed. While Jesse got the fire going in the grill, the younger boys were practicing some soccer moves they'd learned at camp and talking about the events of the day. Jason and Maury were bonding with their new vehicles, simply sitting in them or stroking the hoods, vacuuming the floorboards and exchanging some car talk. Daniel was in the middle of the fray, attempting to act as referee. Unfortunately, Aengus had also joined the impromptu game and was jumping, barking and chasing the ball.

"Hey, Mom, watch this," Jonathan shouted.

Lilah turned and watched her son bounce the ball on top of his sneaker, then toss it in the air and kick it hard. The other boys cheered his move, and Lilah laughed. Her son was flourishing in his new life, thanks to these boys. Her gaze drifted to Daniel. And thanks to this man. Could it be, was it possible, that she was flourishing, too?

She watched as Daniel encouraged the boys, cheering every bounce and kick. Bruce had made her want never to be with a man again, but Daniel was different from any other man she'd known.

He was kind. Patient. Funny. Appealing. Watching him play with the boys, Lilah noticed the graceful way he moved, as if he were comfortable in his own skin.

Her gaze lingered, and a tingle ran through her. Well, of course, it was hard to be a female and not tingle at the sight of him. He was great to look at, but he wasn't just a pretty face. He radiated energy and life, and when he smiled, he could take her breath away.

There was danger here. She could so easily get caught up in that circle of energy and lose what she'd so painfully acquired over the past three years. She could find herself relaxing, staying right here, taking care of his house, mothering his boys, not even realizing she'd lost her independence and had given him control of her life.

He must have sensed her looking at him because suddenly he stopped, and then he sent her that slow smile of his. Lilah felt attraction dance down her spine like a caress, and without thinking, she found herself smiling back.

For a long moment, Daniel simply gazed at her. She

wished she knew what was going on in his mind. She hoped he didn't know what she was thinking.

"Aargh!" In pursuit of the ball, Aengus knocked him flat. For a moment, he lay on the summer-green grass, laughing while Aengus frantically licked his face, either apologizing or trying to bring his master back to life.

"Enough, enough," Daniel told the anxious dog. "I'm fine." Still laughing, he rolled up onto his feet, dusted himself off and headed toward Lilah's chair.

"Chow time," Jesse yelled.

"For the record, guys, you may not eat in your cars or sleep in your cars," Daniel megaphoned to Jason and Maury. "That's enough soccer for tonight," he called out to the younger boys. "Come over here and have a hamburger."

A light breeze cooled their picnic. The black flies seemed to have gone to bed, and even though it was still light at seven, citronella candles were lit to discourage the mosquitoes.

"The idea was to have an easy dinner so everybody could go on the field trip to used car lots," he said, spooning up baked beans from the gallon-sized crock. "So what's all this other stuff doing here?" He was sitting beside Lilah, and the twinkling gaze he rested on her made her feel warm inside. A little too warm.

His thigh brushed hers, a firm, muscular thigh, and the heat inside her intensified. Her appetite, for food, at least, flew away in the evening air.

This was ridiculous. What if the boys noticed her flushed face? She was their housekeeper. She had no business gazing at Daniel with her mouth hanging open.

She closed it tightly, but she couldn't reason the feelings away. "Are you boys going to learn everything you

can about engines?" she asked brightly. "So you can do
some of your own repairs?"

They were on second and third helpings and having a lively discussion about suspension systems when
the candles suddenly flickered and the leaves from the
maples rustled. Seconds later, a jagged flash of lightning crackled above them, and to Lilah's amazement,
the younger boys immediately began counting. "Seven,"
they shouted when the thunder rolled.

They gazed at each other and at the sky. "Dessert
inside," Jesse said succinctly. "Everybody scramble."

"We need rain," Daniel said.

"Not this much of it," Jesse grumbled.

Lightning lit up the picnic scene outside, and thunder
rattled the old glass of the windows. They'd barely made
it indoors with the food when the heavens opened. Rain
pelted down on Jason and Maury while they gathered
up soggy paper plates after putting their cars to bed in
the carriage house. Maybe even with a good-night kiss.

But Daniel really did need the rain. In the first place,
Lilah's fragile body so close to him had stirred his blood,
and he didn't want his blood stirred. He was walking a
fine line here, having a woman in his house, a beautiful woman, and he didn't dare cross it. He needed the
rain to cool him down.

In the second place, he'd been looking for just the
right time to explain the foster-care center to her in a
casual way. "Before we have shortcake, I have some en-
tertainment planned."

The boys were pitching in, filling trash bags with
the used plates, refilling plastic cups from the pitch-

ers of lemonade. "I'll need some tech help in the living room," he added.

"Whoa!" He blocked the kitchen doorway as all five boys attempted to trade kitchen duty for tech assistance. "Jason and Jonathan, come with me."

"Is it a movie?" Nick asked, when he saw the screen set up against the living room windows.

"No, I need to practice the speech I have to give in a couple of weeks to a bunch of people who need to approve the foster-care center. If I wow 'em, they might even donate money."

The boys wriggled uneasily. "Come on," he said. "I help with your homework, right? Well, this is my homework. Pretend you're a roomful of big shots deciding whether to trust me with a great big project I want to do, using their money."

Lilah, who'd been looking interested, winced when he mentioned "other people's money." Bad news. If she wasn't looking forward to the speech, either, he might as well give up on it, he thought, since she was his prime target. He wanted to be able to talk to her about the center. She seemed to understand human nature. She might have some good advice for him.

Jason was at the computer and Jonathan stood by the light switches. First, Daniel delivered a short introduction explaining the purpose of the center.

"The kids would live in houses with parents, just like we live with you?" Maury said. "That's cool."

Jason gave him a look. "Sorry, Daniel," Maury said. "Go on."

The first of the PowerPoint visuals appeared on the screen, presenting a picture of rolling land, grassy and shaded by trees, partially surrounded by a forest of evergreens, maples and birches, with the mountains rising up in the background. Sheep dotted the landscape. "This is the land where we'll build the center. "It's…"

"It's Uncle Ian's land," Nick said with an air of authority. "I know from the sheep."

"That's right," Daniel said. "Jason?"

The second image appeared. "This is the architect's model of the center, as you'd see it from the air."

"Like from a helicopter?" Jonathan asked.

"Big shots don't ask that kind of question," Jason informed him.

"Yes," Daniel said, "it's like an aerial view, but these are small models on a tabletop, so the photographer just leaned over them with his camera."

"It looks real," Will said.

An impatient sigh came from Jason, but Daniel said, "Good, because I want the development board to see how it will look."

He hazarded a glance at Lilah. She wasn't wincing now or looking bored—or as if she wished she could go to the kitchen and help Jesse clean up. She was spellbound. Her hair swung over her shoulders as she leaned forward, her eyes sparkling and her cheeks flushed with excitement.

She is *beautiful* flashed through his mind, before he thought, *and she's interested.* He was so anxious to hear what she thought about his impending presentation after the boys went to bed that he had to force himself not to rush through the rest of his speech and to be patient when the boys interrupted him with questions. The slides got pretty boring anyway toward the end—not for him but for his restless audience, which became increasingly fidgety as the smell of baking shortcake wafted in from the kitchen.

Lilah didn't look bored, not even by these slides. When the estimated costs came up on the screen, her forehead wrinkled in concentration. In reaction to the list of potential donors, he could almost see ideas buzzing in her head.

"Any questions?" he asked, when he wound up.

"No," Will said forcefully, gazing toward the kitchen.

"No questions?" He gave them his most disappointed face, then his hopeful one. "Does this mean you're ready to donate?"

"I'll give you all the allowance I've saved, if you'll just let us have that strawberry shortcake," Will said fervently.

Daniel looked severely around the room. "Anybody else?"

"Dessert's ready," Jesse bellowed from the kitchen.

"Good night, then," Daniel said, bowing. "I'll be in touch with you soon, and have your checkbooks with you."

He said it to an audience of one—Lilah, who was still gazing at the final slide showing the projected time frame for building the center.

A brilliant flash of lightning and a deafening clap of thunder punctuated the moment. *Gotcha,* Daniel thought.

Once again, bedtime didn't happen exactly at nine, but at last the boys and Jesse were, if not exactly quiet, at least tucked away behind closed doors. Lilah was so wrapped up in the center proposal that she realized she'd done a pretty poor job of seeing the kids off to bed.

"I could stand another cup of coffee," Daniel said. "How about you?"

She heard him, but couldn't concentrate on anything as trivial as coffee. "Wow," she said softly, "what you're doing here is, well, it's just…just the most wonderful thing imaginable. And you have it so well thought out. You must have been planning it for years."

He paused at the door, walked back toward her and sat across from her. "You think I'm on the right track?" he said. "You think I can convince the Regional Development Board it's a good idea? Because without them, I can't get the permits to build, and without those, there's no point in fund-raising."

"Of course you'll convince them…" Her voice trailed off.

"But?" he said. "You have to tell me. That's what this trial run was all about."

"I was thinking…"

"What were you thinking."

Okay, she'd go for it.

"I was thinking about some ways you could jazz up the presentation."

His eyebrows lifted. "Tell me. I need to bowl these folks over."

"Well, entertaining them would be a good start. What about a film with a voice-over." She warmed to her subject. "What about a panoramic view of the property, which is beautiful, by the way, then a…well, almost a realistic tour of the architect's models." She paused for a moment, thinking. "Are there other centers like these?"

"Several," he said. He seemed mesmerized. It gave her courage.

"Maybe someone could do some filming at one of

them, show the children engaging in activities there, a clip of the kids having dinner at one of the houses—I thought of that because dinner is such fun here, a high point in the boys' days. No close-ups of their faces, of course," she added in a hurry, "for obvious reasons, but maybe a clip of them in their recreation center, and on their playing fields, and maybe even one of them piling into the bus that takes them to school every day."

She'd been letting her gaze wander as ideas spilled out, but now she focused on him and found him staring back at her.

"It's my turn to say, 'Wow,'" he said after a long pause. He began to pace. "You are so right."

A thrill ran through her. He'd listened to her, and he liked what he'd heard. It made her feel more worthwhile than she'd felt in years.

He went on, "There's a guy in the valley who could do it, Ray Colloton, lives in LaRocque. I think he'd give us a good price. We could fly him to one of the centers...."

He stopped pacing and sat down, looking her straight in the eyes. "Maybe you could go with him and show him what we want."

"Oh, I couldn't," she said. "I have a job to do here."

"I," Daniel said, pointing in the direction of the clinic, "have a job to do there."

"I know how busy you are. I have no idea how you can keep up your practice and give this project what it needs. The details, the endless details, are simply staggering."

His gaze hadn't wavered. "Think you could handle a few of them for me?"

Chapter 7

Lilah stared at him. "I'd like that coffee now," she said.

At least she hadn't said no or argued that she already had enough to do. "Coming right up," Daniel said, "so don't go away."

He got the coffee started, then thought he'd better wait for it with Lilah in his line of sight so she couldn't escape. He went back to the living room, and there he found her gazing at a blank wall. "Hello?" he said. "Are you still with us here on earth?"

She shot him a smile and seemed to relax. "To answer your question, of course I'm happy to help in any way I can. The house is running smoothly, and I have time to think about the center, too."

"You wouldn't feel imposed upon?"

"Of course not. I'm full-time. I'll use that time however you want me to." A shadow crossed her face. "Is the coffee just about ready?" she asked, sounding as if she really needed it.

As always, he had no idea what he might have said to cause her sudden look of doubt. "I imagine so." The coffee wasn't, quite, so he waited and watched it drip while he pondered her contradictions, her happiness, her unexpected moments of...of what? Worry? Sadness? Was she grieving for her husband?

The muscles of his back knotted. How did that scar on her forehead fit into the picture?

He relaxed a bit and laughed at himself. His knee-jerk reaction to protect the young and the helpless had probably made him imagine the scar was a result of abuse. She'd probably fallen on the ice or been thrown by a horse. And of course she'd be grieving for her husband.

He'd felt her response to him, though, the few times he'd accidentally touched her. The truth was, he'd like to touch her on purpose. What he wanted... He suddenly knew what he wanted, and it unnerved him. He wanted to take her in his arms, hug her tight and kiss her. The way her full pink lips had opened as she gazed so raptly at his presentation—maybe even at him—had opened up something in him he'd wanted to keep closed.

But she was his employee. He'd practically coerced her into taking this job, and to make a sexual approach to her would violate every principle of an honorable employer/employee relationship. Not only that, but an affair wasn't what he wanted at this point in his life. He was pretty happy. His life was stable.

Someday, maybe, he'd be ready for love of the romantic kind, but he could never "take a chance on love." He had to have certainty. He'd have to trust the woman completely. Rejection, betrayal, could destroy him.

He had no clue as to what went on inside Lilah or what her life story was, what had driven such a valuable woman into the situation in which he'd found her. Until he learned the answers to those questions, there was no certainty, and he needed those things more than he needed love—or even sex.

He sighed. His libido, so long suppressed, had inexplicably sabotaged his good judgment. What he really wanted was simply to have her working for him.

That was his story and he was sticking to it.

The coffeepot seemed to take forever. He focused on the bouquet in the middle of the kitchen table—his Siberian Irises had just started blooming and Lilah had stuck some of them in here and there with more of the snowball heads. It looked pretty, even on the same old tablecloth. That hadn't changed. Even she knew cloth covers would be a laundry disaster.

Maybe he'd just confused flowers and a neat living room with stability.

When at last the coffee seemed to be ready, he spilled it all over the counter, because he was trying to pour it as fast as he could. One more minute of worry that he was getting too close to her might have led to heart failure. Arrhythmia, anyway. He had to keep her at arm's length—literally.

Before he could carry the cups into the living room, Lilah appeared in the kitchen with a sheaf of copy paper in her hand and a look of intense concentration on her face. "The slides of the financial stuff aren't exactly gripping," she said, sitting down at the kitchen table, "so I was thinking zippier graphics might perk them up. Catchy fonts, larger, too, lots of color, bullets and arrows. Here. Look at this. It's just a rough plan of how the pages might be laid out."

He put the coffee on the table and sat, amused by her seriousness but feeling his senses tingle, coming back to life after years of numbness. She handed him several sheets of paper.

"You could put the same material in a handout that they could take home with them."

He grinned at her. "Maybe we should skip the house-keeping and hire you as public relations officer for the center."

"Oh, no, these are just some ideas..."

He felt confident enough to tease her. "Think about it. We'd send out a press release, "Lilah Jamison has accepted the position of..."

"No press release." She snapped it at him. "No news-papers." She must have seen how she'd startled him, because her mouth twisted in a rueful smile. "Sorry. I overreacted. I'm just averse to publicity, always have been." She sighed. "My mother always said your name should never be in the newspaper except at birth and death. I guess it sank in."

He gazed at her, then relaxed, just as she had done, and said, "She must have been a real lady. Tell me about her."

He saw her tense up again. "Oh, she's just a mom," she said lightly. "A working mom. My dad's an auto me-chanic. We were poor but happy, as the saying goes."

She'd obviously ended that conversational thread. He gave up—for the moment—on trying to glean a scrap of personal information from her. "Okay, let's look at those sketches of yours. Do you do computer graphics?"

She gazed at him, and it was as if a veil dropped over

her face, and when she spoke, she sounded bitter. "I do very compelling computer graphics."

Lilah had a secret. Until he knew the secret, he wouldn't know her, and he couldn't trust her completely. With the boys, yes, but not with his heart.

Lilah said good-night to Daniel as soon as she could. When she reached her apartment, she fell across the bed and buried her face in the pillows.

She had done the fliers for Bruce's nonexistent housing development. She'd learned to keep his books, and then she'd had to learn how to do computer graphics. She'd found it fun, much more fun than spreadsheets. He'd handed her blueprints and sketches of finished houses, and she'd scanned, reduced, enlarged and cropped to make the envelope of promotional material as appealing to potential purchasers as possible. She didn't know he'd simply bought the blueprints from a home-building magazine.

She'd had no idea she was facilitating his scam, but still she felt guilty for making such a good case for North Woods, the development that would never be built.

What had shaken her this evening was the memory of Bruce commanding her to learn how to do the graphics and produce the materials. He'd said, "I support you, so you'll damned well do what I want you to do with your time."

What she'd said to Daniel was, "I'm full-time, so I'll do whatever you want me to do with that time." Which meant the same thing. And when she'd heard the words spilling out of her mouth, she'd felt sick.

But Daniel wasn't like Bruce. He hadn't commanded her, he'd asked her. The center must be real, although she'd had a moment of worry as he talked about asking for donations to build it.

She needed to put her life with Bruce behind her. And she'd thought she had—until she found herself in close contact with a man who could just as easily rob her of her independence, even though he'd do it nicely, make her think dependence was just what she wanted.

But she couldn't spend her life looking for similarities to Bruce in every man she met. She had to get over it.

At breakfast the next morning, Jason and Maury slipped envelopes into Daniel's hand. Surprised by the gesture, he found an excuse to leave the room in order to see what was inside.

The note from Maury read,

Dear Daniel: Thank you so much for my car. I promise to be careful driving it. I'll keep it clean and try to get the best gas mileage I can. I can't wait until my birthday when I can drive it by myself, but I like it when you're in the front seat, Jesse and Lilah, too. So anytime you want to ride with me is fine. Your friend, Maury.

Daniel smiled. He was touched by Maury's note. He was a great kid. Maybe he'd never be a great poet, but he didn't need to be because he'd be a great cook.

Next, he opened Jason's letter.

Dear Daniel: I want to say some things I can't say to your face. You changed my life. When I came here, I was so mad I wanted to make things as hard for everyone around me as I could. Now I

can't even remember how it felt to be that mad.
You made me know I could trust you. You acted
like you liked me, so I started to think maybe other
people could like me, too. I found out they do, and
everything in my life feels different.

When you gave Maury and me these cars, it
meant you trusted me. I don't ever want to let you
down. You are too good a man for anybody to let
you down. Thank you for the car, for making me
feel this way, and for being the greatest person I've
ever known. Jason.

Daniel read the note, then read it again. His eyes
stung. This might be his finest moment. Building the
foster-care center would pale in comparison.

When he felt in control, he went back to the kitchen,
where the boys were talking about Harry Potter's latest
adventure over stacks of French toast. Jason and Maury
were sitting side by side, and he paused between them,
ruffling their hair. "Thanks," he whispered.

It was enough. Maury blushed, and Jason looked up
at him. Daniel tried to transmit, without words, the message, *You're special to me. I love you as if you were my
own sons.*

He saw Lilah across the table, taking in the scene,
her facial expression ever-changing, as if she were wondering how the boys' notes had affected him. He had no
doubt that writing the notes had been her idea, but the
words had come straight from the boys' hearts.

And had gone straight to his.

"I think we've got Jason's party together," Jesse said.
"I'm off to take a shower before he and Daniel get home."

"Good plan," Lilah said. "I'll make a cup of tea and keep an eye on the scalloped potatoes."

"Call me if they get home with good news," Jesse said as he limped out of the room. "I'll come out stark naked to congratulate Jason if I have to."

"I'd love it if you didn't," Lilah said.

She went to the window and rested her forehead against the cool glass. This was such a big day for Jason. His sixteenth birthday, and he would get his Junior Operator's License if he passed the test. They were blowing it all out for his party, and he'd invited five friends, four of them kids who were in and out of the house all the time and wouldn't run screaming from the noise and general confusion. Lilah had her fingers crossed for the fifth one. She smiled. He'd pass the test. His party would be a victory celebration.

"Mom?"

She whirled. "Jonathan! You scared me. I guess I was daydreaming. How're you doing, sweetie? Pretty big day, huh?"

"Yeah. Mom, where do you think Dad is?"

She led him to the kitchen table and sat down across from him. "I don't know," she said, wanting to be honest. "I know he's out of prison, and I know he told a reporter he wanted to be with us again, but that's all."

"Do you want to be with him again?"

What had brought on his anxiety? "No," she said. Then, dreading the answer, she asked, "Do you miss him?"

"Uh-uh. No way."

His head was downcast, and his sneakers kicked the chair stretchers. "Honey, what's worrying you?"

He answered with another question. "Are you happy here?"

"Why, yes," she said, realizing it was true. "And you are, too, I think."

He raised his head and his face brightened. "Oh, yeah. I have kids to play with all the time, and everybody's nice, and you're right here when I need you."

"So what's the problem?" She smiled at him.

"I'm scared he'll find us, and we'll have to run away again."

Her smile faded. She leaned back in the chair, then was suddenly filled with resolve. "Maybe we won't run away anymore, Jonathan. Maybe we're ready to stand up for ourselves."

"They're home!" Will shrieked. His yell rattled the windows. Jonathan was up and running, his worry temporarily forgotten in the excitement of finding out if Jason had passed the test. Looking out the window again, seeing Daniel standing beside Jason, who seemed even taller now, both of them trying to look casual and failing to, she knew it was a victorious homecoming.

Her gaze went to Daniel and lingered there. He wore chinos with a white polo shirt. She smiled. She'd already washed that shirt half a dozen times. It must be a favorite of his. Or maybe it was just the shirt on top of the stack.

Even this early in the summer, his arms were browned by the sun, his nose sunburned. His sun-streaked hair was windblown from the ride in the sports car. He started toward the house and Lilah watched his easy, ambling gait, graceful and confident, never hurried. Nick and Jonathan clung to him, and as she watched, he captured each one in the crook of an arm, picked them up and swung them around in the air.

He was an amazing man. She wished...

She sighed. If wishes were horses...

She bolted through the kitchen door and headed for the celebration, wanting to be a part of it as much as Jonathan did.

Or did she just want to be closer to Daniel.

"As soon as Jason's friends get here we're ready," Lilah said, wiping her hands on her apron—Jesse's apron, actually.

"They'd better hurry," Jesse groused. "Will's gonna eat the dog if they don't turn up soon."

"A car's pulling into the drive right now," Daniel said from the hallway. "I'll call Jason."

"He's already outside," Jesse said.

Daniel joined Lilah at the window, watching four kids spill out of a van belonging to Ray Waller, Jeff's dad. "I thought Jason said five friends. I only see four."

"Somebody got sick, I imagine," Lilah said. "What a shame."

"Or lives close enough to walk." Daniel watched as Jason reached the car and saw him engage in serious conversation with Jeff and his dad. "Looks like 'sick and can't come,'" he said. "Jason looks too serious for a birthday boy."

"I'll keep an eye on him," Lilah said.

An image butterflied through Daniel's mind, of Lilah hugging Jason when they got home, and Jason letting her.

And then he saw another image. When the whole crew had come back, he'd caught her eye, and the impact of that look of shared emotion—*Jason's happy, you're happy, and that makes me happy*—had made his pulse race.

But, then, it had been an emotional day.

The avalanche hit the kitchen, Daniel's boys, Jason's friends, and Aengus in the midst of them. The party had begun.

"Down!" Daniel sped toward the kitchen counter where the cake was on display, and moved Aengus's paws from directly in front of it. "Dogs eat steak, not cake," he told his pet.

The dog had the good grace to look faintly ashamed before he loped away in search of dinner leftovers on the picnic tables outside.

Daniel took a close look at the cake. A yellow sports car, and a darned good replica of one, too, except that it sat a lot lower and looked a lot longer than Jason's car, because you needed a lot of cake to feed this bunch. Lilah had artistic skills, that was for sure. And the way the presentation visuals were shaping up was…

"Daniel."

He jumped. Lilah had sneaked up behind him, and the breathy way she said his name made him shiver. Instead of turning, afraid of what she might see on his face, he continued to gaze at the cake.

"I'm afraid you're right. Everybody's having a great time except Jason."

He turned to face her. "Because of the guest who couldn't come, you think? Maybe a girl he's interested in stood him up." He sighed. "I'll talk to him."

"Her father wouldn't let her come."

Jason had come to him. Daniel hadn't had to corner him to find out why Melissa hadn't come to the party. That was the only positive note in the situation. Jason's shoulders drooped, and his face was downcast. Aengus put his head on Jason's knee and he rubbed the dog behind the ears.

"Why?" Daniel asked him. "She's too young? Not allowed to date yet?"

Jason stood up, angry now instead of dejected. "Not allowed to go out with me. Her father won't let her go out with anybody unless he knows the family."

"I'm your family," Daniel said, unable to control the tensing of the muscles in his face.

"Try telling him that. Jeff's dad tried when they went to pick her up. He was really mad when he got back to the car."

A range of feelings shot through Daniel, empathy for Jason, and the feeling he feared most, absolute, consuming fury at a man who mistrusted a boy just because he was in a foster home. It was the only reason the man could have had. Jason was an excellent student, skillful at basketball and soccer. Whoever this father was, he should be proud Jason had shown an interest in his daughter.

He had to hide his rage from the boy, keep his voice down and his fists from clenching. "What's Melissa's last name?"

"Wilcox."

Daniel sighed. "Oh, boy. That is really too bad."

Jason's eyes asked a question.

"Ed Wilcox is a dairy farmer. He's one of the most vocal opponents of the foster-care center, so he's not too fond of me. Besides that, he's a skinflint, never gives to any cause, doesn't even take proper care of his cows. He's negative about everything, Jason. It's not you, it's just the way Ed is."

"But he's Melissa's father, and she's the nicest girl in the whole school," Jason protested.

"It happens sometimes," Daniel said.

"It wasn't her fault it happened." A suspicious moisture glazed Jason's eyes, and his body drooped. "She'd already asked her mother, her mother said yes, then her father wanted to know who she was going out with and freaked. She feels really bad. She says we can still see each other at school. She's not the kind of girl who'd sneak off on a date."

"Which is one of the reasons you like her. I'm so sorry, Jason," Daniel said. "I could have a talk with Ed, but I don't want to make things worse."

"They couldn't be any worse." Suddenly Jason straightened his shoulders and rose. "It was a great party, Daniel. Aengus and I are going up to bed. I'll talk it over with Maury."

He paused at the door. "You can tell Lilah and Jesse," he said. "I don't want them to think I didn't like the party."

Daniel joined him in the doorway and put his hand on Jason's shoulder. "You're a fine person, Jason. Don't let one man make you think you're not."

"Thanks." Jason gave him a crooked smile. "Lilah makes a heck of a car cake, doesn't she?"

Lilah was a heck of a woman. Maybe she could help him decide what to do about Ed Wilcox.

Chapter 8

"That horrible man," Lilah said. Her eyes flashed dangerously. "He's closed-minded, disrespectful of his daughter's judgment…"

"And bad to his cows," Daniel said gloomily.

The flashing eyes landed on him. "From anybody else, I'd think that was a joke," she said.

"Well, not from me. He's a bad man all around."

"He must have some good in him," she protested. "Everybody does."

"You find it. I can't. He's as stingy with his goodwill toward man as he is with his money."

"All right, I will." She simmered for a few minutes.

"He's dead set against the center, for the same reasons he's dead set against Jason dating his daughter. He and Virginia Galloway are our most formidable opponents, I think. Virginia can influence churchwomen all over the valley, and Ed, believe it or not, has somehow established himself in the Dairy Farmers' Association."

"You'll just have to win them over," she announced.

"How the heck am I supposed to do that?"

"I don't even know them. Let's think about it."

She'd come into the living room brandishing her latest drafts of visuals for the meeting, and for the first time she'd sat down beside him on the sofa so they could look at them together. That meant he was close to that slim, serious face, with the frown she always had when she was thinking. It helped his anger fade.

He drummed his fingers on the arm of the sofa. "The only way I can think of to win Ed over is to give him a whole bunch of money."

"That would be bribery," she said primly.

"As for Virginia, hmm, something to run. Something to star in."

She snapped her fingers. "Give them important volunteer jobs for the center."

"Huh?" He was flabbergasted. Last thing he wanted was to have Virginia and Ed messing with his center.

"Yes, volunteer jobs. If they get involved, well, you know what they say in politics."

"No, I don't know what they say in politics," Daniel said, wondering where the conversation was drifting.

"A volunteer is a vote."

He contemplated the concept. "That makes sense."

"What job could Virginia do that would make her feel important?"

"I don't know. Take over the whole project?"

She gave him a look. "Be serious. What sorts of jobs need to be done right now?"

He began to list them, and after he said, "We'll be

asking for grants, and the grant proposals will require projected capital expense and operating expense reports. You know, the cleaning, maintenance, food, equipment of various sorts..." he trailed off.

"What?" Lilah said. "What did you just think of?"

"Well," he said slowly, "Virginia used to be a nutritionist. Maybe she'd be willing to plan a month of menus, estimate the cost."

"That's a great idea! She can form a committee. She'd be the chairman, of course, and she could command her minions to do the pricing and then have total control over the menus."

"Okay," he said, still feeling doubtful. "I'll give it a try. Any ideas for Ed? Volunteer strangler?"

"Money," she said thoughtfully. "Virginia would be pricing food without actually buying it, so what could Ed do that would make him *feel* as if he were spending a lot of money?"

"Sports equipment," Daniel breathed. "He was a star football player in high school." He wagged a warning finger. "Don't ever ask him about it unless you have an hour or two to listen to him say, 'And then there was that win against Brattleboro High...' Anyway, he could figure out what we'll need and check all over the state to price the equipment."

"Good," Lilah said. "That problem's solved. Now could I show you these charts?"

"I'm at your service."

To look at the charts, he had to lean closer to her, look over her shoulder. Her hair, which looked shinier and healthier every day, tickled his cheek. He began thinking really dumb thoughts. For example, imagining that she was his dreamcatcher, sent by fate to banish his nightmares. And that she'd flown into his life unexpectedly to inspire him to achieve greater things. And worse, he was realizing how much he didn't want her to fly away.

She was so close, just a kiss away. Her generous mouth shone, blinding his common sense. He moved a millimeter nearer, or maybe it was only his heart that moved.

"We'll look at these visuals tomorrow," she said, leaping up with all her papers clutched tight in her hands. "Virginia and Ed were a much more important issue."

She gave him a bright smile and did what he was afraid she'd do—she flew.

If you run fast enough, the monster won't catch you.

In the safety of the carriage house she laid out her drafts on the coffee table and tried to regain her earlier excitement, to no avail. All she could see was Daniel's face so close to hers, hinting at a kiss that would have been so easy, so natural, so wonderful—a moment that might be gone forever.

Would she regret it? At the moment, yes. She sighed, rearranged the papers in a neat stack and went to bed, wondering what it would be like to be kissed by Daniel. She had a strong and scary feeling that it would be absolutely blissful.

The two weeks Lilah and Jonathan had lived in their car had seemed like an eternity, but the following two weeks hurtled by with the speed and force of a tidal wave.

The Fourth of July came and went with the proverbial bang. Fireworks, a parade in town, barbecued chicken that the Rotary Club members had gotten up at four in the morning to have ready by noon, and a great picnic in the backyard in the evening.

Lilah had paid a visit to the photographer Daniel had suggested. "Don't let him scare you," Daniel had warned her. "His skills are camera skills, not social skills."

She was glad he'd prepared her. Ray Colloton was a dour man with a growly voice that he used as little as possible. She struggled valiantly through her spiel, to which he appeared not to have the slightest reaction, so she was shocked when she finally stopped talking and he said without even a ghost of a smile, "Sure. I'll donate my time and materials. You pay travel expenses."

"Free!" She was so excited she tackled Daniel right outside the clinic door on his way into the house. "All Ray wants is travel expenses."

"Nothing like smart, informed female charm," Daniel said.

"It wasn't me, it was the center. You have a fan." But his smile shone above her more brightly than the late-setting sun.

For Maury's birthday, Mike closed the restaurant on Sunday evening—an unprecedented event—and produced a gourmet multi-course dinner, whose various dishes the younger boys either devoured enthusiastically or passed on surreptitiously to Lilah for covert disposal. It ended, whimsically and sentimentally, with the traditional birthday cake and homemade ice cream. Maury's cake, of course, was decorated to resemble a chef wearing a tall white hat.

Maury beamed all evening. Lilah wasn't sure whether it was the reaction to the excitement of the party or the presence of a very pretty girl he pretended not to be gazing at—or the fact that now he could work at the restaurant every afternoon, evening and weekend.

The diner was crammed full. The rest of Daniel's kids were there, of course, plus Maury's school friends. Mike was conspicuous because he was in charge, and Ian was there, too. Mike seemed to be warming to her. Even Ian's glower seemed less fierce.

If only Jason's party could have been so uncomplicated. The winning-over of Ed Wilcox and Virginia Galloway still hung oppressively in the air. Lilah had discovered that summer was Daniel's busiest season, with cows to attend to, horses, pigs, Ian's sheep, tiny Chihuahuas and big huskies, Labs, golden retrievers and Burmese mountain dogs—they seemed to need more attention in the summertime.

Just like kids. As long as you could keep them penned up, they were safe. Let them loose, however, and there was no end to the trouble they could get into.

"Virginia," she reminded Daniel. "Ed. You have to buck up and go for it before the presentation."

"Nag, nag, nag," he said.

She gave him a look. "If you'd already done it, I wouldn't have to nag. And here's some more nagging. We have to schedule the filming. The meeting's two weeks from Tuesday. Ray needs time to edit and splice, to choose background music, all that stuff. You're the one who should go with him," she insisted. "So don't argue with me."

"When you have him in the palm of your hand? When I have more piglets coming, cows with unacceptable cream levels and Bob Frost with an acid reflux reaction to cheesecake? Oh, yes, and there's the fungus between Banjo Galloway's toenails. How he got a fungus is a mystery to me. I don't think Virginia lets him run loose…" He paused, gazing at her face, obviously realizing he'd sealed his own fate.

"When," she asked pointedly, "is Banjo's appointment?"

"Okay, okay."

She could see his exhaustion in the dark circles under his eyes. "Let's make a deal," she suggested. "I'll go with Ray, and you'll pounce on Virginia and Ed."

He threw up his hands in surrender. "Deal. If I can just figure out a way to get to Ed."

"You will," she said, flashing him a smile.

A few days later, the trip with Ray to a foster-care center in Connecticut, celebrated as a model for all future centers, had been interesting. Unique, even. It had meant a long drive with Ray instead of a short flight, which had meant a long interval of silence instead of a short one.

Amazingly, the end result, produced a week later, was a compelling film. Lilah thought about inviting him to dinner with Daniel, Jesse and five energetic boys, and decided that might drive Ray into a deep depression, so instead she made a batch of peanut-butter cookies and hand-delivered them.

With the film behind her, the visuals under control and a week still left before the presentation, she turned her attention to the project that was almost as dear to her heart as the center was to Daniel's.

"Virginia!" Daniel beamed as she swept regally into his examination room with Banjo in her arms. He took the dog from her tenderly, already checking out his toenails. "Looking good," he said. "The ointment's working."

With his hands on Banjo and his eyes on Virginia, he said, "I have a big favor to ask of you. This grant money we're going after for the center…"

Fifteen minutes later Virginia agreed to take charge of the nutritional component of the center's proposal for funding.

He'd spent sleepless nights deciding how to approach Ed, but now Daniel thought he had it aced, so he took a deep breath and dialed Ed's number. The first minute or two of the conversation were uncomfortable, what with Daniel at one end trying to pretend he didn't know Ed had refused to let his daughter come to Jason's party and Ed at the other end obviously wondering if Daniel knew. But at last he got to the clincher.

"Ed, a salesman has dropped off samples of a food supplement for milk cows, and he wants me to test them. If you're agreeable, I'd like to try them out on your cows."

He could almost hear Ed's brain working. Free food supplements, and the doctor does the driving! What veterinary services can I hit him up for while he's out here asking me for a favor?

Then there was the trip to Ed's farm with the supplements, which Daniel had actually bought with his own money. And finally it was Ed wondering if he wanted to go to the trouble of giving the cows the supplements.

But he couldn't resist getting something for free. Daniel took a look at a couple of the cows—no charge—and then wangled a glass of water. In the main room of the farmhouse he found the football trophies that Mike had told him would be there, which Mike had found out by quizzing his customers.

"Ed, I just realized that since you're a legendary football star, you're just the guy I need."

It took fifteen minutes more to make sure Ed understood it was a volunteer job.

And then Ed set himself up for the kill. "Talking to dealers all over the state's going to take a lot of gas." Ed sent him a shifty look.

"It will," Daniel said, "but not necessarily yours." Ed's eyes brightened. "I'm assigning you an assistant. He'll drive you around. Great guy. Tell you what. I'll treat you both to breakfast at Mike's Diner on Tuesday morning."

Sold. Ed was already thinking, "Free breakfast!" Daniel gleefully looked forward to the moment he could say, "Ed Wilcox, Jason Reeves."

"War council," Lilah said to the boys one day when Daniel mentioned he'd be late for lunch. "We're going to give Daniel a birthday party."

"I'm not sure he'll like that," Jason said, frowning. "Jesse always makes him a cake, and he sort of, you know…"

"Huffs and puffs," Maury said.

"Men are like that when they grow up," Lilah said. "Never want you to make a fuss over them. But I'm not sure that's how they feel inside. So we're going to be brave and find out."

"What do we have to do?" Nick said.

"Not tell him is the first thing," Lilah said. "It'll be a surprise party so he can't do anything to stop it until it's too late. Then we have to get Ian and Mike to cooperate."

"They'll sure do that." Jesse grinned evilly. "They get a kick out of embarrassing each other."

"How can we keep him from finding out?" Nick asked. Nick of all people, so skilled at keeping secrets.

"We can do the cooking while he's working and stash it in Lilah's refrigerator," Maury said, "and when that gets full, we'll use one of the diner's fridges."

"Yeah," Will said, "and he can walk in for breakfast and see Jesse making the cake, just like last year, and he can do his…"

"Huffing and puffing," Lilah said. She smiled. "Then how can we keep him out late, so we can put it all together?"

"Uncle Ian," Nick said. "He can have a sick sheep. Maybe he'll have a sick sheep for real, but I hope not."

"Maybe just a vitamin deficiency," Jason suggested.

"Whatever," Nick said, "and then they'll talk, and after that Daniel will come home and we'll yell, 'Surprise!' and then Uncle Ian will drive up."

"That'll work," Lilah said. "Uh-oh, I hear the clinic door opening. Everybody scatter."

They scattered straight into Daniel. "What's going on?" he said.

"Lilah was checking our summer reading lists," Jason said.

"And I have to finish *Treasure Island* fast, so I won't get behind schedule," Will said.

When he stepped into the kitchen, Daniel's expression was puzzled, to say the least.

Daniel went out the kitchen door in search of Jason and found him washing his car. Cleanest car in the valley, except for Maury's, which was practically sterilized.

Daniel had made a commitment to Ed without first consulting Jason, and he'd been worrying about it. He wasn't sure he could convince Jason the plan would work.

The plan being that Jason could charm cranky Ed into recognizing him as an acceptable human being. Maybe it wouldn't work. Daniel had no idea how Ed would react, and he had no idea how Jason would react. Ed was the last person on earth Jason wanted to see, talk to, or, worst of all, drive around the state.

But life had taught Daniel that if you had a problem, you had to face it and deal with it. This conversation required considerable tact and diplomacy, so he began by picking up a brush and starting to scrub the fenders. "Still like the car?"

"You're kidding, right?" Jason turned to look at Daniel and grinned. It must have been something in Daniel's face that made the grin fade. "Is this about Melissa?"

"You're way too intuitive for your own good," Daniel growled, at the same time reminding himself he was trying to get that grin back on Jason's face. "But yes. I wondered how you were doing."

Jason went back to washing the car. "Better. We talked a while at soccer camp. She still likes me. It's just her dad."

Daniel picked up a sponge and started on the hood of the car. "Ed can be difficult."

"He's a jerk."

"Yep," Daniel agreed. "But have you ever heard the expression, 'You catch more flies with honey than with vinegar?'"

"Of course you can. What's that got to do with Mr.

Wilcox? He's pure vinegar. Never caught a fly in his life."

"Ed is the fly," Daniel explained. "You're the one with the jar of honey." He shifted to the side of the car. "I got to thinking that if you want to change Ed's mind about you, you need to sneak up on him and show him what a great kid you are. Acting mad won't get you anywhere. But getting him to decide he might have been wrong about you will."

Jason stopped scrubbing. "How?"

"Let me tell you about my afternoon with Ed. He's even more dead set against the center than he is about you, so I…"

He told Jason the whole story, doing impressions of Ed that got Jason laughing so hard he was snorting, and then said, "so I told him you'd be his driver."

Jason dropped the sponge. He looked as if he'd swallowed a worm, a live one. "I'd have to sit in the car, *my* car, with him? Talk to him? No way."

"I'll buy the gas," Daniel said, hoping to get him laughing again. It didn't work.

"I can't do it. What about Uncle Ian? He's expecting me to work on the barn roof."

"Ian will understand. I know it sounds grim," Daniel admitted, "but it seems to me this is the best way to get to him. He'll be able to see for himself that you're good enough for his daughter. Heck," he added, "he may figure it out when the three of us have breakfast at Mike's Tuesday morning."

"Daniel!"

"All you have to do is be calm and polite and tell Ed how much you're looking forward to working with him. Don't mention Melissa. Don't mention the party. Just mention how awesome it is that he has volunteered. A sports hero like him will know all about sports equipment. And don't look at him the way you're looking at me right now, either." He smiled at Jason's dark expression as he explained. "Look earnest." He demonstrated looking "earnest."

"Think of it this way, Jason. It's a game, and it's one you're sure to win. Think of it as getting the best of Ed." He looked Jason directly in the eyes. "And I know it will work, because if I had a daughter, I'd be in hog heaven if she snagged you for her boyfriend."

Jason broke eye contact and didn't say anything for a few minutes. Finally he reached out and took the hose away from Daniel. "Okay, I'll give it a shot," he said, "but I'm not looking forward to it."

"Mr. Wilcox," Jason said, looking extremely earnest, "it's great you're doing this. Being a football star and all, you must know all about the equipment the center will need." He gave Ed an easy grin. "And I just got a car, so there's nothing I like better than driving it. This'll be fun. Well, thanks for breakfast, Daniel. I'd better head out to soccer camp." He held out his hand to Ed. "Great to meet you, Mr. Wilcox."

Daniel said goodbye and waited, his heart in his throat.

"Seems like a nice enough kid," Ed muttered. "Ay-uh, he'll be okay. Miss!" He summoned the waitress. "Have anything like a cinnamon roll or a…"

Bingo.

Each Wednesday when the Northeast Kingdom's paper came out, Lilah scanned the news online. There had been no further mention of Bruce. This could be a good sign or a bad one. He must be working somewhere. She assumed he'd been left as penniless as she was, but maybe not. For all she knew, he'd stashed away money in a Swiss—or Cayman Islands—bank account.

She went on to the News from Whittaker column. "Eleanor McDougal was admitted to the hospital on…"

Mrs. McDougal had been her home care patient these past three years. Lilah had loved her. At ninety-four, comatose and fading away, this might be her last trip to the hospital. Lilah wanted to do something for her—a note to her son?

No, a note would have a postmark, and Mrs. McDougal's son, at least, would know where she was. Yes, Lilah was being paranoid, but if she made a mistake, she'd pay the price of Bruce's finding her and Jonathan.

Flowers. If she went to a florist here, paid cash and didn't put her name on the card, maybe she could get away with it.

"I have a quick errand to run," she told Jesse. "I need…colored pencils."

"Would you pick up a couple of pounds of butter while you're out? And ten pounds of flour? Oh, yeah, I'd feel better if we had a backup jar of mustard. I'm using the last one. And, let's see…"

Lilah sighed, got out her notebook and made a list.

At the Rose Red florist shop, she selected the types of flowers she wanted in the arrangement—flowers that were blooming now in Vermont. Lush pink peonies, deep-purple irises, accented with delicate white sprigs of lily-of-the-valley. "The florist in Whittaker will have these flowers," the Churchill florist said. "It will be a beautiful gift."

"It will have the Whittaker florist's name on it, won't it?" Lilah was still feeling nervous about what she was doing.

"Yes," Melinda said, looking miffed. "Even though I was the one who helped you design it. What message for the card?"

"'Please feel better,'" Lilah told her. "'I miss you.' And that's it."

"Got it. It will be delivered tomorrow."

When she got home, she had phone calls to make. "Mike?" she said, when he answered with a cheerful, "Mike's Diner."

"Hey, Lilah." He paused. "Everything okay there?"

She'd never phoned him before, and he sounded worried.

"Everything's great," she assured him. "I called because I want to give Daniel a surprise birthday party, and I'd like to know what you think about that."

"Great idea," Mike said. He sounded surprised himself. "It will embarrass the heck out of him. What can I do to help?"

Those few words made her feel amazingly good. "Thanks so much," she said gratefully, "but we think we can…"

"Come on. What we do here is cook. Maury and I can do some of it ahead of time and store it here."

"I have to admit that would be a big help." Daniel's brother being nice to her gave her the wonderful feeling that he'd accepted her. "Any ideas about what Daniel likes most? I'm still thinking about the menu."

"Sure, but it might give me a kick to present him with the things he likes *least*." Mike chuckled. "Come by the diner tomorrow afternoon when Maury's here and the lunch crush is over, and the three of us will put together a menu."

"Thanks," she told him. "I'll be there."

"How are you going to surprise him when he works right there in the house?"

She swallowed hard. "The boys suggested Ian might come up with a sick sheep. Daniel would run to the rescue and…"

Mike's chuckle escalated into a burst of laughter. "Let me know how the conversation goes," he snorted.

"I was hoping," her voice faltered, "you might ask him."

"Nope, you ask him," Mike said, and was still laughing when he hung up on her.

Then she had a brilliant idea.

"You want me to call Uncle Ian?" Nick said.

Lilah had surmised that Ian and Nick had some special bond, maybe because they were both so closed inside themselves. From Nick's smile when Ian picked up the phone, Lilah gathered that Ian hadn't growled. "We're gonna give Daniel a surprise birthday party."

Nick's smile grew wider. Then he said, "But you have to help. If we're gonna surprise him, you have to have a sick sheep." After a long pause, he said, "Because you live the farrest away and if you had a sick sheep he'd come, even on his birthday." Another pause. "Can you think of something else?" Another pause, and then, "Thanks, Uncle Ian. Lilah will call you to tell you the time and all that." Another pause, but this one was Nick's. "When are you coming over next?"

Nick had obviously liked Ian's answer. "He'll do it," Nick reported, his bright-green eyes shining. "He says he doesn't ever have any sick sheep and Daniel knows it, but he'll think of something else."

"Bless you, Nick," Lilah said, hugging him, and, seeing that Jonathan beamed as brightly as if she were hugging him. "You did it!"

"I like Uncle Ian," Nick said.

"We all like Uncle Ian," Jonathan said.

There was something in Ian that Lilah hadn't penetrated yet. She should work on it, and keep working on her relationship with Mike, because if you married a man, you married his family, too.

Married? Where had that come from?

"Mom, why are you blushing?"

"It's gotten so hot in here," Lilah said, and scurried to the cleaning closet to get the furniture polish.

When Daniel woke up from a restless sleep, his first thought was about Lilah, how right she'd been about winning over Ed and Virginia, how smart she was, how...totally appealing.

His second thought was that Elmer Winslow was bringing in his six-month-old husky mix to be neutered. Funny that men acted so squeamish on these occasions, while women seemed rather cheerful about it. He might have to give Elmer a dose of the anxiety drug he kept on hand in case somebody's pet panicked in the clinic waiting room.

Last of all, he realized it was his birthday. Not just his birthday, but his thirty-fifth birthday. The number depressed him for a minute, then he thought about the path he'd traveled in those thirty-five years.

He was the luckiest man alive was his conclusion, and with that in his mind, and thoughts of Lilah half-successfully shifted onto the back burner, he showered, shaved and dressed in the best of moods.

Feeling ready to face the day, Daniel strolled into the kitchen. Lilah turned from the stove to give him a brilliant smile and say, "Happy birthday! Jesse just told me."

"Happy birthday," Will said. He was already at the table, munching on dry cereal to stave off starvation until his real breakfast was ready.

"Thank you," he muttered. "Had to tell, didn't you?" he said to Jesse, who returned a defiant look from the counter where he was working.

Daniel looked at the counter. "Aw, no, Jesse, not a birthday cake. I want to ignore my birthdays. So you can just…"

Will pinned him down with soulful eyes. "*We'd* feel bad if you didn't have a birthday cake."

"Right," Jonathan said as he stepped into the kitchen with Nick a half step behind him. "And besides, birthday cake is good."

"It's chocolate," Will said reverently.

"You're not cutting it to look like a cow."

"I know at least that much," Jesse retorted.

Daniel grumbled some more and kept grumbling as Maury and Jason joined them and annoyed him with still more birthday wishes.

It was pure pleasure to vanish into the clinic, where life was calm and—clinical. As always, he kept an eye on the window to watch the boys' day shaping up. Lilah drove them to soccer camp this morning. Jesse was probably fixating on that darned cake.

Jesse brought them home at noon. Lilah was probably getting their lunch together.

Birthdays made him remember parts of his life he

wanted to forget: made him realize he needed the comfort of predictability every bit as much as his boys did. Would he ever get past it completely? No. He could only remember it and then put it into the perspective of his life now, every day of his life.

Which he'd do right now. Spurred on by a delicious aroma, he stepped into the kitchen briefly to pick up something for lunch. He usually took it back to his office rather than eating with the boys in a preoccupied way. Lilah didn't even spare him a glance. She was too busy trying to keep up with the Philly cheese steak sandwich demand. He put one on a plate, turned down the offer of French fries and coleslaw, and took a minute to stroll through the house.

It had been amazingly clean and neat since Lilah took over. The boys still helped on Saturday mornings, but she'd taught them how to do it right. Today it was downright gleaming.

He sighed. If she took a notion to leave, his life and the boys' lives would take a severe downturn.

He wouldn't think about it. She was here. He'd enjoy it while he could.

Mike called to wish him a happy birthday. Daniel snarled, "Thanks." Just as he was thinking he might get away from the clinic early, Ian called.

"I need you to come out and take a look at my lambs. Oh, yeah, and happy birthday."

"Thanks. What's wrong with the lambs?"

"The lambswool didn't come up to standard this year. I had to sell it cheap. It's something they're eating, or not eating."

"Okay. When do you want me to come?"

"Right now."

"On my birthday?"

"Don't give me that bull—"

"Language."

"That bull. I know what you think about your birthday."

Daniel sighed. "Okay. I was about to close down, anyway."

Twenty minutes later, his fingertips were rolling through the wool on a lamb. "Feels good to me."

"Well, it isn't. The lanolin level's low. They're not getting enough…something."

"That isn't my field, really," Daniel said, rubbing the lamb behind its ears. He stood up, feeling the softness of his fingertips from the lanolin that Ian said wasn't there. "The health of the lambs is, and this one looks great."

Ian frowned. "At least come in and look at some catalogs. There are all kinds of vitamins and minerals that are supposed to increase fleece growth and improve quality, but I don't want anybody scamming me." He gave Daniel a pleading look that wasn't anything like Daniel's image of Ian. "If I lose my reputation with the buyers," he said, "I'm sunk. The corporation's income goes down. It affects all of us."

"Okay, I'll look at the catalogs with you, but I should be getting home soon. Hang on a sec." He called to say he'd be late and that the kids should go ahead with dinner, then followed Ian into his office.

He'd never seen the guy so chatty. Of course, sheep were his passion—sheep and managing money—and maybe he was equally chatty with other sheep herders and wool merchants. It was almost seven when he said, "I think we've got your order wrapped up. I really have to go. The kids will think I've abandoned them."

"Yeah," Ian agreed. "Thanks for the advice. Sorry I used up so much of your birthday."

"Sooner it's over, the better," Daniel said gruffly.

When he pulled into the driveway, everything was quiet. The boys were usually outside kicking soccer balls or pitching baseballs. They must have finished dinner, because the kitchen was dark. Lilah probably had them doing something like playing Scrabble. She wasn't hurting their spelling abilities any, that was for sure.

He pulled into the carriage house beside the van and strode toward the side door. They couldn't be playing games in the living room, because the downstairs was dark. Even though it would be light outside for another two hours, the shade of the maples made lights necessary by six. He glanced skyward. The upstairs was dark, too.

Oh, no. A power outage. With an eight-man household, a power outage was a crisis of the first order. That did it. He was getting the generator he'd been meaning to have installed for years. He dashed through the clinic door, then into the dark hallway. "Jesse, Lilah," he shouted. "No electricity?"

Nobody answered. Had they all been abducted? His heart thudding, he grabbed a baseball bat from a stone crock that stood at the bottom of the stairs and started his search in the living room. The door was closed. Cautiously he inched it open, holding the bat high, and rushed into the room.

The room suddenly lit up, a camera flashed, and as he recoiled, startled beyond belief, more people than he could count yelled, "Surprise!"

Chapter 9

"You sure caught me looking like a complete fool," Daniel said, staring at the screen, on which his picture, complete with raised baseball bat and mouse-sees-snake expression, was on display. "Thanks loads, you guys."

"You looked just like that," Virginia Galloway said. "The camera doesn't lie."

"You looked worse," Jason said. "The photo is actually kind of flattering." He turned from the laptop to give Daniel an evil grin. Melissa Wilcox stood behind him, and Daniel gazed at her in awe. How the heck could Ed have fathered a girl this polite, cute and sweet? Life was full of contradictions, or maybe somehow Ed had managed to woo and win a wife just like Melissa. How in the world could he have managed that?

"Who's responsible for all this?" Daniel asked, waving his arm toward the bustling scene.

"You know it wasn't my idea," Ian muttered.

"Accomplices do time, too," Daniel said, glaring at him. "Lambswool crisis, my eye. Mike?"

Mike shrugged and delivered a slow smile. "My roasted asparagus, but not, absolutely not my idea."

"Jesse?"

"Disobey the general? Never!"

An embarrassing number of guests were chortling at his photograph, but Lilah was just about the only one left of his adult "family" to accuse. "Your idea," he said.

Her idea, too, to win over Virginia and Ed, and here they were at his birthday party, of all things, with Melissa Wilcox's eyes shooting stars at Jason's moonstruck face. He wanted his eyes to shoot stars, too. He wanted Lilah's face to be moonstruck. He wanted her.

Which was why he had to stand here glaring at her. The entirety of him, heart, soul and inflamed body, needed that glare to hide behind.

But then he took another look at her. Her stomach was clenched so tightly she could have fit into Scarlett O'Hara's dress with the seventeen-inch waist.

"Will you ever forgive me?" she asked, sounding as if she really was worried.

His heart sent a smile to replace the glare. "It'll take time. Ten minutes, fifteen…"

She relaxed and returned the smile.

Daniel could manage a smile, but inside he felt sort of crumpled or melted, vulnerable, anyway. Mike and Ian seemed to sense that he'd withdrawn for a moment, was looking at the party from the outside, and they sidled over to him.

"We could have stopped her," Mike said, "but not without telling her stuff we don't want to tell."

"It might be a good idea for us to go through a couple of things like this," Ian surprised him by saying. "Might get a handle on some of that 'stuff' we all have."

"Examine my inner feelings? Get in touch with my feminine side?" But his voice cracked when he said it.

Each brother gripped his shoulder, then moved away.

Yeah, another step toward getting "a handle on that stuff." Now he had more "stuff" to get a handle on, the unnerving knowledge that he was falling for Lilah and falling hard.

He turned down the heat that suddenly flooded him, squared his shoulders and scanned the room, deciding which group to join next. The house was filled to overflowing. Groups clustered at, on and around the picnic tables in the yard.

The boys had been allowed to invite their friends. Jason was still in the living room with Melissa. Daniel could glimpse Maury in the kitchen, aiming a self-conscious, adolescent grin toward the same pretty girl who'd come to his party. Lilah had invited everyone in Churchill he'd ever met, plus some spouses he hadn't even seen before. She'd clearly had a lot of help with the guest list.

The food was stand-up fork food and it looked amazing. Maybe that's what he should do next, sample it, but he felt too tense to eat. Back to the original idea—pick a group to join and turn on the charm.

Before he could do that, however, someone jangled a bell—a cowbell, he thought. The people who were gathered outside came indoors until everyone was sardined into the living room, the hall and all the way up the staircase.

It was Ed Wilcox who stood in front of the fireplace, ready to speak. He held a large vase in his hand, and Daniel dreaded to find out what was in it. A hand grenade? Jason's thumb?

No, Jason was fine, standing close to Ed, with Melissa at his side.

"Folks," Ed said, "a lot of us men don't like presents, so Miz Lilah said on the invitation, 'No gifts, except contributions to the foster-care center we're building in the valley.'"

Wow. Ed had made a one-hundred-eighty-degree turn in the last week or so. He'd accepted the center, and he felt a part of it. He'd accepted Jason. Wilcox-wise, things were looking good. And what had Ed been talking about? Contributions to the center?

"So here's your present, Doc," Ed said, and crossed the room to hand Daniel the vase.

He peered inside and saw envelopes. Envelopes with checks in them, and cash. When he picked up an envelope that appeared to be filled with change, he recognized Nick's handwriting.

Stunned again, he gazed out at the assembled group. Several long, painful seconds went by before he could say, "I don't know how to say thank you in a way that will tell you how *much* I thank you," he said. He knew Nick's entire net worth in allowance savings was probably in that envelope. He held back his emotions. "A Maserati, fully loaded, couldn't make me as happy or as grateful as these gifts have made me."

He got himself out of the limelight, clutching the precious vase, and worked his way toward Ed. "Thanks," he said. "You're doing a great job for the center."

Ed didn't exactly beam. He looked at the floor and shuffled his feet. Same thing as beaming, when you were talking about Ed.

Virginia Galloway bustled her way through Daniel's well-wishers, dragging Reverend Galloway behind her and then thrusting him in front of her. "We've seen the light," the reverend said ponderously. "We're one hundred percent behind the project."

"Virginia," Daniel said, "I can't tell you how much I appreciate the work you're doing."

Then he caught Lilah's eye. She was watching him in the way she often did, trying to read his emotions. He crossed the room toward her.

"This is the best thing anyone has ever done for me," he said softly. "Especially the present."

"You needed a vase really badly," she said with a mischievous smile. "I'm glad you like it."

But her face shone with pleasure. She had no idea how much she'd already done for him. Turned his life around, that's what she'd done. He had a sidekick now, somebody to share things with. She'd offered Daniel the possibility of living a normal life, of finding a woman he loved enough to marry her.

In fact, he thought he'd found her.

"There weren't any leftovers," Jason complained. He and Maury were doing KP duty, and the younger boys had been sent to bed.

"Just a few," Lilah said. "Aengus got a stingy-looking plate, and for some reason we have half a rhubarb pie, about a cup of sautéed brussels sprouts and a half cup of the celeriac remoulade."

"Clearly," Daniel said, "I'm the only one who liked those things. How did you know what I liked?"

"Jesse, Mike—especially Mike—and Ian. You think we didn't cook enough?" She looked worried.

"No, if we'd had any more food, everybody would still be here," Jesse declared. "I'm glad there weren't any leftovers. Made it easier to clean up. Daniel, get away from that pan. We said you couldn't help and we meant it."

Lilah noticed how gently Maury removed the pan from Daniel's hands. Looking resigned, Daniel sat down at the kitchen table.

"Thank the powers that be for paper and plastic," she said. The kitchen actually looked pretty neat. The dishwasher was already on its second load. The rest of the pans and serving dishes were rinsed and stacked on the counter, taking up the least amount of space possible, ready for the next dishwasher load.

"We're quitting," Jesse said. "I'll get up in the middle of the night and load the dishwasher again."

"I'll come over early and do it," Lilah said.

"You'll find it done," Jesse said, staring her down. He gave Jason and Maury a sharp salute. "Dismissed!" They fled, and then Jesse said to Lilah, "You, too, young lady."

"I'll walk you home," Daniel offered.

The idea of being alone with Lilah had been simmering in his mind all evening, and now it was at full boil. A minute alone with her was all he needed to show her how he was coming to feel about her, how he felt about her after she'd done this for him, organized the party,

which was so…what should he call it? Kind? Affection-
ate? Caring?

Loving? He had a hard time even thinking the word.

He still knew nothing about her past. He'd made many
attempts to draw her out, which had netted him only a
too-bright smile and zero information. Maybe she was
hiding from the law. Jamison might not even be her real
name. She might be a professional crook with a forged
driver's license. She'd renewed hers just after she'd arrived, and he'd have given anything to see the old one,
read the address on it.

But he, of all people, knew you had to share your
secrets in your own time. He hadn't shared his deepest ones with her, either. Would he be able to someday?

A cool breeze blew her hair around her shoulders. In
the moonlight it shone, honey shot through with gold.
Her face was sweet. Yep, the perfect profile of a professional crook.

"I know I acted like a grump tonight," he told her.
"But I think every man secretly wishes something like
that party would happen for him."

"I figured that was the case," she said. She turned
toward him, gazed at him for a heartbeat, then seemed
flustered by whatever it was she saw in his face. Without a transition, she shifted her gaze to the sky.

"I haven't traveled much," she said cheerfully. "Just
enough to know the stars are more beautiful in Vermont
than anywhere else."

Daniel laughed at himself. She sounded like a professional crook, too. She'd given him an opening to ask
questions about her travels, but suddenly he didn't want
to. He just wanted to be with her, whoever she was.

What he wanted was to step five feet away from the

kitchen door, pull her into the darkness and kiss her senseless. But he cautioned himself to go slowly, slowly, not scare her. So he looked at the stars with her. "There's the Big Dipper," he said.

"That one," she said, "looks like The Scales. I wish I knew them all. There's a children's book of the constellations I've been meaning to give Jonathan...."

"I know a lot of them," Daniel said, drawing a little closer to her. "There," and he pointed to a waterfall of stars, "is the Overturned Apple Cart, discovered in the seventeen-hundreds by a farmer with an orchard."

Her laughter traveled like a bell through the darkness. "I thought the Greeks and the Romans did the naming."

"No, no, that's an unfounded rumor. Truth is, most of the constellations were identified and named by sharp-eyed Vermonters who were standing out in the dark looking up."

Her eyes sparkled at him. "Okay, so what's that one?" She pointed to the Little Dipper.

He wanted to see that sparkle of fun in her eyes again. "Measuring Cup," he said confidently, "named by a wife who was thinking about how she had no business standing out here in the dark when she needed to be starting her bread dough."

"Fascinating," she murmured. "And that one?"

And then it just happened. She leaned into him, he put his arm around her. He knew what would happen next, knew it would change everything, and he was ready for the change. "That one," he said softly, "was named by a young man who'd met a girl at a dance that night and couldn't get her out of his mind. It's called The Kiss."

He leaned down to her and brushed his lips against her satiny cheek, heard her sharp hiss of breath, felt her hesitation, and then, with a deep sigh that might have meant anything, relief, resignation, she turned her face to his.

Her mouth was soft, warm and yielding. When she reached up to cup his cheeks, he closed his arms around her, held her tight, kissed her with all the hunger and need in his soul. She responded to him, her breath coming faster, her hands sliding to the nape of his neck to draw him closer.

He pulled her tighter, feeling the length of her body against his. It inflamed him. *Hold back, hold back.*

In the circle of Daniel's arms, enraptured by his kiss, she floated in the purest pleasure and ached with the deepest agony. She shouldn't be kissing him. As long as she hid her rapidly accelerating desire for him, she could continue to hide her past. How could she spill out her feelings for him in a kiss, then deny him the truth about who she was, what she'd hoped to escape when she fled to the valley?

Her heart, her body, had taken over her mind. She wanted him, felt she'd burst if she couldn't have him, and everything logical and pragmatic had flown away on the wind.

She'd be sorry someday, but she couldn't seem to feel sorry now. All she could feel was his mouth on hers, the electricity generated by the flicker of his tongue, the ache of his aroused body against hers. She couldn't breathe normally, couldn't think sensibly, couldn't do anything except throw herself headlong into the moment she'd been waiting for almost from the day he'd charmed her and Jonathan into the warmth and comfort of his home.

A dog barked. Aengus. She felt Daniel shift gears just as she was doing; felt him break free of the magnetism that held them together. She was suddenly aware of lighted windows behind them, of a house full of innocent, trusting boys, including her own.

She slid her lips away from his. "Reality check," she said shakily.

She could feel his smile against her hair. "A houseful of chaperones." But he didn't let go of her.

"It's even possible that this was Aengus's watch and Jesse will take over in a minute."

"Yeah, and Jesse will ream him out for not sensing the danger sooner." He drew away, then cupped her cheeks and held her gaze with his. "Is there any dan-ger here?"

"Oh, yes," she said, knowing he had no idea how much danger and still not telling him, unwilling to give up the moment. "And Aengus knows it. Think we could go with his judgment for now?"

For now. If she made love with Daniel, would the dog's barking—or silence—tell her all she needed to know?

Because it was Daniel's heart Aengus would be guarding, not hers.

As he'd predicted, everything had changed. If Daniel had ever wished for a middle-of-the-night emergency, it was now, and, of course, every animal, large and small, was in great shape that night. Nothing to distract him from his aroused, heated state. He slept restlessly, dreaming of nothing but the feel of Lilah's body against his. When he made his appearance in the kitchen, he couldn't just say, "Pancake day!" His gaze met Lilah's and electricity sparked again, followed by renewed longing, and instead he said, "Hi," watching her face flush, before she turned back rapidly to the griddle where pancakes were browning.

"Good morning," she said, sounding short of breath.

"It's hot standing over the stove," he observed, moving up beside her. "I'll flip a few of those."

His arm brushed hers. He felt a shock wave pass through him, saw her blush deepen.

"Okay, thanks," she said, but she lingered a moment before she slipped away.

No, it will never be the same.

Jesse stood beside Daniel, turning bacon in the skillet, adding more crisp strips to the pile of them that was rising next to the stove. "You've finally come to your senses." He muttered the words, because the younger boys had just barreled into the kitchen.

"Or lost them," Daniel muttered back. He was grateful to have an extremely busy day ahead of him.

Lilah didn't know how she'd get through breakfast. Her body zinged with nervous energy. All night she'd moved restlessly between her sheets. When she slept, she dreamed of Daniel, of his kiss going on and on until there was only one way to end it, and then she'd wake up flaming with frustrated desire.

Walking to the house, she'd chanted a mantra: *I have a job. I have a son. I have a former husband lurking somewhere. I can't have this man until I've tied up the loose ends of my life.*

It was a kiss, just a kiss. But one look at Daniel and her mantra had turned into gibberish.

With Daniel flipping pancakes now, breakfast seemed to be under control, so she went to the makeshift office area in the living room, two long, narrow tables Daniel had found, which the boys had dragged down from the attic and placed at right angles. There she'd set up her work for the center. Now she stared down at the many drafts of visuals, at the file on the monitor, at the open DVD drive with the film in position on the disc without seeing any of it. Anything could happen, anytime. She had to have a full presentation worked up for Daniel before her life fell apart again. She could perfect it if the fates gave her time, but she had to give him something. Immediately.

Her mouth twisted. After breakfast. Stoically, she returned to the kitchen, to find breakfast ready and only one spot left at the table—on Daniel's right.

Chapter 10

Daniel had never been so relieved to retreat from the breakfast scene to the serenity of his clinic, the comfortable routine of his career. Sitting next to him, Lilah's body had seemed to throb with heat and her scent had dizzied him. It had been a struggle to be his normal, familiar self.

He couldn't let the boys see that anything was different between him and Lilah. His life might be changing, but theirs couldn't. They needed their ordinary routines and the promise of his reliability.

Still, at the high point of his day, his first reaction was to share it with Lilah. At his first break between patients, he burst through the clinic door, pounded toward the living room where he knew he'd find her working and yelled, "Lilah! Great news!"

She leapt from her chair, scattering papers everywhere, closed what she'd been working on with one swift click of the mouse and faced him, her eyes wide and blue.

"Sorry, sorry," he said, kneeling down to retrieve the papers.

"Hey, this is good," he said, examining a page of the handout.

"Forget the handout. What's the news?"

She sounded too cool for his comfort. He looked up to find her standing with her feet apart, her hands on her hips.

"I shouldn't have blown in here like that."

"You certainly blew my concentration," she said. "You owe it to me to tell me what's happened. Right now."

He was momentarily distracted by thinking how cute she was standing there pursing her lips. The heat rose stealthily inside him as his gaze skimmed over her cocked arms, slim and tanned in her simple white sundress. He picked up more of the scattered papers in an effort to remember why he'd stormed in here in the first place.

"I got a phone call today," he said. "Someone has volunteered to be the chief financial officer of the center."

"Volunteered? He'll do it for free?" Her hands went to her mouth. "Who is this saint?"

Daniel smiled. Her fit of pique had vanished, and she'd embraced his excitement. "He told me he 'did well,' that's the way he put it, in the construction business and had decided to take a few years away from that and use his skills to 'benefit others,' his words again."

"Daniel, that's wonderful!" She came around her

desk, her eyes shining now. She was even more beautiful, more desirable than before. "What's his name?"

She was so close to him, and he was so distracted, that he stammered, "T-Ted Hilton." He cleared his throat, which also seemed to clear his head. "I told him I'd call him when we had the board's approval and knew it was a done deal, then I went to the Web site he'd listed on his card. He's just what he said he was. The owner and CEO of Hilton Construction Company in Philadelphia."

"When can he come onboard?"

"Ten days or so, if the ship floats, so to speak."

"Wow!" She shone a brilliant smile at him. "No wonder you're so excited."

Their gazes locked. Her lips parted and her smile changed into one that was more personal, more for him than for his good fortune. Drawn beyond his resistance, he reached out to her. She tilted her head toward him.

"Doctor! Celia Hennessey is here with Otis." It was Mildred, yelling from the clinic door. He resented her timing.

Lilah drew back, her mouth curved in a wicked smile. "Thanks so much, Dr. Foster, for dropping by."

He regarded her gloomily. "Take two aspirin and call me." Then he smiled. "Any time, day or night."

"Yes, I should be working," Lilah told Jesse, "but if I don't get out of the house for a while, I'll mildew."

"Okay," Jesse said, resigned in the face of Lilah's determination. "Here's the grocery list." He handed her two full handwritten pages he'd been about to take to the supermarket.

"We eat a lot."

"You noticed."

"So here I go. I'll be back by lunchtime."

She set off in her own car for the local supermarket in a lovely, shivery, anticipatory mood. She'd been on *The Kingdom Dispatch* Web site when Daniel surprised the heck out of her, and once again she'd seen no men-tion of Bruce, nor had there been an obituary for Mrs. Mc-Dougal. She could relax again, and however short these relaxed periods were, she appreciated each one of them.

But it had been the sight of Daniel popping in that had created the shivery, anticipatory mood. If only, if only…

Churchill being a small town, she hadn't had much time to agonize over the "if onlys" before she'd parked and prepared herself to empty the grocery store. For-tunately, the local supermarket was usually stocked for the frequent Foster onslaughts.

She snagged a cart and set off for the meat counter. Ground beef, tons of it. A stack of juicy chuck roasts that Jesse would turn into pot roast and a hefty stew. Pork country ribs. The boys loved them. Chicken.

She eyed the cart and wondered if she should leave this one by the checkout and start on another one. Dan-iel's household seemed to revolve around food.

She was sailing past the lamb, which Ian had banned from Daniel's menu and heading toward the bacon and sausage when she saw the florist poised over the cooler.

"Lilah!" the woman bubbled. "I'm so glad to see you. I should have called, but you know the flower business."

"Um, well…"

She shook her finger at Lilah. "What I wanted to tell you was that you forgot to sign the card when you sent those flowers. But don't worry. I did it for you."

Lilah's wonderful mood sank. Now Mrs. McDougal's son knew who'd sent the flowers. But on the other hand, what bizarre circumstance would cause Harold to tell Bruce she'd sent his mother flowers? And how many of her steps would Bruce have to trace in order to find her here in Churchill?

If anyone could do it, he could. Feeling like a lump of lead, Lilah forced herself to finish shopping, help Jesse put away the food, paper supplies and cleaning products, and greet the boys with her customary exuberance. Even a single, unimportant connection could end her comfortable new life here, the happiest life she and Jonathan had ever known.

For once, good news followed good news, and when Daniel came in from the clinic that afternoon, he went directly to Will's room. "Will," he said, "talk to me a minute?"

At dinnertime, he made his big announcement. "Will's parents are doing so well with their physical therapy that the doctor says Will can go home in about a month."

Besides Will, who looked excited enough to pop, only Jason understood the full import of the news. "Will we ever see you again after you go home?" Jonathan asked mournfully.

"All the time," Daniel said. "At school, at Sunday school, we'll invite him to all the family events, and he can come over anytime he wants to."

"We'll still be friends," Nick said to comfort Jonathan.

"And I'll always be here if you need me," Daniel said to Will.

He glanced around the table. Jason wore a half smile, happy that Will was happy but with no desire to have the same thing happen to him. If Maury, who was working at the diner, had been here, he would have reacted in much the same way. Lilah and Jonathan were studying each other, a mother and son who hadn't had to be separated.

Nick came last in Daniel's clockwise scan. In the boy's eyes, he saw a flicker of fear.

Fear of what? Daniel longed to know.

"Tonight we're celebrating," he said.

"How?" Will asked, undoubtedly wanting to know the menu rather than the activity.

"We're going stargazing." He flicked a glance at Lilah, watching the pink rise in her cheeks.

The boys gave him expressionless faces.

"At Uncle Ian's."

They perked up a bit.

"Build a bonfire and roast marshmallows," he concluded.

That got them excited. The room exploded into action. Aengus, knowing something good was about to happen, bounced through the chaos, barking frantically. Jesse began packing supplies.

Jason cleared his throat. "Could I, um, is it okay if—"

"If Melissa could come, too? Sure thing." He took it seriously, didn't smile, didn't want Jason to feel he was being teased.

Jason went straight for the phone. Daniel caught phrases of his end of the conversation. "Tell your dad it's the whole family." After a pause, "By nine. It's the younger kids' bedtime."

He shuffled back toward Daniel. "She can go," he said casually. "I'll pick her up while you guys are getting your act together."

Daniel hid a smile. Apparently the answer had been yes.

Lilah stood to one side, smiling indulgently at the furor. "I'll stay here and clean up," she said.

"Don't even think about it," Daniel said. He put his arm around her and gave her a gentle push. "Get a sweater." He heard his voice hoarsen as he touched her. "See you at the van in five minutes."

A car pulled into the driveway. "Maury's home," Nick yelled. "He can go, too!"

Daniel must have known, just as Lilah did, that if he stargazed right beside her, it would be too much torture to endure. They all lay on blankets spread over the lush green grasses of Ian's acreage, coincidentally on the very spot where the center would—God and the Regional Development Board willing—rise over the next few years.

Jesse tended a bonfire he'd started in a huge metal barrel beside a sheepherder's shack. Will was more interested in the marshmallows than the stars and only paid attention occasionally when something in the conversation caught his attention.

Unbelievably, Maury, the worst student of all Daniel's boys, turned out to be the house expert on constellations. Soon everybody was searching for the star formations that he saw so easily.

Lilah smiled, thinking of Daniel's constellation expertise, and shivered, remembering his kiss. Jonathan lay beside her, looking at her occasionally, as if he was thinking about Will, who'd been away from his mother so long.

Nick and Will were on opposite sides of Daniel, with Nick as close to him as he thought he dared to be without looking babyish.

Jason, his head resting on Aengus's haunches, gazed

up at the sparkling sky, probably wishing he was alone with Melissa, who lay a proper distance away. They hadn't touched each other all evening, behaving in front of the family as if they were just friends. They were thoughtful kids, both of them.

Maury, exhausted from his shift at Mike's Diner and his constellation lecture, had fallen asleep.

Ian leaned against the shack, his arms folded across his chest, not participating, just observing as he so often did.

Lilah closed her eyes for a moment. It was so tranquil. Was this the beginning of a worry-free life for her and Jonathan, or was it the calm before a violent, destructive storm?

Enjoy the peace for now. It could be your last chance.

"I'm going to faint."

Daniel turned toward Lilah. She did look pale. In white trousers and a blue silk shirt, the same shirt she'd been wearing the morning she'd joined their lives, she was lovely. She'd be lovely lying on the floor in a faint, too, but it wouldn't go over well with the audience.

"Calm down," he told her. "It'll wow them."

"Let's start then, and get it over with."

He smiled. "Ladies and gentlemen," he whispered to Lilah, "take your seats. The show will start in one minute."

She sat down, looking like the next in line on death row, and he stood before the audience. After a short introduction, he signaled for the film to begin.

It was smooth and beautiful, the rolling fields of Ian's farm gradually turning into a mockup of the center made with the architect's models. Ray had done a remarkable job. Lilah had had a brainstorm, and had conscripted Reverend Galloway to narrate the film. His sonorous voice vibrated throughout the packed room.

The film segued into scenes of the center in Connecticut, with children gathered at the table in one of the homes, playing baseball on a field with mountains in the background—just as they would on Ian's land—and gathered in the recreation room for a movie.

The last segment had been Ray's idea. "Need to shoot the reactions of the townfolks," he said, "then cut and splice to weed out the cuss words."

"Reverend Galloway would never, um, cuss."

He gave her a "where did you come from?" look. "This part will be a talkie."

They'd ended up with a balanced set of responses, from a gushing, "We love the feeling that our community is doing something good for these poor, abandoned children," to "What center?" which netted a laugh from the audience.

As for background music, the Churchill Consolidated High School band played a soothing and relatively recognizable version of "Climb Every Mountain." Daniel had suggested, "With a Little Bit of Luck," which had earned him a look from Lilah, the kind of look that made him smile each time he recreated it in his mind.

It didn't matter if the band was good. Every kid in that band had a parent or two, and they'd all come to the meeting.

When the film ended and the lights went up, the room was hushed. Then slowly the applause began, rising to a crescendo that rocked the room.

Daniel was consumed by elation. He didn't want to

break the spell. Every element of the PowerPoint presentation was duplicated in the handout.

"I'll give you time to glance at the printed materials, and then I'll be happy to answer your questions."

There was only one question, and it came from Ed Wilcox. "I just wanna know how soon we can get going on this thing."

The board withdrew to vote. The center had its unanimous approval.

Daniel and Lilah said their goodbyes, then went to the van with impeccable propriety. As soon as they were inside, though, Daniel gripped her hand and raised it in a victory salute. "We did it!"

The powerful aura of success vibrated through the van. "You did it. Oh, Daniel, I'm so…"

He lowered their hands, putting hers to his lips. "We did it. You've been my inspiration."

He gazed at her, drew her closer. Excitement still hummed through him, spiked by desire. He started the engine, drove a few blocks, then said, "I'm too keyed up to sleep. Know what I want to do? Go to Ian's farm and walk the site."

Her soft voice throbbed through him like a jungle beat. "I'd like that."

They must have talked on the fifteen-minute drive across the river to LaRocque, then down the narrow road to Holman, but he couldn't remember what they'd talked about. He wasn't listening to anything but the music in his own mind, absorbing the scent of Lilah next to him and feeling the want and need surging through his body.

He parked beside the sheepherder's shack. It took all his self-control to get out of the van, take her hand and begin the walk across the dewy grass. The land seemed to stretch out into space just as the sky did.

"If I have my bearings right," he said, hearing his voice crack, "the main building should go up about here."

"And the houses in a circle around it, with gravel drives circling around from the main road to them and on to the…"

"The playing fields over there," Daniel murmured. "And…"

"Children everywhere," Lilah said. "Happy, having fun, getting over the sad circumstances that brought them here."

Her voice quivered. He couldn't hold back any longer. He spun her toward him, took her in his arms and pressed her face against his chest. "You made it all happen," he told her. "Not just the presentation tonight, or having the genius to catapult Reverend Galloway to stardom…" He felt her soft laugh against his chest. He pulled her tighter and laced his hand through the silk of her hair. "You gave me the support I needed to believe in myself and in the center. All of those things, they made my dream come true." He tilted her head to look into her eyes. "You are my dream come true."

Her lips met his with certainty this time, her need and his meeting in a flash of lightning that made their kiss sizzle with pent-up passion. It was a kiss filled with the joyous energy of flicking tongues, caressing hands, each body seeking the heat of the other. He trailed his mouth across the corners of hers, across her cheek to her ear, which he outlined with his tongue, relishing her soft moan and the way she went limp in his arms.

He slid his hands down to her buttocks, pulling her

closer to his raging heat, fitting her to him, feeling her move instinctively against him. The sky lit up with electricity, and thunder rolled through him.

"Daniel," she panted, "I think that actually was thunder and lightning."

And the rain began to fall, huge drops splattering their heads. "Run to the shack," he told her, and together they raced to the little building, bursting through the door soaked and laughing.

Had the storm saved her from herself? What she was doing here wasn't fair to Daniel. She couldn't make love with him when she was living a lie. Or *had* it sealed her fate? She was more alone with him than she'd ever been, and she wanted him with a desperation she hadn't known she was capable of feeling.

While these thoughts spun frantically through her head, he wrapped a blanket around her and another around himself. They were the blankets they'd lain on as they stargazed on that recent night, and now a stack of them sat at the foot of a rustic bed.

Resisting Daniel would be easier if the cosmos weren't conspiring against her and providing a perfect place to make love. She shivered—from excitement rather than cold. She wanted nothing more than to be in that bed with Daniel. And she could read on his face, in his eyes, in the touch of his hands on her, that he wanted her just as badly.

But he doesn't know the truth about me. He doesn't know I'm living a lie.

"You're cold."

The low throb of his voice and his steady gaze were enough to warm her. When he wrapped his arms around her, he made her feel alive and cherished. He brushed her mouth with his, teasing her lips with his tongue.

Suddenly it wasn't like teasing anymore. Now he kissed her hard and deep, his hands moving over her back in an exquisite rhythm as his tongue explored her mouth. She slid her arms around his neck, too aroused to remember why she was supposed to be pushing him away. Thinking at all was impossible with Daniel touching her, so she stopped trying and let herself be a mindless creature of pure sensation, reveling in the joy of being close to him. She slipped the blanket off her shoulders, and in a second, his joined hers. Now they were much closer. It was better, but it still wasn't enough. She wanted him to surround her. She wanted him inside her.

She freed her lips from his and said breathlessly, "I think now is when you're supposed to say, 'We have to get you out of those wet clothes.'"

It was all the permission he needed. He groaned as he reached slowly for the top button of her shirt. One after another, the buttons slipped free until her blouse fell open. He leaned forward and kissed the valley between her breasts.

The sensual feeling of his lips on her skin made the last of her control evaporate. He must have felt the same way, because his breathing was ragged as they frantically tugged off clothes.

Just before the last garment dropped to the floor, he fumbled a condom out of his wallet. Then he picked her up, stretched her out on the bed and lay beside her, pulling her body over his. As he kissed her deeply, he also caressed her, running his hands over her skin until she was nearly insane with desire. At last she knew the whole of him, hot skin, muscular body, flat stomach, his intense need for her.

In her aroused state, she felt powerful. She sat up, straddling him. Never letting go of his gaze, she lowered herself onto his erection, melding their bodies, their hearts. She'd never believed in fate until now, but the sensation of being with Daniel was so perfect that she truly believed they were meant for each other.

Slowly she moved over him, savoring the sensations that were engulfing her. She knew she was pushing him to the edge of his willpower with her deliberate, provocative movements. He reached up to cup her breasts, his fingers teasing her taut nipples.

Unable to contain her desire any longer, she moved faster, faster, her breath coming in tight gasps. His hands moved to her hips, urging her on, pushing her toward the brink. With one last frenzied motion, she flew over the edge, the world exploding around her. She heard the deep, desperate groan that seemed to come from his very soul and collapsed onto his sweat-slicked chest, tingling with pleasure.

She lay there, both of them gasping for breath, for a moment, then she slid to his side, resting her head against his arm. "Wow," she murmured.

He drew her close. "Yeah. Wow."

All the reasons they shouldn't have made love flickered dimly at the back of her mind, but they were no longer important. Nothing mattered except what she felt for him, and what he felt for her. What problems existed could be resolved and overcome.

He shifted her to her back and smiled as he kissed her slowly, his tongue slipping inside her mouth, his leg slipping between hers.

"Yum," she moaned.

"Yum. Definitely yum," he said, and made love to her again, more slowly this time. When she climaxed, she felt as if her bones would dissolve.

In the deepening darkness she clung to him, deliciously sated at last. The rain had stopped. Thunder rumbled in the distance, matching the beating of their hearts.

Even if she could never have him again, she'd have this memory in her heart forever.

Chapter 11

She'd allowed herself those wonderful hours of love with Daniel and had relished the delicious dreams that followed it. In the morning Lilah confronted the fact that she'd made a selfish mistake, one she couldn't take back.

If only she could believe Bruce had given up trying to find her. If only she could give herself completely to Daniel without reservation. She'd known him for such a short time. How long had she been in love with him?

Until now, it had been a hopeless love. She wasn't in his league and she could never have *him,* just dreams of him. But now they'd kissed, touched, blended into one person. If she had to run away again she'd be left with, not merely dreams, but memories she'd never be able to forget.

She'd told Jonathan they were through with running away. She just hoped she could keep her promise.

She put on a cheerful face and went about her morning routine. When Daniel stepped into the kitchen, her heart thudded, her cheeks, her whole body flushed with heat. When he managed a kiss behind her ear in the split second they were alone, the ache of desire curling inside her was pure agony. She wanted to make love with him again and again and again.

Instead, her life seemed to consist of flipping pancakes, again and again and again.

When Daniel removed himself to the clinic, she felt as if he'd been torn away and had taken most of her with him. But by the time the boys were off to the pool, she'd managed to calm down and focus on reformatting copies of the PowerPoint slides that the head of Child Services would need for writing the first and most important grant proposal, which they'd submit to a well-endowed private foundation. The support of that foundation would be the bedrock of their fund-raising efforts.

Daniel came in for lunch with the boys. He seemed to be trying hard to treat her casually, but he wasn't succeeding any too well. His gaze kept meeting hers. She tried to look away, but found herself captured in his spell.

She had to rechannel both their minds before the boys began to notice that their behavior seemed different. "Has your new man, Ted Hilton, gotten here yet?" she blurted out.

"Got here today," Daniel said. He seemed as relieved by the distraction as she was. "He's pleasant, sounds smart and seems to know his job. He's already started setting up a budget for the construction. He's gone through the donor lists, targeted the ones he has some connection to and has estimated what they might donate."

"When do I get to meet him?"

"Soon, I hope. I suggested lunch tomorrow, but he has to meet with the architect."

"Well, I'm anxious to see what he's like," she said. "I know you shouldn't look a gift horse in the mouth, but..."

"I wouldn't look any horse in the mouth without protective gear." His eyes twinkled, and the vestiges of a smile hovered at the corners of his mouth.

Even the hint of a smile was enough to send her reeling.

Jonathan, whose gaze had been ping-ponging from her to Daniel while they talked, suddenly dropped his fork, a rare occurrence during a meal for any of the boys, and was staring at Daniel with his mouth hanging open. "Do they bite?"

Now Daniel had the full attention of the younger boys. "Sometimes," he said. "You and a horse can get to know and love each other, but some of them are skittish. Something scares them, they might throw you off, kick you or even bite you." His eyes moved toward Lilah. "Treat 'em nice. That's my advice about horses."

She knew what he was saying. They'd gotten to know each other, and she had come to love him. Was he waiting for her to get scared and throw him off, kick him or even bite him?

"Kids at school, mainly the girls, ride horses and think it's cool," Will said.

Jason and Maury, who'd been talking, tuned in. "Girls and horses," Maury said, shaking his head.

"Why do you think it's girls who like to ride?" Nick said. "In the westerns on TV, it's the cowboys riding the horses."

"Because it was their transportation then," Jason said,

his smile so like Daniel's that Lilah had to catch her breath. "Women rode them for fun. Now," and he paused to beat his chest with his fists, "us guys have wheels, man. Who needs a horse?"

"Now the girls ride for fun and think you only need a car for transportation," Maury said, shaking his head. "Especially the town girls, who drive out to where they ride the horses."

"You got it," Daniel said, openly laughing now. The conversation was off and running.

Lilah sat back and listened. She was perspiring. True, the old house didn't have air-conditioning, but it had walls like a fortress, plus ceiling fans, so it rarely felt hot. It wasn't even hot outside, only a balmy seventy-five degrees. She was being tortured by the heat within, so to speak.

Too many things tortured her, invading her dreams and her daydreams both. Her love for Daniel. Her dread that Bruce would find her. Her fierce protectiveness of Jonathan. Why couldn't she just relax and admit that life was good right now, enjoy the moment and deal with the letdown when it happened?

Because she was so certain it would happen, and she had to be ready for it.

Daniel was trying to concentrate on his patient, a Yorkshire terrier so small you could miss him on the chair you were about to sit in, but he was distracted by noise in his backyard. A soccer game, sure, but louder than usual, with more shouting. He handed the Yorkie back to his owner with a comforting "Healthy as can be," and sped to the scene.

Yes, it was a soccer game, but the difference was

that this time Lilah was playing along with the boys. Jesse was acting as referee, and Jason, back from work on Ian's farm, had joined in. They whooped and yelled as they raced across the grass, kicking and passing the ball with a fair amount of skill.

That didn't surprise him. What surprised him was Lilah. She'd never played soccer with the boys before, and since they were stopping now and then to show her how to make a move, he quickly realized it was because she didn't know how to. But she surely did look determined.

He had to give the boys credit. They seemed more interested in coaching her than in worrying about which team was winning.

"Shoot the ball, Mom," Jonathan yelled. "Shoot it into the goal really hard."

Lilah took aim and kicked, but she only grazed the ball, so it spun off to the side.

"I'll never learn to play soccer," she told them.

She was wearing navy shorts and a blue-flowered T-shirt. Her hair was pulled back in a loose ponytail, and her cheeks were flushed with exertion. He'd never seen a more beautiful woman.

When she saw him, she held his gaze for a long moment. The way she looked right now, wild and reckless, struck a blow to his midsection. She'd come to mean so much to him in such a short time. How had he gotten so lucky?

She came toward him. "I stink at this game."

"You have to focus on what you want. Then go after it." Her eyes sparkled. He could tell she'd read his meaning. His gaze slid down to her lips. What wouldn't he give to kiss her right now, in front of the boys, Jesse, the whole world? The desire was so strong, it was all he could do to hang on to what little self-control he had left.

Lilah blushed, as if she knew what he was thinking. Rather than looking away and breaking the spell, she met his gaze straight on. "Sounds like good advice. And what I want right now is to learn to kick."

With some effort, he stepped back from her and pointed at the soccer ball. "Stand directly in front of it and kick it squarely in the center."

She did as he said, and kicked the ball with such ferocity that it startled him. Again, she missed the net. "I'm hopeless," she said.

"You're...delightful," he said so softly that only she could hear.

Her lips parted. The air around them seemed to crackle with attraction. He'd never felt this way about a woman before. His love was all-consuming.

"Watch out, you two," Jesse yelled. "If you're not playing, then move."

He and Lilah had both stepped back a couple of feet when the ball flew into the air and headed directly toward them. Daniel moved out to intercept it, but before he could, Lilah ran forward and slammed it with her right knee.

The ball soared across the yard, flying into the makeshift goal so hard it knocked the net flat. For a second, they all stood still, amazed. Then Jonathan shouted, "You did it, Mom. You made a goal!"

The other boys began to cheer. Lilah held up her fingers in a V, smiled her thanks, then turned to Daniel. "Pure luck," she said. "Who knows if I can ever do it again."

"I do," Daniel said, longing to hug her. It was pure

luck that she'd fallen into his life. A woman like Lilah wouldn't happen to him again. So he was going to keep her, no matter what it took.

The supermarket had become Lilah's social club. She spent so much time and so much of Daniel's money there that it was rare not to run into someone she knew. Ahead of her in the Baking Time aisle, she saw a dark-haired woman who looked very professional in a tan skirt and top with a white blazer.

"Dana," she said, pleased to see her. "I didn't know you had time for grocery shopping."

At the sound of her name, the head of Child Services whirled, and seeing it was Lilah, gave her an oddly hesitant smile. "Now and then, my husband reads me the riot act and insists on food in the house."

Lilah nodded. "Men are like that. They don't understand eggs and toast for dinner."

"And don't tell me he should share the shopping, because we decided to get along with one car—which I have."

It was just pleasant small talk, so why did Dana seem increasingly nervous?

"Lilah," she said suddenly, "do you have a few minutes to talk to me this afternoon?"

"Of course." Now she felt uneasy. "I'm going to the center volunteers' meeting at three—can you make it?"

"Unless there's an emergency. Right now I have to run the groceries home."

"Me, too."

"What about two o'clock?"

"Sounds fine."

Jesse came around the aisle with a second shopping

cart. "Sale on spareribs," he told them both, and pointed to a tall stack of plastic-wrapped packages that were kept in place by an equally tall stack of pork loin roasts on the bottom and chicken parts on the top.

"I'd better get some—if you've left any," Dana said, smiling at him in the genuine way she'd smiled at Lilah in the few times they'd met before today, and whisked toward the meat section at the back of the store.

Lilah finished the shopping trip in a fog of worry. Dana was always so pleasant and kind. She doubted, somehow, that grocery shopping had made her lose her smile. Were there problems with the financial projections she'd given Dana? Something was certainly wrong.

She left Jesse with the job of putting away the groceries, telling him she needed to supply Dana with more information for the grant proposal, and almost sick with unease, she went back into town.

Dana was waiting with a pitcher of iced tea and a plate of cookies, but her eyes were worried and her mouth drooped at the corners.

"What's wrong?" Lilah said quietly. "Just tell me."

Dana sighed. "I got a letter this morning from the group of former foster children who intend to form a foundation to collect money for the center. Did Daniel tell you about them?"

"Yes. It's very good of them to want to pay back. But?"

"They sent me a letter, telling me they'd received it from someone who claims your husband isn't dead. That, in fact, Bruce Jamison was imprisoned for a fraud in which you participated fully, that might even have been your idea. According to the letter, he took the rap for you."

Lilah was suddenly stifled by the air in Dana's office. She could hardly breathe. Her worst fear had become a reality. Bruce had found her, and this was how he'd chosen to pay her back, by spreading rumors that would discredit her. If the valley residents believed those rumors, she'd have to leave the valley and start all over. Maybe he thought he could make her feel helpless enough to come back to him.

It wouldn't work. She wouldn't let him destroy her. He couldn't make her feel helpless any more. She and Jonathan had lived on the edge for more than three years, and she'd never once thought of going back to Bruce. Tears of anger and frustration filled her eyes and threatened to pour down her cheeks. "May I read it?"

Dana handed her a copy of the letter. Was she afraid Lilah would grab the original and run? She read slowly, her anger building. It was worse than she'd imagined, pompous, sanctimonious, and she could hear Bruce's voice in every line. It ended: "Jamison sinned, knew it, admitted it and paid for it. Ms. Jamison sinned, decided she didn't want to face the consequences and turned Jamison in. Is this the sort of person who should be caring for children?"

She halted, and her heart almost stopped beating. Clearly, Bruce even knew she was working for Daniel. He knew about Daniel's foster boys. She'd brought danger into all of their lives.

"I find this letter hard to believe," Dana said. "We ran a criminal background check when Daniel first hired you. Everything was fine."

"Have you discussed it with Daniel?" Was that her voice, so rasping and uneven?

"I'll have to, of course, but I wanted to talk to you

first. Are these accusations true?" Dana looked as sick as Lilah felt.

"It's true that my former husband is alive. I lied about that because I'm afraid of him and didn't want to do anything that might help him find me. It's true that he's been in prison. It's also true that I turned him in. But I did *not* participate in his scam and would never have dreamed up a fraud of any kind." She was shaking with anger.

"I couldn't imagine you had," Dana said. "But I have to know that you're fit to be so involved with Daniel's boys." She paused. "And I also want to make sure you're able to take care of Jonathan."

Delivered sympathetically, it was still the worst threat Dana could possibly have made. "Will you let me tell Daniel about the letter?"

"You're in love with him, aren't you?" Dana's voice was soft now, gentle and understanding.

"I think so."

"I don't want him to get hurt."

"I would never hurt him," Lilah said, "but nothing in the world would make Bruce happier."

"Tell me about him."

Lilah sighed, getting control of her anger. "I was very young when I married Bruce. I'd grown up on the edge of poverty with parents who weren't happy together, and when this attractive, obviously well-to-do young man arrived in Whittaker—that's where I'm from—I saw him as my salvation. He moved me out of my parents' rundown house into a beautiful old one that we restored, got me out of thrift-shop clothes and into nice ones, and for a while I was happy beyond belief."

"I can understand that," Dana said, nodding.

"But soon after Jonathan was born, he changed." She

felt sick, remembering how uneasy she'd been at the time. "He was tense, belligerent. He was in the construction business, and he'd decided to go on his own with a housing development in Whittaker. There was a beautiful property on the lake, where he was going to sell building sites and then proceed with construction. He said I should realize that he was worried about money—he had plenty of capital to make a down payment on the property, but he'd need to sell those sites to get loans for construction."

A slight frown appeared on Dana's forehead. Lilah didn't know what she'd said to cause that frown, but she kept going.

"He said I'd have to do his bookkeeping, in order to save money. That was fine with me. I took a basic course in bookkeeping at the community college and then took over his financial records. But soon…"

"When money got tight, he took it out on you."

"How did you know?" She'd felt so hot a few minutes ago, and now she began to shiver.

"It's a familiar story in my profession," Dana said. She leaned forward, and the gaze she fastened on Lilah was penetrating. "My guess is that first it was yelling, then pushing, and finally hitting."

"You guessed right," Lilah said shakily. "Jonathan…" she bit her lip, fighting back tears, "witnessed a couple of incidents. The first time he tried to get between me and Bruce, tried to protect me. He wasn't even three yet. It broke my heart. No child should ever have that kind of experience."

"It's a credit to you that he's such a well-adjusted child."

"It's a miracle," Lilah said. "He's everything to me."

"When did you actually leave Bruce?"

"When he began selling the sites and we did have money, his attitude toward me didn't change. It was as if he wanted me to be afraid of him. As I got madder at him, my eyes got sharper. He's a great salesman and at last quite a lot of money was rolling in, but he wasn't doing anything with it except stashing it away. No architects' fees. No negotiations with contractors. No applications for loans to begin construction. It was pretty clear he was just accepting the money and had no intention of building the houses.

"When I confronted him, he…hurt me, threatened me, warned me to keep quiet. But I went to a lawyer, got his advice and then turned Bruce in."

"That took a lot of courage."

"I took Jonathan with me. I was scared to death that Bruce might—" She halted, feeling that fear again.

"I understand," Dana said, and this time she spoke gently.

"I didn't divorce him until after the trial. I didn't want to have to testify against him. But after he was sentenced, I insisted on the divorce. No settlement, because all the money we had went to pay back investors." She paused to square her chin. "It wasn't quite enough. I made up the rest from our savings, cashed in our insurance policies, sold the house, took a nursing job and kept just enough for Jonathan and me to scrape by."

Dana winced. "Then he got out of prison and you ran."

"Yes." Did Dana believe her?

"I'll have to think this over," Dana said. "I believe you, but we still have to do some investigating."

"Of course," Lilah said. She'd been hoping Dana

would absolve her on the spot, but apparently it wasn't going to be that easy.

"You will tell Daniel." It wasn't a question.

"I'll skip the meeting and tell him as soon as he has time to talk to me."

Outside Dana's office, still shaky, Lilah flipped open her cell phone and dialed Jesse. "Jesse, there's something I have to do. How easy is dinner going to be? Yes, grill those ribs. Sounds great. Maybe we could grill the corn, too. Because I need to ask you a favor. Would you have time to go to the pool and keep an eye on Jonathan? He... he was a little sniffly this morning. I don't want him get too tired." She listened. "No, nothing's wrong," she lied. "It's just a bad connection. And Jesse, is Daniel in the clinic or making farm calls?"

Daniel was at the volunteer meeting. She'd have to go now. It would be agony waiting for it to be over. How would he react? Would he be shocked, horrified, or would he hold her close and tell her he believed in her, that everything would be all right?

She was sick at heart. Bruce had figured out the right people to target with that letter full of lies. He had probably figured everything else out, too, including the kids' schedules and their activities. She wished Jonathan were with her and not at the pool, but Jesse wouldn't let any strange man, anyone, for that matter, take Jonathan away.

Shoulders squared, she walked to the church where the meeting was being held. On the way, she ran into Virginia Galloway, who spoke politely enough but gave her an odd look as she scurried on toward the church.

Lilah's stomach cramped. Surely not...

She made her way down the stairs to the basement, a large room with a small stage at one end. The local pediatrician passed her on the stairs, giving her no more than a brief nod. At the bottom of the stairs, Sarah Mc-Nally, principal of the LaRocque Elementary School, turned away instead of speaking. Everyone turned away from her, until the mayor of Holman, a beautiful young woman from a political family, came directly toward her, gave her a sympathetic look and put an encouraging hand on her arm.

How many people had gotten that letter? Dana had spoken as if she'd been the only one. Having no idea whom she might safely sit beside, she found a chair at the back of the small group and tried to make herself invisible.

For the first time, she didn't light up inside at the sight of Daniel. He didn't seem to see her. Maybe she *was* invisible. She half heard his encouraging speech to the volunteers. Behind her, she heard the door open and close, indicating that another volunteer had made it to the meeting, but she didn't turn around. She couldn't stand the possibility of another cool stare from someone she'd begun to think of as a friend.

She sank into her own thoughts. Terrible thoughts. If other people in the valley had already seen the letter, and believed Bruce's lies, she'd have to uproot Jonathan right now and leave without trying to defend herself. She'd lied to them about Bruce, told them he was dead. She could almost hear them saying it: "Lie about one thing, and she'll lie about another."

Worst of all, statewide child services wouldn't trust her to care for Daniel's boys. Maybe Daniel wouldn't trust her, either.

What if they tried to take Jonathan away from her? It was a thought too horrible to bear.

As soon as the meeting ended, she'd tell Daniel it was imperative that they talk immediately. For now, she had to wait. In spite of her worry, she finally managed to tune in to what Daniel was saying.

"I'm proud to introduce a new volunteer who has offered to be the financial manager for the center. A businessman himself, he brings his expertise to our project, temporarily deserting his own business, which is an act of great generosity. Ted Hilton, will you step forward, please?"

From a spot directly behind Lilah, a man moved confidently toward the stage. He turned to face the audience, and Lilah found herself looking at Bruce.

Chapter 12

Lilah felt as if she'd been thrown overboard into the deep waters of the Atlantic. Her blood ran cold, her fingertips were icy. Struggling toward the surface, running out of air, she listened to Bruce deliver an exemplary speech, thanking all the volunteers, telling them how much he looked forward to working with them. He said the words looking straight at her. She felt certain that she, and only she, could see the hint of malevolence behind his polished smile.

Bruce did have talent. He was, beyond doubt, a superb con artist.

The meeting ended with a few final words from Daniel. Lilah made a beeline for him, but she wasn't as swift as Virginia Galloway. She and Daniel exchanged a few words that made Daniel nod soberly, then several other volunteers followed. She hung back, waiting her turn.

"Lilah."

Bruce's voice. She stopped in her tracks.

"Be with you in a minute," he said, smiling at several obviously smitten volunteers who'd surrounded him, "but someone told me this is Lilah Jamison, and we haven't met yet. Give us a minute."

She turned to face him. He held out his hand and smiled, performing for his public, but when he spoke, his words were for her alone.

"It's been a long time, Lilah."

"Not long enough," she spat at him, not caring who heard her. "What are you trying to do to me?"

Now his smile was the one she remembered all too vividly, cold and cruel. "You blew the whistle on me. Now I'm blowing the whistle on you."

"But I haven't done anything."

"Apparently you haven't read the letter that's circulating around the valley."

She clenched her fists. "Lies, and you know it."

"You lied about me," he said in a singsong voice, "and now I'm lying about you. Fair's fair."

"You—"

"Now, now," he said in a gently chiding way, "hear me out. I have a plan."

"To hurt me as badly as you can."

"Oh, no. To help you."

He couldn't con her any more. She didn't answer, just waited to hear more of his lies.

"Too bad about the letter," he said with false sympathy. "The townspeople will shun you. Saint Daniel," he hooked a thumb toward the stage, "will fire you. But I will resign from my exalted position, outraged at the community attitude toward you, and whisk you and Jonathan away from the scandal to an upper-middle-class life in, um, Pennsylvania."

"Forget your plan. Stay away from me," she said fiercely, "and don't get anywhere close to Jonathan, or Daniel, or his kids. Jonathan and I would go on welfare before we'd leave town with you. When I tell these people who you really are…"

The smile stayed in place, but his voice was like an icicle, sharp and cold. "Cooperate with me, Lilah. Don't even think about blowing my cover. You'll be sorry if you do."

He stepped away from her, and without missing a beat said jovially, "Sorry about that, ladies. Now I'm all yours."

Lilah made her way toward Daniel, but now she moved more slowly. Bruce had threatened her if she told anyone who he really was. But she'd told Dana the truth about herself and had promised to tell Daniel. Almost, not quite, as a condition of being regarded as a fit mother for Jonathan.

Threat or no threat, she *would* tell Daniel. The person she most needed to tell him about now wasn't herself, but Bruce.

Behind her, Lilah could hear him saying, "I got lucky with some investments, which gave me the capital to start the company. Then it did well and I…"

And, "I'd be happy to offer financial advice. I follow the market closely, and I…"

She had to drive him out of Churchill before he did irreparable harm to the community. She hurried toward Daniel, who saw her and ended the conversation he'd been having with the pediatrician.

"Daniel, I have to talk to you."

"Seems like everybody wants to talk to me right now, but you first," he said.

He whisked her out of the church and into the red pickup. Lilah saw no sign of Bruce. "So let's talk." He sounded busy—or harried.

"I… I have a lot to tell you." Her voice shook. "I want to show you something. Just drive. I'll tell you how to get there."

They made the trip in silence, except for the terse directions she occasionally gave him. At the end of the logging road, she said, "We're here." She turned to face him. "This is where Jonathan and I lived—until we met you."

She led him to the fallen tree trunk where she and Jonathan had spent so many hours, reading, talking, living on sandwiches and cereal. The memories of those two weeks were so painful that she hated to relive them, but Daniel had to know everything.

"What I have to tell you may change everything between us."

He raised his eyebrows.

"I'm not the person you think I am. I've lied to you. I've lied to the whole community."

His expression changed completely. "I know," he said. "I got the letter, too." His voice was calm, but in his eyes she saw that he felt betrayed.

"It was full of lies," she said, longing for that look to go away.

"Your husband isn't alive?"

"He is. I lied about that because it was a gentler story than the truth," she said, shaking with anxiety. "Jonathan and I were hiding from him."

"Why?"

Dappled sunlight shot through the tall trees, mocking her sadness, her bitterness, as the dam that had held back the truth inside her burst and the words flooded out of her.

Daniel listened, his face tight. She found herself stumbling over her words, sounding, probably, just like a person who was telling a lie.

When she told him that Bruce had hit her, his expression changed briefly, encouraging her. "He gave you that scar," he said.

"Yes. When he found out I'd turned him in, he hit me with a cast-iron frying pan. Jonathan was there, screaming." Tears flowed down her cheeks at the memory. "I could hardly stand up, but I made myself stay awake and alert. I had to, to protect Jonathan. Bruce rushed out of the house, maybe thinking he could get out of town in time, but the police caught up with him. They stopped him for speeding, of all things, and as soon as he handed over his driver's license, they knew who he was and they took him in."

"He was a brute," Daniel murmured. "He could be dangerous to my boys, too."

"I thought I'd escaped him," she said, beginning to sob uncontrollably. "I was going to tell you now, tell you I have to leave, and tell you—"

His eyes were sad. "If you leave, you'll change all our lives. You charmed Jesse, the boys love you, and I…" he hesitated, "I love you."

Her breath caught.

"Until you, I'd never met a woman I trusted enough to love. See," he said, with such pain in his face that her heart wrenched, "I wasn't always the person I am now. Learning to trust has been the hardest struggle of my life."

"I'm so sorry," she whispered. "So sorry."

"I'll take you back to town." His shoulders drooped.

"I'll leave with Jonathan tonight."

"I guess that's what we'll have to do." He sighed. "Because of my boys. But not tonight. I don't want you driving with Jonathan when you're upset."

His instinct to protect Jonathan as well as his boys touched her. "Tomorrow, then. But I have one more thing to tell you."

Her heart had turned to stone, but it allowed her to calm down enough to deliver her biggest blow. "I didn't know until today, but this con artist, this violent man, was going to handle the cash flow of the center. Ted Hilton, your new financial manager, is my ex-husband, Bruce. You have to get rid of him."

His shock built to rage that was frightening in its intensity. "Because you lied to me, I was going to let this…this con artist, this violent man, handle the cash flow of the center?"

"That's not my fault! I didn't know he was doing this. I told you I wanted to meet him. Now I've met him, I've told you, and I assume you'll get rid of him."

"Damned right I'll get rid of him," Daniel said, suddenly sounding angry.

And you'll be rid of me tomorrow morning, too. All's well that ends well.

Chapter 13

Lilah huddled in her car, trying to calm down before she drove back to Daniel's house—for the last time.

Her heart was breaking, but she *had* to stay calm, cold as ice inside, until she'd done what she had to do. She had to tell Jonathan, and she'd decided she'd tell him the truth. She had to pack up her possessions. She had to give her son time to say his goodbyes, maybe have dinner with the family as usual and spend the night with Nick. She knew Daniel wouldn't punish Jonathan for his mother's sins.

Her sins. She'd handled everything so badly, when she'd thought she was doing just the opposite. Why had she decided to remain silent, try to be a different person in this new community? Fear of Bruce was a big factor, certainly. Pride? She didn't want anyone to know the kind of man Jonathan's father was. Didn't want any-

one to know that she'd let that man abuse her verbally
and physically.

It wouldn't help to beat herself up. It was over. She
and Jonathan would run again. This time they'd have
more money—she'd saved most of her salary, and they
should be able to afford some sort of shelter. She should
choose a larger city this time, in a state other than Vermont, would change her name.

They'd survive. But she was afraid they'd never be
as happy as they'd been here.

The ice in her heart threatened to melt into tears. She
took a deep breath, then started the car. She'd drive to
the pool first, make sure Jonathan was all right, maybe
even take him home with her. He'd protest, wanting to
stay with Nick and Will, then ride his bike home—with
Jesse driving right along with them.

Every thought that came into her mind reminded her
of some moment during her stay with Daniel. Now she
was remembering the family council Daniel had held
to decide if the younger boys would be allowed to ride
their bikes to the pool. He'd insisted that they be chaper-
oned everywhere, explaining to Lilah that sometimes the
parents of foster children tried to get them back without
going through proper channels, kidnapping them, effec-
tively. And often the children went with them willingly,
imagining everything would be all right. Especially with
the mystery of Nick's past, Daniel couldn't take any
chances, even if the boys thought he was overprotective.

But when they told him everybody in town rode their
bikes to the pool except them, he'd been forced to realize that it was something that made them different
from the other kids, the very thing he had struggled to

avoid. So the compromise was bikes plus a grown-up in the caravan.

Sadness rose up inside her. It had all been so wonderful, and now it had come to an end.

She reached the pool just as Jesse drove away slowly in the van with three young cyclists following him in single file. Lilah pulled up behind them at a safe distance. This afternoon they'd be sandwiched in between two bodyguards. In her rearview mirror, she glimpsed another car she'd seen parked on the street beside the pool. She felt sorry for the driver. Passing two cars and three boys on bicycles would be dangerous on this narrow, curving road. He or she would be traveling at five miles an hour until the Foster cortege got home.

Home. Not her home anymore. She gritted her teeth. She had to gear up for the talk with Jonathan, which she was dreading more than she'd dreaded anything in her life.

Daniel hadn't made afternoon appointments because of the meeting. When he got home, he saw that Lilah's car wasn't there. Maybe she was following the boys home from the pool. Or maybe she picked up Jonathan and left in spite of her promise to wait until tomorrow. Aching inside, he strode into the house, needing badly to spill out his anger and sorrow to Jesse, then make plans to increase security around the house until they were sure Bruce Jamison had left town.

Jesse wasn't there, either. Frustrated and let down, he got out Bruce's business card and dialed the man's cell number. Bruce didn't answer. Daniel left a deceptively polite message for the nonexistent Ted Hilton, then glanced at the card again.

If Lilah was telling the truth, there was no Hilton Construction Company in Philadelphia. So he'd call the number and see what he got. What he got was an "invalid number, please redial." He redialed, and got the same message.

So she *was* probably telling the truth about Bruce. Just a little too late. A lot too late, in fact. He sank into a kitchen chair. He'd known better than to let himself fall in love, and he'd gone ahead and done it anyway. He should have listened to Mike and Ian.

He grew angrier as he sat there. He dialed Bruce's cell number again, and this time he said, after the beep, "Bruce, I know who you are." *Anger won't help,* he reminded himself. *Sound like a man in charge, a fearless man.* "Leave the valley immediately and don't show your face here again. Lilah and Jonathan are under close surveillance." Right. He had no idea where Lilah was, and Jonathan was under the surveillance of a seventy-five-year-old man and two young boys. "You can't touch them. The chief of police knows about you," or would in a minute, "and I imagine your parole officer in Whittaker is expecting a visit from you. If you don't do exactly as I say and get out of here, the chief can get you on a parole violation. So leave, *now!*"

He dialed the police station and filled in the chief. "Nothing to charge him with yet," Daniel said, "but if you can find anything to pick him up for, do it."

He slammed the receiver onto the cradle, then picked it up again and called Dana at home. "Daniel, I'm so sorry," she said. "This is such a mess. I strongly feel that Lilah couldn't have—"

"Dana, Lilah *could* have done anything. She's been lying to me from the start."

"Daniel, are you sure?"

"The man who wrote that letter is her ex-husband, Bruce Jamison, an ex-con, who is currently calling himself Ted Hilton, the center's new volunteer financial manager."

There was total silence at the end of the line. Finally Dana said, "Well, Daniel, I've spent the past two hours trying to check out Lilah's story, so now I have information to refine the search." She hesitated. "Have you and she talked?"

"Yes. She says she had nothing to do with his scam and that he was brutal to her. And maybe he was. She has an ugly-looking scar on her forehead, says he hit her with a cast-iron pan."

"I believe her," Dana said. "Give me time to check out both of them."

"Let me know what you find. I know the guy's an impostor and there is no Hilton Construction Company, but is there any reason to think he's dangerous?"

"And Lilah? Do you think we might need to take Jonathan away from her?"

All the energy went out of him. "No, he loves her. He couldn't be faking it."

"Take it easy, Daniel," Dana said, and her voice was gentle. "We'll figure out the truth."

"She's leaving in the morning," Daniel said, feeling worse and worse. "I told her to."

Another silence, then, "I guess I have a lot of work to do tonight." Dana was brisk now. "Okay to wake you up if I have news?"

"I won't be asleep," Daniel said, because he knew it was true.

He began to pace the floor, waiting. Waiting for the

phone call Bruce would never return. Waiting for Lilah, who would never come home to him again.

Lilah was barely aware she was driving as she followed the boys down the shaded road to the older part of town and Daniel's house, which faced another wooded area. It was a beautiful setting. Elderly neighbors on both sides, and a view of parkland across the street. She'd miss that, too.

The driver behind them was keeping a respectful distance from her car. A nice person. Maybe had a child in the car, too. Although she had her gaze focused on the boys, she was lost in wistful thoughts when the house loomed ahead, fanciful outside, comfortable and loving inside.

It happened so fast. The car behind them suddenly sped forward, then screeched to a halt. The driver flung the door open, and moving like a predator he snatched Jonathan off his bike, thrust him into the backseat and sped away.

Will and Nick, who were riding behind him, crashed into the fallen bike and dominoed onto the asphalt. Jesse screeched the van to a halt.

Lilah was already out of the car. "Leave the bikes!" she screamed. "Get into the house right now and call the police!"

She slammed her accelerator to the floor and went after Bruce.

Daniel had heard the noise and was already on the drive when Nick reached him, sobbing hysterically and flung his arms around Daniel's knees.

"Daniel," Will said shakily, "JJ's been kidnapped!"

"Don't wait for me," Jesse shouted from the street. "Call the police!"

* * *

Daniel had never been so scared in his life. He hadn't been this scared when the Canadian guards had cuffed him and taken him into custody as a teen. Frustrated, but not scared.

"What kind of car was it?" He was running toward his truck.

"A station wagon like Maury's and Uncle Mike's," Will said, sprinting along beside him. "Lilah went after it."

Great. Thirty percent of the cars in Vermont were Subaru station wagons. "Go into the house and stay there with Jesse. I'll call the police from the truck," he said, and sped away.

He called the chief's direct line. "Bruce Jamison has kidnapped his son," he said succinctly. "My best guess is he's taking Route 30 over to I-91, and I'm seven, eight minutes behind him."

"I'll get a car out right now, then I'll alert the state police," the chief said. "You get any more information, call 9-1-1."

He should also have told the chief to look for Lilah and stop her from pursuing Bruce and her son. He'd deserted her, rejected her when she needed him most. How could he have been so selfish as to put himself, the boys, the center, first? Too wrapped up in his own feelings at having been lied to, he hadn't stopped to consider how much trouble *she* was in. Because he'd been so self-centered, now she was going to try to face down her ex-husband alone, and he knew she couldn't handle it. His panic escalated with every second that went by. He wasn't catching up to her, and he hadn't seen any gray station wagons.

In an agony of regret, Daniel drove like a maniac. He wasn't sure what he'd do if he came upon cows being herded across the road, blocking his path. The road out of the valley was rough, but it would be rough for Bruce, too, and he wasn't as familiar with the terrain as Daniel was.

He had a chance. There was hope. He chanted the thought to himself as he drove and drove and drove—toward what, he dreaded to find out.

There was no hope. She couldn't catch Bruce's car. Sobs choked Lilah's throat and tears streamed down her face. For a few seconds she'd had the station wagon in her sights, and then it was gone, too far ahead to see.

This was all her fault. She should have gone to the pool, commanded Jonathan to get in the car and then fled the valley with nothing, not even the near-nothing with which they'd left Whittaker. She knew how cruel and resourceful Bruce was. She should have been ready for anything.

Now he had the most precious person in her life. Jonathan, probably scared to death, was under his control. She wouldn't give up until the last shred of hope vanished, but the road had twisted and turned, smaller roads had forked off in this direction and that. She had no idea if she was actually following Bruce anymore, but the one thing she couldn't do was go back to the apartment above the carriage house where she'd once been so happy to sit and wait. She'd go crazy.

In the distance, she heard the wail of a siren. She told herself the police were on their way to rescue Jonathan, and felt a second's relief until she realized the sound wasn't behind her, but off to one side. They were aiming for the freeway, and Bruce had gone in a different direction.

She had to call the police and tell them.

She braked and pulled over to the side, and just as she opened her phone, it rang. It could be Daniel, saying Jonathan was home safe and sound. Shaking with nerves and exhaustion, she answered the call.

"Mom?"

She had to calm down for his sake. "Jonathan. Are you all right?"

"I'm scared." He was crying. She felt as if she were bleeding inside.

"Lilah. Lilah, the good mother. Do you want your beloved son back?"

Bruce had taken the phone. He actually sounded amused. She leaned her head on the steering wheel and willed her voice to level out before she said another word. "What have you done to him?"

"Absolutely nothing except pick him up from the pool, just as any dad would. He's fine." Airline-pilot drawl. "But he sure misses his mommy. He's hoping you'll join us, so we can be the happy family we used to be."

"Where?" she said. It wasn't the moment to lash out at him. All that mattered was getting Jonathan back.

"We're up in that place where you took your boyfriend this afternoon." He delivered a stagy sigh. "I wish I'd thought to bring a camera to that meeting. The look on your face… Anyway, I followed the two of you when you took off, of course. And the rest is history. Oh, Lilah, poor woman, you've always underestimated me. I know how to get what I want."

"What *do* you want?" She bit her hand, just to keep from screaming.

"Like I said, meet us here, and the three of us will go away together. We'll go to another state, start all over. You are *such* a good bookkeeper, considering that you've only had one course in bookkeeping, but this time, Lilah," and now he dropped the fake country tone, let his innate cruelty show, "you *will* work with me, because you know what I'll do to you if you don't. And to Jonathan. By the way, come alone. No police, no boyfriend, just you. If I hear sirens, we're out of here."

If Bruce had called a second later, she would already have called the police and the cruisers would even now be exiting the freeway, heading in his direction with sirens screaming.

She felt faint. "I'll come alone. If Jonathan isn't all right when I get there, I'll kill you, Bruce, with my bare hands."

"As if." He chuckled, and hung up.

He'd always underestimated her, too, but he didn't know it. That was her trump card. Hands shaking, she dialed Daniel's cell. The voice that answered sounded as panicked as hers. She spoke rapidly. "Bruce has taken Jonathan to our hideout in the woods. Call the police and tell them they're on the wrong track, just to go back to the station and call off the search, because Bruce said I had to come alone."

She slammed the phone shut, turned the car around and drove as if a pride of lions was chasing her.

Daniel swore as he hadn't sworn in years. He'd almost reached the freeway, far from where Bruce held Jonathan captive.

He made a screeching U-turn, then called the police dispatcher. He wouldn't call them off, he'd tell them where to go. "Here's where they are," he said, and tersely gave directions, "and *no sirens!*"

Lilah left the car blocking the bottom of the logging road and hid the keys in the crook of a small tree. Bruce would find it difficult to escape with Jonathan. Halfway up the hill, she made a megaphone of her hands and called out, "Jonathan, everything's going to be okay. I'm here."

"Come on down," Bruce said, doing a passable impression of a game show host. "Or up in this case."

She entered the clearing. It was darker in the woods than it had been on the road, but she could see Bruce standing beside his car and holding Jonathan in front of him. Not holding him so much as containing him. Jonathan wriggled, trying to run to her, but Bruce got an even tighter grip on him.

Jonathan was crying, holding out his arms to Lilah. She couldn't stand it. She rushed toward him fiercely. She'd rip him away from Bruce, run down the road with him, get him into the car—and Bruce would catch up with them in about fifteen seconds, probably before she'd even started the engine.

No, she had to ignore Jonathan's distress, startle Bruce with her calm, collected behavior, take the upper hand. "Don't worry, baby," she said soothingly. "Dad and I are going to talk. We'll work things out." She smiled at Bruce, enjoying the surprise on his face.

How had she dredged up that even smile? No time to think about it now, just keep using it on Bruce.

Several feet away from them, she said, "Okay, Bruce, I give up. You're right. We should all be together again."

The startled look Jonathan sent her broke her heart.

Trust me. Go along with me. She said the words over and over in her mind as she went toward him, hoping he'd somehow receive the message.

Miraculously, he calmed down. Maybe he knew, or maybe he just felt better the closer she came to him.

"You are so smart!" she said to Bruce. "How did you get my cell number?"

"It was no trouble at all. Jonathan was happy to call you for me." His tone was teasing.

"And I was happy to hear from him," Lilah said smoothly. "So, here we are. Tell me again, Bruce, what do you have in mind for us?" She'd stall him until she could make a plan of action, because whatever she came up with had to work. She'd only have one chance.

He tilted his head toward the sky. "I've always liked the idea of settling into one of those midwestern states. You know, good schools, polite people. People with a certain…innocence."

"Oh," she breathed, "I see where you're going. Do you already have a new money-making scheme?"

"Yes." He looked smug. "But you don't think I'm stupid enough to tell you about it yet, do you?"

"Heavens, no. But I know it will be a good one." She gave him a thoughtful look, moving another step closer. "What will we live on while you're just starting up?"

"I managed to stash away quite a bit of money before you—" He halted. "But that's in the past, isn't it?" he said genially. "We're moving forward now."

She was, at least, inch by inch. "Bruce, if we do resume our former lives, we have to agree on a couple of issues. You have to treat me nicely. You can't use verbal or physical abuse. No secrets this time, either. We work together as a team."

Bruce's eyes narrowed. "We'll be like Bonnie and Clyde," he said. "I'll do the scamming and you'll fix the books. We'll look like everybody else in Podunk until somebody uncovers us, and then we'll move and start all over again. Jonathan will be a well-traveled young man, won't you, son?"

Lilah felt sick. But she had to maintain the act. Bruce seemed to be buying it. "It sounds as if you've thought it out well." She took one more small step. "So let's start by being friends again. We can work out everything else later."

He let go of Jonathan, which was all she'd hoped for, and he ran straight into her arms.

Daniel's heart was thudding when he reached the bottom of the logging road and found Lilah's car blocking it. He parked the truck and started up the hill. He wanted to run, but he knew he had to move slowly and silently.

At last he heard voices, two voices at least, and it gave him hope that at the end of his quest he'd find all three of them, Lilah, Bruce and Jonathan. When he was as close to the clearing as he could get without making his presence known, he saw the scene ahead of him.

Jonathan was behind Lilah, clutching her waist. She stood close to Bruce. She was smiling. Bruce seemed to be taken by that smile. *What was going on here?*

Daniel wanted to throw himself into the space remaining between the two of them, somehow get both Lilah and Jonathan behind him and destroy the man, but something held him back. Could she actually be making a deal with Bruce, or was she conning him in the way he'd conned so many innocent people?

He wouldn't blame her for making a deal to save her

son. He supposed he'd do almost anything to save one of his brothers, one of his boys—or Lilah and Jonathan.

He crept closer, ready for anything.

"So you agree to my conditions? You get your temper under control, we cooperate with each other, and above all, we do the best thing for Jonathan."

"Whatever works for you, baby, works for me."

She was conning him! His head spinning, Daniel crouched down, ready to leap forward when he needed to. He couldn't count on the police to arrive in time. When he moved, he'd have to move fast.

Lilah's only connection to reality was the tug of Jonathan's hands on her waist, the stifled sounds of his sobs. Except for that, she was in another sphere, where the real Lilah had ceased to exist and a stranger had taken her place. Confidently, she took yet another step toward Bruce.

I'm almost there. She had a plan in place now. "When I said we'd start by being friends," she said, batting her eyelashes, "you know I didn't mean *just* friends."

Surely she'd gone too far. He sounded wary for the first time. "Hey," he said, "what's made you so friendly all of a sudden?"

She sighed, held out her hands in a defeated gesture. "Well, Bruce, I've had to admit you're smarter than I am. You've won. I want Jonathan to have a happy life, so I might as well try to make it work with you, turn this back into a happy marriage. You are his father. I'm sure that with a lot of attention and affection he'll grow to admire you as much as I have. Besides," she said, daring a smile again, "I've tried being poor, and I found out it was a lot more fun to be rich. And you know how to make us rich better than anybody I know."

He seemed mollified. "I can sure do that."

Now. Do it now. Fighting down her disgust, she took that last crucial step. "And I know that once we're working together toward a common goal, we'll become closer, in every way—"

A glance at his leering smile was all she needed. When he held out his arms to her, she gathered up all her strength and drove her knee hard into his groin.

He yelled in pain and fell to the ground. She delivered a solid kick to his shin and then, for good measure, another one to his shoulder.

Footsteps thundered close behind her, but there was no fear left in her anymore. She had only had one person to fear, and he was down for the count. She'd won the match.

Daniel lifted Jonathan off his feet and wrapped his arms around both of them. "Oh, Lilah, Lilah," was all he was able to say. Her adrenaline sapped, she was shaking like an aspen tree in fall. He held her upright. On her own, she would have collapsed. She buried her face in his chest, and he held them both, whispering comfort, delivering love.

"I've been so unfair to you," he choked out. "I'm not the person I seem to be, either. Mike and Ian aren't my brothers in the way you think. I'll tell you everything later. Now all I want to do is tell you how much I…"

"Daniel," Jonathan interrupted him. "Mom did it. She saved us. All by herself! With the soccer moves we taught her."

His eyes were so wide, shining in the gathering dusk,

and his pride so evident, that Daniel had to smile down at him. "She sure did. She's wonderful, isn't she?" Lilah made a slight movement against his chest.

"Awesome," Jonathan breathed. "You are, too," he said kindly. "But I was sort of thinking if you married her, she could take care of both of us."

Lilah's head shot upward. "Jonathan!"

Daniel snuggled her back against him. "I've never had a finer proposal, Jonathan, and I accept. Lilah, is there any reason we three should not be joined in holy…"

Her soft laughter echoed in his heart. She gazed up at him. "No matter what's happened in your past, no, absolutely none."

Jonathan's arms tightened around Daniel's neck, Lilah's around his chest and his heart beat with a love so strong that it overwhelmed him. Inches away, the chief of police and one of Churchill's two deputies were handcuffing a groaning Bruce and reading him his rights, but the scene couldn't get inside his head.

Only one thing mattered to him now. At long last, Daniel had a real family.

Epilogue

Three weeks later...

"How do I look?"

Lilah smiled. How Jonathan looked was very grown up in his navy suit, white shirt and blue striped tie.

"Movie-star handsome," she told him, bursting with pride in her son.

"I feel kinda dumb," he said, fiddling with his tie.

Lilah pointed out the back door. "You're dressed exactly like the other boys."

And like Daniel. She caught a glimpse of him and wanted nothing more than to rush into his arms. She loved him, she loved Mike and Ian, the boys, Jesse. She'd be marrying all of them—gladly.

She gazed affectionately at the boys as they escorted guests to the folding chairs that filled the backyard, each of them so prim and proper as he held out an arm for a female guest. The yard was green, manicured and lovely. The arbor where she and Daniel would take their vows was surrounded by vases of white lilies mixed with dark-blue flax. A thrill went through her. She'd be standing before that arbor soon, saying, "I do," and thinking, *Oh, yes, I do.*

Quite a crowd had come to see him get married. Rightfully so. He was the most wonderful man she'd ever known.

"You know, Jonathan, I have you to thank for this."

"Because I proposed?" he said. "Well, somebody had to."

She laughed. "That, too," she said. "If you hadn't wanted to spend the night with Nick so badly, we'd have gone back to the forest and we would never have seen them again."

"Hey," he said, "I did do it, didn't I?"

Dana, who would be Lilah's only attendant, rushed into the room, resplendent in a long, lovely blue-flowered dress that complemented Lilah's pale-blue organdy one. She put her arms around Lilah. "I'm so happy for you," she said. "I'm even happier for Daniel." She stood back and looked at Lilah. "When you ran away," she said softly, "I'm so glad you ran away to us."

So was Lilah. Two months ago, who would have thought her life would turn out so wonderfully? Bruce was now just a memory. He'd been arrested, charged not only with kidnapping Jonathan but also with frauds he'd committed before he moved to Whittaker that had just now come to light. This time he was facing many years in prison, and, to Lilah's relief, he had lost his parental rights to Jonathan. When she and Daniel got back from their honeymoon at a romantic seaside resort in Maine,

Daniel would start the process of adopting Jonathan. Her heart swelled with love. They'd be a real family.

Mike stepped through the kitchen door, interrupting her thoughts. She'd gotten closer to Daniel's brothers since they'd realized how much she and Daniel meant to each other.

"It'll be good to have a woman in the family," he said, giving her a bear hug. "Keep him in line, okay? Ian and I are sick and tired of doing it all by ourselves."

"He is a wild one," she said, laughing as she hugged him back.

"Am I interrupting anything?"

It was Ian, and she still wasn't sure what to expect from him. She was touched when he patted her arm and said, "Make him happy."

"I'll do my very best," she said. Better than best.

"Daniel's fit to be tied," Jesse said, banging the door behind him. "Are we about ready in here?"

Daniel fidgeted as he tried to concentrate on greeting each guest in a personal way. He could only think about Lilah. In just a few minutes, she'd be his, and he intended to make her the happiest woman in the universe. In a couple of months, Jonathan would be his, too. He loved Lilah's son. He hoped they'd have a dozen more just like him, maybe with a girl thrown in somewhere.

He gazed at each of his boys, one at a time. Maury, happy beyond belief to be working for Mike at the diner. He'd already found his dream.

Will, who'd soon be back at home with his parents.

Nick. Would he ever solve the mystery of Nick? The boy was happier every day and no longer had nightmares, but he still kept his secret locked tightly inside him.

Then Daniel's gaze drifted toward Jason, who was standing straight and tall at the back of the rows of chairs, his eyes on Melissa, whom he'd just seated. He might ask Lilah how she'd feel about having one more child right now, a big one, already toilet-trained. He smiled. He knew what her answer would be.

But where in the heck was she? If she'd backed out, he'd…

"She's ready," Jesse said at his elbow. "Everybody and his next-of-kin wanted to congratulate her. The kitchen's plumb full."

The music swelled, filling the air with a melody as close to "The Wedding March" as the high school's chamber music quartet could reach. Ian and Mike stepped out the kitchen door and stood beside him at the arbor, where Reverend Galloway, looking properly solemn, stood waiting.

"Keep it short," he whispered, and Galloway gave him a reproving look.

Dana came down the aisle and stood on the other side of the arbor. Now Daniel could only gaze longingly toward the kitchen door, waiting for the glorious moment when—

His heart lurched. There she was, so beautiful in her pale-blue organdy dress she made his heart skip a beat. Jonathan stood by her side, his arm through hers, looking happy to be giving his mother away. As she came down the aisle, their gazes met and held.

And kept on holding as they said their vows, and as he shared his love for her in his kiss and accepted hers with joy. It wasn't easy to end that kiss, but when he did, he smiled down at her.

"Have I told you today that I love you?"

"One or two…" She paused. "Or maybe thirty times. But don't stop now. I'll never get tired of hearing it."

"So I can say it again?"

"Oh, yes," she said, "but I'll go first. I love you, Daniel, with my whole heart, and I always will."

There were tears in her eyes. He put his arm around her as they walked up the aisle to cheers and clapping, then bent his head to whisper in her ear. "My turn. I love you, Lilah Foster," he said. "I love you, I love you, I love you, I…"

What miracle had sent her into his life? What miracle had sent him here to wait for her to come into his life? At long last, they'd both found the place where they belonged—beside each other.

* * * * *

Hard to imagine a more glamorous life than being an accountant, isn't it? Still, **C.J. Carmichael** gave up the thrills of income tax forms and double-entry bookkeeping when she sold her first book in 1998. She has now written more than thirty-five novels for Harlequin and invites you to learn more about her books, see photos of her hiking exploits and enter her surprise contests at cjcarmichael.com.

Books by C.J. Carmichael

Harlequin American Romance

Colton: Rodeo Cowboy
Remember Me, Cowboy
Her Cowboy Dilemma
Promise from a Cowboy

Harlequin Superromance

For a Baby
Seattle After Midnight
A Little Secret Between Friends
A Baby Between Them
Secrets Between Them

Visit the Author Profile page
at Harlequin.com for more titles.

HER COWBOY DILEMMA

C.J. Carmichael

This is for my aunt Eleanor Schatz, who only
this summer reminded me that she was the one
who introduced me to Harlequin romances.
Thanks for sharing your books—here's one for you!

Prologue

It was strange to think of Brock getting married today. He was the youngest of her brothers and, Cassidy Lambert would have asserted, the least serious and least responsible of the bunch.

Yet falling in love with Winnie Hayes had changed him—in good ways. And at twenty-eight, he certainly wasn't too young for marriage. Not that his brothers had set good examples on that score.

B.J. at thirty-four and Corb, thirty-two, were both still single. Could it be they'd talked Brock out of taking the plunge?

Or maybe he'd come up with cold feet all on his own.

How else to explain the fact that Brock, who was supposed to be the groom, and Corb, who was supposed to be the best man, and their driver, friend and foster brother, Jackson Stone, were fifteen minutes late for the ceremony?

Everything else was in place. Guests filled the pews of Coffee Creek's pretty white church. The organist was doing her best to drive them crazy with important-sounding music. And the bride and bridesmaids—Cassidy included—were waiting in the antechamber for their big moment.

"What time did Corb say they left?" Winnie asked. She was perched on the ledge of the windowsill with Cassidy, both of them peering out on a warm, sunny July afternoon.

With her dark hair, creamy skin and lovely figure, Winnie made a perfectly gorgeous bride. She was also fun, a good cook and strong enough to set Brock straight when he needed a firm hand.

Cassidy approved.

She also liked Winnie's friend from New York City, Laurel Sheridan, who was checking her watch for the umpteenth time.

"Thirty-five minutes ago," Laurel replied.

"What's happened?" Winnie stared out the window as if she could will the Coffee Creek Ranch's black SUV to suddenly appear.

"Don't worry," Laurel said. "Could be they ran out of gas or had a flat."

"Or maybe they got halfway here only to realize that Corb forgot the ring." Cassidy made the joke halfheartedly. She was actually starting to worry—something both Corb and Brock would tease her about if she admitted it later.

She swung her new cream-colored cowboy boots, admiring how they went with the sage-green dress that

Winnie had picked out for her and Laurel. She and Laurel were dressed like twins, except Laurel was wearing pretty, high-heeled pumps with her dress.

Cassidy didn't do pumps. Cowboy boots and running shoes were more her style.

"But if they've been held up," Winnie said, "why haven't they called?"

Laurel held out her hands to Winnie. "You're making me dizzy up there." Winnie jumped, and then Cassidy followed.

"I'll call them," she said, unable to stand the waiting anymore. "I'll go get my phone."

She slipped out of the antechamber, intending to head for the minister's office at the other end of the hall. All three of them had left their purses—including their phones—in the bottom drawer of the filing cabinet.

But a late-arriving guest caught her eye. Dan Farley, the local vet, was as darkly handsome as ever, and the distraction of seeing him unexpectedly like this made her momentarily clumsy. As she tripped over her own feet, Dan gave her a quick, dismissive glance.

Not quick enough, however, for her to miss the disapproval in his expressive dark eyes.

Or was it dislike?

Probably both, Cassidy decided, as she continued down the hall, trying not to think about the broad-shouldered vet or the beautiful woman who'd been standing by his side.

Who was that woman? Her brothers hadn't mentioned anything about Farley having a new girlfriend. She entered the minister's office, went to the filing cabinet at the back and pulled open the drawer.

Then again, why would they tell her? No one had

any reason to assume she'd be interested in Dan Farley's love life.

Nor was she. Not particularly.

She grabbed her phone and called up Brock's number.
As she waited for him to answer, she made her way back
to the antechamber. As she slipped inside the door, she
heard Winnie whispering something to Laurel, but she
stopped talking as soon as she saw Cassidy.

"Brock isn't answering." Cassidy ended the call, frustrated. "I'll try Corb."

No answer there, either. "Damn."

Finally, she called Jackson. Again, nothing. "If this
is some sort of prank, I'm going to kill them."

Actually, if she saw them right now, she'd be more
inclined to give them all hugs. She was really worried
and—

"Someone's coming!" Winnie was back at the window. "I think it's Jackson's SUV."

Cassidy hurried to Winnie's side. *Please let her be
right!* But one glance dashed all her hopes. "No. It's the
county sheriff's vehicle."

She looked at Laurel, then Winnie, seeing in their
eyes the same fear that was making minced meat of
her stomach. They watched in suspended dread as the
local sheriff made her way out of her vehicle toward
the church.

"Who is that?" Laurel asked.

"Sheriff Savannah Moody," Winnie answered. "She's
a good friend of Brock's. We were going to invite her to
the wedding, but he said there was bad blood between
her and B.J. I don't know the details."

Neither did Cassidy. One of the drawbacks of being
the youngest in the family was that no one told her any-

thing. Still, she knew the trouble went back a long time, to the last year B.J. had lived at home.

Cassidy rushed out of the antechamber in time to see Savannah make her grand entrance. The crowd—expecting to see a bride—was quelled at the unexpected sight of the sheriff.

Aware of Winnie and Laurel coming up behind her, Cassidy made room for all three of them to follow in Savannah's wake.

"I need to talk to someone from the Lambert family." Savannah's official-sounding voice lifted and carried through the silent church.

B.J. stood first. "Savannah. What happened?"

Olive Lambert rose next, clutching her son's arm. "What's wrong?"

"I'm s-sorry, Olive. There's been an accident. Jackson's SUV hit a moose on Big Valley Road, about five miles from town."

A collective gasp by the congregation was followed by a few seconds of stunned silence.

Cassidy flashed back to the days when her father had been teaching her to drive. "Always drive slower at dusk. That's when your chances of hitting wildlife are the greatest. And pray that you never hit a moose, Cassie. They're lethal."

"Brock?" Winnie whispered.

Savannah rotated slowly, not having realized the bridal party was standing at her rear. "I'm so sorry, Winnie. Brock was in the front passenger seat—the impact point with the moose. He didn't have a chance."

Cassidy felt as if she'd been kicked in the solar plexus. She was doubling over, just as she heard B.J. ask, "What about Corb? And Jackson?"

"Jackson was driving, wearing his seat belt, and the air bag was able to cushion him from the worst of it. He's badly bruised and shaken, but he's okay. Your other brother was in the backseat. He should have been fine, but I'm afraid he wasn't wearing his seat belt. As we speak he's being medevaced to Great Falls. I can't say how bad his injuries are. You'll have to talk to the doctors for that."

"Is he conscious?" Desperately Cassidy prayed for Savannah to say yes.

But the sheriff shook her head. "No."

Brock, dead. And maybe Corb, too? *No, no, no, no…*

Cassidy wanted to run screaming from the church. But Laurel tugged on her arm, gesturing to Winnie. The bride was tottering on her heels, shaking violently. Cassidy reached out for her and, between them, she and Laurel managed to keep her from crashing to the floor.

"We need a sweater or a warm jacket," Laurel called out to the crowd.

A second later, a man's suit jacket was settled over Winnie's shoulders, and a white cotton handkerchief was pressed into Cassidy's palm.

She glanced up to see Dan Farley ordering the crowd to step back and give Winnie some space as he swooped the bride into his arms and carried her out into the fresh air.

Cassidy stood back to let them pass, her hand fisted over the handkerchief. Farley must have given this to her. Only then did she realize that tears were cascading down her face.

Chapter 1

Ten months later

What did it say about her relationship with her family that the person Cassidy Lambert was most excited to see when she got home wasn't a person at all, but her border collie, Sky?

Sky had been her father's birthday surprise for her fourteen years ago. Sky was loyal, loving and, most important, *uncomplicated*. Cassidy knew, no matter what, that Sky would always love her and think she was the most wonderful person on the planet.

The same could not be said of her family.

Cassidy lowered the driver's side window of her vintage 1980 Ford pickup to let in the warm spring air, then cranked up the tunes as she barreled along the 80 toward home. She knew she should reduce her speed, not only to avoid a ticket but also to prolong the drive, which she was quite enjoying.

But she was on a high. After five long years she was finally done with late nights at the library, relentless assignments and tough exams. She'd worked hard to complete the Accounting Master's Program at Montana State University, but she'd done it, and hopefully soon would follow a high-paying job at one of the top accounting firms in Billings.

Josh Brown—her friend and would-be boyfriend if she could make up her mind about that—also had plans to move to Billings. Josh had wanted to come with her to Coffee Creek Ranch. He said it was time he met her family.

"I wouldn't be so anxious if I were you," she'd told him. He thought she was teasing, but she wasn't.

"They can't be that bad. Look at you. Unless you were adopted?"

"No such luck." She had her mother's delicate features and the long, lanky body that came from the Lambert side of the family. She had a soft heart—like her father. But was also headstrong and stubborn—like her mom.

Yet despite all the family resemblances, she'd always been a misfit. Part of the problem came from being the only girl in a family with three boys—four if you counted her foster brother, Jackson, who'd been with the family since she was nine. She knew it wasn't her imagination that her mother was harder on her than the guys. And her father had treated her differently, too, when he was alive.

For one thing, he'd built three cottages by the small lake on their property for each of his sons to live in. But nothing for her.

No doubt he'd expected her to one day get married and go live with her husband. But being excluded that way had hurt.

And it still did.

The boys had been relentless teases, too. They didn't mean to be cruel, but they never cut her a break, either. Even though she could ride as well as any of them, she couldn't match them in strength. And, oh, how they'd loved to taunt her about that. Especially Brock...

Tears fogged her vision, and she slid her sunglasses up on her head so she could rub them away. Though almost a year had passed since the accident that had taken her youngest brother's life—just an hour before he'd been about to marry Winnie Hayes—the loss still felt fresh.

Brock may have driven her crazy, but she'd loved him, living in hope that one day he'd stop treating her like a bratty little sister and they might become friends.

Now they would never have that chance.

Cassidy drove over a series of three gentle hills before arriving at the smattering of buildings and the weathered sign proclaiming that she'd arrived at the town of Coffee Creek. She put on her indicator light, intending to stop at the Cinnamon Stick Café for some fortification before continuing the last fifteen minutes to the ranch.

It was Wednesday morning, the last week of April, an hour before noon. She'd written her final exam the previous afternoon, had spent a night on the town with all her friends, including Josh, then loaded her car for an early departure that hadn't included breakfast.

So she was hungry.

She angle-parked in front of the pretty café that was owned by Brock's former fiancée. Winnie had taken Brock's death really hard and had gone to live at her par-

ents' farm in Highwood immediately following the funeral. Cassidy stayed in touch with her via Facebook and
knew that Winnie hoped to return to Coffee Creek eventually. Apparently she'd developed some health issues
that weren't serious, but required some time to settle.

In the meantime her café was being operated by Winnie's best friend—and Cassidy's new sister-in-law—
Laurel. Laurel Sheridan had flown in from New York
for Brock and Winnie's wedding and had ended up ex-
tending her stay to take care of Winnie's café while her
friend was convalescing. She'd also fallen in love with
Corb and the two had been married last September in
New York City.

Then in March they'd had a baby—adorable little
Stephanie Olive Lambert was another reason Cassidy
was stopping at the Cinnamon Stick. Hopefully Laurel
and the baby would be there.

She was dying for a cuddle with her new little niece.

Cassidy parked, hopped out of her truck, then paused
to stretch her back and her arms. One thing about older
trucks—they sure weren't built for comfort. Still, she
patted the hood affectionately before heading toward
the café.

A hand-painted sign hung over the door, and two
wooden benches promised a place to sit in the sun and
enjoy your coffee once you'd placed your order.

Inside she was welcomed by the scent of freshly
ground coffee beans and the luscious aromas of butter,
sugar and cinnamon. She'd come during a lull and the
place was quiet. Two older women sat at one of the two
booths, engrossed in conversation. Behind the counter,
Laurel was softly singing a silly song about hedgehogs.
She had her back to the door, busy with dishes, but she

spotted Cassidy's reflection in a carefully positioned mirror and broke into a big smile.

"Cassidy! You're home!" Laurel stopped to scoop up her two-month-old daughter from the playpen. "Look who's here, Steph. It's your auntie Cassidy."

Cassidy was already holding out her arms for the bundle. "I hope she isn't making shy yet."

"Oh, she's still too young for that. Besides, she's getting used to new faces. We just got back to work last week and I swear our business has tripled. It seems everyone in the area is finding an excuse to drop in for a coffee and to say hello to the newest Lambert."

Cassidy listened to all of this with a smile, at the same time noticing how happy her sister-in-law appeared. Pretty, too. Her long red hair was pulled back in a ponytail, but it seemed thicker and glossier than ever. And her fair skin was literally glowing.

Laurel deposited a kiss on Cassidy's cheek as she handed over her daughter, who had gained several pounds since Cassidy had seen her last.

"Oh, you're so cute! Look—she has Corb's dimple."

"I know. Isn't it adorable? And only on the left cheek, just like her dad."

Cassidy sighed as Stephanie cuddled in, soaking up the smooches that her aunt couldn't resist planting on her downy soft head. Her wispy hair was coming in orange. And curly.

"How are you doing, precious? Do you like working with your mommy in the café?"

The baby looked up at the sound of Cassidy's voice, and Cassidy was amused to see that she had the Lambert green eyes, as well. Stephanie was staring at her intently, and only when she raised her little hand, awkwardly reaching up, did Cassidy realize she was entranced by the sunglasses that were still resting on her head.

"She's just started noticing her hands a few weeks ago," Laurel commented. "Sometimes she stares at them for minutes at a time. It's so cute. But here I am, talking endlessly about my wonderful baby, again." Laurel rolled her eyes. "What's new with you? How were your final exams?"

"They went well, I think. I won't have my marks for a few weeks."

"Can I get you a coffee and a cinnamon bun for the road?"

Hearing the door open behind her, Cassidy moved out of the way so the newcomer could enter. "You read my mind, thanks."

"Make that a double order, Winnie," said a deep voice behind her. "And leave some space for cream in the coffee."

Cassidy *knew* that voice. Slowly she turned, holding Stephanie like a shield between her and the tall, broad-shouldered man who'd just entered the café.

Sure enough, there stood Dan Farley. The local vet had some Native American blood, which accounted for his high cheekbones, jet-black hair and dark, almond-shaped eyes. Though he'd spoken to Winnie, it was Cassidy he was looking at, with cool dislike.

"Hey, Farley." Darn her voice for coming out so soft and weak. She lifted her chin. "How are things?"

"Busy."

He knew she'd been going to college in Bozeman, and must have noticed the suitcases and boxes in the back of her truck, but he didn't ask about her studies or show any interest in whether or not she was moving back to

Coffee Creek. Stepping past her as if she were nothing more than an inanimate obstacle, he made his way to the counter, where he pulled out his wallet.

Heck and darn, but the man had a way about him. Cassidy glanced at the two women at the back to see if they felt it, too. Sure enough they both had their eyes on Coffee Creek's sexy vet. One of them pretended to fan her face with her hand. The other laughed and winked at Cassidy.

Cassidy didn't wink back.

He wasn't *that* good-looking.

She gave him another glance, seeing only his profile and long, muscular build.

Okay, maybe he *was* that good-looking.

Still, he probably hated her and she had only herself to blame.

Winnie set two coffees in to-go cups on the counter, then bagged them each one of the homemade cinnamon buns baked fresh every day by ex-bronc rider Vince Butterfield. A veteran of the rodeo circuit and a member of the Cowboy Hall of Fame, Vince had licked a lifelong dependence on alcohol and in his sixties had begun a new career as a baker. His mother's old recipe for melt-in-your-mouth sticky buns, thickly topped with frosting, was his new claim to fame.

Five minutes ago, Cassidy had been craving one of them desperately. Now her stomach churned at the thought. What were the chances that she and Farley would happen into the café at the same time? Pretty darn slim. So slim, in fact, that she hadn't run across him here once in the past four years.

Other than at the church last July, she hadn't seen him anywhere else, either.

If he was called out to the ranch when she happened to be home, she always made herself scarce. She'd avoided him at the funeral. If his name came up in conversation with her brothers, she tried not to listen.

And now here he stood, just a few feet away. Making it very hard not to remember... But no. She would not think back to that night. She couldn't bear it.

"So where are you off to now, Farley?" Laurel asked, her tone friendly. Everyone in the Coffee Creek area called the vet by his last name. Probably to avoid confusion with his father, also named Dan, whom he'd worked with before the elder Farley and his wife had retired to Arizona.

Farley glanced briefly at Cassidy again, before answering. "Coffee Creek Ranch."

Though there were plenty of reasons why the vet might have been called out to her family's ranch, Cassidy's first thought was for Sky. At fourteen years of age, every day was a blessing. "What's wrong?"

"Your mother's young palomino is sick. Sounds serious."

"Lucky Lucy? Oh, no." She was glad Sky was okay, but this news was almost as bad. Her mother had bought the beautiful three-year-old palomino just this year and Cassidy loved her. Lucy had a wild heart but a gentle soul. Though she was her mother's horse, Cassidy had felt a special connection with the mare from the first time she'd ridden her.

"Any idea what the problem is?"

"From the symptoms Jackson described, sounds like strangles."

"Really?" In all of her twenty-five years they'd never had a case of strangles on the ranch. She didn't even know that much about it, other than it was a highly contagious, serious infection of the nose and lymph nodes.

"I'll have to examine the horse and run some tests to be sure." He added a generous amount of cream to his coffee, fitted the cup with a lid, then grabbed one of the bagged cinnamon buns. "See you later, Laurel. And thanks."

No word to Cassidy, whose ranch he was heading for. She might as well be an empty bar stool for all the attention he'd paid to her. Wordless herself, she watched as a half-dozen long strides took him out the door.

The café fell silent then, and Cassidy realized that Laurel was looking at her, eyebrows raised.

"What's up with you and the vet?"

Cassidy shifted Stephanie to her other arm. She'd planned on staying for a while to visit, but the bad news about the ranch had her suddenly anxious to get moving again.

"Why do you ask?"

"Are you kidding? Sparks were flying here, and they weren't the good kind. Farley isn't the chattiest of people, but I've never seen him be downright rude before. And the way he all but ignored you? That was rude."

Yes. It sure had been.

"I guess he figures he has his reasons." Cassidy went around the counter to deliver Stephanie back to her playpen. She didn't seem very happy about being set down until her mother wound up a musical mobile that had been affixed to the side of the playpen.

"How do you get any work done with such a cute distraction around?" Cassidy bent to give her niece one last kiss.

"It's taken some adjusting, by me and the staff. Eugenia and Dawn have been great. And even Vince has taken a few turns at rocking Stephanie when she's being fussy."

"That I'd like to see." Vince was the epitome of the tough, silent cowboy from another era.

"I know. Isn't it amazing what babies bring out in a person?"

"It sure is." Though Farley hadn't seemed moved by the baby at all. Of course, if she hadn't happened to be there, he probably would have been much friendlier to Laurel and her daughter. "Is there anything I can do to help you before I leave?"

"We're fine," Laurel assured her. "Eugenia's shift is starting in about half an hour. That'll give me a chance to take Stephanie upstairs, feed her and put her down for her nap. She's a great sleeper, thank goodness. Gives me a couple free hours every afternoon."

"Sounds like a good system." Cassidy counted out money for her order, then picked up her drink and her pastry. Now that Farley was gone, her appetite was returning. "I'd better get going."

"Wait one minute. You're really not going to give me the scoop on you and Farley?"

"Nope." Cassidy gave Laurel a warm hug. "I'll be back to have a longer visit in a few days. Or I may drop in on you and Corb at the ranch one evening."

"I'll look forward to it. But be warned. Next time I see you, you better be ready to tell me what's going on with you and the vet. He's considered the most eligible bachelor in town, you know."

Cassidy wasn't surprised. The guy had *presence*. And those eyes…

"The single women of Coffee Creek needn't worry,"

she assured Laurel. "I'm not going to be any competition where Dan Farley is concerned."

She was out the door before Laurel had time for a comeback. Not that it mattered. She was so *not* going to tell Laurel about the history between her and Farley. She'd never told *anyone* and she'd bet Farley hadn't, either.

Chapter 2

Dan Farley settled his coffee cup into the holder of his truck, then wolfed down the cinnamon bun in two minutes flat. Sweet and spicy…just like Cassidy Lambert.

The little witch.

So she was back in town. Judging from all the baggage in her truck, she was done with school. Would she be staying in Coffee Creek? Or moving on? Corb had mentioned she was studying accounting and thinking of working in Billings, but that her mother had other plans.

He didn't really care how it panned out. The little minx was trouble. And he intended to keep his distance.

For the longest time she'd been nothing but the cute younger sister of his best friends B.J., Corb and Brock. With no siblings of his own, he hadn't really minded when she tried to tag along with them—but Brock was always looking for ways to get rid of her.

He said she talked too much. Which was true.

He complained that she tried to boss them around. Also true.

But she had redeeming characteristics, among them a soft, yet courageous heart. So many times she'd come to him and her brothers expecting them to help a baby chick that had fallen from its nest, a fawn struggling with a lame leg, a farm cat with distemper, eyes weeping from disease, matted fur over a scrawny body.

Brock and Corb would brush her off, but he'd always done what he could to save the animal.

And then Cassidy turned twenty-one and the person who needed saving was himself....

An incoming call prevented him from dredging up further unwanted memories. He pressed the button on his steering wheel to patch it through.

"Hello?"

"Farley?" It was Liz Moffat, his right-hand woman at the office. Besides being his receptionist, the thirty-three-year-old mother of four also did a pretty good job of running his private life, as well. "I just had a call from Maddie Turner."

"I'm on my way to Coffee Creek Ranch right now." The Lamberts' place was only fifteen miles from Silver Creek Ranch. Maddie Turner and Olive Lambert were sisters, though they hadn't spoken to one another in over thirty years.

"When you're finished there, could you swing by Maddie's place? One of her cows is having a difficult birth."

"I'll do that."

"Oh, and Amber wants to know about tonight. If you think you'll be able to make it in time for a movie."

He wanted to say yes, but knew better. "Tell her probably not. I still have to check out the Harringtons' lame cow."

"Maybe things will go well at Maddie's and you'll be able to do both." Liz had fixed him up with Amber and was lobbying hard for the relationship to work.

"Maybe." But he doubted it. Maddie Turner didn't have the head for business that her older sister did, and she'd been struggling financially for the past five years. She wouldn't be asking for his help if the situation with her cow and unborn calf wasn't dire.

But first he had the situation at the Lamberts' to deal with. *And maybe another chance to see Cassidy?*

No. If she knew he was there, she'd avoid the barns, the way she usually did.

Cassidy was driving about ten miles over the posted speed limit on the secondary road out of Coffee Creek. Plus, she was taking sips of her coffee. And nibbling on her cinnamon bun. So she couldn't claim to be the injured party when she saw the flashing lights of a patrol car behind her five minutes after leaving town.

She pulled to the side of the road, turned off her music and waited.

Sun beat in warmly through the windshield and she could hear a meadowlark's song drifting on the fragrant spring breeze that wafted through her open windows. Ahead of her the pavement curved and she tensed as she saw the flower wreath affixed to the simple white cross that marked the spot of the accident where Brock had died last July.

She'd been so busy thinking about Farley—and feeling unjustly hurt at his obvious disdain for her—that she'd almost passed right by the scene of Brock's accident without noticing.

In her rearview mirror, she saw an officer step out of the patrol car. Her nervousness increased when she recognized Savannah Moody.

The last time she'd seen Savannah had been at Brock's funeral. Savannah hadn't stayed long, but she'd paid her respects. Now Cassidy took a deep breath as the sheriff stooped so she could look in the open window.

"Hey, Cassidy. On your way home from Bozie?" Savannah wore her long hair in a braid when she was on duty, but even without her thick chestnut hair framing her face, she was stunning. She'd been blessed with large, thickly lashed eyes and smooth olive skin that she'd inherited from her French Canadian mother.

"Yes. Just finished my exams yesterday."

"I'm sure you're anxious to get home, but slow down, okay? I'm not giving you a ticket this time. Just a friendly warning."

Her gaze shifted up the road a bit, and Cassidy knew what she was thinking. Knew, too, that the warning shouldn't have been necessary.

"You're right. I'll be a lot more careful in the future." She studied the wreath again, noting that the flowers appeared fresh. "Is Maddie Turner still tending that?"

Maddie was her mother's estranged sister. No one in the family knew the whole story behind the family feud, but they'd all grown up understanding that their mother would consider it a grand betrayal if they acknowledged their aunt by so much as a smile or a word of hello.

By the same token, none of them had understood why Maddie was being so diligent in tending Brock's memorial tribute, until Corb took it upon himself to drive up to Silver Creek Ranch and ask her.

Apparently Brock had been in the habit of visiting their aunt every now and then and had even helped her out with some handyman work on occasion.

No one knew why he'd done this. But if any one of the Lambert kids was wont to break their parents' rules, Brock was definitely the one.

"I guess so." Savannah patted the side of her truck. "I'm not a fan of roadside memorials, myself. Anything that draws your eyes off the road is a potential hazard."

"I'll be careful," Cassidy promised again.

"Good. Say hi to your mom for me, Cassidy. And welcome home."

She was gone before Cassidy could tell her that this wasn't a true homecoming. She was just going to stay a few weeks until she found out about the job she'd applied for in Billings. Her first interview had gone well. Now she was hoping for a second, soon to be followed by an offer of employment.

Josh had applied to the same accounting firm, and he felt they both stood a good chance of being hired since their marks leading up to finals had been the top of their class. Competition was tight, though, since the accounting firm was only looking for three new articling students, and at least five other members of their graduating class had applied, including the woman who'd been president of the business club.

Cassidy checked for traffic—and signs of wildlife— before pulling back onto the road. Savannah was long gone, having made a U-turn and driven off in the opposite direction. Meanwhile, Cassidy continued toward home, driving a sedate five miles per hour under the limit until she came to the fork in the road where she slowed down even further.

To the right lay Silver Creek Ranch, where Maddie still lived on the Turners' homestead property.

The road to the left led to Coffee Creek Ranch, which had been in the Lambert family just as long as the Turners had owned theirs. Cassidy's father had passed away years ago, and ever since then her mother, Olive, had been running the ranch—with the help of her youngest sons and Jackson. Her mother had a good head for business, and despite some ups and downs in the cattle business, she'd done very well.

One of her strategies to combat the uncertain economic times had been to diversify into breeding American quarter horses. Now the horse breeding side of their business was bringing in as much revenue as the cattle. And even more profit, according to Jackson, who was in charge of the books.

Now that she had her business degree, Cassidy suspected her mother was going to pressure her to take over the administrative side of the ranch from Jackson. She'd made it clear that she hoped Cassidy would move back home after graduation and join in the family ranching business.

But that wasn't going to happen. Cassidy loved her mother, but it was the sort of love that did best when there were at least a hundred miles between them. And much as she loved the ranch, she thought a business career could be exciting, too. She could hardly wait to get started.

Cassidy's tires rumbled as she drove over the cattle guard that was meant to keep Coffee Creek cattle from roaming beyond their property line. A hundred yards farther down the road, she came to the small wooden bridge that crossed over one of several unnamed creeks that ran through their property.

She drove up the final hill, then paused, looking down on the homestead that had been in her father's side of the family since the mid-eighteen-hundreds. It was hard not to feel a sense of pride. From here she could see the white barns with their green roofs, stacks of rolled hay, sorting pens and chutes, and the neatly fenced paddocks and larger pastures. All the outbuildings had been constructed in the hollow of a wide valley, high enough that there would be no danger of flooding in the spring, but protected from the worst of the winds that came off the mountains.

The main house sat above the other buildings, backing onto a grove of pines and with a view out to Square Butte—a flat-topped mountain that dominated the skyline to the north.

Through a stand of ponderosa pines to her left, Cassidy could see glimmers of Cold Coffee Lake around which their father had built homes for all three of his sons.

Driving past the graveled turnoff to the lake and the cabins, Cassidy crossed through the main gate, with the wrought iron detailing of the double *C*s that were the family brand. Her tires rumbled yet again on another cattle guard. And then she was home.

Four other vehicles were already parked in the yard. Her mother's white SUV, Jackson's black one, Corb's Jeep and, of course, Farley's charcoal-and-silver truck, with the Farley & Sons logo on the side.

Cassidy slid in next to her mother's SUV, where she wouldn't block any of the other vehicles. She cut off the ignition and waited to see if her arrival had been watched for.

Given the trouble Farley had described, she hadn't been expecting a welcoming committee. Probably everyone was down at the barn with the sick horse. But there was one faithful soul waiting to greet her.

Sky, still trim and healthy-looking despite the gray flecks in her black coat, must have been sleeping on the front porch. She was sitting now, head cocked, waiting for the cue.

She'd been trained not to go near any vehicle if there were people inside. But the moment Cassidy stepped out, she came running as fast as her old hip joints would let her.

"Hey there, Sky! Oh, it's so good to see you." Cassidy crouched by her dog, wrapping her arms around her and burrowing her face in Sky's sun-warmed coat.

Sky wriggled and grunted, panted and smiled, demonstrating in every way possible her extreme happiness at having Cassidy home again.

"Has Corb been taking good care of you? You sure look pretty." Cassidy gave her dog a lot of pats and scratches, then sat up on her haunches to look around. The place was almost eerily quiet. Not even the housekeeper, placid, middle-aged Bonny, was here. Must be one of her days off.

They'd had many housekeepers over the years. Olive had exacting standards and most didn't last more than six months or so. But Bonny was made of stern stuff and had been here almost four years now. Cassidy was glad. Besides having loads of common sense—that helped her deal with Olive—she was also an excellent cook.

Cassidy patted Sky again, wondering why her dog

wasn't up at Corb and Laurel's cabin. When Cassidy had left for college five years ago, she'd been living in residence and unable to bring her dog with her. Poor, lonely Sky had turned to Brock for companionship, then after his death, to Corb.

Now she lived almost full-time with Corb, Laurel and Stephanie…and yet somehow she'd known to wait at the main house today. Possibly Sky had heard Cassidy's name spoken more often than usual and had guessed she was coming home?

Cassidy didn't put it past her. Sky was a remarkable dog. When she was younger, she'd been as useful as an extra hand at moving and herding cattle. Now she was too old to work, but she was as smart as ever.

Finally, Cassidy stood, brushing the fine gravel from her knees. She could go into the house and wait for the rest of them to join her. But she'd seen Farley at the café and the world hadn't fallen apart. Besides, she was anxious to find out if Lucy was going to be okay.

She gave the signal for Sky to follow. "Come on, girl. Let's head down to the barn and find out what's going on."

When her mother decided to go into the quarter horse breeding business, they'd built a new equine barn equipped to accommodate twenty to twenty-five broodmares with a separate wing for the stallions. The family's riding horses were pastured and boarded in a smaller, less high-tech barn, closer to the house. This barn—they called it the home barn—had also been updated at that time, including the addition of a new tack room and office, both of which Jackson had designed.

It was to the home barn that Cassidy headed now, Sky

heeling obediently on her left. She was glad she didn't need to waste any time changing. Even when going to school in the city, she'd continued to dress the way she always had: in jeans and cowboy boots. She'd grown up in Western wear, and that was how she felt most comfortable.

In fact, her main concern about going to work for an accounting firm in the city was adjusting to the suits and high-heeled pumps she knew she'd be expected to wear. She'd bought such an outfit for job interviews and so far every time she'd worn it, she'd ended up with blisters on her heels.

Voices became audible as she drew nearer to the barn. The main door was open and her mother, Corb and Jackson were watching while Farley examined the golden palomino in the first stall. Cassidy stopped in the doorway, as yet unnoticed, waiting to see what would happen.

Her mother looked trim in jeans and a pressed gingham shirt. No doubt hard work and a healthy diet had helped preserve her petite figure, but her silver-blond hair, styled in an attractive bob, was the result of regular monthly trips to the salon.

She had her hands on her slender hips as she watched over Lucky Lucy's examination, offering Farley pointers as he worked, which were no doubt exasperating to the experienced vet.

"Be careful," Olive said. "You don't want to hurt her."

No response from Farley.

"See how she's holding her head?" Olive continued. "Low and extended? That's not usual for her."

Farley, who would not have needed to have this pointed out, replied calmly, "She's probably doing that to relieve the pain in her throat and lymph nodes."

Of the four of them, he was the only one Cassidy couldn't see clearly because he was in the stall with the horse. Just the sound of his voice, however, made her feel nervous and excited, the same odd cocktail of emotions she'd experienced earlier in the café.

"You seen any other cases of strangles lately?" Corb asked. Her brother's shoulders were hunched with worry, as were Jackson's. Both men had their backs to her, until Sky came up between them.

"Hey there, girl." Corb bent to pat the border collie's head. "What are you doing out here? You're supposed to be on the porch, enjoying your retirement."

With that, blond, green-eyed Corb looked back toward the house, and a smile slowly broke through his serious expression.

"Look who's home. How're you doing, Cass?"

Of all her family, Corb was Cassidy's favorite. He was easygoing, like their father had been, with a warm smile and eyes that sparkled with good humor. With his blond hair and green eyes, he was also the brother that looked most like her. If they'd been closer in age, people probably would have taken them for twins.

He gave her a one-armed hug, pulling her up between him and Jackson.

Her foster brother had dark, brooding good looks, and a natural reserve that made him difficult to really know. But the smile he gave her now was kind and friendly. "Hey, Cassidy, good to see you."

"You, too, Jackson." She felt her throat tighten. "Hi, Mom."

"Sweetheart." Olive swooped in and gave Cassidy a hug and a kiss. "How were your exams?" Then, Olive continued without waiting for an answer, "I was saddling Lucky Lucy for a ride this morning when I spotted some nasal discharge. I don't blame Jackson for not noticing sooner, even though the horses are now his responsibility."

"Jackson has a lot on his hands these days besides overseeing the care of the home horses," Corb said mildly, countering his mother's implied criticism. "Spring is the busiest time of year for all of us and he's had four new foals birthed this week alone. Plus he's busy with the mare breeding program for the quarter horses."

Cassidy admired the way Corb managed to stand up to their mother without getting upset. All her brothers—except maybe B.J.—were better at that skill than she was.

Every time she came home, she did so with the resolve that *this time* would be different. She wouldn't let her mother get to her. She wouldn't lose her cool. But neither would she let her mother derail her. She had her own plans for her own life. And that was that.

"My exams went well, Mom, but I'm sorry about Lucky Lucy. Is it strangles for sure?" She moved in closer and Farley, who'd been collecting a sample of mucus, now sealed the cotton swab into a vial.

Then he straightened. For the second time that day he took her measure.

"I'm pretty sure. She's got some swelling around the jaw area, as well as a fever and clear nasal discharge."

Cassidy shifted her gaze from the vet to the horse. Lucy was gorgeous, and as recently as her last visit home for Stephanie's baby shower, had been very healthy. She patted Lucy's flank, then moved in closer.

"Remember me, sweet thing?" she murmured. "We

had a great ride together last February. 'Course there was some snow we had to contend with back then."

As if in answer, Lucy coughed, and more discharge gathered in her nasal cavity. Cassidy glanced at Farley, hoping for reassurance. "How bad is it? Is she suffering?"

"Feel here." Farley took her hand and guided it to a swollen area on Lucy's neck. "Her lymph nodes are pretty enlarged. I'm sure it's causing her pain or she wouldn't be distending her neck like this."

"Oh, you poor thing." Cassidy gentled her with soft strokes, trying to erase the feeling of Farley's strong, capable hands over hers. Lucy nickered, voicing her appreciation of the extra attention.

"I'll run a test just to be sure," Farley said. "But for now we'd better assume that she does have strangles."

"Crap." Jackson sounded disgusted. "We'll have to disinfect everything, won't we?"

"Afraid so." Farley kept a hand on Lucky Lucy as he walked around her, then out to the aisle. "Good thing you keep your riding horses separate from the breeders. Hopefully the quarter horses will be fine. But I'd recommend no sales or purchases until the strangles is under control."

Olive made an impatient sound. "Is that really necessary? You said yourself, we have the two operations completely separate."

"Just to be sure, I think it is. You'll have to set up a quarantine area here in the barn. Watch the other horses carefully. Any of them show signs of the disease, then they'll need to be separated, too."

Jackson rubbed his unshaven chin. "This is going to mean a lot of extra work. Frankly me and my men are stretched to our limits right now…and Corb and his wranglers are, too."

"Jackson's right about that," Corb was quick to agree. "Most of the calves have been born, but we've got branding and vaccinating…and soon we'll need to be moving the herd to higher ground."

Suddenly it seemed like everyone was looking at Cassidy. *Heck and darn.* "You know I'm only home for a couple of weeks, right?"

Olive frowned at that, but Corb wasn't deterred.

"A couple of weeks could see us through the worst of this. If we're lucky." He turned to Farley. "What's involved, exactly?"

Farley shook his head. "Strangles is incredibly contagious. It can be passed on through indirect contact with buckets, feed, grass, fences and especially water troughs."

"I don't see why our quarter horses should be under quarantine then," Olive said sharply. "We feed, water and pasture them entirely separately from the riding horses."

"The infection can also be transmitted by flies," Jackson replied calmly. "Still, I have to wonder how Lucy caught this. I haven't heard of any other cases in the area."

"Have you brought any new horses onto the property lately?" Farley placed the vial for testing into his black case, then went to the sink at the corner of the barn and washed his hands.

Jackson shook his head no, then glanced at Olive. "Didn't I see you load Lucy in the trailer last week?"

"That wasn't Lucy," Olive said shortly. "I *did* buy some secondhand tack at auction on the weekend."

"That could be your culprit. I hate to say it, but your whole tack room should be disinfected. You're going to need to stock up on chlorhexidine soap."

"We have some," Corb said, pointing to a gallon by the sink.

"You're going to need more. But I have a few gallons in my truck I can give you for now." He turned to Cassidy. "If you're in charge of containing this infection, we should sit down somewhere and talk." He looked as excited as if he'd just sentenced himself to an hour in a dentist's chair.

Cassidy felt the same way herself. After a semester of studies, she'd hoped to spend most of her break on the back of a horse—not cooped up in a barn with a bucket and a rag.

"You two might as well talk in the office." Olive waved to the door next to the tack room. "I'll bring out some coffee and sandwiches. I know Corb and Jackson will be happy to get back to work."

"Over the moon with excitement," Corb teased. He gave Cassidy a tap on the shoulder. "We'll catch up later, okay? Come by tonight and say hi to Laurel and Stephanie?"

"I did drop in at the café for a visit on my way through town, but I'll still take you up on that offer."

"Better disinfect your arms and hands, if you've had any contact with Lucy," Farley warned as the two men and Olive left the barn. "And your boots."

"I'll set up a boot dip right now." Cassidy found a plastic tub in the tack room and mixed up a disinfecting solution. She set the tub by the door so that anyone leaving the barn would be able to disinfect their boots on their way out.

Corb, Jackson and her mother all made use of the new boot dip then headed off to their respective chores.

And then it was just the two of them in a barn that was suddenly, uncomfortably silent.

For a second Cassidy considered trying to clear the air between them. But how could she possibly do that? What she'd done had been inexcusable, even if she'd only been twenty-one at the time.

Instead, she headed for the office, trusting Farley to follow, which he did, along with Sky.

The border collie settled at her feet when she sat in the oak chair behind the desk. Farley took the upholstered chair opposite, dwarfing the thing with his tall, muscular frame.

It took a lot of physical strength to be a large-animal vet, and no one could doubt that Farley had that. But it was more than his size that she found intimidating right now. When Farley looked you in the eyes, you could tell he wasn't one to compromise.

Or make allowances.

Cassidy found paper and a pen for taking notes, then waited for her instructions. As the silence stretched on, she forced herself to meet the vet's gaze.

"What can I do to help Lucy?"

"Hot compresses on her swollen glands. The abscesses will probably rupture on their own in about a week, but if they don't, I'll need to lance them."

Cassidy made a note. *Hot compresses.* "Anything else?"

"It's important that she keep eating and drinking to maintain her strength. You can try feeding her gruel— that might go down easier than her usual hay mixture.

But the majority of your effort should go into keeping the infection contained."

She nodded, well aware of the risks.

"As well as keeping Lucy quarantined from the other horses you'll need to clean and disinfect her water buckets and feed containers daily. Bedding should be burned, walls and fences scrubbed down." His gaze fell to her hands, which were smooth and pale after so many months of study. "You up for all of that?"

"Guess I'll have to be."

"There's more. Any contaminated pasture areas should be rested for at least four weeks."

"You want those scrubbed down, too?"

One corner of his mouth turned up slightly. "Fortunately for you, ultraviolet light from the sun has natural antibacterial qualities."

"Yeah. I'm feeling really lucky right now. As is Lucy, I'm sure."

Once more Farley seemed to struggle not to smile. And seeing that, she felt an ache for the easy friendship that they'd once shared.

Though *friendship* wasn't quite the right word. She'd had a crush on him dating back to the days when he and her brothers would hang out together. As a young girl, she'd followed them around the ranch until Brock ran out of patience and came up with some devious plan to get rid of her.

"Remember the time you, Corb and Brock lured me up the hayloft in the old cattle barn, then pulled down the ladder and stranded me up there?"

Farley blinked. She'd disarmed him by bringing up a story from so long ago, before the trouble between them.

"I do. How did you get down, by the way?"

"One of the hired hands heard me yelling and came to the rescue."

"You were quite the tomboy back then. But I guess it's going to be accounting offices and city life for you now, huh?"

"You say that like it's a bad thing."

He shrugged. "I'm not the only one who's surprised."

This was true. Corb, B.J. and her mother had all tried to talk her out of studying business when she'd first told them about her plans to go to college. She didn't know if they didn't think she was smart enough, or what, but they certainly hadn't been supportive.

"Yoo-hoo," her mother's voice rang out. A few seconds later she breezed in the door with a tray. "I don't mean to interrupt, just wanted to bring you some lunch."

She'd brought out a carafe of coffee with mugs and a plate of sandwiches. After setting the tray on the middle of the desk between them, she stood back and looked from Cassidy to Farley with a smile of satisfaction.

"Actually," Farley said, "we were just finishing up here."

"Don't be in such a rush. You have to eat, don't you? Take your time. I'm sure you two have a lot of catching up to do."

And with that, Olive left, making a point of closing the door behind her.

Olive didn't often make herself scarce, so Cassidy couldn't help but be suspicious. Was it possible her mother was hoping she and Farley…?

No. It couldn't be.

She risked a quick look at the vet's expression, trying to judge if he'd felt any weird vibes from her mother, too.

"Olive seems to be in a good mood for a rancher who

has just had her livestock quarantined," he commented, reaching for one of the ham-and-cheese triangles.

"Yeah. She's up to something." She felt the hot color rising on her neck.

"Matchmaking?" Farley suggested.

"Kind of looks that way, doesn't it?"

"A little," he admitted. The light in his eyes grew darker, colder. "Guess you forgot to tell her that I'm the last man on earth you'd ever want to be with."

Chapter 3

It wasn't true. Farley *wasn't* the last man on earth she'd want to be with. But she *had* told him he was. One minute before leaving the dance she'd gone to as his date—on the arm of another man.

At least, she'd *tried* to leave with another guy. Oddly enough, she couldn't remember the name of that other guy anymore. But she did recall that *she'd* been the one to ask *him* to dance. With Farley on the sidelines, silent and angry, they'd danced an entire set together before she'd convinced the other guy that he wanted to drive her home.

They'd left the dance floor arm in arm. But Farley, in a voice that was not open to negotiation, had stepped in at that point. "You came to the dance with me. I'm damn well seeing you home safely."

The other guy had stepped aside hastily then, no

doubt having assessed Farley's size and the girth of his biceps, and decided he liked the current shape of his nose just fine, thank you very much.

Cassidy had endured a fifteen-minute drive in Farley's truck during which time not a single word was spoken. When they'd pulled up to the ranch house, he'd been out of the truck so fast that he had her door open before she'd even located the lever to do it herself. With his arms crossed over his broad chest, he'd stood watching until she was safely inside her home. Only then had he driven away.

And he'd pretty much never spoken to her since then.

Did she blame him? No.

Was she embarrassed for the way she'd acted? Hell, yes.

The truth was, she never should have accepted his invitation to the dance in the first place. But he'd caught her off guard in the Lonesome Spur Bar on the night of her twenty-first birthday. She'd been out having her first legal drink with a group of friends when he caught her eye and crossed the room.

She'd been ridiculously excited. Farley was older, hot and sooo handsome. And suddenly he had noticed her, too.

"Is it true?" he'd asked her, dark eyes smoldering with an emotion she'd never seen in them before. "Pretty Cassidy Lambert is no longer jailbait?"

"I stopped being jailbait a long time ago," she'd announced with a voice full of sass and vinegar. That didn't mean she wasn't quaking inside. She'd assumed Farley was completely out of her league. But now he was finally seeing her as someone other than his friends' annoying little sister.

He'd asked her to the Harvest Dance being held in the community hall the next evening. She'd accepted. And then all it had taken was one dance in his arms and she'd panicked.

Simple as that.

"Is it too late for me to apologize for my behavior that night? I was just a kid."

"No." Farley placed a hand on the desk. "If you'd still been a kid, I wouldn't have gone near you."

"I suppose that's true. But I was young."

"It wasn't the classiest move I've ever seen, Cass. But it was honest. You always were one for knowing what you wanted." He paused, then added pointedly, "And what you didn't."

She stared at him mutely. How could he talk as if he knew her so well, when she, herself, had never quite figured out why she'd acted the way she had that night? She hadn't been then, and wasn't now, a man-crazy sort of woman who liked to go on lots of dates and play one guy off another.

"I should get going. I've got another call to make before I head back to my office. You're clear on how to handle the strangles?"

She nodded, not bothering to point out that he'd only eaten one of her mother's sandwiches. She guessed that her company wasn't conducive to a good appetite on his part. She'd been so wrong to think that talking about that night would clear the air between them or ease her guilty conscience.

If anything, she felt worse.

It wasn't the classiest move I've ever seen, Cass.

God, she felt about four inches high right now.

Clumsily she got to her feet, almost knocking over her mug of coffee as she moved out from behind the desk.

Farley's eyes stayed cool. "I can see myself out."

"I know." She followed him, anyway. "But I just wanted to ask you about something else."

"What is it?"

"You said I should watch the rest of the horses in case they get sick, too. But what, exactly, should I be looking for?"

"Glad you asked that." Farley opened the office door, waited for her to pass through, then exited himself. "Don't wait until you see nasal discharge or hear the horse coughing. If any of your horses go off their feed, or seem to lack their usual energy, separate them from the rest of the herd immediately and give me a call."

"Okay." They both washed up at the sink again and used the boot dip before leaving the barn.

Midafternoon sun had Cassidy wishing she had the sunglasses she'd left behind in her truck. Squinting, she glanced at Farley, who was setting a quick pace toward his own vehicle.

"How long will we be under quarantine?"

Farley tossed his black case into the passenger side of the truck. He paused a moment to consider her question. "*If* you're diligent with disinfecting, *if* Lucy recovers quickly and *if* none of the other horses come down with it, I'd say about three weeks."

"That's a long time."

"Yeah, but better to contain this thing now before it spreads and becomes a bigger problem." He narrowed his eyes. "Or were you not planning to stay in Coffee Creek that long?"

"That depends on whether I get a job offer or not."

"You excited about spending your life as a pencil pusher in a city high-rise?"

"Why not?" she countered, placing her hands on her hips and narrowing her gaze. "You think swabbing mucus from a sick horse's nostril is so much better?"

"Actually, I do." He reached for his hat, settling it on his head, before giving her a final, parting nod. "But I wouldn't expect you to understand why. Though the little girl who grew up on this ranch would get it."

"Take a look at these paint chips, sweetie," Olive said. "Which one do you like better with these fabric samples for your new duvet cover?"

Cassidy had just hauled her suitcase into her old bedroom, halting when she saw her mother sitting amid piles of fabric swatches and paint chips spread over the blue-and-white quilt she'd had as long as she could remember.

The handmade quilt was an heirloom from her grandmother Lambert. Cassidy had always loved it, though admittedly the fabric was now threadbare on the edges.

"What's this about, Mother?" She was tired after the long drive and the stressful encounter with Farley. Bad enough that they had strangles on the ranch and that she was in charge of containing it. If only her mother could have called some other vet rather than Farley.

"We haven't decorated your room since you were a little girl. Don't you think it's time to spruce it up a little? I thought we'd paint and order new curtains and bedding. That desk in the corner is too small for you now. What do you say about replacing it with an armoire? A beautiful antique would look lovely in that corner. I saw one in Lewistown the other day that would be perfect."

Since the bed was unavailable, Cassidy hoisted her heavy suitcase up on the desk that her mother had just pointed out. "What's the point in fixing up the room when I'm only here for a few weeks?"

"That's if you get the job," Olive reminded her. "It's always good to have a backup plan and you know you always have a home and a job here with us."

"Mom, I've told you that isn't what I want to do with my life. If I don't end up getting this job, I'll apply for another."

"So you really mean to follow in B.J.'s footsteps, do you?" Her mother did nothing to hide her disappointment.

B.J. had been traveling the rodeo circuit for almost as long as Cassidy could remember. He'd left home at eighteen and though he made the occasional pit stop at home, he never stayed long.

"I'm not planning to start competing in rodeos, Mom."

"That's not what I meant and you know it. This land has been in our family for five generations. Your father and I planned things so we have room enough and work enough for all of you."

Then why didn't Dad build me one of those cottages he had made for the boys?

Cassidy didn't voice the question, even though it was often on her mind. The truth was, she'd never wanted to live so close to her mother. Nevertheless, it did rankle that she'd never even been offered what had been so freely given to her brothers.

"Mom, you just finished helping me get five years of higher education. Surely you must want me to put it to good use."

"You could take over the bookkeeping and taxes here

at our ranch. Handle our dealings with the bank and manage our investments."

And be under the thumb of her mother and brothers for the rest of her life? "Mom, I have to make my own way. Do my own thing."

"You think you'll be happy living in Billings for the rest of your life?"

"It's not that far. I'll visit. Like I did when I was going to school in Bozeman."

Her mom pressed a hand to her forehead. "That is not the right plan for you. I promise you, Cassie, you'll be making a big mistake if you walk away from your heritage."

Stay calm. Stay firm. That was Cassidy's new mantra and she was determined to stick to it. "It's my life, Mom. And my decision."

Olive sighed. She turned her gaze to the view out the window, then back to Cassidy. "Let's drop it for now. I don't want a big argument to spoil your first day home."

Right. 'Cause it had been such a great day so far.

Cassidy took a deep breath and reminded herself that she'd vowed to try harder with her mother. "Why don't we go to the kitchen, brew a pot of tea and talk about something else?"

"In a minute." Olive picked up two paint squares. "I promised Abby at the hardware store I'd phone and place my order this afternoon. Which do you prefer? The sage-green or the buttercream?"

Dan Farley drove away from Coffee Creek Ranch feeling disappointed, unsettled…frustrated. He wasn't usually a man given to complicated emotions. What was it about Cassidy Lambert? After all these years she ought to be nothing to him.

But it didn't help that she'd shown such concern for the sick horse. He'd always been a sucker for her soft heart.

And it helped even less that she still filled out her jeans in all the right places. Add in that beautiful blond hair and those disarming green eyes—hell, any man could be excused for losing his head over a girl like Cassidy.

But he didn't want to do it twice.

To distract himself, he decided to check in with Liz.

"Just finished at the Lamberts' and I'm on my way to Silver Creek."

"That took a while."

Liz was probably worried he wouldn't make the date with Amber. Why did all women assume a man wasn't happy unless he was suitably married?

"Yeah. I've put the place under quarantine. We'll have to run the tests, but I'm pretty sure about the result."

"Bad luck for them," Liz allowed. "Good luck at Silver Creek. Hopefully things will go better there."

Maddie Turner was waiting for him when he arrived, a stocky woman with wiry gray hair and plain features—quite the contrast to her fine-featured, well-coiffed sister, Olive. The two border collies flanking her were younger versions of Cassidy's dog, Sky. The dogs looked anxious, just like their owner.

Maddie was wearing faded overalls and a threadbare shirt—both smeared with blood. Her face was damp and she appeared exhausted. He knew from experience that helping a cow with a difficult delivery was hard, physical labor.

"You okay?"

"Been better. Thanks for getting here so fast," she said, as he grabbed his gear out of the truck, then slipped on a pair of overalls.

"I was next door at Coffee Creek."

She didn't blink an eye at the mention of her sister's place. "Lucky you were so close. I don't think we have much time."

She led the way to the barn, where he could hear the sounds of distress from the mother-to-be. They found the poor thing on the stall floor, with terror in her wide brown eyes.

She looked on the small side. Young. "This her first calf?"

Maddie nodded.

A quick exam confirmed that the calf was positioned backward and upside down. A C-section was their only hope. "Anyone else around?" he asked hopefully.

"Nope."

"No hired help?"

She avoided eye contact. "I've had to cut back lately."

"Too bad. We could use an extra set of hands here." Or two, or four. He started setting out his equipment, going through the steps in his head. Since he didn't have an assistant, he needed to have everything at the ready before he prepped the cow for the incision.

"I can secure her head," Maddie offered.

He wasn't so sure about that. Maddie looked pretty exhausted. "How long has she been in labor?"

"I brought her in from the field a few days ago. Just had a feeling she was going to have some trouble. Sure enough when I came out this morning I could see that her labor had started, but wasn't going anywhere."

He sighed. "Okay. We better not lose any more time."

"I agree." Maddie moved behind the prone cow, sinking to the straw bedding and then locking the animal's head to prevent her from moving around. The exhausted heifer didn't even resist.

"Poor thing," Maddie said softly. "Don't you worry. Doc Farley is going to get this critter out of you."

The tender caring in Maddie Turner's voice and the firm yet gentle way she handled the animal reminded Farley of her niece, Cassidy, trying to comfort Lucky Lucy earlier.

He shelved the thought, returning his focus to the job at hand. Maddie couldn't afford to lose the calf or the cow. More than money was at stake here, though, and Farley was determined not to fail.

An hour and a half later, the new mother and her matching black calf were resting in the barn, and Farley and Maddie were in the kitchen having coffee. Farley was tired, but pleased. Helping to bring new life into the world was one of the most rewarding aspects of his job.

He ought to be on the road, heading to the next ranch. But he sensed Maddie wasn't ready to be alone, so he'd agreed to stop in for a bit. Now Maddie placed a plate with crackers and cheese on the table.

"Sorry I don't have anything more substantial to offer. You must be starving. I know I am." She opened the upper freezer compartment of her fridge. "I could fry up some sausage and eggs if you have twenty minutes to spare."

He thought about the lame cow and the forty-five

minutes it would take to drive to the Harringtons' spread. Then he thought about Amber and the movie she'd been hoping to see. That was out of the question now. But hopefully he could still manage a late dinner. "I really don't."

"Didn't think so." Maddie closed the fridge door, then sank into a chair and reached for her coffee. Her dogs were in the room with them. Farley thought he had them straight now. Trix was sleeping on the mat by the back door and Honey was curled up under the table. As well as the dogs, there was a cat prowling the place, too. Short-haired and ginger-colored, she'd slunk into the room earlier, taken Farley's measure, then exited with nose held high.

Maddie's kitchen was a warm, cozy place. The wooden table and chairs had the sort of "distressed" look that came from decades of being used and not coddled, as did the wooden floors and cabinets. The counters were cluttered, but clean, and the big farm sink gleamed as if it had been disinfected recently.

The focal point of the room was the antique, black, wood-burning cookstove. Warm air drifted from the stove to soothe the sore muscles of Farley's shoulders and upper back. He fought the urge to close his eyes, knowing that if he succumbed to sleep he might find himself still in this room an hour later.

He crunched down on a couple of crackers and a slab of the cheddar, then followed the food with a swallow of hot, almost scalding, coffee. Maddie made it the old-fashioned way, boiled in a percolator on the stove.

"So what's up at Coffee Creek?" Maddie asked him.

He hesitated before answering. Everyone in the community of Coffee Creek was aware of the rift between the Turner sisters, though no one knew the exact cause. Some people felt that Olive's marriage to neighboring rancher Bobby Lambert had been the start of it. One fact was irrefutable: Maddie hadn't attended their wedding. And despite the size of the wedding—apparently several hundred—the absence had been very conspicuous.

"One of their horses has strangles," he finally said.

"Sorry to hear that." Maddie sounded genuinely concerned.

"Hopefully it hasn't had time to spread. They have the sick horse quarantined and Cassidy is going to be disinfecting the barn."

"Cassidy? So she's home from college, is she?"

Maddie seemed to know a lot about her sister's family. He supposed he shouldn't be surprised. Since she'd never married herself or had children, the Lamberts were her closest relations. Which only made the feud between the sisters that much sadder.

"Only for a few weeks, apparently. She's hoping to get a job with some accounting firm in Billings."

"Really? I can't imagine Olive letting her do that."

"I'm not sure Olive has much say in the matter."

Maddie's lips tightened. "Then you don't know my sister very well."

"She hasn't been able to keep B.J. from the rodeo circuit," he pointed out.

"All the more reason she's going to fight like hell to keep her daughter close to home."

"You think? Cassidy's no pushover." Tenacity was in her DNA. And growing up with all those brothers had only made her tougher and more resilient.

"You don't know Olive," Maddie repeated.

"Not as well as you do, obviously," he allowed. "But my money's still on Cassidy."

Chapter 4

Cassidy took the time to have tea with her mother, then changed into rubber boots and gloves and headed back to the barn. She had her faults, but avoiding hard work wasn't one of them.

After diluting the disinfectant that Farley had left with her, she started with the horse troughs and feeding buckets. Once those had been thoroughly washed and rinsed, she went to check on Lucy.

Oh, how she hated to see the sweet mare in obvious discomfort. Lucy had a fierce spirit, but she was also gentle and trusting with her rider. Olive had purchased her from one of the best trainers in Montana and it showed. Cassidy had known she'd spent a pretty penny on her, too, when Olive demurred from sharing the purchase price with them.

Privately, Cassidy thought Lucy's potential was being

wasted as a working horse on a cattle ranch. She had lovely footing. Cassidy bet she'd make a great barrel-racing horse. And she was so pretty, she'd be a real crowd favorite.

In high school Cassidy had dabbled in the sport, coached by her brothers and encouraged by her mom. But in her final school year she'd decided she needed to focus on her grades and she'd given up competing.

She hadn't run a course since.

"Hey, Lucy. Think you'd like being the center of attention in a rodeo ring?"

The worst waste of all, of course, would be if Lucy didn't recover from the strangles. Cassidy took some comfort from the fact that Farley hadn't seemed overly worried.

Cassidy went to the tack room to heat some compresses, then returned to Lucy's stall.

"I have something here that should help you feel better."

Lucy nickered and shuffled restlessly. Her nostrils were oozing pus again and she looked as miserable as a horse could look without actually collapsing to the ground.

Cassidy pressed the heated pads against the mare's swollen lymph nodes. "How does that feel?" She'd wash down the stalls next, then mix up some warm mash for Lucy. She had fencing to clean and the tack room, too, but that might have to wait for tomorrow because she needed to examine the rest of the riding horses before nightfall and make sure none of them were exhibiting signs of the sickness.

Three hours later, Cassidy finally made it back to the ranch house, where she showered and had dinner with her mother. Olive was hurrying the meal because she had a meeting in town at seven.

"I'm sorry to rush out on your first night home. But if I don't go they'll just make a bunch of silly decisions that I'll have to fix the next meeting."

The committee was working to build a historical site at the intersection of Highway 81 and Main Street, kitty-corner to the Crossroads Gas and Snack. A life-sized bronze of a quarter horse had been donated to the town and the idea was to have a walking loop around the statue with wooden signposts detailing the history of the area.

Olive had been shepherding the project from the start and had contributed a significant chunk of cash to the fundraising efforts.

"That's fine, Mom. I'll run over and visit Corb and the gang."

"I hate to leave you with the dishes…"

"Not a problem. Have fun at your meeting."

Her mom grabbed her leather coat from the closet at the side door, then slipped on her best pair of go-to-meeting boots. "If you think fun is even a possibility, then you haven't met Straws Monahan."

Cassidy chuckled at that, knowing that even the strong-minded Straws whose property was on the other side of Coffee Creek, closer to Lewistown, would be no match for her mother.

Fifteen minutes later, the kitchen was spotless and Cassidy slipped outside to walk to her brother's. Sky followed at her side for the quarter of a mile to Cold Coffee Lake Road. Trees—a mixture of aspen and ponderosa pine—separated each of the brothers' cabins, giving them some privacy from one another.

Jackson lived in the cabin closest to the main house. Originally built for B.J., when it had become clear that he was going to be on the road most of the time, Olive had reluctantly given permission for Jackson to take up residence.

The other cabin had been Brock's. It was vacant now, and Cassidy had no idea what would become of it. She'd heard Corb suggest that Olive offer it to Winnie, but that idea had gone over like a lead balloon.

Olive and Winnie had been like oil and water from the start. Cassidy knew, since her mother had confided in her, that Olive had hoped Brock would marry someone else. And that she felt Winnie fell short of the mark as far as being the wife of a cattleman.

Cassidy hadn't bothered arguing.

Nothing she said had ever changed her mother's opinion on anything, anyway.

Cassidy helped Sky up the stairs to Corb and Laurel's front door. Exhausted from the walk, Sky seemed happy to curl up on a plump cushion on the plank floor of the porch that was obviously a favorite sleeping spot.

Since the door had been left open a crack, Cassidy gave it a nudge. "Hello?"

"Come on in!" It was Laurel who answered. "We were hoping you'd drop by."

Cassidy left her boots in the foyer and found Laurel in the kitchen, where the counters were littered with stacked dishes and pots and pans.

Laurel didn't seem perturbed by the mess. She was at the sink, her hands in soapy water. "Hey, Cassidy, some homecoming. I hear you spent the day disinfecting in the barn. But I bet that wasn't as bad as this mess." She wrinkled her nose at the stove behind her.

Cassidy came round the counter to give her sister-in-law a hug. Once more she thought how smart Corb had been to marry this woman. Laurel's easygoing nature and sense of humor were a good match for him.

"Yeah, it's been a chaotic day." Cassidy glanced at the stove, which was splattered with baked-on tomato sauce and something that looked like egg yolk. "You, too?"

"Every day's chaotic when you have a new baby. After two months you'd think I'd have things figured out and be on some sort of schedule, but you'd be wrong."

Cassidy laughed. Already she felt more relaxed than she'd been all day. "Where's the rest of the family?"

"Corb's giving Stephanie her bath upstairs. They'll be down in a sec." She glanced at her own T-shirt, which had some stains matching those on the stove. "I could use a bath myself. Not to mention some clean clothes. Sorry to be such a slob."

"You look just fine." Cassidy picked up a towel to dry the dishes Laurel was washing. "Babies must be addictive. I can't wait to see the little peanut again and kiss every inch of that adorable little face."

"Maybe I should shave first." Corb was down the stairs, with Stephanie tucked into one arm like a football. "Gosh, Cass, I had no idea you were so fond of your older brother."

For answer, she snapped the towel at his back. "Hand over that cutie-pie. Your wife needs your help in the kitchen."

"This is so not a fair trade," Corb grumbled. But he smiled as he handed his daughter to his sister. "Do you think her hair is red? I think it is, but Laurel swears it's blond."

"Maybe strawberry-blond?" Cassidy said, in compromise, though she agreed with Corb. Stephanie felt wonderful in her arms. She'd lost the fragility of a newborn, but was still, definitely, an infant. All soft and sweet and cuddly, with wide green eyes that stared right at her.

"Jeez, why wasn't I assigned child-care duty instead of put on the quarantine detail?" Cassidy started swaying, in a way that felt instinctual.

"Wait two hours and you'll be glad you ended up with the job you have," Laurel advised. "Stephanie is a great baby, but evening is her cranky time. She doesn't usually settle until around midnight, and then she's up like clockwork at three for another feeding."

"That sounds tough," Cassidy said with a grimace. "Still, it's great to have a baby in the family."

Corb and Laurel exchanged a glance. Then Corb said, "Actually, there are two babies in our family now."

"What?" Her brother wasn't making any sense. But Laurel knew what he was talking about. Cassidy turned to her sister-in-law. "What the heck does he mean by that?"

Laurel looked nervous. She glanced at Corb, then said, "Winnie had a baby. A little boy."

Cassidy collapsed on a handy stool. "Is it Brock's?"

Laurel nodded. "Winnie was two months pregnant on their wedding day. She hadn't told Brock yet, so he didn't know."

"Wow." Cassidy felt numb at the news. Then slowly she took in the ramifications. "Brock left behind a son." There was some comfort in that.

She did the math next.

"But if she was two months pregnant last July, then Winnie would have had her baby sometime in January."

"That's right," Laurel agreed.

"So that's the 'health issue' that's been keeping her at home with her parents?"

"Winnie almost lost the baby after Brock died. Her doctor prescribed bed rest. And calm."

"I get that she had to stay with her parents. But why didn't she tell any of us about the baby?"

"She did make a few overtures to your mother. But Olive never returned her calls. To be honest, I think Winnie is still bitter that Olive wasn't warmer to her during the engagement period."

Cassidy couldn't fault Winnie for feeling that way. Still. "Winnie's baby is our nephew. Mom's grandchild. She should have told us."

"That's how I feel," Corb said.

"As Winnie's best friend, I've been conflicted. I promised her I would let her decide on the right time to tell your family. But obviously I had to tell Corb. And he's been patient, but—"

"Enough is enough." Corb shook his head. "Winnie's had her chance to break the news. Since she hasn't, Laurel and I have to be the ones to tell the family. You're the first one to find out. We'll tell Mom next."

"Can you do me a favor and do it when I'm not around?"

Corb laughed, then asked how things had gone in the barn. "I meant to check on Lucy after I finished my chores, but I knew Laurel couldn't wait to see me."

"More like you couldn't wait to see Laurel," Cassidy guessed, bending down to smooch the baby while her brother and his wife exchanged a kiss.

"So what was up with you and Farley earlier?" Corb asked. "God, the tension in that barn was something else. You two never had a thing, did you?"

Of course Laurel picked up on the suggestion right

away. "I'll bet you anything they did. They were both in the Cinnamon Stick at the same time today," she told her husband, passing him a bowl to dry at the same time. "Wicked sparks."

Corb looked at the bowl he'd just dried as if he'd never seen it before, then shrugged and placed it on the table. "Anyway, I thought you had a boyfriend in college? Jed something or other…"

"His name is Josh. Josh Brown. And he's not really a boyfriend."

"Though he'd like to be?" Laurel guessed.

"Maybe…"

"Let's get back to Farley. Fill in the blanks, sister dear."

Cassidy had never considered her family to be an especially sensitive or perceptive bunch. So why was everyone picking up on all these vibes between her and Farley?

She had to set them straight. And now.

"Farley and I don't have a *thing*. He just doesn't like me very much. And I guess the feeling is mutual."

"He doesn't like you very much," Corb repeated, as if sounding out the words for someone with limited understanding. "Right. That's totally believable, Cass. Good cover."

He had inside information of some sort, she realized. Which could only have come from one source. "What did Farley tell you, Corb?"

Her brother just gave her an innocent grin. From experience she knew that nothing she did or said would get him to spill the beans.

Brothers.

Why couldn't her parents have given her at least *one* sister?

* * *

"At some point you have to put your own life on your priority list, Farley."

Liz sounded more upset than Amber had when he'd called to bow out of their date. He couldn't make the movie—*or* the dinner.

Farley pulled into the lane leading to the home where he'd lived all his life—except for the years he'd spent going to university in Bozeman and Washington. The ranch house had been built on the south end of four sections of wide-open meadows with timbered ridges and a mile of Careless Creek flowing through it.

Once upon a time his ancestors had tried their hand at cattle ranching, but his grandfather and father had both abandoned those efforts in favor of veterinary practice, renting out the rest of the land to their neighbors who used some for grazing and the rest for hay.

The old barn had long since been converted into an office, with examining rooms and stalls and pens for housing animals that required overnight stays.

"The situation at the Harringtons' was serious, Liz." If only they'd called him in three weeks earlier, instead of trying to diagnose the problem themselves. "I couldn't just walk out on them to go watch a movie."

"You need to partner with another vet, Farley. There's too much work for one man alone. Frankly, you could use more office staff, as well. You may be willing to forgo a personal life, but I have four kids and a husband. I hate to leave my work undone at the end of the day, but lately I've had to do it."

"I know you work hard. And I appreciate it." No way would he put up with all these lectures she gave him if he didn't.

"Thank you. But you're missing the point. I wasn't looking for a pat on the back. It's time you made room for more in your life. To put it plainly—besides a business partner, you also need a wife."

If he was talking to anyone else, he would have hung up at this point. But Liz was right about one thing—she kept his life running as smoothly as possible and he couldn't do without her.

"I don't have time for a girlfriend, let alone a wife." He pulled up to the garage and shifted into Park.

"That's because—"

"I'm home now. Gotta go, Liz."

He turned off the ignition and the Bluetooth cut out, truncating the rest of his very capable assistant's advice. He loved Liz. Usually. And then there were times when he'd like to trade her in for a quieter model.

His dogs met him as soon as he stepped out of his SUV. Tom and Dick were mongrel terrier mixes, part of a litter dropped off at his clinic five years ago. They'd proven to be great companions, much less trouble than either a girlfriend or a wife. If only he could train them to answer phones and work the computer, he'd be set.

"Hey, guys. You hungry? I know I am." Farley made his way in through the side door into a large mudroom with a bathroom attached. He always had a shower and changed after work, no matter how tired or starving he was.

The dogs knew this and they waited patiently for him to finish.

Next on the priority list were his dogs. Not a big believer in doggy kibble, Farley fed them a special, homemade mash that he kept in the refrigerator. Both dogs loved it and went straight to their ceramic bowls by the far wall to gobble and enjoy.

Now it was his turn.

Farley surveyed his gourmet kitchen.

Five years ago when his parents retired, he'd sold one section of his land and pumped the money into the sprawling ranch house. He'd put in heated slate floors, new maple cabinetry and all the high-end appliances, as well as redoing the bathrooms. The old windows were replaced with triple panes that blocked UV light and a new red metal roof replaced the aging asphalt shingles.

He'd bought furniture, too, the kind you saw when you booked into an upscale mountain resort. His house was now his castle, in every sense of the word.

Maybe it was a little on the big side for just one man and two dogs. But you never knew. One day another dog might come along and join the family. As a vet, it was bound to happen sooner or later.

Sometimes his mom got on his case, too. Like Liz, she thought marriage and children were the holy grails of life. She didn't seem to get that when you were doing the work you'd been born to do, a family sometimes seemed more like dessert than the main course.

Not that he didn't enjoy the company of a woman now and then. And Amber had her charms. He found her intelligent, attractive and pleasant company. Fortunately she was easygoing, as well, since so far he'd had to cancel three of their seven dates.

He'd told her he would call her when he got home but it had been five hours since the crackers and cheese Maddie Turner had fed him and he was getting light-headed.

Farley took out a full carton of eggs and a loaf of

bread. He felt as if he could eat all of this and more. It had been a while since he'd used his fancy kitchen to its full potential. Maybe on the weekend he'd invite Amber over for dinner.

But when Farley tried to imagine Amber standing by the stove or sitting across from him at the table, all he could see was golden-haired Cassidy. Sweet as honey one minute. As fired up as a bumblebee the next.

Easygoing did not describe Cassidy. But she was so deliciously *alive*. She'd been around seventeen when he'd stopped seeing her as a spunky little girl and saw her as a desirable woman. He could still remember the exact moment. He'd been watching TV with her brothers when she'd come down the hall dressed in a jean skirt and T-shirt. Her long blond hair had been freshly washed, and she'd been wearing makeup—for the first time that he'd ever noticed.

Wow, he'd thought. He hadn't stared, but it had taken all of his self-control not to. She was too young. The sister of his best friends. He knew his feelings weren't appropriate and he'd done his best to deny them.

But when he saw her at the bar on her twenty-first birthday, he hadn't been able to resist asking her out. The date started perfectly. Olive had smiled at him warmly when he arrived to pick up Cassidy, letting him know that she approved of him dating her only daughter.

And Cassidy had looked beautiful—quieter than usual—but absolutely lovely. They'd danced the first set as if they were the only two people in the room— gazes fused, bodies coming together like two pieces of an interlocking puzzle.

And then she'd asked for a drink and by the time

he returned with the requested glass of punch, she was dancing with someone else.

This had all happened a long time ago. Four years. He'd thought he'd put it all behind him.

But then he'd seen her today and he'd felt the old punch of attraction.

What had been up with that? It didn't make sense. Once Cassidy Lambert had seemed like his dream girl.

But the reality was different. She'd grown up into a spoiled brat who treated men like dirt and wanted to live the high life in the city. Not that he had anything against city folk. But he sure had no use for a woman like that in his life.

Chapter 5

Cassidy got up around three in the morning to check on Lucy, then again at dawn. Both times the horse seemed to be holding her own, no better, no worse. By six o'clock, Cassidy was hungry. Usually they had oatmeal or boiled eggs and toast for breakfast, but wanting to surprise her mother—and make a special effort to please her—Cassidy decided to cook crepes using a recipe Josh had taught her.

She passed Corb and Jackson on her way from the home barn to the house. They were heading out to the cow and equestrian barns, respectively.

"Want to join Mom and me for breakfast later? I'm planning something special."

"*You're* cooking? No, thanks."

She smacked her brother's shoulder. "I'm better than I used to be." She had a reputation for burning anything she tried to make, thanks to her impatient habit of cooking everything on high heat so it would be ready faster.

"I'm sure you are. I was just kidding. But I want to head back home and make Laurel something to eat when I'm finished here. She had a rough night with the baby."

"What about you, Jackson?"

"I'm kind of tied up today," her foster brother mumbled. "Thanks, anyway."

"Okay, fine, boys. Your loss. I'm making crepes." She thought that might tempt them, but both men just kept walking. Corb, she could understand—she was actually proud that he'd turned into such a caring husband and father—but Jackson lived alone. You'd think he might enjoy a little company and a meal he didn't have to cook for himself.

In the old days, when their father was alive, Jackson had seemed like another brother to her. But lately—and most particularly since the accident—he'd been distant. Cassidy didn't think it was only to her and she made a mental note to talk to Corb about this.

In the kitchen Cassidy put on a pot of coffee, then whipped up the batter, prepared the fruit and started a small nonstick frying pan on medium-low heat.

When her mother came in from her morning "rounds" as she liked to call them, Cassidy had a stack of crepes ready. She waved a hand at the table. "Sit down, Mom. I'm waiting on you for a change."

"What's this?" Olive looked from the table, to the stove, to her daughter.

"I made you breakfast." Cassidy handed her mother a cup of coffee with the cream and sugar already added. Then she plated two crepes with some fruit salad and set it down along with the pitcher of syrup.

"Well. Isn't this something."

Cassidy waited for her mother to take a taste.

Olive took a tentative bite. "Sweet, isn't it?"

"Is it too sweet?"

"I wouldn't say that. Stop standing there, watching me. Aren't you going to eat, too?"

Cassidy joined her mother, and dug into the meal with a keen appetite. Must be all the fresh air and the hard work from yesterday. When she was finished, she went to the stove to help herself to seconds.

"Can I give you some more, Mom?"

"I don't think so, sweetheart. This was lovely, but I find eggs and toast and oatmeal stick to the ribs when you have a long day ahead of you."

"Oh."

"Since the frying pan is already out, I think I'll cook a few eggs. Want me to put some on for you?"

"No, thanks." She put the syrup back in the fridge and her plate in the dishwasher. It was silly for her to have hurt feelings because her mother preferred a more robust morning meal.

She wondered when Corb and Laurel were going to tell their mother about Winnie's baby. "Any plans to see Corb today?"

"No. I'm leaving in about thirty minutes to negotiate a sale of some of our yearlings with a rancher out Lewistown way. If the meeting goes too long, I may end up taking a room in town and coming home in the morning."

"What about the quarantine?"

"Yes." Her mother sighed with annoyance. "We'll have to delay delivery until that's cleared up, I guess."

"Speaking of clearing it up, I'm going out now to check on the rest of the horses."

An egg splattered as her mother added it to the hot frying pan. "Good. If any of them seem even a little off, make sure you call Farley right away."

"Mom thinks Farley walks on water," Cassidy confided to Sky as they headed out of the house toward the pasture. "So do my brothers."

Sky cocked her head as if to say, *Go on*. Cassidy did.

"Well, he is a pretty good vet. I'll give him that. But most eligible bachelor in Bitterroot County? That has to be stretching things."

Cassidy's mood lightened when she spotted the ranch's working horses munching on the hay Jackson had rolled out for them earlier. She slipped between the rungs of the wooden fence.

"You stay here, Sky," she told the border collie, and Sky promptly lowered onto her haunches.

Cassidy had grown up with most of these horses and considered them just as much family as she did Sky… and her brothers. She made the rounds, saying hello to each and every one of them, at the same time checking for signs of the dreaded strangles.

Finally she came to her own coffee-colored mustang, Finnegan. She'd owned him since she was eight, and he was now twenty-one years old.

"Hey, old man. How come you're not chowing down with the others?" She offered him a hunk of a carrot she'd snatched from the fridge earlier. Finnegan just gave it a sniff.

She patted his neck and some of his light brown hair

went flying. "You could use some pretty serious grooming, huh?" In fact, all of the horses were looking scruffy.

"Hey, Cass!"

She swiveled, following the sound of Corb's voice. He'd just left the cattle barn and was walking in her direction.

"If you have time today, they could all use a little action with the shedding shears."

"I noticed."

"It's been hard without Brock." Corb shrugged. "We can't seem to get enough done in a day, despite the extra workers B.J. hired."

Their eldest brother had returned to the rodeo circuit a week after Brock's funeral. Cassidy suspected he'd hired the extra workers to assuage his guilt for leaving them all so quickly.

Not that she'd been any better. She'd gone right back to school, hoping she could run from the heartbreak of losing her brother.

Focusing on her studies had helped some, but she'd spent a lot of tearful nights. "I guess it would take more than one hired wrangler to replace our brother out here," Cassidy said sadly, eyeing the neglected herd.

"Jackson used to take care of these guys as well as handling all the admin work and accounting. But I asked him to step in and manage the breeding program, so he's pretty much run ragged these days."

"Is that why he's being so standoffish?"

"Overwork?" Corb gave the idea less than two seconds of thought. "No. I think he still feels guilty about the accident."

"But it wasn't his fault. There was nothing he could have done." Savannah Moody had made that clear after the investigation was completed and no charges had been laid.

"He still blames himself, and I guess I understand how he feels. I'd probably feel the same in his shoes."

"Have you tried talking to him?"

"Of course I have. But it doesn't help that Mom is treating him even more coldly than she used to."

For some reason their mother hadn't been keen when her husband came up with the idea of taking on a foster son. But while Bob Lambert usually gave in to whatever Olive wanted, on this point he'd been surprisingly firm, and Jackson had come to Coffee Creek Ranch where her father had treated him the same as one of his own.

"If only Dad was still with us. He'd know what to say to make Jackson feel better."

"Maybe he could." Corb sighed. "But we might as well wish the accident had never happened. Dad and Brock are both gone and we have to deal with it."

He glanced at Cassidy then, and she wondered if he thought her plans to work in Billings were selfish, when she was so obviously needed here.

"Do we have the money to hire more help?"

Corb nodded. "When Jackson moved to the breeding program, the plan was to find a new accountant so he wouldn't have to bother with the desk work anymore. But so far Mom hasn't given the go-ahead on that."

Cassidy could guess why. Her mother expected *her* to fill that role.

"I'll do what I can to help while I'm here, Corb. But I can't stay. I worked hard for my degree and I want a chance to use it."

Besides, after living apart from her mother the past

five years, she could never go back to living in the same house as her.

The crepes episode was a perfect example of how a simple little thing could get her all upset. Life was too short to keep doing that to herself.

"I just couldn't come back here to live. I'm sorry."

"Hey." Corb patted her shoulder. "I didn't mean to make you feel guilty. I get it."

"By the way, you'll have to wait to tell Mom about Winnie's baby. She's off to Lewistown today and may not be home until tomorrow."

"Thanks for letting me know that." He stepped back from her and gave the horses a good look-over. "So how do they seem to you? Any signs of strangles?"

"Nothing obvious. But I noticed Finnegan seems to be off his food. He didn't even want the carrot I just offered him." She unclenched her fist, where the untouched chunk of carrot still sat.

"Damn." Corb checked the mustang more closely, then shook his head. "Doesn't look sick to me, but just to be sure, we better put him up in a separate area of the barn. Keep him away from both Lucy and the other horses."

Cassidy nodded. She'd already decided the same thing, though she was almost positive that Finnegan didn't have strangles. He couldn't.

Still, she brought him into the barn, settling him into the stall farthest from Lucy's. An hour later Corb and two hired hands tacked up four horses and went out to sort calves for branding. Cassidy busied herself cleaning Lucy's stall and hauling the soiled hay away and burning it as per Farley's orders.

Two hours later, she had to admit that Finnegan was

looking worse. She'd offered him some oats and given him a thorough grooming, but he still wasn't eating and seemed decidedly lackluster.

Much as she didn't want to, she could see no alternative.

She had to call Farley.

Cassidy made the call from the barn, using the phone in the office where she and Farley had talked just one day earlier. She'd hoped to clear the air with him then, but the truth was she felt even more awkward now than she had before.

So she was relieved when his phone was answered by someone else.

"Farley & Sons," said a woman with a brisk, no-nonsense voice. "Liz speaking."

Even though Farley now worked on his own, he hadn't changed the name of the business to reflect this. "Hi. This is Cassidy Lambert from Coffee Creek Ranch. Farley was out here yesterday looking at one of our horses."

"*Cassidy* Lambert?"

"Yes."

"I see."

Was it her imagination or did the woman's voice shift from businesslike to frosty?

"Well, if you're wondering about the test results for your palomino, it's going to take several days before we know for sure."

"I was actually calling because we have a second horse off his feed and I was wondering if Farley could come take a look at him."

"Dan has a full schedule today. And plans for dinner with his girlfriend tonight."

Dan Farley had a girlfriend? She knew she shouldn't be surprised, or even interested, but she was both. Fighting the urge to ask questions that weren't appropriate, Cassidy refocused on the issues that *did* matter.

"This second horse is older, and I'm afraid if he has strangles it could hit him hard. I'd really appreciate it if Farley could come as soon as possible."

"Well, he could maybe squeeze in a visit tomorrow. He was planning to swing by Silver Creek then, anyway."

Tomorrow. Cassidy hated to wait that long. But it didn't seem she had any choice. "Do they have strangles at Silver Creek, too?"

"Not at all. Far as we know, you're the only ones in the area."

Which meant the mystery of how Lucy had contracted the bacterial infection was still unsolved. Maybe it *had* been that secondhand tack. Cassidy ended the unsatisfactory call and went back to check on the horses.

While she was applying a fresh compress to Lucy's neck, Corb and the hired men came back with their horses. They looked dirty and tired and she offered to brush down their horses and clean the tack for them.

The men gave her grateful smiles, passing off their horses before taking off for their well-deserved dinners.

Careful to protect the horses from infection, Cassidy brushed them off outside before letting them loose in the pasture. Then she turned to the tedious job of disinfecting the tack room. The job took several hours and she was tired, sweaty and hungry by the time she was finished. Still, rather than head in for the shower and meal that she craved, she washed thoroughly and went back to Finnegan.

There wasn't much light left in the day at that point, but she didn't need it to see that Finnegan had deteriorated. He had discharge in his nostrils and he still hadn't touched either the oats, the carrot or the hay she'd left out for him.

Heck and darn.

Lucy was doing worse, too. Not only were the glands in her neck visibly more swollen, but she seemed to be struggling with each breath.

Mentally Cassidy went over the instructions Farley had left with her and wondered if she'd missed something. She wished she had someone to ask, but it was past eight o'clock now and there was no one around. She could always call Corb at the cabin. But he had no more experience with strangles than she did, and he already had precious little time to spend with his wife and baby daughter.

Liz had said Farley might make it tomorrow morning. So she'd just hang on until then.

"Looks like it's going to be a long night," she said, speaking out loud as she set up the cot they used when keeping watch over pregnant mares. She made a pot of coffee in the office and found a box of granola bars stashed in a bottom filing cabinet. She ate one for herself and broke up a second for Sky.

They had an old radio in the barn tuned to a local country station and she put that on.

It helped to have a little music and the radio announcer for company, though she could have done without the ads, which were jarring at the best of times.

She wondered what Josh was doing and took her phone out of her back pocket. Two missed calls and three text messages.

Going out for lunch with Kate and Liam—two of their college friends. Then, an hour later, *Wish you were here, too.* And the final message, sent just fifteen minutes ago. *You're quiet. What's up?*

She thought about answering, but her heart wasn't in it. Josh had grown up in Great Falls and had never even owned a pet. He'd try to be sympathetic, but he wouldn't really understand why she was so upset. Besides, she didn't feel like talking. She hated to see any animal suffer and when they were animals she knew and loved it was even harder.

She sat on an overturned wooden bucket at the back door of the barn, with one arm looped around Sky's neck. The sun was setting and the rolling hills to the west had never looked lovelier against the swirls of vivid orange and red.

"This must be the most beautiful place in the world, don't you think?"

For answer, her dog rested her muzzle on Cassidy's knee.

"They'll be okay, right? I mean, strangles isn't fatal." *At least not usually.* Gosh, she was tired. She'd only managed a few hours of sleep last night and today she'd been a lot more active than usual.

Thankfully the rest of the horses seemed fine. The four horses she'd groomed earlier were enjoying their evening feed with the rest of the small herd.

Once the sun was down, Cassidy decided she might as well try to catch a little sleep. Leaving on the lights in the office and the tack room, so she didn't feel quite so all alone, she sank onto the narrow mattress and closed her eyes.

A few minutes later she became aware of a high-pitched noise rising above the music on the radio. Sky growled and went to the closed barn door, whining to be let out.

Coyotes.

"Come back here, Sky. Ignore them."

It was a mark of Sky's obedience that she listened and returned to lie at the foot of Cassidy's cot.

But by the dog's uneasy stirrings, Cassidy could tell she wasn't going back to sleep. They'd always had coyotes here on the ranch. Just like moose, elk and white-tailed deer, they were part of the natural order.

But tonight their nighttime cries sounded closer than normal.

Eventually they quieted, though. Probably they'd moved on, farther down the valley.

Cassidy relaxed and finally drifted to sleep.

Farley was surprised to find the Lamberts' house completely dark when he pulled up in his SUV at ten o'clock that evening. He felt like a fool for taking Amber home early after their dinner and for driving out all this way.

He started to pull a U-turn, then he noticed a couple of lights on at the home barn where Lucy was quarantined.

So he parked and grabbed his black kit from the passenger seat. A series of motion-activated lights illuminated the path for him as he made his way to the barn.

His boots crunched on the graveled path, mixing in with the chorus from the frogs in the nearby lake. As he drew closer to the barn a new sound rose softly in the night air.

He recognized the melancholic refrain of a popular

country tune. The radio was on. He'd been listening to the same station on his drive over here.

Sky was waiting at the barn door for him. Where you found Sky, you were bound to find Cassidy, but at first he saw no sign of her.

Two horses nickered at him. One was Lucy. The other—at the opposite end of the barn—had to be the second horse Liz had reported Cassidy suspected was sick, too. A closer look told him it was Finnegan—the mustang Cassidy had ridden when she was growing up. This wasn't good news. Finnegan had to be getting on in years by now. The older horse would have a tougher time with strangles.

Once his eyes had adjusted to the low light in the stables, he finally spotted Cassidy. She was sleeping on a cot next to Finnegan's stall, curled up with a blanket that he'd seen in the office the other day.

A feeling that was both powerful and tender welled up in him. Why? It didn't seem to matter that she'd treated him like dirt. That she'd spurned his way of life. He wished like hell that he could transfer those feelings to Amber, a woman for whom such a longing would make a hell of a lot more sense.

The song ended, and the radio announcer started in on a weather update.

Cassidy's eyes slowly opened. She stared right at him. Blankly, at first. Then her eyes rounded and she whispered, "Farley? I can't believe you're here."

"Liz said it was an emergency." He turned away, fighting an impulse to hold out his hand and help her up.

She didn't need one anyway. Quickly she stood up, planting her feet—she hadn't taken off her boots—on the concrete floor. "What time is it?"

"About quarter after ten," he guessed.

"Really? Thanks for coming out so late."

"Don't worry about it," he said, brushing aside the thanks. "Just wait till your mother gets my next vet bill. You'll probably hear the shriek all the way to Billings."

"Well, it was still awfully nice of you." She was up now, moving to Finnegan, stroking the horse and crooning. "Hey, baby, don't worry. The vet's here now and he's going to help you." She turned to Farley.

His heart clenched at the sight of her face, and all that he could read in it. It seemed so genuine, her concern for her horse. But in a few more weeks she'd be in Billings—how much would she care then?

He put a hand on the mustang's flank and began his inspection. "How was he acting today?"

"Kind of listless. Wouldn't eat, not even his oats or a carrot." She exhaled despairingly. "Everything you said to watch out for."

"Well, he is running a fever," he confirmed ten minutes later. "And there is a little clear discharge. I'll take a swab for testing, but I think in this case it would be smart to start on antibiotics right away. Maybe we've caught it early enough that it will help."

He moved to Lucy next. "How's our other patient doing?"

"She hasn't eaten much today, either. And starting late this afternoon, she seems to be struggling to breathe. I've been changing her hot compresses every twenty minutes—except when I fell asleep," she added guiltily.

"Lucy's having trouble breathing because those swollen lymph nodes are pressing right up against her airway. We need to relieve the pressure and soon."

"Poor Lucy. Should I get some more hot compresses?"

"No. I was hoping the abscesses would burst on their own, but since they haven't, we'll have to lance them."

"Will it hurt her?"

"Not if we do it right. Are you willing to help?"

She looked insulted. "Of course I am."

"It won't be pretty."

She put up her chin. "You don't think I can handle a little pus?"

"Not a little. A lot. And I don't know what you can handle, Cass. I just thought it was fair to warn you."

Chapter 6

Why did being around Farley always have to be so complicated? She'd been so relieved, at first, that he was here, and she was no longer alone with her worry and fear. True, she could have called Corb or Jackson, but handling the strangles outbreak was her responsibility and her brothers had already put in long days.

Besides, what could they have done that she wasn't already doing?

Farley was different. He was a vet, obviously. But he also had a calm, take-charge attitude. Just his presence was enough to make her feel better.

For a while. But it didn't take long for other emotions to tangle up her heart. She felt defenseless, confused... and even angry.

He had this disapproving way of looking at her that made her feel so small.

Yes, she'd behaved abominably at the Harvest Dance four years ago. But it had been four years. And she'd finally apologized.

So what was he holding against her now?

She felt sure it was something.

"I'll need some clean rags," Farley said as he pulled equipment from his open case. She saw a bottle of antiseptic, cotton swabs, a big, ugly-looking knife... Suddenly she felt woozy. She went for the rags, glad to have an excuse to look the other way for a while.

She'd put on a brave front, but the truth was she hated icky things like pus and vomit...and especially blood. But she would get past all of that tonight. She had to do it for a horse whose heart was as wide and open as the Montana skyline.

Cassidy's determination to be brave was sorely tested in the next twenty minutes. It was awful watching Farley cut through the abscess.

Lucy was a trouper throughout, a model patient, Farley said. And, fortunately, once the pus was gone, her breathing immediately returned to normal.

When it was done, he showed her how to prepare a tamed iodine solution.

"You'll need to flush the wound once a day to keep it clear of infection."

They were arm-to-arm as he said this. She could feel his warmth, the solid bulk of his broad shoulders against her slight ones.

"Like this." He demonstrated, then handed the solution and gauze to her.

She followed his example, feeling pleasure when he nodded his approval.

"Good job," he said. "Most people wouldn't have been able to stomach a procedure like this one."

"It was tough," she admitted. "But I was so worried about Lucy, I kind of put it out of my mind."

"I guess you haven't changed all that much, after all. Still can't stand to see an animal suffer."

Cassidy's breath caught in her throat. He was so close she could smell his cologne over the pungent odor of the iodine. But wait a minute. The scent was too sweet and floral to be something a man would wear.

And then she remembered what Liz had told her.

"So how was your date?"

Farley dropped his syringe, then recovered it from the straw bedding and tossed it in the bag containing all the pus-soaked rags. "What makes you think I was on a date?"

She followed her nose, which led her to the collar of his shirt. "It's either that, or you've started to wear Joy. Not the first choice for most men who wear cologne."

"Stop *sniffing* me."

She backed off, amused. "Why not? It's nice. I bought a bottle for Laurel this Christmas."

"I do *not* smell like perfume."

He was embarrassed, she noted with glee. "My mistake. It must be Lucy, that silly horse. I keep telling her the stallions prefer her natural pheromones."

Farley looked pained. And then he laughed. "If you must know, I was out for dinner with Amber Ellis. I had no idea she wore Joy perfume. But at least now I know what to get her for her birthday."

Amber Ellis. Corb had dated her a few years back. Cassidy remembered liking her a lot. So why did she feel this sudden flash of irritation toward her?

Farley packed up his bag, instructed her on the various medicines and treatments for the horses, then rolled up his sleeves and washed at the sink.

"Should I stay out here and keep an eye on them?" she asked, when what she really wondered was whether Farley would be heading home now...or to Amber's.

"We've done all we can for tonight. Go inside and get a decent night's sleep. They'll be okay until morning. In fact, I'm expecting Lucy will be a whole lot better by then."

Cassidy didn't ask about Finnegan. She was too afraid of getting the wrong answer.

The next morning Cassidy was up early to check the horses. As Farley had predicted, Lucy was much improved. Cassidy fed her warm mush, administered the antibiotics and mucked out the stalls. After, she burned the soiled bedding as before and disinfected the feed and water buckets.

There wasn't much she could do for Finnegan, though, who still had little appetite and the tell-tale strangles nasal discharge. While his glands hadn't swollen as much as Lucy's had, Cassidy prepared hot compresses for him anyway.

She was on her way back to the ranch house when she spotted Corb on the other side of the yard.

"Want to come out for a ride?" he asked. "I need to fix a section of fencing on the northern boundary."

The sun was shining in a cloud-free sky. There was nothing Cassidy would rather do. But she shook her head. "I better stay close to home and keep an eye on Finnegan."

"How's Lucy?"

"A lot better. Last night she was having trouble breathing but Farley came by and lanced the abscesses. She's almost her old self today."

"Farley came by, huh? Must have been pretty late. Now that's good service, I say."

Cassidy noticed the teasing gleam in her brother's eyes, but she knew how to keep him under control. "Yes. Unfortunately he had to cut his date with Amber Ellis a few hours short. You remember Amber, don't you, Corb?"

He flushed, just as she'd hoped he would. "You pest. Better get to the kitchen. If you're not coming out riding today, Mom has some errands she wants you to run. She got back about an hour ago and is in the kitchen making a list."

"Before you saddle up any of the horses, make sure they seem healthy," she reminded him before she left. "Let me know if any of them aren't eating or seem listless."

"You got your phone on you?" he asked.

She nodded.

"Okay. I'll call you if there are any problems."

As she headed to the house, Cassidy wondered what mood her mother would be in. Olive had stopped by the barn earlier, making her morning rounds later than usual, as she'd spent the night in Lewistown. They hadn't talked much, though, since Olive hadn't wanted to risk spreading the strangles by stepping inside the barn.

Having their riding horses in quarantine was bad enough. It would be a disaster, though, if the quarter horses were infected.

She found her mother in the kitchen, making a fry-up in the huge cast-iron pan that had been in the family pretty much forever. Cassidy cringed as she thought of her crepe-making fiasco of the previous day. She should have known better than to try something new with her mother.

Mother only liked new ideas when she thought of them.

"Help yourself to coffee," Olive said. "This'll be ready in a minute. How's my Lucy doing?"

Cassidy caught her mother up with the latest developments, then listened to her mom talk horse prices while they ate their scrambled eggs mixed with sausage, tomatoes and onions. When they were finished, Olive asked her to move her belongings into Corb's old room.

"The painters are coming today."

"That was fast."

"The curtains and duvet cover won't be ready for a few weeks," Olive said. "But the new armoire is being delivered on Friday."

"New armoire?"

"I paid for it in Lewistown yesterday. After my meeting," she added, looking at her daughter as if she thought she was a little slow for not keeping up.

In Cassidy's opinion, the last thing they needed to be worrying about at this busy time of year was redecorating her bedroom, but she knew better than to complain. "That sounds great, Mom."

"Nothing is too much trouble for my kids." Her mother got up and patted Cassidy's cheek, then pulled out a shopping bag. "And look at what I found for Stephanie."

Inside were the tiniest pair of cowboy boots that Cassidy had ever seen. "Gosh, these are cute."

Also in the bag was a tiny jumper with Cowgirl

printed on the front, a velvety-soft stuffed horse and a picture book about farm animals.

With the Lambert family, indoctrination started early.

"That's so nice, Mom." She set the bag aside, feeling a pang for the other new baby in the family. Corb better tell their mother soon. The longer they delayed, the worse Olive was going to take it.

Just then, her phone signaled an incoming text message. It was from Corb and the message was simple.

Tell her.

Heck and darn. Was he serious? Not my place, she texted back.

Please?

Cassidy sighed. She really did hate her mother not knowing this. "Mom? I found out something major last night when I dropped in on Corb and Laurel."

Olive frowned. "This sounds like bad news."

"More like a big surprise. Sit down, please."

She waited until her mother was actually in a chair before she continued. "You know how Winnie has been staying at her parents' because of health issues?"

"I always said that woman didn't have the strength to be a rancher's wife."

"Actually, she's had a good reason for not returning to Coffee Creek sooner. She was two months pregnant when Brock died."

Olive gasped and Cassidy jumped up to get her mother a glass of water.

"Winnie had a little boy in January."

"Brock's son?"

Cassidy nodded.

"Oh, my word.... Why didn't she tell us?"

"Think about it, Mom. Can you guess why she might have been reluctant?"

A rare flush rose on Olive's cheeks.

"She was grieving. And according to Laurel she had a very difficult pregnancy. So we've got to be understanding. Besides, if we get Winnie angry, we may lose out on the chance to be a part of Brock's baby's life."

Olive nodded slowly. "You're right."

"Good. So don't go doing or saying anything you might regret later."

Again Olive nodded. "I'll have to think about this."

"In the meantime, do you need anything from town? Corb said you had a list of errands and I'm planning on going to the library this morning."

The radio had been good company last night. But a book would be even better.

"I do." Her mom handed her a shopping list. "And would you mind taking this outfit to Laurel?" She handed Cassidy the little cowgirl duds. "I can't believe I have another grandchild. Seems like I have a lot of shopping to catch up on."

Cassidy took Sky along with her for the drive into Coffee Creek. She went to the Cinnamon Stick first, and she and Laurel shared a laugh at the ranch-themed gifts from Olive.

"I'm not sure about the boots—I don't think Stephanie will be wearing shoes for a long time. But everything else is wonderful. Olive sure does like to spoil her granddaughter. We've had a gift from her almost every week since Steph was born."

"Hopefully they didn't come with too many strings attached."

Laurel raised her eyebrows, but didn't say anything further. After the way Olive had tried to commandeer the wedding plans for Laurel's marriage to Corb, Cassidy thought it was big of her not to add her own complaints to the list.

"By the way, Corb asked me to tell Mom about Winnie's son. So I did it."

"Really?" Laurel's eyes grew huge. "How did she take it?"

"I didn't give her much of a chance to react. I just warned her that if we didn't treat Winnie very carefully we might end up not being part of Brock's son's life. I left her to mull that over for a while."

"Gosh. I have to call Winnie and let her know that Olive's been told. She'll be glad she didn't have to be the one."

"Does she have any plans to bring the baby back to Coffee Creek?"

"Eventually," Laurel said. "But I don't think she's ready yet. On top of all the other problems she's had, it seems her son is really colicky."

Laurel handed her a cup of coffee. "So how was your night? Corb tells me that Farley dropped by for a while? He also said that Farley is dating Amber Ellis."

"Really? He passed that along already?"

Laurel smiled smugly. "Text message about five minutes after you told him."

Cassidy laughed. "Well, at least the lines of communication are working in your marriage."

"That's all you have to say? What about Amber? Are you upset?"

"Why would I be?"

Laurel just raised her eyebrows.

Cassidy took her coffee in a to-go cup, plus a bag containing several cinnamon buns that Laurel pressed on her. She certainly wasn't going to admit, not even to Laurel, that she didn't like the idea of Farley dating Amber one little bit.

Cassidy headed to the library next. Every time she entered the historic old building she wished she'd been alive when the children of the area had all gone to school here. A one-room schoolhouse combining six grades' worth of pupils must have been a lot of fun.

The librarian, Tabitha Snow, was on her computer when Cassidy arrived. She broke out in a welcoming smile and left her desk to give Cassidy a hug. "You're back! How did it go?"

"Very well. Though I must admit I'm glad to put all that intense studying behind me. I'd like to read something fun for a change."

It was nice to see Tabitha again. She'd encouraged Cassidy's love of books and learning from an early age. But it was a little disconcerting as well to see new gray hairs and tiny lines around the attractive librarian's mouth. A reminder that things had changed in the years she'd been away from Coffee Creek.

"Oh, I know just the story. This one kept me up all hours last week." She pulled a book from a wheeled cart next to her desk. "And the ending is perfectly wonderful—you never see it coming but it feels so true when it happens."

Cassidy gave the back cover a quick read and agreed it sounded interesting. "Thanks, I'll take it." She dug her library card out of her pocket and handed it over, interested to see that even their small local library had gone electronic, with bar codes, scanners and everything.

"So how are things with you?"

"Oh, the same." Tabitha looked surprised that she would even ask. "I adopted a new cat this fall. That makes six now." She sighed. "I suppose I'm becoming something of a cliché. The old lady who lives alone with her cats and her books. Next thing you know I'll take up crocheting."

"Why not? Since Winnie went to live with her folks, she's taken up knitting. And what's wrong with cats and books, anyway? Both sound like wonderful things to surround yourself with."

"Ah, you always were the sweetest child. Not a child anymore, of course, but I'm glad you kept the sweet part." Tabitha handed her the book. "There you go. You have three weeks, but if you like the story as much as I did, I predict you'll be back within a few days."

As it happened, Cassidy left the library at the same time as the postmaster from the building next door was crossing the street for his usual lunch at the Cinnamon Stick.

"Hey, Burt."

"Cassidy." He nodded.

Three years ago Burt and Tabitha had been married. When they separated they set up rules so they could continue to live in the same small town without causing each other too much grief.

One of their agreements was that Tabitha would frequent the Cinnamon Stick in the morning, and Burt at noon. That way they wouldn't have to worry about running into one another.

Cassidy had assumed the arrangement was temporary, but it seemed they were still sticking to their schedule. "Any mail for Coffee Creek Ranch today, Burt?" she called out across the street.

"Nope. Your mother picked it up yesterday afternoon on her way to Lewistown." He nodded again, then disappeared inside the café.

Cassidy shrugged, then continued to her truck, which she'd parked outside of the café. She was surprised to see Maddie Turner standing at the open passenger-side window, petting Sky. She was so short, Cassidy didn't see her until she was only a few feet away. Sky had sure noticed Maddie's presence, though. She was wiggling, panting and smiling, the way she always did when greeting a friend.

Cassidy stopped, not sure what to do.

When she was growing up, she had witnessed both her mother and her father cross the street rather than exchange a greeting with Maddie. She herself had never spoken to the woman who was her aunt.

But to ignore her now seemed just plain silly.

"Hi. My dog sure seems to like you."

"I hope you don't mind. I couldn't resist stopping to say hello. And it seems like she remembers me." Maddie's voice sounded hoarse. She pulled out a tissue and coughed.

"Corb mentioned something about Sky coming from a litter of yours."

"That's right. Her mother was a direct descendant of the border collie your mother and I had when we were growing up."

Cassidy frowned. "So how exactly did I come to own her?"

Though her dog had been delivered to their door in a

basket on her fourteenth birthday, she'd always assumed her father was behind the gift.

Maddie smiled shyly. "I had a feeling you would like one another. Was I right?"

Cassidy didn't know what to say. She was surprised that Maddie Turner even knew her birth date, let alone that she would have given her such a special gift. She wondered if her mother had guessed that the dog had been from her sister. Given the breed, she probably had. So maybe that was why she had been so annoyed.

"I don't know what to say. Thank you. Sky was my best friend when I was growing up." She thought for a moment. "And she still is."

"That's the way I feel about my dogs, as well. I have two border collies on Silver Creek—"

Maddie stopped abruptly, her gaze shifting to the door of the café, where Vince Butterfield, the ex-bronc rider turned baker, was just stepping out at the end of his shift.

"Hello, Maddie," Vince said, his voice deep and rusty. "It's good to see you. Next time you're in for coffee you should come back to the kitchen and say hello."

Cassidy was surprised. Vince hardly ever did anything more than nod at the people he met. She glanced back at her aunt and was surprised to see that pain had clouded over Maddie's lovely eyes.

"I don't think so, Vince." Without another word to either of them she turned and walked away.

When Cassidy returned home, her mother's SUV was in its usual parking space in front of the garage. Cassidy pulled in beside it and went inside through the back patio doors.

Her mother was just hanging up the phone and

seemed startled to see her. "Oh, hi, sweetheart. How was the trip to Coffee Creek?"

"Great. Laurel said thanks for the gift. And she sent you back this." She handed her mother the bag with the cinnamon buns. "Who was that on the phone?"

"Oh—it was nothing important." Olive glanced at the cinnamon buns, then set the bag on the counter. "I've already had my lunch. I'm off for another meeting this afternoon. The Heritage Site Committee again."

Which explained why her mother had changed from the jeans she'd been wearing earlier, to the Western-styled skirt she had on now. Plus, she'd touched up her makeup.

"You look pretty, Mom."

"Thank you, dear." Olive picked up her satchel, then hesitated. "Would you consider joining the committee? We have a treasurer but she doesn't seem to know much about investing money and we've got a fair amount of funds just sitting in a savings account. You would be a real asset."

Her mother looked so hopeful, Cassidy felt like a heel turning her down. "I'd be glad to give your treasurer some investing advice. But I can't join full-time since I'm moving to Billings. It would be too far to travel for regular meetings."

It seemed like every muscle in her mother's face tightened. "So that's still on then?"

"Why wouldn't it be? I haven't got the job yet. But I'm hopeful. And even if I don't get that position, I'm sure I'll find something else."

Her mother said nothing to that, just sighed and changed the subject. She gave Cassidy a list of chores to do for the afternoon, including checking on the quarantined horses, which Cassidy had been intending to do anyway.

Once Olive had driven off, Cassidy went to the phone and scrolled through the recently called list. She had a funny feeling about that look she'd surprised on her mother's face. Sure enough, Josh's number topped the list of recent callers. Scrolling back further, she noticed he'd phoned her yesterday, too.

She pulled out her cell phone and hit his speed dial number.

"Finally!" He sounded breathless above the background noise of city bustle. "Why haven't you answered any of my texts or phone calls?"

She didn't tell him that her mother hadn't passed along his messages, since she hadn't responded to his calls on her cell phone, either. "It's been crazy here. We've got strangles and all our riding horses have been quarantined."

"Strangles? What's that?"

"It's a very contagious bacterial disease that—well, it can be really serious. And I've been put in charge of making sure it doesn't spread and nursing the infected horses."

"Wow. Sounds like you could use some help…"

Cassidy ignored the hint. Josh had been keen to visit her family ranch for some time now, but she had her doubts on how well he would fit in. He'd never even been on a horse and knew nothing about the cattle business. She was afraid Corb and Jackson would have a field day with him. And her mother… Well, the fact that she hadn't told Cassidy about any of Josh's calls pretty much demonstrated the sort of welcome *she* would give Josh if he came.

"I'm doing okay. What's new with you?"

"I got the second interview! I've been dying to tell you. We set a date for next week. How about you? Have you heard anything?"

"Not yet." She wouldn't put it past her mother not to tell her if she had, but she hadn't seen any calls from the firm on the recently called list. Besides, she'd given her cell phone number and email as her primary contact information. The home number was just for backup.

"Not to worry," Josh assured her. "I'm sure you'll hear something soon. Oh—and you should check for your marks. Mine were posted last night."

He reeled off a list of marks that were all impressive.

"Good for you. Look, Josh, I've got to go. I'll call you later when I have time to talk, okay?"

She hurried to her computer and went online. In minutes she was relieved to see that her final marks were even better than Josh's.

So why had he gotten the call while she was still waiting?

Deciding it was too soon to worry, she changed and was heading out to the barn, when she was intercepted by Jay Owen, one of their hired workers.

"We've got another sick horse," the short, wiry wrangler told her. "Chickweed. I just put him into the stall next to Finnegan."

Chapter 7

The one person Cassidy didn't expect to see in the barn examining the newest sick horse was Farley. She watched him, unseen for a while. Despite his height and his broad shoulders, Farley was light on his feet and sure with his movements. If you could call a vet graceful, then Farley was graceful.

A slight movement from Sky, as always in her shadow, betrayed her presence.

Farley glanced up from the vial he was putting in his case. "Looks like we have another one."

"Oh, no. But you sure got here fast. I didn't even have time to call you."

"I was already on the property doing some preg testing in the cattle barn."

Since a grove of pine trees separated the cattle barn

from the house, that explained why she hadn't seen his truck.

"That was lucky for us. So how is Chickweed doing?" The sturdy quarter horse was her brother Corb's favorite. They'd had him about ten years.

"Hey there, Chickweed." She patted the horse as she walked around him, doing a quick visual exam. Chickweed was a smart, sure-footed horse with terrific cow sense.

But she could tell right away, by his posture and the position of his neck and his head, that he wasn't feeling well. "Is he running a fever?"

"Afraid so. And he's definitely suffering some pain— see how swollen he is under his jaw?" Farley placed her hand over the enlarged lymph nodes, and she nodded.

Not only did she feel the evidence of strangles in the horse, but she also felt the rough calluses of Farley's hand. And the strength. And the warmth.

She remembered what his hands had felt like on her waist and on her shoulder, when they'd danced together four years ago. She'd never forgotten and never would.

Did he ever think about the good part of that night?

Or just her inexcusable behavior afterward?

She glanced at his face, and saw that he was looking at her, his dark gaze as always intense, but inscrutable.

"Should I prepare some hot compresses?" she asked.

He blinked. "Yes."

The moment between them—if indeed, it had been a moment—was over. Farley went to his vet truck to get some more antibiotics, while she warmed up compresses for all three of her patients.

Lucy was restless as Cassidy washed her dried-up

abscesses and when Cassidy offered her the warm oat mush, she gobbled it up.

"She's definitely feeling better," Cassidy noticed.

Finnegan, unfortunately, seemed to be worse. He ate only a few mouthfuls of the mush and hardly reacted when she called out his name and tried to give him a little loving.

"This is odd," Cassidy said. "His neck isn't as swollen as Lucy's was or as Chickweed's is right now, yet of all of them, he seems the sickest."

"You have to remember he's older," Farley reminded her. "And it's possible…"

"What?"

Farley removed the latex gloves he'd been wearing and tossed them into the trash. "There can be various complications from strangles. We'll have to keep a close eye on Finnegan."

"What sort of complications? What should I watch for?"

But Farley was frustratingly vague. "Just let me know if anything changes, okay?" He was at the doorway now. "I should get back to those cows. You okay in here?"

She was. But she liked it better when he was here with her.

Which was odd considering how much he disliked her.

"I'm fine," she insisted.

He hesitated before leaving. "Heard anything about that job in Billings?"

"Not yet. But I got the results from my finals and they were good."

"Congratulations."

"Still no word from the accounting firm, though.

Some of my fellow students have already been called. Maybe I won't be getting a second interview."

Farley's gaze dropped to her boots, then returned to her eyes. He gave her a small smile—a shadow of the ones she could remember from earlier days—and nodded. "I'll bet you will."

Farley pulled on a pair of OB coveralls and disinfected his boots before rejoining Corb in the cattle barn. It was breeding season and Corb needed to know which of his cows were pregnant and which were not. It was messy, physical work that required Farley's full concentration.

Corb's job was lining up the cows for examination, then sorting them into pens when they were done.

"No wonder we pay you the big bucks," Corb said, as Farley unblocked an unusually large amount of fecal matter from one of the cows.

Farley shrugged. He was used to this. And the hard work was good distraction from a woman who could mess up his mind without even trying. Seeing how much she cared about her horses was making it hard for him to keep up the distance he'd planned with her. He'd assumed that part of her had calcified—around about the time she discovered how much fun she could have playing one guy off another.

But now he knew it hadn't.

She was as soft-hearted as ever.

Which meant that it was just him she had a problem with.

Self-preservation required that he stop noticing all the sweet, womanly things about her. But he couldn't seem to stop himself. He loved the soft curve of her ear that was exposed when she pulled back her hair, the incredible green of her eyes, the way she drew in one brow when she was confused or disbelieving.

The phone on his belt clip vibrated, reminding him that he still hadn't answered last night's phone message from Amber. She was the woman he should be thinking about right now. So why wasn't he?

He knew he owed her, at the least, a phone call. But how was he supposed to pursue a relationship with one woman, when he was all the time thinking about another?

He felt the small, squishy sac of the cow's uterus and something harder inside, about the size of a baseball. "She's pregnant."

"Great." Corb released the animal with the other bred cows and Farley moved on to the next one.

If only women were as easy to understand as cows. He knew one thing for sure. His life would be a lot less complicated once Cassidy took that job and made a permanent move to Billings.

It was a long week for Cassidy. Chickweed turned out to be lucky. His case of strangles was mild and within seven days both he and Lucy seemed as good as new. Finnegan was different. His spirits dragged. His appetite was sporadic. Though terribly worried about her mustang, Cassidy was growing weary of her assignment, which kept her cooped up in the barn when she really wanted to be outside enjoying the warm May weather.

During her long nightly vigils—she refused to sleep in the house until she knew all the horses were out of danger—she'd finished the book Tabitha had recommended and another besides.

While the stories were pleasant diversions, she still felt increasingly restless. Plus she was getting really sick of the smell of disinfectant.

She could have spent more time in the house, rather than the barn, but she was also avoiding her mother who, when she wasn't complaining about Winnie keeping Brock's son a secret, was stepping up her campaign to get Cassidy to join the Coffee Creek Heritage Site Committee.

"We could schedule our meetings to coincide with your visits home," she'd offered last night during dinner.

"I don't think so, Mom."

"But why? Don't you care about this community? You could make a real difference here."

Her mother had gone on, talking about the importance of remembering the past and keeping alive the cowboy tradition. It was as if she was purposefully ignoring the fact that Cassidy planned to work as an accountant and live in Billings.

Though even that plan was beginning to look doubtful.

She *still* hadn't been called for a second interview and the waiting was driving her mad. Her marks had been top of the class, even better than Josh's. She'd thought she'd done well at the first interview.

So why wasn't she getting the second interview invitation that Josh and several other classmates had received?

Cassidy stopped to kick a wooden fence post. Just because she felt like it.

"Did it help?"

Heck and darn, Farley had seen her. He must be here doing more preg testing today. She hadn't seen his vet truck, but he'd probably parked it by the cattle barn again.

"Not really," she admitted.

"What's the problem?"

Even in an OB uniform covered with cow manure, Farley still looked ridiculously handsome. Something about those regal Native American cheekbones and his jet-black hair, which always fell perfectly in place and didn't even seem to show the indent from his hat when he removed it from his head.

Speaking of hair, hers was a mess. Something her mother had pointed out yesterday and again today.

"Just because you're living on a ranch doesn't mean you should get sloppy with your appearance, Cassidy."

"Spring fever," she said, after taking a moment to consider Farley's question. "I think Lucy and Chickweed have it, too. They're itching to get some exercise but I'm afraid to let them out with the other horses."

"Can't do that until we know they're not contagious," he agreed. "But they looked pretty spirited to me the last time I examined them. We could take them out for a ride. Clear their cobwebs—and our own, besides."

She glanced at him, intrigued by what she thought he'd just suggested. "*We* could take them? You have time for a trail ride?"

Even more surprising was the idea that he would want to go for a ride with *her* along for company.

He smiled. "I think I deserve a reward after all the cows I've felt up the past few weeks."

Cassidy didn't know who was happier to finally be free—her or Lucy. Farley on Chickweed was right behind them as they left the barn behind, then the yard, and then the pasture. It felt great to be out on the open range, knowing they could ride for hours and not run into another human being.

After ten minutes of pure exuberance, Cassidy brought Lucy down a couple of notches. "Easy, girl. I know you're happy to be out of that barn, but I don't want you to get sick again."

She turned to look at Farley, who was also transitioning Chickweed into a slower pace.

Cassidy couldn't help noticing…he'd cleaned up crazy good.

Gone were the gooey overalls and the latex gloves. Now Farley was in faded jeans and a mossy-green shirt and a hat about as dark as his hair.

He looked sexy, handsome and just a little dangerous.

Just the way he'd looked to her four years ago at that dance. Back then the feelings had been more than she could handle. Now she couldn't help wondering what it would be like to kiss him.

Not that she saw it happening.

But what was the harm in a little daydreaming?

He urged Chickweed closer. "You and Lucy were made for one another."

"I feel that way, too. But she's my mother's horse."

"Yeah." He eyed the palomino thoughtfully. "But she's so agile. She'd make a lovely barrel racer."

"I *know*. I think the very same thing."

"Didn't you compete in high school?"

"Yes, with Finnegan. Much as I love my boy, though, I think Lucy has it all over him in the raw talent category. Not that it matters. I really can't imagine Mom taking up barrel racing any time soon."

"Your mother is in great shape for her age. But barrel racing? I don't think so."

"What about you? Do you still steer wrestle?"

"Every now and then," he admitted. "To let off a little steam."

"I remember watching you and my brothers practice. It used to scare me. I was so sure one of you was going to get hurt."

"Trust me, the hits were a lot easier to take when we were younger. I don't know how B.J. can keep up the pace he does. He called me the other day. Tried to talk me into registering in Central Point at the end of the month."

"The Wild Rogue Rodeo? Are you going to do it?"

"I might. What about you?"

For a moment she was tempted. Then she shrugged. "It's difficult for me to think about the future right now. Each day that passes without a call for that second interview just makes me realize how much I was counting on landing that job."

"You didn't look too worried a minute ago."

She hesitated. Then laughed. "That's true. Thanks for suggesting we do this. Isn't it a beautiful day? I mean, look at that view of Square Butte." She waved her hand at the mountain rising from the hills to their left. "Doesn't it just take your breath away?"

"I know what you mean." His voice sounded thoughtful, and she turned to look at him, trying to figure out his mood. He was looking at her, though, not the mountain.

Was he changing his mind about her?

"Forgiven me yet?" she dared to ask.

"Thinking about it."

"Yeah? What else are you thinking about? You looked so serious there for a minute."

"I was just wondering what made you choose accounting as your field of study?"

She had a feeling he'd pulled that question out of his hat, but she answered anyway. "Math was my best subject. The guidance counselor at school suggested I study business and the program at the U of M looked interesting."

"And did you enjoy it?"

She shrugged. The classes on accounting, statistics, management and finance had come easily to her. "I was good at it."

"Math and science were my best subjects, too. Did you ever consider something else like, say, vet school?"

"Mom mentioned the idea," she admitted. "But as you've already seen, I'm too squeamish."

"Yet, you have a way with animals. Your dog. Your horses."

"Yes. But I love them so much I can't stand to see them suffer." A vet had to have the ability to be rational and objective. She could never stand back dispassionately when an animal was hurting. "I even have a hard time helping with branding. I know it's necessary, that the calves don't hurt for long, but it always breaks my heart, all the same."

"And here I thought you were so tough."

"Did you really?"

"I remember you jumping off the bluffs on the far side of Cold Coffee Lake. That's a thirty-foot drop."

"Brock dared me."

"You were only ten years old at the time." He shook his head as if he still couldn't believe it.

"And scared to death," she confessed. "But it was fun after the first time." When it came to her *own* safety, she could be daring enough. It was the suffering of others—particularly helpless animals—that got to her the most.

They talked some more.

Farley told her about going to university, then vet school. He talked about his parents and how they'd decided to move to Arizona when he turned thirty.

"One thing I'll always be grateful for. My dad sat me down for a talk when I finished high school. He told me that while my grandfather and father had both been vets, I shouldn't feel pressured to follow in their footsteps. He told me I could do whatever I wanted with my life, and even though I had no doubt about choosing the veterinary field, I was always grateful to him for making sure I knew I had a choice."

"Wow," Cassidy said. "I couldn't imagine my mother having a talk like that with any of us kids."

"She wants you all to work at Coffee Creek."

"You noticed that, too, huh?"

He laughed, and after a second, so did she.

At one point Cassidy noticed a movement in some brush about twenty yards in the distance. The long grass swished and she caught a glimpse of gray. "Was that a coyote?"

"Yup. The females are nursing the young in their dens this time of year. Which means the males have been booted out and are feeling a little nastier than usual. There seem to be more around than usual. I was at Straws Monahan's the other day and he said they lost a couple barn cats last week. They suspected a coyote was involved."

"Oh, those poor kitties. I heard the coyotes howling last night. I was safe in the barn, yet even so it was kind of spooky."

"They won't bother us on the horses," Farley assured her.

It was Farley who first noticed the time. "We'd better head back. I should check in with my office. Liz will be having a fit."

"She likes to keep a tight rein on you," Cassidy said, remembering how protective the other woman had been on the phone, how quick to tell her that Farley was dating Amber Ellis.

"Too tight at times. But she's so darn good at what she does I put up with it." He glanced around the landscape. "It would be good to give the horses a drink. Is that a creek bed over there?"

Cassidy shielded her eyes and looked where he pointed, to a grassy bank and a large grove of shrubbery with some stunted pine trees, as well. They'd gained quite a lot of elevation and trees never grew as tall at this altitude.

"You're right. I think we've actually run up to the boundary of the Turner ranch. That's Silver Creek over there."

"Perfect." Farley signaled Chickweed to move toward the creek and Cassidy followed on Lucy. They dismounted by a clearing in the trees and let the horses free to drink their fill.

Cassidy scanned her surroundings, realizing that they'd ended up at the site of an old cattle shelter that had been used by the Turner family in the years when their operation had been as large as the Lamberts'.

Sure enough, on the other side of the creek, partially

hidden by the bushy ponderosa pine, were the charred remains of an old barn.

Farley noticed it at the same time as she did. He whistled.

"This is the place where that vagrant died, isn't it?"

Cassidy nodded. B.J. and one of his buddies, Hunter Moody, had been out partying here with some friends when a storm blew in. Lightning had set the place on fire, and while all of B.J.'s friends had escaped without harm, unknown to them a young vagrant—passed out in the loft above their heads—had perished. The body had never been identified and everyone assumed the man was a vagrant from another state.

"I was only nine at the time, but I'll never forget Sheriff Smith coming to our door and taking B.J. and my dad in for questioning. I thought they'd been arrested and were going to jail and I'd never see them again."

"I was worried, too. Not that I believed B.J. had done anything wrong, but my parents weren't keen on letting me hang out with your brothers for a while. A lot of people in the community believed B.J. and Hunter set that fire on purpose."

"Small towns and rumors." Cassidy shrugged them off. She knew her brother would never do anything like that. Still, she had a morbid impulse to check out the old barn. She decided to toss a challenge to Farley. "Want to take a look?"

He hesitated. "We'd have to cross the creek."

At the narrowest point, the creek was still a good eight feet across. And about two feet deep.

"We could do it on horseback," she replied.

"That we could."

They swung back up into their saddles, and Lucy and

Chickweed gamely waded to the other side. As Cassidy dismounted, she realized this was the first time she'd ever set foot on Silver Creek Ranch property. Thinking back to her brief encounter with Maddie Turner earlier that day, she didn't think her aunt would mind.

"I'm amazed this place is still standing." Farley circled the charred structure, which was leaning decidedly to the east.

"Rain saved it from burning completely to the ground," Cassidy remembered.

"That's right. They said the vagrant died of smoke inhalation."

"I wonder if we'll ever know who he was."

"He must not have had any family, or someone would have tracked him down by now. I wouldn't suggest you go in there, Cass. It doesn't look safe."

"I agree." Cassidy took a last glance at the decrepit old barn, then whistled for Lucy.

Instead she found Farley. He'd moved closer to her and was looking at her in a way that reminded her of that night four years ago.

She hitched her thumbs in the belt loops of her jeans, trying to pretend her heart hadn't suddenly started to pound.

He moved a little closer, this time near enough to reach out and touch the side of her face.

How could a finger so hard with calluses feel so tender?

"At the Harvest Dance…was that some game you were playing?"

"Why are you bringing that up again? I said I was sorry."

"That's fine. I'm still wondering why you did it. That guy. Did you ever see him again?"

"No. It wasn't about him. I just felt…over my head. That's all."

Understanding shone in his eyes then. "You were scared."

She nodded.

"There are nine years between us. It's a big gap."

"Back then it was." She could hardly believe she'd said that. As if to imply it *wasn't* a big gap now. That she and Farley…

"Well, it was probably just as well. If you hadn't pulled that stunt, I would have ended up kissing you good-night. And God only knows what would have happened next."

She swallowed. He hadn't kissed her then. But she was pretty sure he was going to kiss her now. And she wanted him to.

In fact she wanted him so badly right now it seemed as if nothing else really signified. She could remember how it had felt to be in his arms, and she wanted that sensation again. And more.

She wanted him to kiss her the way a real man would kiss a woman. As if he meant it. As if he were claiming her for all time.

Chapter 8

But Farley didn't move any closer. And he made no move to kiss her, either.

Instead he handed Cassidy the reins to Lucy, which he'd been holding with his other hand.

She stared at him for a moment, confused. What had this been about? Was he toying with her? Or had he just told her that the age gap between them had been too big before and still was today?

"Is this about getting even with me?" she finally asked.

"What the hell does that mean?"

"It means you were going to kiss me. Then you backed off. Like you're trying to teach me a lesson or something."

He looked exasperated. "You're the one who just told me how desperately you want to work in Billings. Explain to me why it would make any sense at all for me to kiss you."

"Then why did you look like you wanted to?"

"Lord, woman, you're going to drive me crazy. For the record, I'm not the kind of guy who plays games when it comes to love. Teaching you some kind of 'lesson' was the last thing on my mind."

"Well, then." She put her hands on her hips, not ready to let this go. "What *was* on your mind, then?"

"Four years ago it seemed like you'd changed into a different sort of person. I guess today I was thinking you hadn't changed as much as I'd thought you had."

"And is that a good thing?"

"Damn it, Cassidy, I don't want to discuss this anymore. You've got your life plan and I've got mine. Let's leave it at that. And now can we please make tracks?"

He was already astride Chickweed by the time she recovered her senses enough to mount Lucy and follow his lead across the creek back onto Coffee Creek land.

They didn't push their horses, but they didn't dawdle, either. They made up time by cutting through to an access road and taking a more direct route back to the ranch.

Suddenly it was all business between them, which left Cassidy disconcerted, but also—*face it*—relieved. Kissing Farley would have been such a huge mistake. Thank goodness he'd been smart enough not to go there.

And now that they were back at the barn, she felt guilty for ever having left. Finnegan didn't even twitch an ear when she went to say hello to him. She noticed he'd drunk some of his water but hadn't touched his feed.

Though they'd taken Lucy and Chickweed a lot farther than they'd intended, both horses seemed better for the fresh air and exercise. Still, Farley wouldn't let them out with the other horses until they'd been tested and found clear of infection.

"They should have absolutely no contact with Finnegan, or anything he touches. Unfortunately, not all horses who've had strangles develop an immunity to it."

Cassidy groaned. So now she had to keep two areas separate within the barn. One for recovering horses and one for horses still battling the infection.

"I know it's more work, but the cleaner you keep things, the sooner this will be all behind you."

Cassidy settled Lucy and Chickweed in fresh stalls, then went to check on Finnegan again. Farley was just finishing up his examination.

She slipped into the other side of the stall and laid her face against Finnegan's dear neck. "You need to eat, sweetie." She looked over at Farley. "There has to be something more we can do."

She was consumed with guilt for having taken off this afternoon, while poor Finnegan suffered all on his own.

"I'm sorry. At this point all we can do is try to keep him comfortable. Anti-inflammatory drugs and penicillin is what we've got. You can try hot compresses, but I don't think they'll be as effective with him as they were with the others."

Cassidy carried Farley's grim words in with her that evening as she joined her mother at the dinner table. "Lucy and Chickweed are almost completely recovered, but Finnegan isn't getting any better. Farley says there's not much more we can do for him."

"Given Finnegan's age, I'm not surprised."

That struck Cassidy as a little harsh, but then her mother had never been sentimental about any of their animals—certainly not Sky, whom she'd tried to ban from the house, until Cassidy wore her out after years of sneaking her into her room to sleep every night.

No, her mother saved all her maternal instincts for her children, and Cassidy supposed she shouldn't fault her for that.

"I've been thinking about Winnie and the baby," Olive said, between bites of her salad. "I've decided to send Winnie a note. I won't mention the baby. I'll just say that I hope she is doing better and hope to see her back in Coffee Creek one day."

Cassidy was surprised at her mother's restraint. "That sounds like a smart plan." She waited a beat then asked, "Any calls for me today?" She already checked for messages. There weren't any.

"Not that I noticed. But I wasn't around much. The meeting took most of my afternoon."

Anxious to avoid that subject, Cassidy jumped into another topic. "Farley and I took Lucy and Chickweed out for a little exercise. They seemed good as new."

"You and Farley? That's nice." Olive smiled at her approvingly. "He's a good man. Did you know his land abuts ours for about a mile on our western boundary?"

"I had no idea. I didn't even realize he owned much land." She'd never been on Farley's property, except when she'd taken Sky for her vaccines to the clinic which was next to the ranch house.

"Oh, yes. The Farleys were big-time ranchers back in the day. Over the years they've sold a lot of their land, but they still own about a thousand acres." Her mother removed their salad plates and returned with bowls of southwestern-style chicken chili. "So where did you go for your ride?"

"Farther than we intended." Cassidy reached for her spoon enthusiastically. "Did the housekeeper make this?"

"Bonny? Yes. She made cookies, too, if you have any room."

Cassidy took a taste and made a note to thank Bonny the next time she saw her.

"You and Farley must have had fun," her mother said. "You were gone for quite a long time."

"The horses needed exercise." She had a feeling her mother's matchmaking instincts were on alert and didn't want to feed that any more than she had to. "Before we knew it, we'd reached Silver Creek. Remember the old barn that almost burned down sixteen years ago? It's still standing, though only barely."

The light drained from her mother's eyes, and her smile vanished, leaving traces of fine lines branching out from her puckered lips. "That place should be razed."

Cassidy had never thought of her mother as old. She had far too much vitality for that. Yet, now she could see that the passing years were taking their toll. Her mother may not be old, but she *was* aging. And clearly she *did not* want to talk about the events of sixteen years ago.

"Eat your chili, Cassidy. It's getting cold."

The next morning a low front moved over central Montana and Cassidy woke up to a heavy, gray sky with the scent of rain on the wind.

Her mother had convinced her to sleep in the house for a change, but first thing, even before brushing her teeth, she pulled on her jeans and a flannel shirt, and went out to check the horses. Sky wanted to come with her, but she convinced her dog to stay inside where it was nice and dry.

It had rained some in the night. The gravel paths were slick and the trees and grasses glistened with fresh moisture. She studied the sky and figured it would likely be raining off-and-on all day.

Rather than head back for a rain slicker, she dashed to the barn where she found everyone in pretty much the same shape as she'd left them the day before.

Lucy and Chickweed chowed down their breakfasts and swished their tails impatiently as she cleaned their stalls.

"I know you want to be out with the others, but trust me. Today you should be happy to be inside."

Finnegan was the same. No better, but hopefully no worse, either. She brushed him down gently, more to give her an excuse to spend time with him than anything else. She put on fresh hot compresses and changed out his water and his feed, hoping something fresh might entice his appetite.

But he just looked at her with listless eyes.

"Oh, sweetie, don't give up. You have to fight this thing, okay?"

Finnegan shuffled his feet.

"That a boy," she encouraged, holding a handful of warm mush to his mouth.

He took a taste, then changed his mind and averted his head, just like a toddler refusing a nasty spoonful of vegetables.

"Oh, Finnegan." She didn't know what to do. She really didn't.

The rest of that week passed in much the same way. Lots of rain, lots of mud and an endless routine of disinfecting, nursing, hoping and praying.

Meanwhile, in the main house the painters came—and went.

The antique armoire was delivered and the old desk removed.

On Wednesday Olive went to town and returned with the finished duvet, cushion covers and a new set of drapes, which Cassidy helped her hang.

When they were done, Olive surveyed the room with satisfaction. "Good. That's one job done."

Cassidy didn't dare say that she'd liked the room better the old way. Knowing that her mother was waiting for a reaction, she forced a smile. "It's beautiful, Mom. Like a posh hotel room. Thanks."

"My pleasure, Cassidy. I'm just glad you like it." Her mom patted her hand, then left the room.

After a week of rain, the air was muggy and close in the barn, yet Cassidy went back to sleeping on the cot in order to be close to Finnegan. As her mother packed for an overnight trip to Billings to look at some stock, Olive rolled her eyes and declared that Cassidy's devotion to Finnegan was overkill.

"You have to remember, he's just a horse. When I asked you to take care of this outbreak, I never expected you to provide 24/7 service. You'll wear yourself out at this rate."

It wasn't that Cassidy enjoyed sleeping on the cot.

If Finnegan had shown even the slightest degree of improvement, she would have been glad to spend a night in her newly jazzed-up bedroom.

But Finnegan still wasn't eating. And he'd lost a significant amount of weight thanks to the strangles.

Running her hand over the horse's belly that evening, Cassidy could count his ribs.

"Oh, I wish you'd eat. Just a little."

But Finnegan refused even water this evening. Another very bad sign.

Cassidy was sitting on the edge of her cot, wondering if she should call Farley, when she heard footsteps crunching on gravel, then the barn door rolling open.

In came Corb. He had a thermos and a paper bag in hand.

"Laurel noticed the light was on out here again. Seems like you're spending a lot of nights in the barn these days, Cass."

"I feel better when I'm close to him."

"You better be careful you don't make yourself sick." He handed her the thermos and bag.

Cassidy checked them out. Hot coffee and a chicken sandwich. "Yum. Thank Laurel for me, okay?"

"Will do." He started to leave, then hesitated. "You know it doesn't help anything, you sleeping out here."

"Maybe. But I couldn't stand it if I woke up one morning and came out here to find—" She couldn't say the rest without giving in to tears. Finnegan had been a good, loyal horse and there was no way she was going to leave him to die alone. No way.

Not that she'd written him off, the way she could tell her mother—and even Corb—had done.

They didn't understand what a proud spirit her horse had. He could beat this. He *would* beat this.

Corb sighed and shook his head. "How about I stay here tonight and you sleep in the house?"

"Thanks, but no. This is my job and Finnegan is my horse. Besides, you have a wife and a baby who need you."

He chuckled drily. "Now that you mention it, I might get more rest out here than I do in there."

"Maybe so. But I need to be here."

"Stubborn girl." He laid a hand on the top of her head, a rare gesture of affection. "I guess I'll see you in the morning, then."

"Good night, Corb. Thanks again for the food." The sandwich was delicious and there was a note at the bottom of the bag explaining that the coffee was decaf so she shouldn't be nervous to drink it all.

Cassidy had to admit that the hot, flavorful coffee went down nicely with her sandwich.

She was just pouring herself a second cupful when she noticed two things. A slight breeze cooling her neck. And Sky was no longer lounging by her cot.

She jumped to her feet, right away noticing that Corb had left the barn door ajar. Had Sky slipped out?

And then Cassidy heard an awful growl, then barking and a cry of pain.

Cassidy grabbed a pitchfork and ran out the open door, triggering the motion detector lights as she raced into the yard, then around to the pasture, following the terrible sounds of canine growling and yelping.

She was out of range of the floodlights now, tripping over the uneven ground as she ran. The full moon was low, casting an eerie orange glow over the field. A flash of movement caught her eye, and then she saw them, the coyote circling Sky, about to make a second attack. Sky, obviously wounded, was a sitting duck.

"Get out of here, you awful thing!" Cassidy charged with the pitchfork and only then did the coyote start to slink away. But not after at least one yearning look at the prey he'd almost felled.

"Oh, Sky! Are you all right?"

Sky's soft whimper was truly pathetic. Cassidy dropped the pitchfork and tenderly caressed her dog. As she touched the fur around her neck, she felt a slick of something warm and wet.

The smell of blood on her hand was unmistakable.

"Oh, Sky, how badly did he hurt you?" She gathered the dog in her arms. Cassidy could haul a thirty-pound bag of feed without too much trouble. She could damn well carry her dog, too, if she had to.

But where should she go? What should she do?

Cassidy moved as fast as her shaking legs would carry her. Her mother was in Billings—should she call Corb?

No. The answer came to her in a flash of certainty.

She had to take Sky to Farley. He was only a fifteen-minute drive away.

The walk to her truck seemed to take forever. Trying not to cry, she murmured comforting words to her dog. "It's okay. Farley will fix you."

But what if Farley couldn't? It would be more than she could stand to lose her dog in this awful way. That damn coyote. And her, too, for not noticing Corb hadn't closed the door all the way.

Cassidy settled Sky in the foot well of the passenger side, then grabbed the blanket she kept in her truck for emergencies and wrapped it around her dog.

As she reached for the keys she'd left dangling in the ignition—a lazy habit of hers when she was out on the ranch—she realized her fingers were slick with blood. She wiped them clean on her jeans, then started driving.

She went as fast as she dared, all too aware of the potential hazard of wildlife crossing the road. She could do nothing to stop her tears, but she opened her window so the wind and cool air would clear her head.

A phone call warning Farley of her arrival would be a good idea.

But she didn't dare reach for the mobile phone in her pocket.

She supposed this wouldn't be the first time the vet had been woken from his sleep by a distraught rancher.

Farley wasn't having a good night. He'd finally found the time to go out for dinner with Amber this evening. When he'd dropped her home, he'd told her that he appreciated how patient she'd been with him, but he didn't think their relationship was going to work out.

"That's okay," she'd said.

She hadn't pressed him for details, not that he would have given any if she had.

How could he tell Amber that it was another woman who put him in a fever whenever he was around her? Cassidy Lambert. If it wasn't for that damn case of strangles she might have come and gone from Coffee Creek without him even knowing about it.

That would have been better.

Maybe then his relationship with Amber would have stood a chance…

But now Cassidy was in his head again. In his thoughts during the day and his dreams at night.

He couldn't stop thinking about her. Wanting her. Cursing himself for not kissing her when he'd had the chance. So what if he couldn't have her forever? Right now one night seemed like it would be enough.

*Really? Just one night? Is that the kind of man you
are now?*

His sheets were tangled from all his tossing and
turning, and a fine sweat had broken out over his skin.
When the sound of a vehicle pulling into his yard carried through his open window, at first he thought he had
to be hearing things.

But there was no mistaking the heavy knocking at
his door.

And then a voice, crying out for help.

"Farley. Please, Farley! You have to help."

Good God, it was Cassidy. What had happened?

He was out of bed and into his jeans and T-shirt in
less than five seconds. Down the hall and to the door in
five seconds more. He twisted the lock and pulled on
the handle. And in stumbled Cassidy, with Sky in her
arms and blood everywhere.

She'd been crying and her hair was windblown and
wild.

"What happened?"

"Sky was attacked by a coyote. Right outside the
home barn. Oh, Farley, she's lost a lot of blood."

He'd already slipped on his boots. Now he gently
eased Sky out of her arms. "Follow me. We'll go to the
clinic and get a proper look at her."

The motion-detector lights flicked on as they hurried
along the stone path that led to his office. He always
locked up at night, protecting the expensive equipment
and drugs that might be the target of thieves. But the
keys were still in his jeans and he shifted Sky's weight
to his left arm so he could pull them out.

He shouldered the door open, then flipped the light
switch. In the sudden bright halogen glare he could see

that Cassidy was drawn and pale. She blinked at the onslaught of so much light, then she shuddered. "The blood. It's everywhere…"

She was sounding like Lady Macbeth now, and he was worried.

But then she'd told him, hadn't she? *I'm terrible with blood…*

"Sit down, Cass. Now. Before you faint." He placed Sky gently on the aluminum examining table that Liz would have disinfected before she went home this evening. Sky, poor thing, was shaking. Though she didn't fight Farley, it was Cassidy she kept her gaze trained on.

And Cassidy, who had done as he'd asked and collapsed into the chair by the table, reached out a hand to her dog. "It's okay, Sky. You're going to be okay."

Though her voice was reassuring, there was fear in her eyes when she looked at Farley. Now that she'd accomplished her mission and delivered her dog to help, Cassidy's tears started again. He could see them welling up, then overflowing to her cheekbones, where they hovered for several seconds before spilling down to her jaw. He wanted—badly—to comfort her.

But first he had to see if he could save her dog.

He found the source of the bleeding, parted the border collie's long hair and examined the gaping wound.

As was to be expected, the coyote had gone for Sky's neck, and had managed to make a good-sized gash.

But it wasn't too deep, thankfully. "We'll clean this up, then a few stitches will patch this nicely."

"So she's going to live?"

"The injury isn't life-threatening," he was happy to reassure her. He gave Sky a quick once-over but found no other obvious signs of trauma. "We'll booster her rabies vaccine just to be sure, but it seems she came out of that fight okay. Strange that the coyote went after a dog this size."

As he reached for his supplies, he glanced at Cassidy. "Tell me what happened."

She explained how Corb had brought her out a sandwich and coffee, then left the door ajar.

"As soon as I realized Sky wasn't in the barn anymore, I jumped up to look for her. And at that exact moment, Sky barked and I heard growling and snarling." She shivered. "So I grabbed a pitchfork and chased off the coyote. But I was too late."

"Actually, you probably saved her life." Farley wasn't at all surprised that Cassidy would be prepared to jump into battle against the coyote to save Sky's life. If the attacker had been a wolf, or even a bear, he knew she would have done the exact same thing. "Sky's older now. Slower and weaker. I guess the coyote figured he could take her."

Fifteen minutes later, Sky was all cleaned and stitched up. He'd had to shave some hair around her wound, so she looked bedraggled.

Not unlike her owner.

Cassidy rose shakily from her seat. "Thanks so much. You'll be mighty tired tomorrow—I'm sorry about that."

As if he cared. He liked the fact that Cassidy had come running to him when she needed help—even if it was just his vet skills she'd wanted.

She assessed Sky doubtfully. "Will it hurt her if I pick her up?"

"Let me." Carefully he scooped the border collie into his arms. Sky barely whimpered.

Cassidy opened the door for him and locked up behind them. As he started on the path back to the house, he heard her behind him.

"Farley? Where are you going? My truck's over here."

"I know where your truck is."

"But it's late. You need some sleep and I should get home and check on Finnegan."

"Has his condition worsened since I saw him last?"

"About the same, I'd say."

"Then he'll be fine until morning."

"That's what Mom and Corb said. It's easier to believe coming from you. So you think he's getting better?"

She looked so hopeful he hated to reply with the truth. "I can't promise that. But he has some time left. And maybe he'll rally."

She pressed her lips together with fresh determination. "Then I have to go."

He studied her pale face, bloodstained hands and clothing, and sagging posture. It would be better for both of them if he let her do just that. But the Lambert family had already suffered a tragic loss due to a car crash. So he pointed out the obvious. "You're in no condition to drive."

"But—"

"Get your ass in the house, Cassidy." He tipped his head toward Sky. "Don't forget—I have a hostage."

Chapter 9

The man was wonderful—he'd saved her dog—but also infuriating. His attitude right now reminded her of his reaction that night four years ago, when he'd insisted that since he'd driven her to the dance, he was damn well driving her home, as well.

She wanted to argue.

But she was too tired.

She also couldn't deny the flood of gratitude she was feeling toward him right now.

She couldn't have stood it if Sky hadn't been okay. To lose her beloved pet of fourteen years in such a bloody and violent way would have been too cruel. It was bad enough that Sky had been hurt and traumatized.

So she fell in behind Farley as he led her around the side of the house. When he paused at the door, she hurried ahead to open it for him, but though Sky was pretty heavy, he still waited for her to enter first.

On her previous visits to Farley's place she'd never seen anything other than his main foyer and the clinic. This first glimpse of his private space impressed her. The large mudroom had tiled floors, stainless steel countertops, a laundry area and a huge closet. It was practical, but also beautiful, with a calm color scheme and some humorous prints of farm animals, including one with a bird on a cow's head.

The clicking of nails on tile announced the arrival of Farley's own two dogs.

Cassidy had met Tom and Dick before and she had a chance to say hello to each of them, before Farley ordered them out of the room.

"You can shower in there." He pointed to a room next to the closet. "A clean robe is on the hook. Use that while I throw your jeans and shirt into the wash. Just hand them out the door."

She shook her head. "I'll shower when I get home."

For an answer, he just pointed at the mirror over the laundry tub sink. She stared at herself for several long seconds before silently going into the bathroom.

Here, again, she was impressed. The place was spotless, modern and almost spalike. The sink was long—like a trough—and the shower was the kind with a half-dozen different body spray heads as well as an overhead rain shower nozzle.

Quickly she stripped and passed out her jeans and T-shirt. The harsh iron smell of blood was deep in her lungs. She thought she'd never be rid of it.

But the mint-scented shampoo helped. So did the massaging jets of warm water. Worried that she was going to empty Farley's hot water tank, she finally forced herself to turn off the taps after fifteen minutes.

There had been no conditioner for her hair, so brushing it out would have been impossible, even if Farley had owned a comb up to the job. His own little brush, set neatly to the side of the sink, would snap in two if she tried to run it through all these snarls.

Still, she was clean.

She slipped into the white robe, disregarding the slippers that were lined up beneath them. They were much too big, and anyway, she was toasty warm after that great shower.

She walked past the churning washing machine into a kitchen that took her breath away. Lights over the stove and recessed around the moldings showcased French Country white cabinets and vintage-looking Heartland appliances.

The kitchen was divided from the family room by a large island and on the other side she saw Farley by a beautiful river-rock fireplace, adding a log to a couple that were already snapping. And right next to the hearth, Sky was settled in as cozy as could be, with Farley's dogs a polite distance away.

There was even soft music playing. And a pot of tea and cookies on the massive wood coffee table.

"Wow. This place is pretty gorgeous."

At the sound of her voice, Sky raised her head, but was too weak, or perhaps too traumatized, to leave the blanket Farley had placed for her by the heat of the fire.

"I did some renovations a few years ago," Farley said as if they had been nothing significant.

"I'll say." She glanced around, noticing the art on the walls, the well-placed area rugs, lamps and an outstanding bronze of a cowboy wrestling a steer on the table behind the sofa.

All the little touches that men weren't supposed to bother with.

"Did someone help you?"

"Like a designer, you mean?"

Actually, she'd been thinking of a girlfriend. But she nodded.

"Not really. The people at the furniture and paint stores offered suggestions. But I had an idea what I wanted."

The way he looked at her when he said that last bit made her very aware of her naked skin beneath the smooth cotton of the robe. Yes, Farley was the sort of person who knew what he wanted.

And what he didn't. The snub he'd given her this afternoon when they were out riding still burned, even though she knew she wasn't being logical.

She didn't want Farley. She wanted the job in Billings. And to give a more serious relationship with Josh a shot.

The strangles infection had sidelined her for a few weeks. That was why she hadn't thought much about Josh since she'd arrived and been too busy to answer his calls and text messages.

Is that really true?

Or is the plain truth that Josh can't stack up next to a man like Farley?

The vet had changed into a clean T-shirt and jeans while she'd been showering. The clothes weren't tight, but they couldn't hide his strong muscular build. His dark hair gleamed and so did his eyes, set off to perfection by those sharp cheekbones.

Everything he was she could see in his face. Proud. Powerful. Most intimidating of all…perceptive.

"Don't be scared. This isn't some grand seduction plan."

"I wasn't thinking that," she said quickly.

She went to sit on the hearth, carefully wrapping the robe around her legs so just her ankles and bare feet were peeking out. She placed a light hand on Sky's back, and her dog relaxed back to sleep.

He could *say* he had no plans to seduce her. But she'd have to be blind not to see the heat in his eyes. Just like she'd seen it earlier when they were at Silver Creek.

"Have some tea and a cookie," he suggested. "Sugar is good after a shock."

Her mind flashed back to the terrible fight between Sky and the coyote. The raw, desperate noises. The smell of the blood. Sky's limp body and her pleading eyes.

She moved forward to the floor, settling in front of the spread he'd laid out, and took a bite of the oatmeal chocolate chip cookies. They weren't the kind from a package.

"Don't tell me you bake as well as excel in interior design?"

A corner of his mouth turned up. "Those are from Liz. Have I ever told you that she manages my life?"

"Right down to baking cookies. That's some assistant you have. I'd keep her, if I was you." She poured some tea for herself and when she looked at Farley and he nodded, she filled his mug, too.

"It's why I put up with her meddling. She's the one who set me up with Amber."

Cassidy had been lifting the mug to her mouth when

he said this. She paused...*steady now*...then sipped. "And how is that working out?"

"Not as good as Liz hoped. Amber's lovely. But she lives a forty-five-minute drive from here and I don't have much free time."

A forty-five-minute drive wasn't that bad. Not in Montana.

"You're going to have slim pickings if you're looking for a single woman who lives closer than that."

She polished off the rest of the cookie, not daring to meet his gaze. *Her* ranch was fifteen minutes from his, but that meant nothing. First of all, she wasn't going to be living there much longer. And secondly, he hadn't really broken up with Amber because of the distance between them. If he'd really liked her, he would be willing to drive double that far to see her.

"Maybe I'm not looking. Period. Me and the dogs, we're pretty comfortable the way we are."

"No one you can count on more than your dog," she agreed. She reached across the table again. "These are so good I'm going to have another."

"Please do. And take a seat, would you? Your legs have to be cramping down there."

"I should go home."

"You don't have any clothes," he said calmly.

Right. She felt such a fool. Awkwardly she made her way to the sofa, settling on the far cushion, then leaning back into the softly plumped, leather-covered seat.

The sound of a buzzer startled her but with his same steady calm, Farley got to his feet. "Sounds like the wash cycle is finished. I'll throw your things into the dryer. Is that okay?"

"Sure. Thanks."

While he was gone, she gave the room a closer look. There were photos of his parents on a built-in shelving unit. Also a picture of him graduating from college and another with him and the dogs.

On the lower shelf she found a chessboard with pieces carved from jade. By the time he returned from the laundry, she had a game set up on the table.

"Do you play?" she asked. Her father had taught her and her brothers during the long, cold winters of their childhood. Corb and Brock had never enjoyed it much, but she and B.J. had both been keen.

"I used to. With my dad."

"Me, too. And since we have time to kill before the clothes dry…"

If he realized she was using the game as a safety barrier between them, he gave no sign of it.

"Okay. Let's do it. You can be white."

Cassidy started with a classic opening, placing her center pawn two squares forward.

Farley countered with a similar move. "So you asked about my love life. It's only fair I get to ask about yours."

"Hmm?" She moved her next pawn forward one space.

"Corb tells me there's a guy in your life. Josh."

She frowned. "Corb shouldn't talk about things he doesn't know about." She'd never mentioned Josh to her mother or her brothers. They only knew about him because he'd phoned the house number a few times—despite her request that he only call her on her mobile phone.

"So you're not serious?"

No question that Josh wanted them to be. "I'm not sure."

Farley moved his next pawn and she countered with a move from her rook.

"Interesting," he said.

"What? My relationship with Josh? Or the move I just made in chess?"

His hand hovered over the board as he contemplated his next play. Her gaze lingered on his hands. They were strong, yes. But they also had a long-fingered grace. As a vet he needed both qualities to meet the demands of a job that required him to handle six-hundred-pound cows and horses and yet also perform delicate surgical procedures.

"I'm just saying, it's interesting. You tell me you're a free woman, and I'm a free man. Just because I didn't kiss you this afternoon didn't mean I didn't want to."

Cassidy narrowed her eyes. He was making moves here that had nothing to do with chess pieces. "You said this wasn't a seduction scene."

If it had been, that would have scared her off. Right? Then why didn't she feel scared *now?*

"I said I wasn't *planning* a seduction. If you decide you'd like to make love, though, I wouldn't say no."

Just hearing him say those words started her pulse racing. "Like I'd do that."

"Agreed, it's a long shot." Still, he reached for her hand. And she let him have it.

"Besides, you aren't looking for a woman in your life."

"I wasn't talking about a lifetime. As I understand it, that isn't what you have to offer, either."

She ought to be shocked at his suggestion that they have a one-night stand. But the way he was touching her hand, running his thumb in slow circles on her palm, was so hypnotizing.

"That's pretty scandalous, Dan Farley."

Was that really her, sounding so bold? But she *felt*

bold. That was the thing. So strange and unlike her. With her eyes she willed him to come closer and when he placed a hand on her shoulder, she touched him, too.

She could see his eyes so clearly now, and what she saw thrilled her. A dark, pulsing energy was swirling around them, blocking out the world.

But all the anticipation was nothing compared to how she felt when he actually lowered his lips to hers. His kiss unleashed something inside of her, a power and a desperate need that she hadn't even realized she possessed.

Oh, Farley! She tangled her fingers in his hair as their kiss deepened. His arms banded around her waist, pulling her closer, and the contact with his solid, heated chest only heightened her pleasure and her desire…for *more.*

But just as she was ready to slip her robe off her shoulders out of an aching need to have him touch her more intimately, a buzzer sounded from the mudroom again.

The dryer.

Damn, awful timing.

Farley's kisses began to gentle. He pressed his lips to her cheek, to the corner of her eyes, then the top of her head.

She struggled to understand. He'd started this. Why was he stopping?

She tried to find the answer in his eyes, but he had them closed. She watched as he swallowed. Then took a deep breath.

"Cass. Honey. It's time you went home."

"You're serious? What was this that just happened?"

"You have to admit it was more fun than chess." He touched the side of her face gently, then stood. "Let's see if your jeans are dry."

* * *

She'd never met a more infuriating man. It was the middle of the night and Cassidy was driving slowly, out of consideration for Sky's injuries, wanting to keep any jostling to a minimum.

So she vented her frustration by pounding her palms on the steering wheel.

He'd kissed her because he'd found the chess game boring.

Really?

So all those sparks—all that sexual tension—that had been in her mind only?

She didn't believe it.

But what if it were true? Maybe he'd just wanted to humiliate her the way she'd embarrassed him that night at the Harvest Dance. Because she'd been ready to strip off her robe and make love with him. And he'd turned her away.

As it had turned out, her jeans were still damp, but she'd put them on without complaint. Farley had walked her to the truck, but only so he could help settle Sky in for the drive home.

"Thanks again for fixing my dog," she'd said stiffly, as she climbed into the driver's seat.

There wasn't enough light to see any expression in his eyes as she drove away. Maybe there hadn't been any expression worth seeing.

Farley stood in the driveway long past the time that Cassidy's taillights had disappeared from view. The cool air helped bring his libido back under control. If he hadn't put a halt to it, they could have been making love right now.

But he'd put on the brakes. He didn't know if he'd just done the smartest thing in his life. Or the stupidest.

With eerie timing, a marauding gang of coyotes let out a series of yips that echoed in the hollow where his great-grandfather had built their home. For all Farley knew one of them had been Sky's attacker, and yet he couldn't feel any animosity toward the animals.

In fact, he felt a certain kinship. He couldn't deny he had an urge of his own to howl at the moon tonight.

At least she was no longer scared of him. If anything, she'd discovered her own power. Maybe now he should be scared of her.

Exhaustion had set in by the time Cassidy reached Coffee Creek Ranch. After checking Finnegan and finding him holding his own, she decided to take everyone's advice and finish out the night in her own bed, with Sky sleeping at her feet as usual.

The unfamiliar bedding, the dark shadow of the new armoire against the far wall and the smell of fresh paint were useful for one thing—distracting her from thoughts of Farley.

Her utter tiredness helped, too. She closed her eyes and the next thing she knew the sun was rising, blanketing the horizon with a wash of fresh orange light.

She convinced Sky to stay inside when she went out to do her chores. The storm system had finally passed on, and the day was breaking clear and bright. She took it as another good sign when she was able to convince Finnegan to eat some mush straight from her hand. She was burning his bedding in an area set off from the barns and pastures when she saw Jackson drive up to the equine barn.

He'd either been up awfully early this morning, or he had spent the night away. Could it be a woman?

Somehow she didn't think so. Jackson looked so morose these days—not at all like a man who was enjoying the excitement of a new relationship. Or even the comfort of an older one.

Once she'd extinguished the fire, she decided to see if he would talk to her.

The equine barn was double the size of the one they used for their home horses. Olive had spared no expense in the design or outfitting. She wanted potential buyers to be impressed when they came to check out their herd.

And she'd been even more careful in selecting the breeding stock for the operation. The result was that Coffee Creek Ranch now had the reputation for breeding some of the finest American quarter horses in Montana.

Cassidy found Jackson giving orders to a couple of the hired men. They were monitoring several mares, trying to pick the optimum time for breeding. She waited until they were finished their discussion and asked him how he was doing.

"Fine." He paused, then nodded toward the door. "Want to go for a walk?"

"Sure." She followed him back into the sunshine and out to the pasture where the mares were grazing. She noticed the spring growth had been picked over pretty well, and Jackson must have been thinking the same thing.

"We need to move them out soon, now that the warmer weather seems to be settling in."

Cassidy eyed the herd, looking to see if any of the horses seemed dispirited or uninterested in grazing. "They all seem healthy."

"Yeah. You've done a good job of keeping the infection contained."

A compliment from her foster brother—always a man of few words—was something to be savored. "Thank you."

"You put your heart and soul into it. The way you tackle everything you do." He gave her a little smile. "But you didn't come to me to talk about the strangles, did you?"

Cassidy knew she had to choose her words carefully. Jackson was a grown man with every right to come and go as he pleased without a family inquisition. "I don't mean to pry. I just want to know if everything's okay."

"That's a tough one. Do I still miss Brock each and every day? Yes, I do. But I'm sure all you do, too. What you don't have to feel every day is the responsibility of knowing you contributed to his death."

"That's harsh, Jackson. And totally unfair. If a bolt of lightning had struck the truck, would you have blamed yourself for that, too?"

Jackson's eyes flickered, but he didn't respond. Cassidy sighed out of frustration. "Is that why you were out last night? Did it have something to do with Brock?"

"In a way." He studied her face for a bit, as if weighing consequences in his mind. Then he seemed to come to a conclusion. Placing a hand on her shoulder he said, "You know Brock used to go over to Silver Creek Ranch and help out your aunt now and then."

"Yes. I heard about that."

"He thought it was totally bogus the way the family had cut her off."

"It never felt right," Cassidy agreed. "But there must be reasons."

"According to Corb, Maddie didn't tell your mother when their father had his stroke. Your mother won't forgive Maddie for denying her the chance to say her farewells before he died."

"That's awful!" Cassidy knew she'd always treasure her own last moments with her father. He'd had his first heart attack in the morning, been rushed to the hospital in Great Falls, then passed away two days later. Her mother had been by his side the entire time and Cassidy and her brothers had all had a chance to see him, too. "Did Brock know that?"

"I don't think so. But I suspect he would have said that there are always two sides to a story. Since he passed on, I've felt it was my duty to continue where he left off and help Maddie whenever I have free time. That's where I was last night—working until dark reshingling her roof. She invited me to bunk over and I couldn't say no. I could tell she wasn't feeling well and didn't want to be alone."

Cassidy didn't know what to think. She felt sorry for her aunt, but she still wanted to know why Maddie hadn't told Olive when their father had that stroke. Why would anyone deny someone the chance to say farewell to their beloved parent?

"Do you think Mom knew what Brock was up to?"

"No, but your father did."

"Really?"

"Yup. Though his loyalty to your mother made it impossible for him to say so, I think he approved."

Cassidy didn't doubt that. Her father had been such a softie. "Jackson, I feel awful about Maddie Turner. Is there anything I should do?"

"Just stay out of it, Cassidy. It's better if you don't get

involved." He glanced back at the barn. She could tell he didn't want to discuss the topic any further.

She sighed. Why was life always so complicated?

"I should go check on Sky. She had a tussle with a coyote last night and I had to take her to Farley's for some stitches." She made a show of scraping some mud off her boot as she said this, in case her expression gave anything away.

"That explains your hair, I guess."

Cassidy put a hand to her head. She'd forgotten that she still hadn't brushed out all the tangles. "I was covered in blood. Farley made me shower at his place, but he didn't have any conditioner."

"Is that a fact." Jackson looked amused. But only for a moment. "I'm sorry I wasn't home to help you last night. Damn, those coyotes are getting pretty brash if they'll come right up to the yard."

"Maybe it was the full moon." It might explain more than the coyotes' behavior.

Chapter 10

After breakfast, Cassidy decided that Lucy and Chickweed needed some fresh air and exercise. She took Lucy first, into one of the training pens. On a lark, she rolled out three barrels and made a makeshift barrel racing track.

"Ever seen one of these before?" she asked Lucy. "I have a feeling you're going to find this really fun." She tacked up the horse, then walked her through the circuit, letting Lucy familiarize herself with the wooden barrels.

At the first barrel Lucy paused and blew air from her nostrils, and then she grew more frisky, as if she sensed that a game was in the offing and she was anxious to get going.

Lucy seemed like a natural as she traced the distinctive cloverleaf pattern around the barrels. And she instinctively made tight, clean turns around each one.

After just their second trial circuit, Lucy tossed her head and gave a snort as if to say, *I get it. Can we do it faster now?*

So Cassidy urged her back to the imaginary start line. She held her in place for about thirty seconds, then let loose with a holler.

"Yeah! Go, Lucy, go!"

Cassidy laughed as her horse took off, following the path that they'd been tracing earlier, only much faster. She nicked the first barrel and totally trashed the second, but sailed around the third with no incident.

"Not bad. Not bad at all."

Cassidy hadn't realized she had an audience. Suddenly self-conscious, she trotted Lucy to the fence. Farley had his arms resting on the top rung, a big smile on his face.

"Decided to train her to be a barrel racer after all, huh?"

She shook her head. "Just having some fun."

His gaze swept over her, and self-consciously she put a hand to her hair, wishing she'd remembered to put on a hat, or at least pulled the mess into a ponytail or something.

Farley didn't seem any worse for the excitement of the previous night. He looked as strong, calm and unflappable as ever.

"How was Sky this morning?"

"Tired, but good. She ate a little breakfast and had a lot of water." Heat was rising up her neck to her face. It had nothing to do with the exertion of the ride and everything to do with seeing Farley.

Would he mention the kiss?

"That's a good sign." He broke away from the fence.

"Jackson wants me to do some work with his mares this morning. I guess I'd better get started. I heard you laughing, though, and couldn't resist coming to see what you were up to."

He started to walk away, then turned back. "You need to laugh more often. It's a beautiful sound."

By noon, Cassidy had finished exercising both Lucy and Chickweed and given them both a thorough grooming. She managed to coax Finnegan into eating a little more mush and dared to hope that before too long her brave, old mustang would be back to normal. When she'd finished scrubbing up, she modified her route back to the house so she could circle around the equine barn and see if Farley's truck was still parked there. It wasn't.

She saw Jackson and Corb, though, mounted on two of the uninfected ranch horses, preparing to move some of the newly pregnant mares to the northwest pasture.

Inside the house, Bonny was washing the kitchen floor on her hands and knees—the way Olive always insisted it had to be done. Cassidy tiptoed around the tiled area on her way to her bedroom.

"Hey, Bonny. Thanks for the chili the other night. It was delicious."

"Glad you liked it." Bonny sat back on her haunches. "Want me to get you some lunch?"

"No thanks. Since Mom still isn't back from her trip, I thought I'd go into town. Do we need anything while I'm there?"

"Not that I can think of." Bonny went back to washing floors and Cassidy took a shower, using copious amounts of conditioner to untangle her hair.

As she grabbed her wallet to leave, Sky gave her a "please stay here and hang out with me" look. But when

Cassidy asked if she wanted to go in the truck—a word that usually had Sky bounding to her feet—Sky turned her head and pretended she hadn't heard the offer.

Cassidy cranked up the tunes in her truck as she drove—windows down, her hair blowing. It would be a mess again, but who cared. She was relieved the rain had finally stopped. Sunshine was always good for the spirit. When her phone chimed she decided to pull over and see who was trying to reach her.

Maybe… Farley?

Or the accounting firm?

But no, it was just another text message from Josh, frustrated as usual that she wasn't answering his calls. The disappointment she felt when she saw his name told her something that she'd been suspecting ever since she arrived home.

Had seeing Farley again been part of her change of heart?

In all honesty, she couldn't say no.

But that didn't change the fact that her friendly feelings toward Josh would never reach the level of passion and excitement that she'd felt for Farley last night.

She couldn't tell Josh this by text message. So she called him.

As she waited for him to answer, she prepped a little speech in her head. *This time apart has given me time to think...and I've realized that we're just not right for each other...*

Of course, the actual conversation didn't go quite as smoothly as she'd planned.

"You've been leading me on," Josh complained.

Cassidy decided to take this one on the chin, as her brothers would say. "If I have, then I'm sorry."

"Are you? You don't sound it."

Oh, he sounded like a petulant little boy. "Well, I apologize for that, too. I'm sorry for all of it, Josh, but I hope we can still be friends."

To her surprise, he mumbled, "Maybe." Then hung up.

She took a minute to review the conversation. Had she been cruel? But sometimes that was what honesty required. And she'd been that, at least. If they ended up working at the same accounting firm, she'd just hope that Josh would be decent about it.

By the time she reached the Cinnamon Stick, Cassidy was starving. Eugenia and Laurel were handling the tail end of the luncheon rush. Both booths and all four stools were taken, but that didn't worry her. She'd order a sandwich and eat it outside.

"Where's Steph?" she asked her sister-in-law after ordering the Black Forest sandwich special.

"She's had her lunch and now she's napping." Laurel patted the monitor located on a shelf above the food prep area. "She's usually good for a couple of hours in the afternoon and when she wakes up, she'll have another feeding, then we'll go home." She winked. "That's the plan, anyway."

Eugenia shrugged. "Babies, they have their own ideas about schedules and such. But I must admit, that little Stephanie is one golden child."

"She sure is." Laurel handed Cassidy her sandwich, then in a lower voice said, "Did you know your mother is here?"

Cassidy frowned, then went to the window. Sure enough, parked on the other side of a big horse trailer

that had blocked her view was the Coffee Ranch SUV.
She scanned the room again.

"Where is she?"

Laurel raised her eyebrows. "In the kitchen. Talking to Vince."

"I didn't think *anyone* talked to Vince."

"Oh, they do. He just doesn't talk back."

Cassidy grinned. "Has she eaten?"

"Not that I know of."

"I'll see if she wants something." Cassidy edged
around the corner, heading for the closed door separating the kitchen from the serving area. She could hear
voices, all right. Her mother was speaking.

"—two years and haven't been for dinner once."

"I was there for the baby shower."

"Not the same thing. Why don't you come this Sunday? I'll invite the whole family."

When Vince didn't answer, she added, "Including
Jackson."

Why would Vince care if Jackson was invited to dinner or not? Cassidy realized she was eavesdropping, but
was too curious to stop.

"I know you mean well. But I'm happy sticking to
myself."

"Come on, Vince. We may be old but we're not dead."

Cassidy gasped. Her mother sounded like she was
flirting. She waited, but again Vince chose to say nothing. She was just about to move before—

And then it was too late. The door swung open and
her mother stepped right in front of her.

"Cassidy?"

"I—I came for a sandwich." She held up the paper
bag Laurel had given her a minute ago.

"Then what are you doing behind the counter?"

"Laurel told me you were here. I was going to ask if you wanted some lunch, too." But then she'd been distracted by something more interesting than ham and cheese on rye.

"I've eaten, thank you." Her mother sounded distracted. "We've been so busy lately, I was hoping we could all get together for dinner this Sunday. Are you and Corb free?" she asked Laurel.

"We sure are. Can I bring something?"

"Maybe one of Vince's pies for dessert? Unless he decides to bring one himself. I invited him, as well."

"Oh." Laurel paused in the act of wiping clean the counter. "I didn't know you and Vince were friends."

"We went to school together. And yes, we were friends before he got caught up in the rodeo circuit."

The scorn on her mother's face made it clear what she thought about *that* lifestyle. Olive assumed that every cowboy was in it for the partying, the women and the alcohol. She never seemed to see B.J.'s trophies and prize winnings as anything but minor accomplishments at best.

But perhaps it was because she'd seen what the rodeo life had done to Vince that she was so hard on her oldest son, Cassidy reflected.

"Corb and I will try to convince him to come," Laurel promised.

"Good luck with that." From what Cassidy had overheard, she guessed it wasn't going to be easy.

The next few days were hot. Summer had arrived in Montana and with a vengeance.

By Sunday, the humidity had risen to intolerable levels and there was talk of thunderclouds, even though the sky was still clear.

Come three o'clock however, it wasn't. As the clouds gathered, so did the horses, moving into their storm shelters, acting skittish and wild. Cassidy finished her chores early so she could peel potatoes for the dinner and set the table as her mother had asked.

By five-thirty all the family had arrived. Cassidy had commandeered her niece, Corb was opening wine, Jackson was on the patio grilling steaks, Laurel was tossing the salad while Olive checked the potatoes roasting in the oven. Amid all that chaos, the doorbell rang.

"Get that, will you, Cass?" her mother asked.

So her mother had convinced Vince to come after all, Cassidy surmised as she headed for the entrance with Steph tucked snugly in her left arm.

She still thought it was odd that Vince had been invited to a family dinner. She'd asked her mom about it earlier and all Olive had said was that Vince had once been a very dear friend.

"Was he friends with your sister, too?" she'd asked, feeling a little daring for even mentioning Maddie's existence.

"Probably," had been her mom's short answer.

There had to be more to the story, Cassidy thought, remembering the look of pain on Maddie's face that day Vince had said hello to her outside the café.

Maybe she'd find out more about the past tonight.

But when she opened the door it wasn't Vince Butterfield standing on the porch.

Words deserted her.

Finally Farley said, "I guess your mother didn't tell you she'd invited me?"

She shook her head no. Three days had passed since she'd seen him last. But had she thought about him?

Oh, yeah.

"How's Sky doing?"

"So much better. And Finnegan is, too. He's been eating a little more, every day." And then she blurted, "You look good."

He'd dressed up in dark jeans and a Western-style dark shirt, and she thought it would be fair to say she'd never seen a man who looked better in black.

Or sexier.

"You look nice, too. Even combed your hair, I see." He took a strand and let it slide between his fingers, then bent in closer for a look at the baby.

She could smell the botanical mint of his shampoo, and also feel the heat of his body. He touched a finger to Stephanie's cheek and she found herself wishing he would touch her, too.

Heck and darn. Get a grip on yourself.

"Isn't she the sweetest baby?"

"Sure is." But Farley was looking at *her* as he said this.

Gosh, she felt like such a fool. She could feel a flush gathering on her cheeks and she wished her mother had given her some warning.

Though Olive's comment about making an effort with her hair and makeup for a change should have tipped her off.

Farley straightened, and his voice deepened as he said he was glad to hear that Finnegan was eating again. "To be honest, I wasn't sure Finn would be strong enough to beat this thing. I'll come by tomorrow and draw a sample for testing. The sooner we can clear your ranch of the quarantine, the better."

"That would be great." She led the way to the combined kitchen/family room, where Farley was given a warm welcome. His friendship with her brothers was reason enough for him to be here tonight, but Olive's smug smile told Cassidy everything she needed to know about her motives for inviting the vet.

On the pretence of helping her mother with the potatoes, Cassidy passed the baby to Laurel, then went to the stove and murmured, "You can stop with the matchmaking, okay? It isn't going to work."

"Don't be silly. I just wanted to thank Farley for all the extra work he's been doing for us. I'm so glad that darn strangles didn't spread any further than it did. I have you to thank as well, Cassidy. You did a wonderful job keeping it contained."

Cassidy waited. There was usually a "but" or an "if only" attached to one of her mother's compliments.

"If only you weren't so set on working in the city. You have such a knack with animals."

"I have a knack with numbers, too, Mom. And a good brain. Is it such a crime that I want to use it?"

"Are you saying we don't have to think because we work on a ranch? That we're somehow *inferior* to people who work in offices and ivory towers?"

"Of course that's not what I mean." Cassidy blew out an exasperated breath. Her mother was unbelievably obdurate. How was she ever going to get the message across that she was not going to put up with her mother nosing in on her love life?

When it came time to sit at the table, certain that her mother was going to connive to sit her next to Farley,

Cassidy wiggled in for the chair between Jackson and Corb. But in a move worthy of a choreographed ballet, somehow Corb got diverted, Laurel moved over a space, and Farley ended up on her right-hand side after all.

He raised his eyebrows at her and shrugged, as if to say he wasn't sure how it had happened, either.

Cassidy fumed.

It wasn't just her mother. Her whole family was behind this scheme. And she was fed up.

It wasn't that she didn't *want* to sit by Farley. But they made it happen so obviously, it was embarrassing.

Besides, what was Farley to think? That her family thought she was so unappealing they had to find her a man—since she couldn't do it on her own.

Cassidy ate very little of the meal, and added even less to the conversation.

Olive focused most of her efforts on Farley.

"Tell me—you don't have plans to sell any more of your land, do you?"

"No. When Dad retired we let a section go to Cooper Madison. He'd been renting it from us for years and was anxious to own it outright. But we're keeping the rest."

"That's good. You know a corner of your land to the west butts right up to Coffee Creek. It's good grazing."

"I know. Why? Were you interested in renting it?"

Olive laughed. "Oh, we've plenty of land for our own needs, Farley. I just thought it was an interesting tidbit."

"Really? An interesting tidbit?"

In the back of her mind, Cassidy heard the percolating rumbles of the approaching thunderstorm. But she had nothing to fear from thunder and lightning. It was her mother who had her all riled up.

And she just couldn't take it anymore.

"Go on, Mom, why don't you connect all the dots for Farley? In case he's so stupid he can't see that if he and I marry it will be so wonderful that our land is connected."

"Whoa, Cass. You're getting a little crazy here," Corb said.

"Am I? It isn't just Mother behind this. You think I didn't notice the way all of you herded Farley and me into these two back seats—like we were cattle going up the ramp to the loading chute."

"Cassidy!" Olive threw down her napkin.

An eerie silence fell over the table. It was as though the entire ranch was holding its breath.

Then, in the next second, came a crash of thunder that had the dishes dancing on the table. Cassidy was already standing by then.

"I think it would be a good idea if I went to the barn and checked on the horses."

No one said a word to her as she left the room.

Farley wanted to laugh. Or maybe cheer. But he didn't think either reaction would sit well with the Lamberts. And though they were friends, Coffee Creek Ranch was also his biggest client.

So he held his tongue and just listened as Olive apologized for the rudeness of her daughter.

"I didn't think she was all that rude," he said calmly. "You gotta admit she was provoked." He glanced around the table. Olive had an expression of wide-eyed innocence, but no one else would meet his gaze. "You all were a little obvious," he added.

"I don't know what you're talking about, Dan Farley." Olive started gathering plates, even though most of them hadn't finished eating. "Cassidy thinks everything is all about her. It never occurred to her that maybe Laurel wanted to sit by Corb and that's why— Oh, bother. It's just too silly to put into words."

Olive was doing a good job of obfuscating, but Corb, Laurel and Jackson were smirking. They knew a con job when they heard one.

"Guilty as charged," said Corb, shaking his head. "Sorry, buddy. Seems real stupid now, but we did kind of arrange things so you two sat together."

"Corb!"

"Cassidy does take a lot of wisecracks from her brothers," Laurel said diplomatically.

"Come on, honey. We're just having fun. It's no big deal."

"Well, it is to your sister," Farley pointed out. "She feels like she's being railroaded." And not for the first time, he guessed. It couldn't be easy being the youngest, and the only girl, in a family as strong-willed as this one.

They didn't mean to run roughshod over her. But what none of them seemed to understand was that beneath her tough, spunky attitude, she was soft and vulnerable.

A side she tended to only reveal when she was around the animals she loved. Sky, Lucy… Finnegan.

He understood better now why she was so determined to start a new life for herself in Billings.

Chapter 11

On Monday the phone rang while Cassidy was having breakfast with her mother. Olive was preparing to give a tour to some buyers who were driving up from Bozeman in about an hour, while Cassidy was waiting for Farley to come by and grab a mucus sample from Finn.

Her mustang had showed a bit more appetite again this morning, and Cassidy was really hopeful that the test would be clear of the strangles bacteria.

Her mother wasn't talking to her much today. She was still wounded by the scene Cassidy had made at last night's dinner.

Cassidy figured she should be the one who was wounded. But as time went by she felt more and more guilty. She hated discord and her mother's silent treatment was the worst.

"It's for you."

Those were the first words her mother had said to her all morning. "Thanks, Mom." Cassidy took the receiver, resisting the urge to move to another room.

"Hello, this is Cassidy Lambert."

"Nice to speak to you, Ms. Lambert. This is Pamela Oswald from Cushman and Green."

Cassidy froze. Finally they were getting back to her. But she'd checked on Facebook last night and several more of her classmates had reported being given second interviews last week.

So maybe now they were calling the rejects?

She tried to prepare herself for disappointment. She didn't want to fall apart. Not in front of her mother.

"I've been looking forward to hearing from you, too," she replied.

"I'm glad. Because we were hoping you would come to our offices for a second interview. We'd like you to meet a few more people in our organization and give them a chance to get to know you, as well."

Cassidy pumped her arm. Yes! "That would be great." Was that too colloquial? "I mean, I'd be happy to come to Billings."

"Would Thursday suit you? Say at nine?"

"That sounds perfect."

"Great. Just go to the main reception desk and ask for me. I'll send you an email confirming the details, in case you don't have a pen and paper handy right now."

"Thanks so much, Ms. Cushman. I mean Oswald." Cassidy's insides cringed at the mistake, but the woman on the phone didn't even seem to notice as she thanked her again, then said goodbye.

Cassidy replaced the phone. Her mother had been watching her, but now she seemed busy stacking the dishwasher. When she was done, she washed her hands, then finally looked at her daughter.

"I suppose that was the accounting firm you've been waiting to hear from?"

Heck and darn. She wanted to be happy about this. Instead, she felt almost guilty. "They've invited me for a second interview on Thursday."

"So soon?"

Three days' notice didn't seem unreasonable to Cassidy, but she nodded.

"Well, I guess we'll all just chip in and work a little harder around here."

There were actual tears in Olive's eyes as she said this. Tears that Cassidy knew would have any one of her brothers jumping hoops to try to clear away.

But Cassidy knew there was no way to do that. She'd told her mom that she wasn't going to be a regular part of the team that ran Coffee Creek Ranch. No matter how many times she said it, her mother never seemed to hear.

Her mother *didn't want* to hear. Maybe a good daughter would behave different. Cassidy knew she couldn't.

She *would* go on that interview.

And, if she was offered the job, she *would* take it.

Monday morning Farley took a few hours at his desk to catch up on paperwork and follow through with test results. He was pleased to see that the cultures for both Lucy and Chickweed from Coffee Creek Ranch were negative for S. equi.

Finnegan's, however, was still positive. But this was the sample he'd taken last week. He'd get another today and hopefully that one would reveal better news.

He pulled up his sheet with the calls he needed to

make today. Liz always prepared this for him, right after she made their morning coffee.

Looked like he had another long day to put in, but that was springtime in ranch country for you. Frankly, Coffee Creek Ranch was getting big enough that they could almost use a full-time vet. Monahan's equine center— a horse training and boarding facility on the other side of town—was his other major client. They employed a full-time farrier, but he was often called out to help there, as well.

And he was still trying to service the other thirty or so ranchers in the area. Thankfully, most of them were a hell of a lot smaller, many more like acreages than real farms or ranches.

Still they all had animals. And most anyone who had domesticated animals, whether cows, horses, dogs, cats, or even—as in the case of the Bernhard family—lizards, eventually needed a vet.

"So."

He heard Liz enter his office and plant herself in the vacant chair.

When she didn't say anything further, he looked up from his papers. Normally Liz was a pretty upbeat person. Today she didn't seem that happy. "Yes, Liz?"

"I have a friend whose son just graduated from vet school in Washington. He met a girl from Lewiston while he was there. She also graduated from vet school, by the way. They're planning on getting married and moving to the area. You could either sit back and let them become your competition. Or you could hire them and train them so they actually learn to become decent veterinarians."

"It's not enough that you arrange my dates. Now you're hiring the staff, too?"

"Look, it's a lead, okay? Would it hurt to interview them?" She set two résumés on his desk. "Don't know why I bother. I give you the best advice in the world and you never follow it."

He sighed. "I take it you spoke to Amber this weekend?"

"You mean the prettiest, nicest and most eligible woman in the county? Yes, I did."

Prettiest? No.

Nicest? Maybe. If by *nice* you meant bland.

And he could name one other woman who was just as eligible as Amber Ellis. Not that it made any difference to him. He was pretty sure after Sunday dinner he'd made it to Cassidy's "no fly" list.

"Liz, you know chemistry is a big *X* factor. You can take a man and a woman that you think would make a perfect couple and it just doesn't work out that way."

"Yeah. Maybe that was the problem. Or maybe Cassidy Lambert came back to town and—"

"Liz." He used her name like a big, forceful stop sign. "Off-limits, Liz."

She looked startled. And well she might. He'd never said that to her before.

But no way, no how, was he discussing Cassidy with her.

Silently, she gave him a resentful look, then left the room. He waited until she'd closed the door before he checked his list again.

How about that? First stop: Coffee Creek Ranch.

Farley drove up to the Lamberts' home barn about fifteen minutes later. Today he was just making a quick trip, to get a sample from Finnegan, then he was off to the other side of the county for a long day of preg-testing on the Double D.

He slipped on his stethoscope and a pair of gloves before stepping into the quarantine area. He found Cassidy giving her mustang a gentle rubdown.

Lucky horse.

She was in those jeans she always wore. He'd noticed the label when he'd washed them. Tuff, they were called. Sexy, was what he called them. They made her legs look long and slender and her rear end unbelievably cute.

She had on an old T-shirt today, only partially tucked in, but he didn't mind that. Cassidy was at her best when she looked disheveled.

"Hey, Farley." She kept brushing her horse, but he could see a flush working its way up her neck to her fair cheeks. "I'm sorry about last night. I hope I didn't embarrass you too much."

"It'd take a lot more than that to get me embarrassed. I thought it was kind of funny to tell you the truth." He went on the other side of Finnegan, listened to his heart and lungs and frowned. Not what he'd been hoping for. "How's our boy doing today?"

"He ate a little. Not as much as I'd like." Cassidy paused. "I wish I could find those scenes with my mother funny. I try to let it all slide off me, the way Corb does. But she gets to me. She really does."

"They say mother-daughter relationships can be tricky. Not that I know firsthand." He pulled a swab kit out of his case and quickly took another sample.

Then he checked Finn's temperature, frowning again when he saw it was thirty-nine degrees. He said nothing to Cassidy, though, not wanting to worry her.

"I'll get back to you on the test. But I have a feeling it may be a while before we get this bug completely out of his system. In the meantime, you can let Lucy and Chickweed rejoin the herd. Their tests came out negative again."

"They'll be so glad about that. And so will I. They've been so frisky lately I can't seem to give them enough exercise."

"Been barrel racing with Lucy again?" He hoped so. He'd loved watching Cassidy on the palomino. The golden girl and her golden horse. Even more appealing than the picture they'd made, however, had been the way they worked together as a unit.

"Maybe I will this afternoon." Cassidy put down the curry brush, then hitched her thumbs in her belt loops and followed him out of the stall. "It's fun for both of us, though I suspect Mom and Corb would prefer I got some more work done."

"Exercising horses is work," Farley insisted. "I still think you should give some thought to registering at Rogue River."

Cassidy laughed. "And give my mother something else to complain about? Believe me, one rodeo cowboy is enough for this family. Besides, if things go my way on Thursday, I won't have much opportunity for that sort of thing anymore."

Her eyes were sparkling, as if she was sitting on some sort of secret. Though he had a sense he wasn't going to like it, he asked anyway.

"What's happening Thursday?"

"I got a call for a second interview with Cushman and Green!"

He forced a smile. "Congratulations. That's the accounting firm, right?"

With her hands pressed together under her chin, she nodded. "Most of my friends had already heard from them. I'd lost all hope that I would be chosen. And then this morning, they phoned."

Farley felt as if a big, black storm cloud had just pushed the sunshine out of the day. But he smiled again and told her she should be proud.

"Thank you. The timing couldn't be better. After that scene with my mother…" Cassidy kicked at a clump of hay, scattering the fibers over the floor. "I truly believe we'll have a better relationship if we don't see so much of each other."

"So what are you thinking? Coming home maybe once a year?" Farley tried to joke so she wouldn't guess how he really felt.

She laughed. "More like once a month. I will miss this place. But I was thinking if I found a ground-level suite maybe I could take Sky with me this time."

"It won't be easy for her to adjust to the city." Farley waved a hand indicating all the beautiful land around them. "Not when she's used to all this."

Once more the smile on Cassidy's face wavered, but then she shrugged. "We'll see. She's getting older. Maybe she won't mind spending most of her days inside."

Farley removed the protective gloves, then washed up at the sink. He thought he could sense some nervousness behind her happy chatter.

But that was only normal, right? It didn't mean she had doubts that she was doing the right thing.

Whereas he did. He couldn't help siding with her family on this one. Cassidy belonged here, in Coffee Creek. But if he dared to tell her this, he'd only be one more person telling her how to live.

Cassidy drove to Billings on Wednesday after her evening chores. Finnegan hadn't been cleared from quarantine yet—and frankly he didn't seem quite himself, anyway—so she asked Corb if he would keep an eye on him for her.

Her brother must have been feeling a little guilty about Sunday, because he didn't tease her or complain, just said it would be no problem.

Even though she knew it was. His days were full with branding and vaccinating the new calves, but she didn't want to ask one of the hired hands to do the job.

Not that she didn't trust them. She just trusted Corb more.

The drive to Billings was long. Three hours. She'd expected to enjoy the journey, but thoughts of home—and Farley—kept intruding.

He'd seemed happy for her when she told him about the second interview. She'd been glad of the support—which she hadn't received from her family.

But part of her had wished he would just grab her and kiss her.

Ever since that night at his house, she'd been able to think of little else but making love with Farley. What would it be like? Would it ever happen?

So much was against them. Their age difference had been a big impediment for a long time. And now there was her mother—pushing them together so hard that Cassidy couldn't help but wonder if she was in danger of making a big mistake.

If she succumbed to her longing for Farley, she'd be trapped. Just the way her mother wanted her to be. Living forever in the shadow of her family and the Coffee Creek Ranch.

Cassidy spent a lonely night at the Super 8. She could have called her classmates—and Josh—but she didn't want to talk to any of them until she had the interview behind her.

If it was a flop, she'd just run back home and consider her options.

If it went well, she'd be in the mood for a little celebrating.

Thursday morning she dressed in the same skirt, blazer, blouse and pumps that she'd worn to the first interview when the firms had come on campus to survey the best of that year's graduating class.

She hoped they wouldn't remember that she was wearing the same outfit. But she had nothing else appropriate.

She winced as she walked out of the hotel to the parking lot. She wished she'd had the nerve to wear her cream-colored cowboy boots. But her girlfriends in college had told her the look wasn't right.

She sighed and slid behind the driver's wheel. She'd gone over the directions on the internet so many times, she had no need to refer to a map as she made her way toward the downtown.

Billings was small as cities went, with around a quarter of a million people. But it was the biggest metropolis in Montana and as she surveyed the busy streets, the traffic and all the people hurrying to work, she wondered if she was going to be happy here.

She'd been fine during her five years in Bozeman.

But that had been college. This could be the rest of her life—at least a big chunk of it.

In her email Pamela Oswald had helpfully suggested a place to park and Cassidy felt more confident once she'd maneuvered her truck into one of the stalls. On foot she felt better. Well, if it wasn't for these darn heels, she'd feel better. Why had she let the girls talk her into three-inch heels?

She hoped she didn't look as if she'd been hobbled as she made her way along the sidewalk toward North Broadway and what appeared to be the tallest office tower in the city. Around her men and women were carrying briefcases and take-out coffees. Many of them had PDAs in hand, checking messages or taking calls.

She felt important, just being among them.

Squaring her shoulders, she entered the lobby and headed for the elevators, squishing into the small space with four men and three other ladies.

She noticed a few glances coming her way, and nervously put a hand to her hair.

On Tuesday she'd gone to Lewistown to get it trimmed. "Chop off three or four inches" had been her instructions. When she looked at the floor, though, she was sure she saw at least six inches of her golden hair—gone.

The new length came to her shoulders, though, and swung nicely as she walked. This morning she'd used a hair dryer and straightener after her shower to make sure it was sleek and controlled.

Stop thinking about your hair, stupid. It's your brain that will win you this job.

She got off on the fifteenth floor and headed to the receptionist, per Pamela's instructions.

She was invited to wait on an elegant leather sofa. Business publications and the *Wall Street Journal* were fanned out on the glass table in front of her. But she focused on all the people coming and going. Some of them cast her a curious look. A few smiled. Most just ignored her.

If her spine had been replaced with an iron rod, she couldn't have sat any straighter. Everything felt so foreign. The people weren't just dressed differently, they spoke differently and moved differently.

Finally Pamela came and she was so polished and elegant that Cassidy felt like a complete country bumpkin. She'd never thought to get gel nails. Or to wear jewelry. Not that she owned anything as chic as the chunky silver necklace and bracelet that looked so great with Pamela's black suit.

Those little touches make all the difference, she thought. And then she reminded herself, *It's about your brain. Okay?*

She was given a tour of the offices. Hallways lined with oil paintings, board rooms with sleek furniture and views that spread out to the Beartooth Mountains.

She was introduced to people she'd never remember. There was a little banter and quite a few smiles, but mostly people were very serious.

Fifteen minutes later, she was in an accounting partner's office. He looked about Farley's age, but was as different as could be from the country veterinarian. Thin brown hair, trendy glasses, an expensive suit that fit his slender build as if it had been sewn in place.

"It's nice to meet you, Cassidy," said Mr. Cushman—not *the* Cushman for whom the business had been named, but a nephew, Pamela had explained in a whisper a few minutes earlier.

"Thank you. I'm happy to be here, too."

He shuffled papers on his desk. "With the downturn in the economy we only have room for three articling students this year. If I was going on marks alone, you'd be a shoo-in."

Cassidy swallowed nervously, then managed a slight smile.

"But we have to see how you'll fit in here. That's why we asked you to come and look around, meet a few people."

They chatted for about ten minutes. Cassidy thought he seemed impressed that she knew the names of the firm's biggest clients and was up-to-date on local business news.

This was all research she'd done a month ago before the first interview.

Then he invited her to lunch. They were joined by a couple of articling students who'd been hired last year, and went to eat at a posh restaurant with names of things on the menu that she didn't recognize and waiters so attentive they folded her napkin on her chair when she went to the restroom.

At the conclusion of the meal she and Pamela had a final chat. "It was a pleasure meeting you, Cassidy. The partners will be making their final decision in a couple of weeks and I'll phone you as soon as I know."

Chapter 12

Cassidy decided to spend the night in Billings, rather than drive home right away. The day had taken a lot of energy out of her. She wandered the streets, finding a charming area with shops and restaurants. She picked up a slice of pizza from a take-out place and found a bench where she could relax and people-watch.

She didn't need to be alone. She could have called Josh or one of her other friends. But she was too worried that if they started comparing notes about their interviews, she would discover hers hadn't gone as well as she thought it had.

Around eight o'clock she went back to the motel room, watched some TV, then went to sleep. She was up early the next day, on the road by seven, and home just before ten.

Her mother happened to be locking the front door

when Cassidy pulled up to her parking spot. But as usual, her warmest welcome came from her dog. Sky was as amazed and delighted to see her as if she'd been gone for a month.

Cassidy was pleased to see her wound was healing nicely and her eyes were bright and lively.

After giving Sky one last scratch, she straightened. "Hi, Mom."

Olive was dressed in working clothes—jeans, shirt, old boots and a bandana at her neck. This could mean only one thing. Corb had organized a big work party to push the cattle farther north.

"How was the interview?"

"I'm not sure. I have to wait a few weeks now for them to decide." She gave her mother a kiss on the cheek, then tugged her bandana lightly. "I take it you're going with the guys to move cattle?"

Olive nodded. "We'll be camping out tonight, home around dinnertime tomorrow." She hesitated. "Want to come along? Dave is staying back to keep an eye on the animals. He knows to feed Sky. And check in on Finn."

Dave was one of the extra hands B.J. had hired after Brock's death. And he'd turned out to be a reliable worker, from what Corb and Jackson said. But Cassidy didn't want to leave the care of her animals to someone who wasn't family.

Normally staying back from a trip like this would have been a major sacrifice. Without a doubt, Cassidy's happiest childhood memories were the family trail rides when they'd moved the cattle up to higher elevations where the grass was just coming in nice and thick. The days were long but there was always time to enjoy the scenery, be amused by the cattle's antics, and indulge in late-night conversations around a campfire.

But that wasn't for her. Not this year, anyway.

"No. I'm tired. And I have things to do."

"Things like what?" Her mother sounded cautious.

"Just things, Mom. You go and have fun. I'll take care of business around here."

Cassidy quickly changed into regular work clothes, then went to the home barn to see everyone off on the trail ride. There were bedrolls behind the saddles and a couple of extra horses carried the tents and food supplies. She felt another pang of regret. Nothing tasted better than a meal cooked over a campfire.

"Sure you don't want to join us?" Corb asked. "We can wait while you saddle up."

"That's okay." She looked over the crew. Besides her mother and Corb, there was also Jackson and three hired wranglers. "What are Laurel and the baby doing while you're away?"

"She's gone to Highwood to visit Winnie and the baby. Eugenia, Vince and Dawn are holding down the fort at the café while she's gone."

Five minutes later they were off and Cassidy headed for the open barn door. She passed Dave Crosby at the boot dip, on his way out.

A smile broke on his weathered thirtyish face. "Hey, you're back. That's good. I was just heading over to check the new calves and moms in the cattle barn, but I'm kind of worried about that mustang of yours."

"Finnegan? What's the problem?"

"Well, shortly after you left on Wednesday he went off his food."

"I thought Corb was looking after him?"

"Yeah, well, your brother asked me to look in on him. And I noticed yesterday morning he hadn't touched his oats. Not today, either."

"But I wasn't feeding him oats. There was this special formula. I left the instructions on a sheet in the feed room."

Dave scratched behind his ear. "Well, I didn't see those. And no one told me any different. So I fed him oats, same as we usually do."

"Okay, Dave." She put a hand on his arm, then nodded for him to go. "I'll handle it from here."

She wasn't going to blame him, and not Corb, either. She shouldn't have left Finnegan. It was as simple as that.

She hurried inside and was not happy at what she saw. Finnegan was visibly thinner and weaker. "Hey, boy, what's the problem?" She patted him down carefully. His belly had swollen, but she couldn't find any of the pustules around his neck or throat the way she had with Lucy and Chickweed.

Obviously, she had been wrong to assume he was out of the woods.

She went to mix up the gruel that she'd fed him with success before, but today he would have none of it. Not even a bite.

"Oh, Finn. You need to eat. I can see how weak you are."

Finn just snorted and looked at her with the saddest set of horse eyes she'd ever seen.

She moved Finn to a fresh stall, offered him water and feed again, but he still refused to eat. Feeling desperate, she called Farley's cell phone number. He didn't answer and the call was routed through to his office.

"Farley & Sons," said Liz Moffat.

"Hey, Liz, this is Cassidy out at Coffee Creek. My mustang has taken a turn for the worse." She'd been so sure he was getting better. There was no way she would have left him if she'd thought he might have a setback. "He hasn't eaten in a few days and he seems awfully weak. Do you think this is a complication from the strangles?"

"I couldn't say. But I do know that last test came up positive, so he still has the bacteria." Liz's voice had been cool at first, but now she sounded genuinely concerned. "Unfortunately Farley's on the Double D again today, working out in the fields where cell phone reception can be spotty."

"Oh, heck and darn…"

"Isn't it always the way?" Liz agreed. "But if I can be sure of anything, it's this. Once Farley gets your message, he's going to be there to help you as soon as humanly possible. Maybe even five minutes faster than that."

Cassidy turned on the radio to keep them company, set out a water dish for Sky and made herself a pot of coffee. There wasn't much she could do for Finnegan, but give him a lot of TLC.

And wait for Farley. He'd know what to do when he got there. They just had to be patient.

But the sun was skimming the tops of the western ranges by the time she heard his truck pulling up to the barn.

Dave had left for home two hours ago. He'd asked if he could do anything to help before he headed off but she'd said not to worry.

"The vet will be here soon."

She had the door to the barn open, hoping the fresh air might help Finnegan. The horse was lying down in his stall now—and had been for about three hours. She watched as Farley climbed out of his truck. He looked tired as he lugged his vet bag out of the passenger seat and he held his head kind of low, so she couldn't see his eyes from beneath the rim of his hat until he was almost beside her.

And when their gazes finally did connect, she saw the same cool, dispassionate look he'd had a month ago when they'd happened into the café at the same time.

Farley didn't say hello or ask about her trip. He looked from her, to her horse, then turned on one of the lights and moved into the stall. "How long since he's eaten?"

"It sounds like he hasn't had anything since I left for Billings on Wednesday." She squeezed her hands nervously together as she waited for Farley to do his thing.

He had his stethoscope around his neck and a rectal thermometer in his hand. After fifteen minutes, he heaved a heavy sigh. "Well, he's still running that fever. And I don't like the sound of his heart. See the way he's sticking his legs out?"

She nodded. She'd never noticed Finn rest in that position before.

"That tells me he's in pain. My guess is that the strangles bacteria has progressed to his vital organs." Farley ran a hand over Finnegan's stomach. "See that swelling? It probably hurts him to eat."

"Poor Finn." She knelt on the soft bedding and wrapped her arms around Finnegan's neck. The horse gave no reaction, but close like this, she could hear the labored sound of his breathing. "So what do we do?"

Farley didn't answer.

The truth crept in slowly with the inevitability of the sun setting behind the mountains. And with it came a pain and a sorrow that Cassidy already had too much familiarity with.

She'd been fifteen when her father died.

Twenty-four when Brock was killed in the accident.

And now it was Finnegan's turn.

Just a horse, some might say. But he'd been family. And one of the last links she still had to her dad.

Farley sat down a few feet from her, leaning his back against the side wall of the stall. He watched Finnegan for a while, then he looked at her.

Cassidy didn't want to see the sympathy in his eyes. She bent her head close to Finn's and murmured words that she hoped were comforting. "Don't be scared, Finn. I'm not leaving you again."

Her voice broke a little on the last word. Would this have happened if she hadn't gone to Billings?

And, as if he had read her mind, Farley said, "There's not much you can do to prevent this kind of complication. Finnegan is an old horse. That made him more susceptible."

"H-he's very near the end, isn't he?"

Farley nodded.

Her eyes started filling with tears. But she smiled. "I remember the day Finn came to us. The whole family had gone to a horse sale. It was my eighth birthday. We didn't have the breeding business back then, Mom and Dad were just looking for good cattle horses. I was the one who spotted Finnegan first."

The memory was fresh and true. She could almost smell the stockyard, taste the popcorn—each of them had been given a small bag—and hear the rapid-fire sound of the auctioneer's voice.

"'Look at that one,' I told my dad. 'Your sister has a good eye,' he said." Cassidy smiled, remembering the approving look her dad had given her.

"My brothers all crowded in to see him, but Finnegan would have nothing to do with them. He walked right up to me, though. And Dad said, 'Look at that. I guess we'll have to buy our girl a horse for her birthday.'

"Mom was appalled. She thought he was too much horse for an eight-year-old to handle. And of course she was right. But Dad told me that if I took care of him for two years, by the time I was ten I'd be able to ride him. I remember sitting on the fence watching as Dad trained him. Dad had such a calm and patient way with horses. I learned a lot just observing him. At the end of each session, it was my job to clean the tack and give Finnegan a good brushing. And while I was working the curry comb I'd be dreaming of the day when I'd finally be able to ride him…"

"And ride him you did." Farley had one hand on Finnegan's back, as if reassuring the horse that he, too, wasn't going anywhere. "I used to think that you were mighty small to be on such a big horse. But right from the start, you knew how to control him. The two of you made quite the pair."

Cassidy swallowed. Those had been such happy days. The strengths and weaknesses of her mother and father had been complementary. Between them, they'd created a family that was strong and loyal with love as a solid core.

The balance had been lost, however, when her dad died.

"When we got home from the hospital after Dad

passed away, I headed straight to the barn and took Finnegan out for a ride. I was a mess, but Finnegan seemed to know that he had to be good and gentle with me that day. We were out for hours, and you know something strange?"

Farley didn't say anything, but his eyes told her he was listening with both his ears and his heart.

"I felt as if my dad was with us. I talked to him and I swear he answered me…" She brushed the tears from her eyes and tried to smile. "Crazy, huh?"

"No. It just shows the bond you had with your father."

Cassidy let out a long breath and looked down at Finnegan. Her heart ached to see him so still and weak. "Are you suffering, Finn? I'm so sorry if you are. You were such a good horse. So brave and true. I won't forget you. Not ever."

She laid her head close to his and Finnegan gave a soft nicker. It was the last sound she heard him make. The barn suddenly felt incredibly silent and cold.

"He's gone. Isn't he?"

"Yes. I'm sorry. But yes."

"No." She didn't want it to be true. She wrapped her arms tighter around her horse and though she'd wanted to be strong, she couldn't help herself. The sobs came pouring out of her, as if she'd had a broken heart for years and was only now letting it all out.

She was crying for Finn. And Brock. And her father.

Crying for a time when they'd all been together. Those glorious years that she'd taken for granted, never guessing how soon they would end.

"Come here, sweetheart." Farley had laid a blanket over Finn. Now he pulled her up and into his arms, not seeming to mind that her face was wet and sticky. He put a hand on her head, letting her burrow into the solid warmth of his chest.

And she clung for a good long minute, then took a deep breath.

"I'm sorry I lost it."

"I wouldn't think much of you if you hadn't."

There were tears in his eyes, too, she saw. She reached up to touch one. Farley caught her hand and held it close.

"Now what?" she asked, her voice coming out in tremolo.

"I know you have a plot where you bury your horses. Let me make the arrangements for that tomorrow. When your family gets home you can have a ceremony."

"Thank you."

"In the meantime, you and Sky should come home with me. You shouldn't be alone tonight."

Hearing her name, Sky came immediately to Cassidy's side. She'd been standing guard at the door all this time, Cassidy realized, as if sensing they needed protection.

"Good girl, Sky." She petted her dog and considered Farley's offer.

Her instinct was to say no. But she knew if she spent the night in her mother's house, or even in Brock's cabin, all she would think about was Finnegan growing cold and stiff in the barn. She shuddered.

Farley took her hand. "Let's get your things."

It was too hot for a fire this evening. Farley went around his house opening windows, but the air still felt humid and close. He made soup and tomato sandwiches, and though Cassidy swore she wasn't hungry, he noticed she ate every bite.

When they were done, they took a couple beers and went out on the porch. Sky, seeing what they were doing, turned back at the door and returned to the hearth with the other dogs.

Not wanting to attract the moths, Farley didn't light the candles that he kept out here. There was enough light filtering out from the living room window that they could see where they were going. They sat side by side on the cushioned swing and listened to the cricket music.

"So how was the trip to Billings?" he finally asked. He'd been avoiding the subject, not sure he was ready to hear the answer.

He'd had a rough couple days while she was gone. It had taken her absence from Coffee Creek to make him realize how far gone he was.

He ought to be protecting himself from more pain and keeping his distance. But seeing her in pain made it impossible for him to stay away.

"It was fine, I hope. They seemed impressed with my academic record. And my meetings went well." Cassidy took a swallow of beer, then pushed out of the swing and went to stand by the railing.

She looked gorgeous. Her hair was shorter, but it suited her and it was still long enough to frame her beautiful face in gold. Before coming here she'd changed into clean jeans and a T-shirt and he couldn't help noticing that her silver belt buckle fell at just the right spot to emphasize both her slender waist and the curve of her hips.

He felt his heart start to pound, hard and fast.

She always did this to him. Always.

He found the courage to ask, "Did you get the job?"

She sighed. "I don't know yet."

But she would, he thought. Who wouldn't hire a smart, beautiful woman like her? Who could resist?

The realization that she was really going scooped all the feeling from his gut, leaving him hollow and exposed. And angry. Why did he care so much? He shouldn't. He'd known from the start what her plans were and frankly, he couldn't really blame her. Being a Lambert wasn't easy for her. In Billings, she could finally just be herself.

"If I hadn't gone, maybe Finn would still be alive." She took a long drink, emptying the can then setting it aside. She turned to stare out at the night.

"I don't think that's true."

"But you can't *know* it isn't." Her voice cracked and then she was crying again. "No one else loved him like I do. I should have known they wouldn't give him enough attention."

"No." He hated hearing her suffering. He went to her, putting his arms around her. "Don't blame yourself. Even if you'd been by his side every second, there was nothing you could have done."

She turned into him, pressing her face, damp with tears, against his chest. He cupped the back of her head with his hands, feeling all sorts of things that were complicated and wrong.

He wanted to comfort her and reassure her.

But he also wanted…

And then she was lifting her face and bringing her hands to his shoulders. "Farley?"

She said his name softly, almost as if she was pleading for something. And then she was on her toes. And he was leaning closer to her. And they were kissing.

Chapter 13

Farley made it all disappear. Every worry, every loss, every problem. Gone.

Instead Cassidy had him and this moment. His bronzed skin and taut muscles, his amazing kisses and his pleasure-giving hands.

She stopped thinking.

There was no need to think. Their bodies were in control now. One kiss led to another. Clothing was discarded. They didn't go inside. She didn't want that. Farley grabbed the cushion from the swing and set her gently onto that.

She supposed she could have seen the stars and the moon as they made love. But Farley's eyes were enough. His eyes told her that he knew what she needed. And knew how to give it to her.

As she cried out his name, she felt as if she were

howling at the moon. And when he gasped her name back to her, the circle was complete. The waves of pleasure slowly ebbed, until all she could hear was his heart under her ear, and all she felt was his body next to hers.

"No wonder I was so afraid of you at the Harvest Dance."

"Why do you say that? Did I hurt you?"

"The opposite of hurt, I'd say. But was I ready for this four years ago? I'd have to say no." She wasn't so sure she'd been ready now. She'd lost herself for a while there. Been consumed by all the things he made her feel.

And while it had been wonderful, it was also terrifying.

She'd only just started figuring out who she was. She didn't want to lose herself to Farley next. And that would be all too easy to do.

"Cass?" He brushed her hair gently with his fingers, letting the strands fall slowly back in place. "I'm sorry I couldn't save your horse for you."

She swallowed as the pain, momentarily pushed aside, started to seep back. "You did what you could. And maybe it was his time."

She rolled over and searched for her clothing. He must be thinking she and her mother were quite the pair. Both of them throwing her at him in the most shameless way.

She pulled on her jeans and top, anxious to be covered. This had not been right. It wasn't the plan. "Farley, will you drive me home?"

He looked stricken. "I thought—"

"This was a mistake. I—I must have been crazy." It was a warm evening, but her teeth were chattering.

"Cass, please, stay the night. In the spare room if you want." Farley was up, pulling on his jeans, then wrapping his shirt around her shoulders. "You're shaking. Are you cold?"

She shook her head, passed him back his shirt. "I can't stay. I can't."

As he drove her home, Farley was reminded of that night, four years ago, when they'd sat silently in a dark truck, both of them desperate for the trip to be over so they could pretend the night had never happened.

Though Farley wasn't so sure he could make that same wish tonight. Making love with Cassidy had been everything and more that he could have hoped for. And she'd been right there with him. He'd heard the pleasure in her voice, felt it in her body, right down to her cells.

But emotionally she hadn't been ready. Maybe her emotions had been too raw. Maybe she saw him as a threat—someone else who would try to keep her from taking that job she wanted so much. Or maybe she just saw him as the man her mother wanted her to be with, and therefore the last man on earth she would ever settle for.

Just like on that other night, four years ago, when he stopped the truck, he went to open her door. Sky jumped out first, then Cassidy.

She wouldn't look him in the eyes. "Thanks for the lift, Farley. And thanks for…what you tried to do for Finn."

Every instinct screamed at him not to leave her this way. But what choice did he have?

"Let me walk you to the door."

She shook her head. "Just go, Farley, okay?"

She was so tired, she was swaying on her feet. Her face was tear-stained and her hand rested on Sky's head as if her dog was the only thing holding her together right now. He wanted to scoop her up and carry her to her bed.

Instead, he got back into the truck and drove away.

Cassidy watched until his taillights were faded to tiny dots in the distance, then contemplated her options. Sleep in the posh bedroom her mom had designed for her?

No, thanks.

She decided to drive to Brock's cabin and spend the night there. Sky was confused, but obeyed her command to climb into the passenger side of her truck. At the cabin, she found the key under the flowerpot as usual and went inside.

Sky seemed immediately at home and went to lie on the sofa. But Cassidy hung back. She hadn't been here since Brock's death and she felt as if she was violating a sacred space. As she moved tentatively from room to room, however, she began to feel a peaceful connection to her brother.

Cassidy looked over his music collection and found an album that he had played incessantly when he was around fourteen. She put it on and smiled at the familiar opening guitar riff.

The music filled up the empty spaces in the cabin and added warmth and life. Bonny had boxed Brock's belongings and given the cabin a cleaning after his death. Dust had accumulated over the passing months, but it wasn't too bad.

Cassidy found clean sheets in the linen cupboard and made up the spare bed. She turned on the shower, stripped and stepped inside. The hot water was soothing, at first. But it didn't take long for her thoughts to start torturing her. First she was sobbing, thinking of Finn.

And not a minute later, her breath was heavy, remembering what had happened with Farley. She ran a soapy cloth over her body. He'd touched her here. And here. And here.

Oh, Lord, what had possessed her? She'd practically begged him to make love to her, then treated him like chopped liver when it was over.

She'd been such a jerk. Just like four years ago. The parallel between the way she'd behaved on the two occasions was mortifying. How could she ever face him again?

Eventually the water began to run cool, and Cassidy switched off the taps. She dried off and then dragged her weary body to bed. Not a minute later, Sky joined her there.

Poor dog must be so confused by now. It had been quite an evening. First she'd been dragged out to the barn, then to Farley's place, and now here they were settling in at Brock's cabin.

Showing a wonderful ability to adapt to new circumstances, however, Sky just put down her head and went to sleep.

And Cassidy, eventually, did the same.

Cassidy couldn't remember the last time she'd slept much past dawn. But she was exhausted—mentally and physically—and not only did the cabin's spare bedroom window face north, but the curtains were drawn. Finally, there was no alarm set in the room. In fact, there wasn't even a clock.

Sky must have been just as tired as she was, because she didn't wake Cassidy up, either.

It was the rumble of her empty stomach that finally roused Cassidy and had her lifting her head from the pillow.

She glanced around the dimly lit room in confusion, then winced as everything came back to her.

She grabbed her phone from the bedside table and could not believe what she saw.

She'd slept until noon?

Hastily, she scrambled out of the bed, then dressed in the clothes from the previous night. It was hard not to remember Farley's fingers on the buttons of her shirt, or the way he'd looked at her when they'd—

No.

She let Sky out for her morning constitutional, then opened the passenger door of her truck and urged Sky to jump in.

For the first time that Cassidy could remember, Sky balked.

"We're not going far," she promised the border collie. "Just home."

The word *home* seemed to convince her and Sky finally took her place. As Cassidy motored back along the graveled road, she could hear the sound of heavy equipment coming from the direction of the horse burial grounds.

Farley was living up to his promise to take care of Finn, and Cassidy was thankful that she wouldn't have to face the body when she went into the barn this morning.

But Dave had already done the chores, she noticed, as she made the rounds of the cattle and equine barns ten minutes later. She went to the home barn last and the first thing she noticed was the missing boot bath.

Inside were more changes. The stall where Finnegan had died last night was empty and perfectly clean.

Only one person could have done all this. She found his note in the tack room.

"I've disinfected Finn's stall, feeding pail and water trough and burned the bedding. You can consider this official notice that the quarantine on Coffee Creek Ranch is ended."

Cassidy read the note several times, closing her eyes and letting a few more tears fall. How could he be so kind and thoughtful when she'd behaved like such a—

Words failed her.

She wanted to call him and thank him, but she guessed he might not be too happy to hear from her right now. In fact, she wouldn't blame him if he never wanted to see her again.

Cassidy got some horse treats from the feed room then went outside to the pasture. Lucy spotted her right away and came trotting over.

"Good girl, Lucy." She broke off a piece of the baked horse treat and gave the palomino a hug. She wondered what Lucy and the rest of the herd had made of the previous night's events.

She was certain that they knew Finn had died. She could tell by the way they huddled closely together, even though the day was sunny and warm.

When she'd finished feeding Lucy the treat, she patted her on the rump, then headed back to her truck. It was past one in the afternoon now and she needed coffee.

The Cinnamon Stick seemed like the logical place to go.

* * *

Straws Monahan was sitting in one of the booths, enjoying coffee and a sandwich. The gray-haired rancher was in his early fifties, a trim, kindly eyed man whose family roots in this area went back as far as the Lamberts and the Turners.

"Thanks," Cassidy said to Dawn, who was manning the café with Vince this afternoon. She picked up her coffee and sandwich. "How's it going? Has it been busy?"

"Steady, but not too bad. I hope Laurel manages to talk Winnie into coming back to Coffee Creek soon. I don't mind working the extra hours, but I miss Winnie. We all do."

"Yes, that would be good," Cassidy agreed. She hoped her mother's note would be the first step in making Winnie want to come back to the town that she had once called home.

Cassidy nodded hello to Straws, who'd been looking her way ever since she'd stepped into the café. She was heading outside, intending to sit on the bench in the sun to eat her meal, when he called her over.

"Cassidy? Got a minute?"

"Sure." She settled herself into the bench seat opposite his. Back when the Monahans had been cattle ranchers, Straws had been a successful rodeo cowboy, as well. He'd retired when his wife had their first child, about twenty-five years ago, and opened the Monahan Rodeo Arena and Equestrian Center.

Over the years he'd built amazing facilities, including an eighty-thousand-square-foot indoor arena and an outdoor stadium with seating for twenty thousand people. These were used for all sorts of rodeo, riding and equestrian clinics.

Cassidy had a lot of time for Straws, who was widely known for his humane methods of training and working with horses. He was scrupulous in the people he hired and the Monahans' full-service boarding was generally considered the best that money could buy for your horse.

"Has your mother talked you into joining our committee yet?" he asked.

It took her a moment to connect the dots. Then she laughed. She'd forgotten that Straws was on her mom's Heritage Site Committee. "No, but she hasn't given up trying."

"Olive never does," Straws said mildly.

Cassidy wondered if he was going to try to persuade her as well, but his next question took a different tack.

"You were a barrel racer in high school, weren't you?"

"That was a while ago. But yes."

"You were very talented. I remember watching you when my own daughter was doing some competing. Ever consider going back to it?"

"Why do you ask?"

"I just lost one of my best riding and barrel racing instructors. She's marrying a fellow from New Mexico, leaving in about a week. Any chance you want the job?"

"Well—I'm flattered." And she was. Straws only hired the best. "But I just graduated from college and I'm planning to move to Billings and work for an accounting firm."

"Really? Olive never said anything about that."

Cassidy rolled her eyes. "She isn't exactly a fan of my plan."

He laughed. "She is skilled at ignoring facts that

aren't to her suiting, isn't she? Well, if your plans change in the next few weeks, you let me know, okay? Even a few weeks of your time would tide me over until I found someone permanent."

"Thanks, Straws, I'll give it some thought."

Straws rose to leave, then hesitated as he noticed someone else come into the café.

Cassidy followed his gaze and was horrified to see Dan Farley at the entrance. He noticed her, too, but she couldn't decipher the look in his dark eyes.

"Hey, Farley. Come and join us." Oblivious to the emotional undercurrents flowing between Cassidy and Farley, Straws made room for Farley to sit next to him. "I was just about to ask Cassidy here how their horses were making out. I heard you had some strangles to contend with?"

Cassidy noticed how tired Farley looked. She hated that it was her fault. She wrapped her hands around her mug of coffee then turned to Straws. "Quarantine was just lifted today. Two of our horses recovered, but…" She steeled herself to say the rest. "We did lose one of our older horses."

"I'm sorry to hear that. I hope it wasn't that beautiful palomino who died?"

"No. You've seen Lucky Lucy?"

He nodded. "I thought your mother was being a little foolhardy when she took her to Joe Purdy's ranch on the other side of Lewistown. Sure, Joe knows what he's doing when it comes to training barrel horses. But Purdy's has been battling with the infection for over a year. Never properly isolated and contained the disease when it first showed up and now it's spread pretty much through their entire herd."

Cassidy could see that Farley was as shocked to hear this as she was.

"I hadn't heard about that," Farley said slowly. "Purdy's ranch is well out of my district."

"When did Mom take Lucy to Joe Purdy's ranch?"

Straws wrinkled his brow. "Must have been mid-April."

Two weeks before Cassidy had come home from college. "Maybe she didn't know about the strangles?"

Straws shook his head. "I warned her myself."

A snippet of conversation came back to her then. "Farley, remember when you asked if any of our horses had left the property recently?"

He nodded, but didn't say anything. She knew he was recalling how Jackson had mentioned seeing Olive load Lucky Lucy into a trailer and she'd insisted he was mistaken.

But this seemed to imply that Jackson had been telling the truth.

It was her mother who had lied. But why?

"Anyway, I'm glad it all worked out in the end." Straws finished his coffee. "I should hit the road. Cassidy, you think about my offer, you hear?" He winked. "I pay real good, in case you haven't heard."

Once the older rancher was gone, Farley lifted his brows. "Straws tried to hire you?"

"He's looking for a new riding teacher. Someone who knows how to barrel race." But who cared about such details now? "Farley, can you believe Mom would have exposed Lucy to strangles on purpose? It doesn't make sense. Everyone around knows that Straws has the best trainers in the area. And his operation is impeccable. If she wanted extra training for Lucy, why not take her to the Monahans'?"

"It doesn't make sense," he agreed.

Unless… "You don't think she did it on purpose because of me? I hate to sound paranoid, but she might have figured that if a couple of our horses came down with strangles, I'd be home in a few weeks and I'd be the obvious person to look after them."

"That's twisted. But there is a certain logic to it," Farley said.

Plus, Cassidy thought, not only had the strangles kept her on the ranch, it had forced her into spending time with Dan Farley—the man Olive thought she should marry.

But that part was just too embarrassing to say out loud.

"This is crazy, isn't it? Mom can be manipulative, but she'd never go this far. She's too good of a business person to risk spreading strangles over her entire herd."

Farley was quiet for a while. Then in a low voice he said, "Maybe she took a calculated risk. She knew the riding horses were separated from the breeding ones, and the chances of the quarter horses getting infected were slim. Plus, she probably knows that only ten percent of the horses who develop strangles ever develop complications. Maybe she hoped your horses would ride it out without any lasting problems."

"Or maybe she'd calculated all that and concluded that the loss of a horse or two would be worth it," Cassidy concluded bitterly.

Farley rubbed his forehead then sighed. "You know what? I think the drama of the past few days is catching up to us. There's a much more likely scenario."

"Really? I'd like to hear it."

"Your mother probably had her own reasons for wanting Purdy to work with her horse. She chose to ignore the possibility of getting strangles, figuring the chances were small. Then, when the infection did show up, she was too embarrassed to own up to her mistake."

His scenario was more likely, Cassidy had to agree. But it still put the responsibility for the outbreak all on her mother. And it didn't change the fact that she had lied.

Chapter 14

Farley left the café with Cassidy. Running into her this way had not been helpful to either the headache pounding behind his eyes or to his spirits, which felt as if they'd been dragged behind a herd of wild horses for a few days.

He'd been up early, wanting to arrange for Finnegan's burial as soon as possible. He'd also disinfected the barn so that Cassidy wouldn't have to face the heartbreak of doing it herself. It had seemed like the gentlemanly thing to do.

Out in the sunshine, standing beside the old truck that she was so ridiculously fond of, she thanked him.

"I slept in until noon. I can't remember the last time I did that. And when I finally made it down to the home barn, you'd taken care of everything. Thank you, Farley."

He had to look away, unable to bear how pretty she

looked with the sunshine glinting like gold in her hair. She'd run out on him twice now. Only a fool would risk that kind of humiliation a third time.

"Don't worry about it. It's part of the job when you're a vet."

He saw that his comment wounded her, but hell, what did she expect from him?

"Look—I'm sorry about running out last night. You must have thought I was crazy."

"You'd had a rough night. And for the record—I wasn't trying to take advantage of that."

"Of course you weren't…"

"Good. I'm glad that's clear." His anger was coming through in his voice. He didn't intend it, but couldn't seem to stop it, either.

"It is," she said softly.

"Well, I'd better get going. I have a busy day."

She nodded.

He hesitated. "I hope you get that job, Cass. To hell with what your family thinks. You have to go after what you want in life."

Last night he'd been crazy enough to think that what he wanted was her.

But he needed a woman with a little more staying power.

On the drive home from town Cassidy noticed something strange. The flowers on Brock's roadside marker were brown and neglected. This was the first time, in her knowledge, that they'd been left to molder. She parked on the side of the road and waded through the grass. When she arrived, she paused for a moment, with her head lowered and her heart aching.

Brock. We miss you.

Then she lifted the wreath off the marker. Immediately the dead blossoms began to disintegrate, scattering in the breeze, until Cassidy was left with only a few dried stems in her hand. She brushed them off into the grass, then went back to her truck.

Obviously Maddie had stopped tending her roadside tribute. But why?

Her family didn't return from moving the cattle until it was almost dark that evening. Cassidy was waiting outside the barn. For some reason her mother had left Lucy behind and Cassidy had passed the time by setting up a barrel racing course and running Lucy through it.

No wonder the palomino had taken to the sport so quickly. Cassidy laughed at herself now, how she'd congratulated herself for being such a great teacher.

But she hadn't been the first to introduce Lucy to a barrel racing course. That would have been Joe Purdy.

Once the initial shock of discovering that her mother had purposefully exposed their horse to strangles had passed, Cassidy had started to wonder about why her mother would want Lucy trained in barrel racing in the first place.

Once again the puzzle pieces came together too easily.

Probably Olive hoped that barrel racing was another lure she could use to reel her daughter back in to Coffee Creek. A beautiful horse like Lucy—practically ideal for barrel racing? What horse-loving woman could resist?

Really, Olive had played all her cards, not leaving anything to chance. She wouldn't be pleased to find out that she had lost anyway.

Around five o'clock Cassidy groomed Lucy and let

her out with the other horses, then she cleaned the arena, and finally she and Sky sat down to wait.

At quarter to six the posse of riders was visible coming down from the north. Cassidy watched until the moving blob turned into individual riders, then identifiable faces. When they finally came up to the barn, she could tell they were all exhausted.

Still, she showed no mercy.

"Finnegan died."

Everyone was silent for a moment, then Corb shook his head. "I'm sorry to hear that. When did it happen?"

"Last night. Farley's already had him buried. The barn's been disinfected and our quarantine is lifted."

"Finn was a good horse, but he was old," Olive said. "I know you did everything you could for him. At least this ordeal is behind us now."

"And who should we thank for that, Mother?"

Olive swung out of her saddle and handed the reins to Dave, who'd come out to help with the horses. Dave led the tired horse into the barn for grooming.

The other two wranglers, Eric and Jay, followed.

That left Corb, Jackson and Olive. Her brother and her mother were gaping at her with surprise. Jackson just looked as though he wanted to escape. When he tried to leave with the other cowboys, Cassidy stopped him by grabbing his arm.

"Please stay a minute. I'd like to get your input on something."

"Sure," he said cautiously. "I'm sorry about your horse. I know how much you loved Finnegan."

"Thanks, Jackson." She blinked away tears. This wasn't the time to be soft.

Speaking slowly and careful not to raise her voice,

Cassidy recounted the information Straws had passed on to her at the Cinnamon Stick Café.

"Is it true, Mom? Did you know Joe Purdy had strangles on his ranch when you took Lucy to him for training?"

Olive's face had been growing progressively paler. Her eyes darted from her daughter's face, to her son's. Then finally to Jackson's.

Undoubtedly she was remembering his earlier assertion that he'd seen her loading Lucy into a trailer. She'd managed to discredit him the first time he'd said it. But this time it wouldn't be so easy.

After almost a minute of silence, she drew her breath.

"You're right. I took a risk that I shouldn't have. It was supposed to be a surprise for you, Cassidy. I originally bought Lucy to give to you as a graduation gift. Remembering how much you loved barrel racing I thought it would be fun to get her a little up-front training."

Despite her resolve to be firm and unyielding, Cassidy felt a little piece of her heart soften at this. Her mom had been right about one thing. She loved Lucy and couldn't have selected a more perfect horse for herself.

"But why risk her getting strangles? You could have taken her to Straws if getting her some training was so important to you."

"I wanted this to be a secret and I was worried someone at Monahan's would blab. You know how fast news travels in Coffee Creek."

The first part of her mother's explanation had tweaked her heart strings. But this—it just didn't make sense. Again, the risk, for a smart business person like her mother, just wouldn't have been worth it.

Unless it had been a calculated risk.

"You knew that a young, healthy horse like Lucy would almost certainly recover completely from a bout of strangles, didn't you?"

"Cassidy! Are you suggesting I *wanted* Lucy to get sick?"

Corb looked as shocked as Olive sounded. But Jackson, Cassidy noticed, didn't seem surprised at all by the suggestion.

She met her mother's gaze again, and in that instant, she knew that she had to stop here. Spelling out the reasons why her mother might have done such a thing would not give her any satisfaction, and would undoubtedly create wounds that would take a long time to heal.

"Only you know the answer to that question, Mom."

Then she asked Jackson if they could talk for a few minutes.

Cassidy and Jackson headed to the office at the front of the barn. Cassidy sank into the upholstered chair, leaving the one behind the desk for her foster brother.

"I was wondering if you knew what was up with Maddie Turner? She's stopped tending the flowers on Brock's wreath. I'd assume she figured it was time to let it go, except she left the dead ones in place and that just doesn't seem like something she would do."

Jackson rubbed the back of his head. He had to be tired, hungry and longing for a good shower. She appreciated that he had taken a few minutes to talk to her about this.

"Well, you're right," he finally said. "It isn't something Maddie would do. Not if she had a choice. But she's in the hospital in Great Falls. I drove her there myself the day before we left on the cattle drive."

"Is she going to be okay?"

"Not likely. It's lung cancer and they didn't catch it early."

"Oh, dear. Does Mother know?"

"Do you think she would care?"

Cassidy couldn't answer that question. After today she could only conclude that she didn't know her mother nearly as well as she'd thought.

"Who's looking after her animals?"

He hesitated. "Vince Butterfield."

"The baker?" This just got stranger and stranger.

Jackson nodded again. "I don't know how he found out she was sick, but he's the one who asked me to drive her to the hospital. Apparently she wouldn't let him do it. But while she's gone, he plans to finish her roof and take care of the animals. She doesn't have a lot left. Mostly pets and about a dozen cattle."

Cassidy remembered how hard her mother had worked to convince Vince to come to their family dinner. He'd turned her down flat. And yet he'd rearranged his entire life in order to help Olive's sister.

"Thanks for telling me that, Jackson. Do you think they'd let me visit her in the hospital?"

He thought about it for a moment. "You're family. Why not?"

Cassidy headed back to the house then and found her mother sitting on the open tailgate of Cassidy's old Ford.

"What's this?" Olive asked, waving at the boxes and suitcases in the back.

Earlier in the day Cassidy had packed her things, knowing that she couldn't wait until she'd heard about the job in Billings to start making changes in her life.

"I'm going to move, Mom. Into my own place. I know Brock's cabin is vacant. I'd like to stay there for Sky's sake. And I'll pay rent."

"Rent? Your brothers never paid rent, why should you? But moving into Brock's cabin is ridiculous. The house is plenty big enough for both of us. You don't really blame me for the strangles, do you?"

And truly, at that moment, Olive looked so small and vulnerable that it was almost impossible to believe.

"Besides," she added, her voice trembling a little, "we just redecorated your room."

Cassidy had expected her mother to take this tack. And while it was still effective, she'd prepared herself to handle it. "The room is beautiful, yes, but I warned you at the time I wouldn't be staying long."

Cassidy could tell her mother didn't know what to say. She'd done everything she could, played every card in her deck of tricks, but it wasn't working. She wanted Cassidy here, living with her. She wanted her working on the ranch and being the treasurer for the Heritage Committee. And, eventually, she wanted her to marry Dan Farley.

"This is crazy, honey." Olive raked a hand through her thick silver-blond hair. "I was planning to offer Brock's cottage to Winnie."

Cassidy didn't argue, even though she knew Corb had suggested this very thing, only to have Olive shoot down the suggestion. He'd also raised the idea of giving Winnie a cash settlement worth at least a portion of Brock's estate. After all, if Brock had died just two hours later, Winnie would have been his wife and entitled to everything.

But Olive was almost pathologically opposed to any

part of the ranch going to someone who wasn't "family." Of course Winnie now had a son who was family. So maybe that was why she'd decided to make a gift of the cottage.

"I'm fine with that, Mom. Go ahead and give the cabin to Winnie and I'll ask her if I can rent the apartment over the Cinnamon Stick."

"Oh, for heaven's sake! Move into the cabin then. Who knows when Winnie Hayes will be back in town, anyway. Maybe never."

"Are you sure, Mom? 'Cause I don't mind—"

"I'm sure," she snapped. Then she shook her head. "What has gotten into you, daughter?"

There were lots of answers to that question. Some Olive would have found quite unkind. So Cassidy stuck with the obvious. "I've just grown up. That's all."

That Sunday Cassidy drove into Great Falls to visit her aunt. When she gave her name and explained that she was a niece, she was allowed to visit her in the semi-private room.

She'd brought flowers. A vase of pretty tulips. It seemed the least she could do for a woman who had tended her brother's roadside memorial so faithfully, for so long.

"Cassidy. This is a surprise."

Maddie was sitting upright in her bed, connected to an intravenous line and dressed in a blue cotton gown. Her face looked gaunt and her hair grayer than ever, but her eyes were still that beautiful green.

"Jackson told me you were sick. I'm so sorry."

"Sit down. And thank you for the flowers. I've always loved tulips."

A curtain shielded the other patient from Cassidy's view, but she heard an older woman's husky voice say, "Me, too. Put them where we can both see them, love."

"Cassidy, meet June," Maddie said. "My partner in misery."

"Hey, June. Nice to meet you. How about I put the flowers here on the ledge at the back of the room. That way, when the curtain is pulled back, both of you can enjoy them."

"Nice to meet you, too, Cassidy. I've heard all about you. But don't pull back the curtain now, love. I'm not decent back here."

June had heard all about her? Cassidy wasn't sure what to make of that. Had Maddie told her *everything* about their family?

"Seems you lucked out with your neighbor," she commented to her aunt and Maddie smiled.

"Indeed. It's wonderful to have someone to talk to."

"Maybe you'd like to talk to me, too, now that I'm here?"

"Why, of course. What would you like to talk about?"

"I'd like to know what the big family feud is about. What in the world happened, Aunt Maddie?"

It was the first time she'd ever linked those two words together. The effect was touching. Her aunt's eyes fluttered and tears blossomed like heavy dew drops.

"Oh, Cassidy. There aren't enough words… Have you tried talking to your mother?"

"I can't. But I've heard that she's angry because you wouldn't let her see her father before he died."

Maddie sighed and turned her head ever so slightly away. "Yes. I suppose that's the story."

"But you wouldn't do that, would you?" Even as she

asked the question, Cassidy knew the answer was no. She could see the genuine pain in her aunt's eyes.

Her aunt was silent for at least a minute. And when she finally spoke again, her voice held a core of steel resolve. "I've been given six months, Cassidy. I don't want to end my days by spreading more discord among the family. It means a lot to me that you came to visit. Thank you."

"That's it? You're not going to tell me *anything?*"

"I can't, sweetheart. It really is better this way."

Chapter 15

Farley was shoeing the first horse of the afternoon at the Monahans' place on Wednesday afternoon when he heard a familiar-sounding voice.

"Come this way, baby. That's a girl."

She sounded so much like Cassidy, he stepped out from the stalls with his alligator clinchers still in hand. There was a round arena right in front of the barn and sure enough, Cassidy was at the center of the pen working with a frisky bay mare.

With a wide-legged gait to accommodate the farrier chaps protecting his thighs, he started toward the fence. Cassidy had on her working boots and jeans, a pale pink tank top and her white hat. She must have stripped off her shirt earlier in the day. He could see it fluttering in the breeze from a fence post by the gate.

It was warm, that was for sure. There was a damp

patch between her shoulder blades. And she paused to swipe the back of her arm over her forehead.

That was when she spotted him.

"Farley?" She let go of the lunge line. As she walked toward him, the gentled bay followed. As soon as she noticed, Cassidy smiled and paused. "Hey, girl, you're getting the idea now, aren't you? Here's your carrot. Hang on a minute now while I talk to my friend."

Disregarding the gate, she climbed over the fence, hopping down to the earth-packed ground right beside him.

"Hey, Farley." Her gaze swept over his chaps and the tool in his hand. "Shoeing some horses today?"

He nodded. "Les Felding and I just started the first one. How about you? What are you doing here?"

Whatever she was doing, she looked good. Like she belonged. An equine training center was the perfect place for someone like Cassidy and he wondered why he hadn't realized that before. A faint hope kindled in him as he waited for her answer.

"When I ran into Straws the other day at the café he said they'd just lost one of their instructors. I called him up later and told him I could help him out for a while. He has me working with some of their new young horses this week. Starting Monday he wants me to run a barrel racing camp for middle-grade girls. By the time that's over, hopefully I'll be starting my new job."

"In Billings?"

"Yeah. I haven't heard yet. But my fingers are crossed."

He should have known. When the hell was he going to stop being such a fool over this woman? The pretty receptionist at Monahan's front office had flirted daringly with him earlier. He should have asked her out.

Cassidy shuffled her boots in the dirt, then glanced up at him, almost shyly. "This is quite the operation, isn't it?"

"Straws runs a first-class outfit. Some of the top names in rodeo have been to his clinics. I'm going to the steer wrestling one next Sunday."

"Preparing for the Wild Rogue?"

"Yeah. B.J. called me on the weekend and confirmed our plans. He's registering in the saddle bronc event and tie-down roping."

"He'll be after the big purse." Cassidy looked proud of her older brother.

Farley hesitated. He should leave it at that. But in the end, he couldn't stop himself from adding, "B.J. wants you to come, too."

He saw a wistful yearning cross her face, just seconds before she shook her head. "If I get the job I won't be able to take the time off. And I'd have no time or place to practice."

She was pretty quick with her excuses. Frankly, he was just as glad. "What does your mother think about you working here?"

"She isn't impressed. But her opinions don't sway me, anymore."

She said this definitively, and he realized that Olive had finally crossed a line that had changed everything between mother and daughter.

"You still living at the house?"

She shook her head. "In Brock's cabin. I was tempted to move into town, but that would have been tough on Sky. Coffee Creek Ranch is the only home she knows.

I wish I could take her with me when I go to Billings. But I've thought about what you said and I realize that wouldn't be fair. She was happy with Corb and Laurel before. They'll give her a good home."

He fought back the urge to tell her that there was another solution here, staring her right in the face. She had to know how he felt about her. How he couldn't stop feeling about her. He knew he was being a fool, but there was just no choice. Not for him.

He loved her. He felt as if he always had.

But even if she wasn't leaving Coffee Creek, she would never feel the same way about him. She'd proven that when she ran out on him the other night.

Cassidy had her plans, and she'd never wavered from them.

And maybe he should be grateful she was going to move to the city. If he couldn't have her, it would be easier this way. Perhaps one day he'd forget her enough to fall in love with someone else.

Then again, she'd been out of his life for four years and he'd come undone after just one look at her at the Cinnamon Stick Café.

"Farley, I want to apologize again for everything me and my family put you through."

"You don't need to apologize for your family. It was you who walked out the door after we made love. Not your mother or your brothers. You."

There. He'd put it to her plain.

She winced. "I was upset. I'd lost my horse, and—"

"Sure, you were upset. And for a while I worried that I may have taken advantage of that. But I don't think so anymore. I think *you* took advantage of *me*. Maybe you thought having sex would make the pain go away for a while. But it wasn't a diversion for me."

Her eyes were huge as she stared up at him. "Farley, I—"

"It's good that you're moving to Billings. I think a little distance from you is just what I need right now."

Tears started to build in her eyes, and his gut clenched at the sight. Damn her for knowing just how to get to him.

"I'm sorry if I hurt you. If you're trying to do the same to me, I have to tell you it's working."

He resisted the urge to wipe away the tears. To hold out his arms. "This isn't about hurting you. It's about me not being someone to help you pass the time until you hear from that damn accounting firm."

"No." She grabbed his arm and held on tight. "You were never that. You mean so much to me, Farley. Can't you see it in my eyes?"

For a second he almost believed her. But then the fates intervened and saved him from himself.

"Hey, Doc," an irritated voice called out from the stables. "You planning to shoe all four of this here horse's hoofs? Or just the one?"

"Be right there, Les." Farley pulled away, then angled his body back toward the stables, giving her one last look over his shoulder. She hadn't started back to the arena yet. She was still looking at him, her expression almost...wistful?

"See you around, Cass."

"Yes. See you around."

Cassidy didn't know why she spent more time that afternoon reliving the encounter with Farley than she did checking her phone for messages from Cushman and Green. She felt as if there was something left unsaid between them and it worried her.

He'd done so much to help her since she'd come home. He'd fixed up Sky after the coyote attack, and he'd been there for her when Finnegan died, too.

He'd been the only one to offer the support she'd needed then. And what had happened after, well, it had been magical and she couldn't understand herself, why she had felt the urge to go home after.

He'd thought she was running from him.

But maybe she'd been running from herself and feelings that were just too big for her to contain.

The end result was that she had spoiled things between them again. And all she had to hold herself together was her work at Monahan's.

She really loved it. At the end of her second week, she was amazed by the progress her teenage girls had made with their horses. Their parents were pleased, too, and so was Straws.

"All of them would sign up on the spot for a second session if I could confirm that you would be the instructor," he told her on Thursday, as he passed over her check.

Cassidy folded the paper in half and tucked it into her back pocket. "It was so much fun. Some of those girls are really talented and there were a few great horses, too. But I can't promise anything beyond tomorrow, Mr. Monahan."

Back at home she ate her dinner outside, sitting in one of the wooden deck chairs looking at the lake, Sky at her feet, still damp from a quick swim.

In the distance, she heard Laurel call for Corb to come

inside for dinner. She and Stephanie had returned yesterday from their visit to Winnie's family farm in Highwood. Apparently Winnie still wasn't ready to come back, though she would one day, since she'd invested all her money in the Cinnamon Stick Café and couldn't afford to sell.

Cassidy picked at the pizza she'd heated for her dinner. Despite the hard work she put in every day, she didn't have much appetite lately. She hadn't been sleeping well, either.

She supposed she was just nervous about the job. Twenty times a day she checked her phone for messages, and every night she logged on to Facebook to see if any of her classmates had been offered jobs. But all week there'd been no word. Everyone seemed to assume that she and Josh were shoo-ins, it was only the third person who was up for debate.

Cassidy wished she could feel as confident. She kept thinking over her interview and second-guessing things she'd said and done.

She laid the unfinished slice of pizza back on her plate and wondered what Farley was doing tonight. Maybe he'd gone back to dating Amber?

She should be glad for him if he had. After all, it was partly her fault that the relationship had broken apart when it did.

But the mental picture of him and Amber together didn't make her feel glad. She felt—*okay, face it*—jealous. She'd told herself that making love with him had been a terrible misstep.

The more she thought about it, though, the less like a mistake it seemed.

But that was a crazy way to think. Farley was part

of the plan that her mother had made for her life. And she wasn't doing that anymore, letting Olive control her destiny.

Besides, Farley had made it pretty clear that he was done with her.

Cassidy started back for the cabin with Sky at her side. She'd feel better once she heard about the job. It was probably just the suspense of waiting that was making her so unsettled.

The call came on Friday. As soon as she hung up, Cassidy paused to let it soak in. She'd been offered the job. Shouldn't she feel elated?

But she'd been through this before, when she'd applied for college and waited to see if she'd be accepted. She'd anticipated the acceptance letter would send her through the roof with excitement, but instead all she'd felt was satisfied and relieved.

Like she did right now.

Cassidy phoned her mom and her brothers to pass on the news. She had to leave messages for all of them; only Corb answered and professed that he was proud of her.

She doubted that she would have received such a civil comment from her mother.

When she'd finished the calls, she picked up the phone, hesitating over another number. She really wanted to tell Farley. But she was pretty sure he didn't want to hear from her.

So instead of phoning Farley she logged on to Facebook and checked her friends' status feeds. Within five minutes the news had been posted. Both Josh Brown and another one of their classmates, Adrienne Itani, had made the final cut. Cassidy confirmed her own good news, then sat back and thought about everything she had to do.

They'd been asked to start work the following Monday. Which meant she had the weekend to drive to Billings, find an apartment and buy some office-appropriate clothing, at least enough for a week.

She looked down at her hands, the calluses, the dirt beneath her nails that was always so hard to clean out. Maybe she should get those fancy gel nails, too.

It was hell leaving Sky. Corb and Laurel promised to take good care of her, though, and to give her lots of love. Leaving Lucy was almost as hard. Even though her mother's motives for buying the palomino were suspect, Cassidy and the horse had developed an amazing rapport.

Leaving her mother was not so hard. Cassidy had moved past her anger into a cooler place where she could still appreciate all that her mother had done for her, while, at the same time, freeing herself of the burden of trying to please Olive and make her proud.

So when her mother turned on the tears, Cassidy refused to be swayed into feeling guilty. She said her farewells, hugged and kissed her family, who had gathered at the porch to say goodbye, then headed for her truck.

A bark from Sky was the only thing that made her cry. She turned for a final look at her dog, then got behind the wheel and drove straight through to Billings without stopping.

She'd done some searching on the Net and had three appointments set up to look at apartments. She chose one on the ground floor of a lovely brick complex, only eight blocks from her office.

Next she went shopping and found a new suit, skirt and several blouses to mix and match.

And then it was her first day. She could hardly sleep the night before, and arrived at the office fifteen minutes early. Josh arrived next, and she was shocked at how little she felt when she saw him.

He gave her a hug and told her he'd missed her.

But inside all she had was a big void.

Adrienne came next, one minute before nine and Cassidy was awed by how professional and elegant she looked. She was wearing a similar outfit to Cassidy— skirt, jacket and blouse. Yet Adrienne wore them with a natural grace that Cassidy just didn't feel.

They were given an orientation by Pamela. Then introduced to the managers under whom they'd be working. The first day involved reviewing manuals and signing lots of paperwork. On Tuesday they were assigned clients and reviewed files and given jobs of photocopying papers and making up schedules. Wednesday Cassidy accompanied her manager to her first client meeting. Thursday she was put to work finding documentation for certain expense transactions, a job that continued to Friday and, she was told, would probably take her the rest of the next week to complete.

Cassidy felt her spirits drop. The job was turning out so different from what she'd expected. She glanced out the window. The blue sky teased her. She wondered about her family, her dog and her horse. Mostly, she wondered about Farley. Was he missing her at all?

Anger drove Farley for several days after Cassidy left Coffee Creek. The damned woman had toyed with him like he was a mouse.

Again.

And he'd let her.

What the hell was wrong with him?

By Thursday, that story wasn't washing anymore. After dinner, when he was out walking with his dogs, he finally admitted the truth. Cassidy wasn't into manipulating or playing games. If she'd slept with him, it had to have meant something to her.

Trouble was, the meaning had been inconvenient. It hadn't fit into her plan.

And so she'd run.

And what had he done? Taken offense and pulled back.

Never once had he told her how he really felt about her. Never once had he put his heart—and his pride— on the line and said the words.

Once, he'd told her that if she wanted something, she should go after it.

Didn't the same advice apply to him?

Farley went into the office to check his appointments for the next day. As usual his schedule was booked solid.

He could always wait for Saturday. But his gut told him no. It had to be tomorrow.

He slashed a black line through his afternoon appointments. Liz would make the phone calls for him.

After lunch, he'd be on the road.

Friday at five, they were all back at the office. Cassidy had never been so happy to see the end of a work week.

"We have to hit the bar," Josh said, clearing off his workstation.

"Absolutely," Adrienne agreed. "My manager tells

me a lot of the first and second years go to the Irish pub on the corner. How does that sound?"

"Good with me," Josh said. "Cass, you coming?"

She walked by the Silver Unicorn every day to and from work. It was a dark, low-ceilinged place. No outside patio. She was longing for sunshine and clean air, but she said yes anyway, just to be sociable.

Her stomach was churning as they rode the elevator down to the lobby level. She'd been on edge all week, anxious to do a good job and, more important, not screw up.

But that desire to perform well had hidden other feelings. Something awful was swelling and intensifying inside of her. She didn't know what it was. But even breathing seemed to be harder with each passing second.

As soon as she stepped out of the revolving door to the street, Cassidy realized that the feeling she'd been unable to name was suffocation.

She hated the new job. Just hated it.

She didn't like the city, the sidewalks, the pollution or the noise.

How could she have done this? She'd studied so hard for her degree. She'd dedicated the past five years to it.

And yet, now that her goal was in hand, she'd never been so unhappy.

She took a deep breath and knew that she couldn't go to the pub tonight.

She couldn't go back to the office on Monday, either. She was no quitter, but there was no sense in spending her life in a place where she didn't belong. It was really as simple as that.

Josh and Adrienne were still by her side. She didn't know what to tell them. But suddenly Adrienne stopped.

"Wow. Check out that cowboy at eleven o'clock. Is he hot, or what?"

Cassidy looked.

Adrienne had spotted one hot cowboy all right. He was tall and broad-shouldered, dressed entirely in black, leaning against a concrete pillar, one cowboy boot crossed casually over the other.

As soon as her gaze landed on him, he touched the brim of his hat in acknowledgment.

"My, oh, my." Adrienne patted a hand over her sleek brown hair. "He's looking right at me as if he knows me or something."

"He's hot all right," Cassidy agreed. "But he's mine."

She reached down and took off the high-heeled shoes that had started blisters on the back of her heels. In bare feet she walked over the hot concrete path and dropped the shoes into a handy trash can. *Good riddance to you.*

"Way to go, sister," cheered a woman wearing white running shoes with her suit.

Cassidy smiled, but kept walking in a line that would take her straight to Farley. He was the last person she'd ever expected to see here.

But, she now realized, he was also the only one she really wanted.

With every step she drew closer to him. And he was smiling. Momentarily she felt a pang of sorrow for all she was leaving behind. She'd had so many hopes and aspirations.

But she saw now that it had never been something she wanted. Only something her mother didn't want her to want.

She'd spent the past five years in a pretty confused state. Between trying to think for herself and avoid her mother's attempts at manipulation, she'd forgotten to do the most important thing.

Follow her heart.

When she reached him, Farley held out his arms and swept her feet right off the ground.

"I missed you," he said. "And I've come to get you. But only if you're ready to be mine. No more running."

She looked into his eyes, so steadfast, so true. There was something powerful between them, and it had been there from the start. At twenty-one it had scared her. But now she understood that far from being subsumed by it, she would be made stronger by it and more fulfilled.

"I love you, Farley."

And then he kissed her.

Epilogue

It was Saturday night at the Wild Rogue Rodeo in Central Point, Oregon. Steer wrestling was just a hobby for Farley, something he did for a change of pace from the relentless hard work of his veterinary practice.

Although he'd brushed up on his skills at the steer wrestling clinic at Monahan's, he hadn't really expected to place at the rodeo. He was just here for fun and the companionship of some people who meant a lot to him.

But he'd done unexpectedly well on Thursday and Friday. And if he did as well tonight, he'd go home with some money. And maybe even a trophy.

But all of that was just gravy to him now.

The announcer was calling his name. "Next up we have Dan Farley, a vet from Coffee Creek, Montana, here to show us that he has a few bulldogging skills, as well…"

The voice faded as Farley concentrated on what he was doing. B.J. Lambert had agreed to be his hazer and he was on the other side of the chute where the steer would momentarily be running from. B.J. would keep that steer moving in a straight line. The rest was up to him.

He urged his mount into position. At the same time he heard a sweet voice holler from the crowd. "You can do it, Farley!"

Cassidy. She was waving her hat, her blond hair blowing crazily in the breeze.

His back went straighter, his head prouder. With a girl like Cassidy Lambert cheering for him, how could he ever fail?

He gave a nod and the chute man tripped the lever. Out raced the revved-up longhorn—six hundred pounds of him, in Farley's estimation.

The second the barrier released, Farley was off, too. His horse was a dream, bringing him right up to the sweet zone. With a leap of faith he leaned over his horse and grabbed for the steer's horns. For a second he was out there—hanging in the air while his horse ran flat-out.

The next, he had an elbow crooked around one horn, a fist over the other.

He wasn't thinking or planning now, just moving on instinct. He felt his boots slip out of the stirrups and he slid to the left, pulling the steer's head until he had the nose nestled up in the crook of his arm.

The legs were up. The horn sounded.

"5.6 seconds!"

Farley released the steer, then found his footing. He was sure he could hear Cassidy cheering above the roar of the crowd. His time wouldn't win him any records. But it might just get him the top ranking for the night.

He brushed the dust from his legs, waved his hat at the crowd, then hurried out of the arena. His shoulders ached a lot. He was getting old for this sport. But what a rush.

Cassidy wanted to find Farley and congratulate him on his performance. She was so proud of him. He'd been competing against some pretty serious cowboys tonight and he'd beat them all!

She hoped to do him proud, too, in the barrel racing event. But she also knew it wouldn't pay to set her expectations too high. She'd been doing a lot of training this past month at Monahan's—Straws had offered her a full-time position when he heard she'd quit the job in Billings—but she'd also been away from the sport for a long time.

And she'd never before competed in a bona fide PRCA sanctioned rodeo.

She wiped her hands nervously on her cream-colored jeans. She'd chosen a golden Western-styled shirt for her top, and her hat had a matching gold band. The colors worked perfectly with both her coloring and Lucy's.

Her mother had made her a gift of the horse when she came back from Billings. She'd been gracious about it, too, but then she'd been proven right, hadn't she?

It still galled Cassidy to admit it.

Her mother had known she belonged in the country. And she'd known Farley was the right man for her, as well. If she had only stepped back and let nature take its course, Cassidy figured she could have saved herself—and those she loved—from a lot of heartache and grief.

But stepping back was never going to be Olive's way.

And for good, and bad, her mother was a force in her life that she was always going to have to deal with.

Before Cassidy knew it, the barrel racing had started. She was the sixth and final contestant. She heard the excitement of the crowd as she and Lucy lined up at the gate.

"And here she is, the golden girl and her golden horse from Coffee Creek, Montana. Don't they make a pretty picture? This is Cassidy Lambert and her palomino Lucky Lucy. I'm betting Cassidy won't be needing any luck tonight. Not based on what we saw from her last night."

Cassidy was so nervous she thought she was going to be sick. And then she caught Farley's eyes, standing off to the side near the chutes for the bucking horses. He nodded at her, and she could almost hear his calm, strong voice inside her head.

"You're my girl, Cassidy. You can do anything."

And she felt that she could. His love took all the best things about her and made them better. She ran a hand down Lucy's neck, then leaned over to whisper in her ear. "Be my lucky girl. Let's go!"

Though it was well-known that Olive did not care for the rodeo, she went to Central Point, Oregon, that weekend to see her eldest son, daughter and soon-to-be son-in-law compete. That was one thing about her mom, Cassidy thought. She always put her kids first. And it did seem Olive was proud when Cassidy came in third for barrel racing. Farley placed first for steer wrestling and B.J. won both the saddle bronc and tie-down roping events, ending up the big winner of a thirty-five-thousand-dollar prize.

Olive congratulated them at the end of the ceremony, then excused herself. Much as she didn't like the rodeo, she especially hated the partying that went on afterward.

Cassidy and Farley, however, were happy to go to the Rogue Saloon and socialize with all the other competitors, with B.J. promising to follow once he'd given an interview to some local journalists.

At the saloon Cassidy and Farley did *some* socializing.

And then all Cassidy wanted was to dance with Farley.

He was holding her in his arms when a song came on that they both instantly recognized. For the first time that night she tripped. And Farley steadied her.

"You aren't going to run away this time, I hope?" he whispered in her ear.

It was the last song they'd danced to four years ago, before she'd panicked and sabotaged their date.

"I'm never running again," she promised him.

"I'll hold you to that." He brushed a thumb over the diamond ring he'd given her two weeks ago. "So—had any thoughts about when we should have the wedding?"

"Soon." She was anxious to move in with him, and figured Sky would adjust okay—she'd already been accepted as a pal by Tom and Dick.

"I'm good with that. Just give me a date so I can tell my folks. They'll want to book a flight."

"Are you okay with something small?"

"Whatever you want."

"Just close family and friends. I'd like it to be at the Coffee Creek Church."

"Are you sure?"

She nodded. Their family needed to purge the painful memories of Brock's wedding-that-never-happened. "And Straws told me we could have the reception in his dining room. It's beautiful and has such amazing views of the mountains."

"Have you talked to your mother about any of this?"

"Not yet. I want you with me when I do. She'll have a place of honor at the wedding as my mother, but I don't want her commandeering the plans, the way she tried to do with Laurel and Corb."

Farley remembered. Olive had organized every detail of that event, only to have the young couple elope in New York.

"I can handle Olive," he assured her. "You, now, that's a different story. You have me wrapped around your little finger. You know that, right?"

She laughed. She'd never been so happy. "I plan to keep you there, too, cowboy. And don't forget it."

* * * * *

WE HOPE YOU ENJOYED
THIS BOOK FROM

◈ HARLEQUIN
SPECIAL
EDITION

Believe in love. Overcome obstacles. Find happiness.

Relate to finding comfort and strength in the
support of loved ones and enjoy the journey
no matter what life throws your way.

6 NEW BOOKS AVAILABLE EVERY MONTH!

HSEHALO2020

SPECIAL EXCERPT FROM

HARLEQUIN
SPECIAL EDITION

*Real estate developer Brittany Doyle is eager to
bring the mountain town of Gallant Lake into the
twenty-first century...by changing everything.
Hardware store owner Nate Thomas hates change.
These opposites refuse to compromise, except when it
comes to falling in love.*

Read on for a sneak peek at
Changing His Plans,
*the next book in the Gallant Lake Stories
miniseries by Jo McNally.*

He stuck his head around the corner of the fasteners
aisle just in time to see a tall brunette stagger into the
revolving seed display. Some of the packets went flying,
but she managed to steady the display before the whole
thing toppled. He took in what probably had been a very
nice silk blouse and tailored trouser suit before she was
drenched in the storm raging outside. The heel on one of
the ridiculously high heels she was wearing had snapped
off, explaining why she was stumbling around.

"Having a bad morning?"

The woman looked up in annoyance, strands of dark,
wet hair falling across her face.

"You could say that. I don't suppose you have a shoe
repair place in this town?" She looked at the bright red
heel in her hand.

Nate shook his head as he approached her. "Nope. But hand it over. I'll see what I can do."

A perfectly shaped brow arched high. "Why? Are you going to cobble them back together with—" she gestured around widely "—maybe some staples or screws?"

"Technically, what you just described is the definition of cobbling, so yeah. I've got some glue that'll do the trick." He met her gaze calmly. "It'd be a lot easier to do if you'd take the shoe off. Unless you also think I'm a blacksmith?"

He was teasing her. Something about this soaking-wet woman still having so much…regal bearing…amused Nate. He wasn't usually a fan of the pearl-clutching country club set who strutted through Gallant Lake on the weekends and referred to his family's hardware store as "adorable." But he couldn't help admiring this woman's ability to hold on to her superiority while looking like she accidentally went to a water park instead of the business meeting she was dressed for. To be honest, he also admired the figure that expensive red suit was clinging to as it dripped water on his floor.

He held out his hand. "I'm Nate Thomas. This is my store."

She let out an irritated sigh. "Brittany Doyle." She slid her long, slender hand into his and gripped with surprising strength. He held it for just a half second longer than necessary before shaking off the odd current of interest she invoked in him.

Don't miss
Changing His Plans *by Jo McNally,*
available September 2020 wherever
Harlequin Special Edition books and ebooks are sold.

Harlequin.com

Copyright © 2020 by Jo McNally

**IF YOU ENJOYED THIS BOOK
WE THINK YOU WILL ALSO LOVE**

LOVE INSPIRED

INSPIRATIONAL ROMANCE

Uplifting stories of faith, forgiveness and hope.

Fall in love with stories where faith helps
guide you through life's challenges, and discover
the promise of a new beginning.

6 NEW BOOKS AVAILABLE EVERY MONTH!

LIXSERIES2020

Love Harlequin romance?

DISCOVER.

Be the first to find out about promotions,
news and exclusive content!

Facebook.com/HarlequinBooks

Twitter.com/HarlequinBooks

Instagram.com/HarlequinBooks

Pinterest.com/HarlequinBooks

ReaderService.com

EXPLORE.

Sign up for the Harlequin e-newsletter and
download a free book from any series at
TryHarlequin.com

CONNECT.

Join our Harlequin community to
share your thoughts and connect
with other romance readers!
Facebook.com/groups/HarlequinConnection

HSOCIAL2020

HARLEQUIN

Heartfelt or suspenseful, inspiring or passionate, Harlequin has your happily-ever-after.

With new books published every month, you are sure to find the satisfying escape you know you deserve.

SIGN UP FOR THE HARLEQUIN NEWSLETTER

Be the first to hear about great new reads and exciting offers!

Harlequin.com/newsletters